D0700520

emerge 20

ABOUT *emerge*

emerge is an annual publication produced by students, alumni, faculty, and industry guests of the Writer's Studio. *emerge*, as its title suggests, is a showcase of new writers emerging onto a dynamic and changing publishing landscape. It has been designed to introduce and promote new talent into the marketplace and for many of its contributors *emerge* will be the jumping-off point to further success writing and publishing their works. From this collection, the readers of *emerge* will get a taste of great things to come.

ABOUT THE WRITER'S STUDIO

The Writer's Studio is an award-winning creative writing program at Simon Fraser University that provides writers with mentorship, instruction, and hands-on book publishing experience. Over the course of a year, students work alongside a community of writers with a mentor, developing their writing through regular manuscript workshops and readings. Many of our alumni have become successful authors, and have gone on to careers in the publishing industry.

The Writer's Studio 2020 mentors:
Claudia Casper—*Speculative Fiction and Writing for Young Adults*
Kevin Chong—*Fiction*
JS Arnott—*Poetry and Lyric Prose*
JJ Lee—*Narrative Non-Fiction*

The Writer's Studio Online 2018—2019 mentors:
Eileen Cook—*Speculative Fiction and Writing for Young Adults*
Jen Sookfong Lee—*Fiction*
Kayla Czaga—*Poetry and Lyric Prose*
Claudia Cornwall—*Narrative Non-Fiction*
Stella Harvey—*Fiction and Personal Narrative*

sfu.ca/write

emerge 20

THE WRITER'S STUDIO ANTHOLOGY

Betsy Warland
Foreword

CREATIVE WRITING
AT SFU CONTINUING STUDIES

Simon Fraser University, Vancouver, B.C.

Copyright © 2020 by Simon Fraser University

Copyright of individual works is maintained by the respective writers.

All rights reserved. No part of this book may be used or reproduced in any manner whatsoever without prior written permission except in the case of brief quotations embodied in reviews.

Cover Design: Solo Corps Creative
Cover Illustration: Sandra Sugimoto
Typesetting and Interior Design: Solo Corps Creative
Printing: Marquis

Printed in Canada

Library and Archives Canada Cataloguing in Publication

emerge 20: The Writer's Studio anthology /
Foreword by Betsy Warland

ISSN 1925-8267
ISBN 978-1-77287-074-9 (paperback)
ISBN 978-1-77287-075-6 (ebook)

A cataloging record for this publication is available
from Library and Archives Canada.

Creative Writing | SFU Continuing Studies
Simon Fraser University
515 West Hastings Street
Vancouver, B.C., Canada, V6B 5K3
sfu.ca/write

SFU Publications
1300 West Mall Centre
8888 University Drive
Burnaby, B.C., Canada, V5A 1S6

To the writers and readers who, in these strange times, turn to stories and poems—for clarity, solace, and to reckon with what it means to be human.

And to everyone who has helped shape, guide, and grow the TWS community over the last twenty years to help make those stories happen.

Invention, it must be humbly admitted,
does not consist in creating out of void but out of chaos.
—Mary Wollstonecraft Shelley

Contents

NON-FICTION

SPECULATIVE AND YA FICTION

POETRY

Foreword

In 1999, it was one of those rare moments: I was the right person, at the right time, for the right task. Simon Fraser University's Continuing Studies Writing and Publishing Program decided to create a certificate in creative writing. Having taught this in a variety of settings, I was hired to design the program.

When I moved to Vancouver in 1980, the writing community was a relatively small but very dynamic community. Writers knew, inspired, and helped one another. The Vancouver-based community that coalesced from writers teaching at Vancouver universities and colleges, as well as from writers associated with small literary magazines, presses, and bookstores began to change for a variety of reasons. As Canadian writing evolved into Canadian Literature, younger writers found themselves adrift.

Prior to moving to Vancouver, I initiated a feminist literary organization that produced workshops, events, and publications in Toronto and witnessed how valuable an intentional community of writers could be. While teaching creative writing in Vancouver, I was impressed by how many talented writers were hungry for more training; more companionship. A certificate in creative writing could address this need, could create a "learning in community" alternative. As the English-speaking world was becoming far more global, creating a writing program for "emerging" writers of diverse backgrounds was paramount.

The design of the Writers Studio had to be practical; realistic. Students needed to learn how to keep their head down for the year and make their writing life fit with their working, family, and intimate life. Over the years, TWS writers' lives and professions have varied wildly—even their ages: twenty-years-old writers work alongside middle-aged writers and writers in their sixties. Educational restrictions are not applicable. Writers with PhDs work alongside writers who haven't finished high school and both proceed to have their books published.

Prior to writing this Foreword, I read the *emerge 20* manuscript. Then, I read *emerge 01*. An obvious difference is that there were nineteen writers in *emerge 01* and seventy-eight in *emerge 20*. The overall quality of the writing was equally strong. The pronounced difference was a far greater variety of racial, cultural, indigenous, countries of origin, and first-language writers in *emerge 20*. As a result, *emerge 20* has expanded the range of topics and points of view in their narratives (regardless of genre). Few things could make me happier than this. This is the world we live in.

When I reviewed the 47 alumni books listed on the website of TWS Goodreads, once again, this increasing diversity is evident. Tangible. I know of twelve more published alumni books not yet on this list, and there are likely more. Considering that it takes a number of years upon graduating from the Studio before alumni can finish a manuscript, this volume of alumni books actually spans about fifteen years. I believe that the diversity of these writers (and their narratives) would have had a much harder time finding their feet without TWS as their springboard. Although literary awards are not the be-all-and-end-all, the fact that TWS alumni have been shortlisted and won numerous literary awards is notable. I can say with conviction that Canadian literature would have notably been poorer without these books.

Here, it is time to acknowledge all the TWS mentors who have nourished, inspired, and challenged their workshop writers. It's an inspiring list. In face-to-face (essential chronological): myself, Lynn Coady, Stephen Osborne, Lydia Kwa, Steven Galloway, Miranda Pearson, Wayde Compton, Caroline Adderson, Ivan Coyote, Rachel Rose, Shaena Lambert, Brian Payton, Timothy Taylor, Jen Currin, Charles Demers, Hiromi Goto, Meredith Quartermain, Kevin Chong, JJ Lee, Carrie Mac, Joanne Arnott, and Claudia Casper. In TWS Online: Jordan

Abel, June Hutton, Claudia Cornwall, Eileen Cook, Jen Sookfong Lee, Stella Harvey, Fiona Tinwei Lam, and Kayla Czaga. I cannot praise these author-mentors enough. Aside from myself directing the program, subsequent directors Wayde Compton, and now Andrew Chesham, have added TWS Online and graduate manuscript workshops. TWS is more vibrant than ever.

Writing is the hardest work I know. Fortunately, it's also the most fascinating and frequently the most illuminating work. Over the years I have watched how TWS alumni who have never met immediately trust one another when they do. Their mutual curiosity and respect is inspiring. Cliché alert! This bond is priceless beyond words.

—*Betsy Warland*, Vancouver, 2020

Fiction

edited by Emma Cleary

Dora Joella Prieto
The Last Wisdom Tooth
AN EXCERPT

The street outside was full of people. Today, people were in the zócalo celebrating San Antonio de Padua, the Franciscan saint of June 13th—and
patron saint of lost things. The activities could be loosely categorized
into the following groups: selfies in front of the parroquía; artesanos
shouting out macramé prices, competing for their customers' attention;
and swarms of large families milling about, the drunk tíos and suegras
looking disapprovingly at their daughters-in-law. It was a normal day.

Seeing the apparent normalcy of the afternoon in spite of the occasion, Andrés felt self-conscious—he wasn't sure how much meaning
to ascribe to the affair. He spotted a family shuffling slowly and put
on his best journalistic enthusiasm, a measured, authoritative kind of
excitement.

"Buenas tardes, Señora," he addressed the matriarch of the group,
deferring to her authority. "My name is Andrés and I am writing about
the last wisdom tooth—¿usted qué opina de la muela del juicio?" He
held his breath; it felt like God was turning up the heat.

Through pursed lips and crossed arms she retorted, "A ver, jóven, I
thought the last wisdom tooth was pulled out, like, thirty years ago. ¿De
qué hablas?" She looked at him severely, clearly galvanized by her chance
to dominate.

Andrés deflated. She didn't even know about it.

"It's for the *Voz de la Nación*." He name-dropped his employer to
legitimize his questions. "And I'm writing about the last wisdom tooth,
which will be extracted today!"

3

One of the younger women, who was holding up her tío, then responded indifferently, "No idea, güey." The tío lurched forward toward Andrés. "A ver, cabrón, I'll remove a tooth for you." He chuckled while swinging his arm. Andrés stepped back. A young kid stuck his tongue out at him.

Andrés turned to the next in the group, an older but more optimistic-looking woman. He once again channelled his journalist tactics, beaming at her and asking, "What are *your* thoughts on the last wisdom tooth?" Even now, Andrés could feel that this question was becoming a metric for his own growing obsession with the story.

"Umm …" she said, embarrassed to be at the centre of attention. "Ya no las necesitamos," was the uninspired reply as she covered her laugh. The suegra scoffed disapprovingly at her daughter-in-law's weak reply.

Andrés sighed, thanked them all for their time, and kept walking around the square, taking notes about the atmosphere and the recent conversation for his feature article. He was hoping to capture the richness of the event for two main reasons:

1. His boss had already planned tooth-related merchandise, so they needed the feature to really sensationalize the event.
2. It was in his nature to feel things deeply.

Andrés pulled his phone out of his pocket to see a text from his boss: *Cuesta de San José 16.* Andrés leaped away; it was starting! A magnetism both repelled him from the town square and pulled him toward the office of Dr. Magola Guzmán. *The last wisdom tooth on the planet*, he thought to himself dreamily.

Caught between her parents' poverty-informed wishes for her to be a doctor and her own self-interested desires to be an artist, Magola became a dentist. That equation didn't make sense to most, but it's what happened. As she was extracting the last wisdom tooth on the planet, in the desert highlands of Soledad, she thought about how future generations might covet the wisdom teeth of their ancestors, finding within those malformed evolutionary mistakes a key to the past. She really hoped they would, but as she was cutting gristle, slicing the gum, and twisting while she pulled the tooth from the patient's mouth with agility, she also doubted it.

Magola had already dipped her own wisdom teeth in gold and studded them with her uncle's emeralds from the mountains, in an effort to persuade her descendants to revere these rare treasures—if not for posterity, then for the timeless language of wealth. This particular mix of logic and creativity was precisely how Magola became a dentist.

The tooth glistened in her forceps as she held it up to the light, rubies of coagulating blood sliding down and forming a small red stalactite on that last anomaly, semiprecious and ridiculous. Below, the whites of her patient's eyes glowed against cinnamon skin, further accented by a deeply furrowed brow. Magola looked down and realized that her delight was her patient's distress. The furrow in the patient's brow deepened, painting worry lines into her young face, as she took in the sight of her bloody tooth, which was now separated from her body and being held by the smiling Magola hovering over her.

"Ya ... está ...?" The patient articulated slowly and laboriously, with Magola's fingers still exploring the left side of her mouth. Magola's patients expected her to display nothing more than competence with a side of boredom.

"Sí. And wow, it was a good one! Very, very clean," she said appreciatively.

Magola had to remember to stay in control of her passion for dentistry. Like prison guards or morticians, it was considered morally compromised for a dentist to take too much pleasure in the gory work they did. The patients didn't want to feel like powerless little mice strapped to the dentist's chair and subject to the maniacal feats of a bloody oral frenzy. An overzealous dentist was not agreeable to people; it made them feel unsettled.

Magola collected herself, moving methodically as she dropped the patient's tooth into a sterile bag and putting down the forceps. She asked the patient whether she would like to keep her tooth. The patient simply said, "No."

"En serio?" She betrayed her feigned stoicism.

"Sí," the patient said sharply. "Y quiero que lo tires a la basura." She emphasized *basura* with the barbed delight of someone enjoying another's distress.

"I don't think you know what this means," said a sombre Magola, mysteriously.

The patient lay there, bleeding and regarding the situation with disgust. She felt the fascination with her tooth was one of generations past—*her* generation had no time for such sentimentalities, having inherited the task of Saving the Planet, not saving teeth.

Magola of course felt differently. As she approached the garbage can, she felt like she moved in slow motion. She pulled the lever to open the airtight lid and dropped in the tooth, which landed with a soft splat, lodging itself into some more fleshy bits of coagulated blood from a ten a.m. root canal. The act felt sacrilegious; she felt the devil in her bones. After, the cleanup and the patient leaving all happened in a blur.

Outside, Andrés was standing awkwardly, peering through the glass and taking notes, trying to make eye contact. Magola took off her gloves and wiped her brow, waving him in.

She was an impressive woman, 1.8 metres tall with thick black hair that she braided elaborately. The braids were born out of practicality, to keep her hair out of the bloody mouths she spent her time in—Magola's magic was to create artistic perfection in precisely these practicalities.

As for Andrés, he fell in love immediately. Andrés felt something chilling enter his bones as he realized this. Magola gestured for him to take a seat in the chair. It was still warm from the patient.

"Ah—hola—soy Andrés," he said, searching for words. He had a quick self-deprecating thought of how he wrote words for a living, and yet was so bad at choosing them in conversation. Very different skills, he decided.

"So, how did the patient react?" Andrés queried.

"She didn't react much at all. It was like a normal extraction." Magola said *normal extraction* with a severe disappointment, making it obvious she wished it hadn't been, which warmed Andrés.

He retired his neutrality for a moment. "But it was the last wisdom tooth on the planet. It was anything but a normal extraction." He wasn't sure if he was reassuring her, or if he was reassured by her. "What was it like for you?"

At this, Magola went on a monologue describing the fantastic gum density, the perfectly formed molar that was beautiful in its lack of necessity, how the white bone had contrasted against garnet-coloured blood clots collecting in the ridges of the molar, and how the pop of the tooth coming loose had a particularly final sound. She was breathless.

As for Andrés, he was slack-jawed and fascinated, his imagination going wild with images of Magola, blood, and beauty in such a way that he knew his report could never capture. He closed his mouth and gazed deeply into her eyes. "Oh, I understand."

Elliott Gish

Grey Dog

AN EXCERPT

The child stood with her back to me, her woollen coat the same dull grey as the bare trees that surrounded us. Under her arm she clutched her doll, its curly golden hair considerably grubbier now than it had been after Christmas.

"Lillian!" I cried, kneeling and seizing her shoulders. She gave a start and a little cry, turning in my grasp to look up at me. Her round blue eyes were so wet and wistful, so full of that odd, unfocused longing common in children, that I had to close my eyes against a sudden surge of rage so strong it left me weak at the knees. The nerve of the little devil, toddling away into the woods and drawing me in after her! "Why did you leave the road? What on earth is the matter with you?"

I said this in my harshest growl, speaking in the voice of a thousand spinster schoolteachers and a thousand maiden aunts. I expected the child to cry—in my sudden savage mood, I *wanted* her to cry—but instead she lifted a chubby finger to her lips and whispered, "Hush, teacher! Look."

And she turned around again and pointed through the trees. My gaze followed the pointing finger up and up, beyond the thick stand of nude birches by which we knelt, and then I saw it.

The doe sat comfortably in the last of the winter snow, her pointed ears twitching, her black nose quivering as she took in our scent. We were scarcely more than ten feet away from her, and yet she did not get up to run. Indeed, there was no fear in her shining black eyes beneath their thick and girlish lashes, no nervous shivering in her delicate limbs.

She stared at us with a brazenness that looked quite unnatural on a creature so famously shy. Although she was thin enough for me to see the outline of her ribs beneath her velvet fur, her belly was hugely swollen, and as I looked at it I saw it tremble and quake like a shaken bowl of water. I could smell the sweat and stink of her; her droppings, her musk, her sun-warmed flesh.

"My word, Lillian," I said, all my anger quite forgotten. "What a discovery you have made! The first deer of the season, I have no doubt—and look, see her little round belly? She is going to drop a fawn soon."

As soon as the words were out of my mouth I rather regretted them, for in my experience, once a child learns that an animal is in a delicate condition, they will not rest until they learn *how* that condition came to be. But Lillian did not pester me with questions about the whys and the wherefores of the thing. Instead she stood there quietly, still in my rather wicked grasp, taking in the scene with the solemnity of a priest.

The tremors in the doe's belly increased. Still staring at us, she shifted in the snow, then turned to nose intently at her hindquarters, a grey-pink tongue snaking out to touch the soft white fur there. The back legs slowly rose, the tail lifted, and I realized that the fawn was not coming soon, but *now*. Dismayed, I reached down to cover Lillian's eyes with my hands. Scientific exploration was all well and good, but I was not in the mood to deal with Mrs. Morice charging into the schoolhouse and demanding to know why I had corrupted her daughter.

But Lillian would not submit to having her eyes covered. She wiggled away from me, tiptoeing with exaggerated care a foot or two closer to the doe. I tried to grab hold of her again, but she was out of my reach, and my position was so unsteady that I nearly toppled over into the slush.

I could have gotten to my feet and reached the child that way, but I was loath to frighten the animal at such a moment. The child was raised in the country, I reasoned to myself. She must have seen eggs hatching, cows birthing calves, horses in foal. Perhaps she had even seen her mother give birth to a younger sibling, a tiny brother or sister. I hoped that this was so, that she would not be too horrified by what she was about to see.

The animal's flanks were now fairly convulsing, ripples disrupting the smooth brown of her fur. Her neck strained as the muscles in her hindquarters clenched and relaxed, a dribble of red running down between her legs. Her mouth opened in a desperate pant, and I could see past the white semicircle of blunt teeth down into the column of her throat. For a moment I fancied I could see beyond that, into her guts, her lungs, her fluttering heart. A thin little whining moan wound through the chill of the morning air, a sound much like the creaking of a door, opening slowly.

Had my sister made that noise on her birthing-bed, her deathbed? Was Florrie as calm as the doe, waiting for new life to slide out of her and into the world? Did she accept her fate as passively as this animal seemed to? Or did she struggle, did she fight?

I have to believe that she fought.

The trickle of red became a stream, a gush, a torrent. The doe's moan grew louder, higher, and her dark eyes rolled back into her head until I could see a fingernail crescent of white in each one. From the trembling hind of the deer emerged not the expected spindly legs of a new fawn, but a kind of mass—pulpy, gore-purple, expelled from the animal in shuddering bursts of flesh. Head lifted, mouth gaping, the deer collapsed onto the melting snow, the white underside of her tail stained like cardinal feathers. Her sides heaved twice more, then stilled.

In front of me, Lillian let out a shivering cry, more of a sigh than a sob. "Miss," she said, turning again to look at me, "what happened? Is she asleep?"

I did not reply. I could not.

Pushing the child behind me, I stepped toward the crumpled brown heap of animal. Her eyes remained open, but the liquid shine that had made them seem so human and bold moments before was gone. The grey-pink tongue lolled out of her muzzle and onto the snow. Her smell was overpowering up close, the stench of blood adding depth and horror to the perfume of her unwashed body. I looked at her ears, waiting for a twitch to indicate that there was life still in her elegant body. They did not move.

"Is there a baby, Miss?" Lillian called. She stood exactly where I had left her, her face troubled and uncertain, but eager, too—hungry for good news, something less frightening than the spectacle of blood and death she had just witnessed. A little fawn to pet and exclaim over, soft and gentle as a newborn kitten. "Can I come see?"

I did not want to look. But I could not leave her wondering.

Slowly, reluctantly, my eyes travelled down the doe's body. Here was the curve of her neck; here were her dainty shoulder blades; here were her pointed black hooves and her legs with their bones pressed up against the skin. And here was something else.

The thing I saw in the snow was not a fawn. It scarcely seemed to be anything. I looked at it as one might a cloud, struggling to see any sense or shape in that amorphous pile of blood and flesh. For a moment I thought—I hoped—that it had no shape at all, that it was simply the last excretion of a sickened animal. But then I saw, all unwilling, the bulbous head, the little blooming hands, the bulging suggestion of an undeveloped eye.

Is there a baby, Miss?

For the second time that afternoon a moan rose up through the trees, this time in a human voice, one so deep and heavy with dismay that I scarcely recognized it as my own.

Yes. There was a baby.

B. B. Randhawa

The Woman Who Thought She Was a Cow

The bull they have selected for me sits under the tree. He seems happy. I wonder what they are feeding him.

"He is not too demanding," says my father.

My mother whispers, "He is easy on the eyes."

This is the first time I have seen him. They expected me to marry him without looking at him.

"I married your mother after looking at her hoofs."

"I refused to see your father."

"I have not even seen him properly," I'd whimpered.

"You will like him. He is handsome."

"Is that all that is needed to be liked by me? Handsomeness?"

"Don't be clever. This is no time for games. Marriage is a serious business."

It is serious. It is the gravity of the situation that makes me want to know the bull I am going to marry. I do not want to marry someone based on his face and hoofs. I want to know if he can carry on a conversation. I want to know his values. I want to know his work ethic. I want to know if he wants to have calves and if he has access to feed to raise them. I want to know if he likes poetry or words. I want to know if he values education. Has he even been to bull college?

I am supposed to serve him and his family so that they can scrutinize me, my body, my fertility, my value, as I parade from one to another offering them food and drink. When I serve him water, he does not look up at me. He seems shy. While he looks at the ground, his mother looks me up and down. She is scrutinizing me for the amount of milk I will produce and the number of calves I will bear. Will I be an asset or a liability? The smile in her eyes appears to tell me that I will be an asset.

"She has big eyes, your daughter, and walks with such grace. I even like her little tail. Such a beauty."

His mother hums with approval as I walk between the guests serving. I am serving now, and after this marriage will be perpetually put to service. Serving my in-laws. Serving my husband. Serving my children, followed by serving their children. Will there ever be someone in service to me?

I highly doubt it.

It is hard to see myself being looked at and evaluated. I want to scream, but I smile and nod instead. I remain docile. I appear submissive. Even he is smiling now. They approve of my demure demeanour. I will not give them trouble. They do not know of the wolf that lives inside the cow that is me. I look like a cow. Act like a cow. Walk like a cow. Talk like a cow, but I am a wolf. I have been called that before by a bull I was seeing briefly behind my parent's back. I will not follow the other cows in the herd. I will do my own thing and be a master of my own fate.

They cannot see this, of course. I show them no signs of the predator in me. Will they be safe from what lives inside me? But at this moment, I fear for myself. The wolf inside me is raging. I want to tear down everything in this perfect grazing patch and howl. I just moo, instead. No howling sounds come out of my cow throat. I submit to my fate.

I am not invited to make the selection. I am the one to be selected, if I am lucky.

"You are lucky," they tell me. "Everyone does not get a handsome bull."

Apparently all cows are not so lucky. Some will never bear calves and their mammary glands will not fill with milk. Milk—the source of solace to so many. It sounds like bad luck, but it seems like a boon to me. I do not like to drink milk. I refuse to drink any milk; I've only ever drank my mother's. She is older now. She no longer produces milk. Her value has decreased with age to others, but to me she is more precious than ever.

My mother is smiling ear to ear. She has already picked out my wedding outfit. She has all the jewels chosen. The bells I will wear for the ceremony have been imported from Switzerland—cow heaven. She even knows what the wedding cards will look like.

"They shall have your hoof print and his."

My father has been busy telling all his friends that his daughter is to be married. He has fulfilled his obligation by marrying off his only daughter. He wants to make sure everyone knows he was generous at his daughter's wedding.

"I want to throw you a party that will be remembered."

"Yes, we must put on a good show."

No one has asked me what I want. I have not been consulted on my favourite food or the bells I like. I do not like cowbells. I do not like this bull. I do not want to marry him. He does not excite me. I still have not spoken to him. I wonder if he even speaks. I cannot imagine marrying someone I cannot talk to. I need someone who will at least listen. I want a partnership. I was not just made to give humans milk and bear calves. There is more to me than my body. I am more than just a source of milk, meat, and more cows. My body belongs to me. It is not for others to use or abuse as they see fit. Even the dung I produce is dried and used as fuel. Even my excretions are not mine. There appears to be no part of me that is not of value.

Even in death I will be consumed as I am consumed in life. Every part of me will be cut up and used. Even in death, I do not return to the earth that I came from. I am a commodity. A property. I am given in dowry and with dowry. I am used in bartering. I have become a transaction. I need to control my milk production. I must take control of my mating life. I am taking my life back into my hands.

Wait.

They do not seem to care about the sounds I make. It is my voice they have not found a use for. My voice is still mine. I will use it. I will use it to say, "No." No to this marriage. No to the destiny that they have forged for me.

I am not just a cow.

I was not just made to mate and give birth to other cows. I am a cow who is also a wolf. I am divine. I am Kamadhenu.

I am more than the name they call me.

Teminey Beckers

My Name Is Badger

AN EXCERPT

Badger and her five siblings are banished to the car
for hours while the adults drink inside the pub.

"Finding anything good back there, Luc?" Badger asked.

"Mostly trash. Lots of empty booze bottles."

Badger saved a crazy eight for last and knocked on the window to let everyone know she was on her last card. Guy looked up from the floor of the car, where he was scribbling on newspaper, and raised a crayon to the window. Unable to reach, he settled back onto the cushion of his sagging diaper.

"Make her pick up," Patti said to John, who was propped on her knee. "It's our only chance." She held John's chubby hand in hers and looked through his cards. "No twos, oh well." She pointed to a card and he placed it on the pile. Just as Badger was about to put down her winning card, she heard a loud burp from the back of the car. She glanced up and saw a silhouette of her brother with an empty bottle in his hand. A prickling sensation travelled the length of her spine.

"What is that, Luc?" Badger said.

He dropped the bottle and hunched over, wrapping his arms around his belly. "I thought it was ..."

"What's wrong?" Patti asked.

"I don't know." Badger scrambled over the backseat and picked up the bottle. It was a cream soda bottle. She noticed a piece of saran wrap with a rubber band next to it. Last week, she had been with Dad when the man at the gas station gave him a sample of marked farm gas, which was cheaper than regular gas and dyed pink to differentiate it. She had watched Dad wrap the top with a piece of plastic and secure it with a rubber band. Holding the bottle to her nose, she recognized the smell. Oh no, oh no, she thought. What do I do?

"Gertrude. Get Mom and Dad," Badger said.

Gertrude was in the front seat chomping her gum and tapping her fingers on the dashboard along to "Help!" on the radio. "We're not allowed out of the car."

Badger raised her voice, "Gertrude, stop messing around. Luc needs a hospital. Now!"

Gertrude turned to face Badger, "What happened?"

"Luc drank Dad's gasoline sample."

"What? No!"

"Just go!"

Gertrude flew out of the car and sprinted across the parking lot. Guy fiddled with the chrome window crank, oblivious, but John seemed to sense something was off. "Luc," he said. "Luc." He tried to crawl over the backseat but Patti pulled him onto her lap.

Badger rubbed circles on Luc's back. Even in the dull glow sneaking into the parking lot from behind the pub's curtains, she could see his face was unnaturally flushed. His legs and arms twitched, jerking from side to side. "You're going to be fine," she said. Luc groaned.

"Luc. Owie," John said. Patti nodded.

Gertrude burst through the pub doors followed by Mom and Dad.

"What's the matter? Is he okay?" Mom flung open the door, letting in a rush of cold air, and kneeled on the backseat. She reached her hand back to touch Luc's cheek. Her eyes darted around the car, as if searching for some explanation.

"Mom, he drank the bottle of gasoline. We have to get him to the hospital!"

"What gasoline?" Mom glanced at Dad who was now seated behind the wheel. "Louis, did you have gasoline in the car? Shit. Shit. Get us outta here." She picked up Guy, who had started to whimper, and handed him to Gertrude, in the front.

Badger hated it when her parents swore, it brought to mind too many drunken arguments that she would rather forget. "Mom, you're gonna freak him out. Just be quiet."

Dad's eyebrows tensed in a grimace. "Stupid kid," he said. "He'll be fine, Ruby. Don't worry so much. Won't ya, Luc? You'll be fine." He put the car into reverse and screeched out of the parking lot. Luc gagged and his body curled inward. Badger strained to look into his eyes, to calm him, but recoiled slightly when she saw they were rolled back, only the whites visible. Vomit dribbled out of the side of his mouth. She grabbed a plastic bag and shoved it under his face.

"Here."

She held it open and he vomited. Badger had to hold her breath so she wouldn't too. "Open the windows!" She leaned forward and threw the bag out. It exploded on the pavement.

"Again," Luc mumbled.

"Out the window, Luc." Badger helped him stretch over the backseat so he could stick his head out the window, like a dog. He vomited again, leaving a trail of puke along the side of the car.

"Oh, man," Dad said.

"You shut up," Mom said. "This is your fault."

"Dad, he's trying his best," Badger said. She and Mom held Luc partway out the window. Mom supported his head and Badger grasped the back of his shirt. Patti squished herself into the opposite side of the car, holding John close.

They pulled up in front of the emergency room and Dad got out to open the back door. Mom scooped Luc into her arms and his limp legs bobbed up and down as she rushed him through the ER door. Badger hugged her knees to her chest and whispered to herself, "He's gonna be okay, he's gonna be okay. Please, please, please let him be okay."

Dad turned to face her, "Don't worry. He'll be fine. Those docs will pump his stomach and he'll be goodasnew!"

"How do you know, Dad? What if he's not?" She swallowed a sob and felt Patti's arm across her shoulders. She couldn't imagine a life without Luc. His playful eyes and mischievous smile. It was her fault. Gertrude was older, but she didn't pay enough attention. All she cared about were the stupid Beatles, with their funny haircuts and silly songs. Badger was the responsible one. She should have been more careful, not playing cards. She should have known. She should have been watching him.

Dad pulled the car away from the ER entrance into a parking spot nearby. He was going too fast and had to slam on the brakes to avoid hitting the curb. The kids put their hands out as they were thrown forward.

"Dad, watch it!"

"Whoops," Dad said. "You all in one piece?" Badger opened the back door but before she was out of the car, Dad stopped her. "Where do you think you're goin', li'l missy? We have to wait in the car."

"But Dad, I want to see if he's okay. Can't we go ask the doctors?"

"The last thing they need is a bunch of kids poking around. Let the docs do their work. You can all go to sleep back there while we're waiting."

Easy for you to say, Badger thought, but she knew there was no sense in arguing. As much as she wanted to fight, she felt drained of energy, like the radio getting quieter and quieter when its batteries were almost out of juice. Plus, Dad was drunk and loud and Badger didn't want to draw attention. She climbed back into her seat and snuggled up next to John and Patti. It wasn't long before they fell asleep, but Badger couldn't. She kept thinking of Luc, hoping, praying, that he would survive.

After what seemed like a lifetime to Badger, Mom came out to give them the news. The doctors had pumped Luc's stomach, removing all the gasoline. He had to stay the night in the hospital so he could be monitored. Luc was not going to die. Not today. Badger let out her breath and the tears she had been holding in slipped down her cheeks. She cried until her body gave in to exhaustion and she slumped against her sister. Resting her head on Patti's shoulder, she allowed herself to be pulled into the inviting darkness of sleep.

Dora Larson

The Apartment

AN EXCERPT

The air in the apartment was dry as dust. I could feel it in my lungs. It drew the moisture from the skin of my hands and face. When I turned the locks and opened the door, I expected it to push a semicircular path through inches of dust as it swung, like a snow plow. But I could see as my eyes adjusted to the dim light that it hadn't. There was a layer of dust, yes, but much finer than I'd imagined, passing easily under the door. The draft of air from the hallway didn't seem to disturb any of the particles. Everything remained still. I had wanted to know what it felt like to step into inches of dust, sink into it, whether it would feel like stepping into a cloud, but instead the apartment was just dirty. I was disappointed.

I hadn't been inside the apartment in eighteen years. I hadn't gone back to that city at all, in fact. Why would I? My parents were dead, I had no siblings, all of my friends had also emigrated. There were so many other places in the world to go. I only went back eighteen years ago because my daughter wanted to. I was still paying the minimum utility bills then, keeping the electricity on and the water running, just letting them deduct automatically from my bank account, even though who knows how long it had been since I'd actually set foot in the place. On paper, the apartment was functional. So we stayed there.

It was July when we went, hot and dry. I gave the floors a cursory sweeping, moving dust around, collecting it in the corners. The rugs felt powdery and thick. I found the ancient vacuum cleaner from the 1970s in the closet where my parents kept it, but it wouldn't turn on, so in the end I just left it. Our feet turned black if we walked around without shoes on, so we just wore our shoes the whole time, even to the bathroom. I wiped down the kitchen counter and bathroom sink with a rag I found, the water sputtering alive out of the taps. It was impossible to tell whether the rag was dirty or just old. The next day I bought some actual cleaner and a sponge, soap, shampoo, and scrub brush for the tub. When I plugged in the fridge, even more ancient than the vacuum cleaner, it miraculously worked, so I stocked up on tomatoes and peppers, salami and cheese, and we ate a lot of sandwiches that reminded me of my childhood. We slept with all the windows open, the sound of the tram and buses coming in until the last bus passed at around two in the morning. I often woke up in a sweat, but there wasn't a fan in the place, and I wouldn't have wanted to blow all that dust around in any case. Anna didn't complain that I can recall, didn't whine about the heat or the stiff, coarse towels or the uncomfortable beds, but she didn't ask to return, either. Looking back, we should have stayed in a hotel.

Anna, then fourteen, had an interest in the apartment, and in the past. When she was older she would start a family tree and try to do research, asking me questions to which I usually didn't know the answers. On that visit, after getting over the bewilderment of the apartment, frozen in time and untouched since my mother died several years earlier, she quietly opened dresser drawers and desk drawers and closets, looking. At first I was curious and did it with her, but when we pulled open the top dresser drawer and saw my father's socks and mother's underwear and stockings in there, I had to turn away. It was everything I could do not to slam the drawer shut and yell at her not to go rummaging through other people's things. Instead I retreated into silence, and found an excuse to go to the kitchen every time she started poking around. Luckily she didn't carry on long. I think she was overwhelmed by the sheer volume of it all. Every drawer was bursting, mostly with clothing, faded, the fabric cheap and unpleasant, but also with tools, hammers and screwdrivers, boxes of nails, piles of pens and broken pencils, pair after pair of eyeglasses, towels, tablecloths, and papers. Some were so full she could barely push them shut again.

Like me, Anna never was particularly interested in clothes, but even if she had been I would have told her not to bother. There were no vintage treasures to be found, just styleless, functional garments. When I peeked inside the closets, I didn't recognize anything as mine. I must have taken everything with me when I left, and I donated all that old stuff long ago. I stood beside my old bed and tried to conjure the old motions of dressing and undressing, the muscle memory of where I had hung my clothes, but they didn't come. When we left at the end of the trip, I locked the door behind us and tried not to think about the apartment again. And I mostly didn't, for nearly two decades. But there I was again, eighteen years later.

I finally dealt with it because of my friend Martha. My parents were both dead before my daughter reached adolescence, so the apartment just sat there, easily ignored for ages. But Martha's parents held on forever, well into their nineties. She was in constant contact with the apartment where she grew up, going back every summer for several months, taking her children to see her parents. In many ways I never understood it. My mother was a difficult woman, and my father isn't worth discussing. When Martha's mother, also a difficult woman, finally died, everything happened fairly quickly. She told me about it later over a video chat, after it was all finished. Her mother took a turn for the worse, fought the doctors with everything she had, and died in the hospital two weeks later, full of rage. A month or two after that, Martha's father fell and broke his hip in the kitchen trying to put a large tray loaded with peaches into the refrigerator. It was clear to him, finally, that he couldn't go on living alone in the apartment. When they were in their sixties and seventies, still mobile and in obscenely good shape, Martha had tried to convince them to make some modifications: remove some awkwardly placed counters with sharp corners, convert the deep tub into a walk-in shower with a seat, put in some handrails, widen the narrow hallway by getting rid of the cabinets stuffed with clothes and shoes from the '50s and '60s that didn't fit anyone anymore, and that no one would have wanted even if they had. But they had refused, and now he couldn't stay. They were so stubborn, Martha said. They acted like children. Martha, from afar, got him a spot in the most expensive nursing home in the country.

That left the apartment where Martha grew up unoccupied, and she proceeded, immediately and efficiently, to sell it. I marvelled as she described it to me. Hauling out her parents' porcelain and silver and Afghan carpets and having them shipped. Getting the antiques appraised and consigned. Emptying the desk drawers: the stacks of old bills, the photos of her kids over the years, of her own childhood, a few of her parents when they were young. The piles of clothes layered within the cabinets, like geological sediments. The real estate market was crazy, and she quickly found a buyer who was willing to pay not just in cash but in dollars. The whole thing was done in a month.

"But how did you clear it all out in a month? How did you go through all the stuff?" I asked. Although I hadn't been to my parents' apartment in nearly two decades, I could imagine it, the papers and files and clothes and dishes and towels and linens, just like she described at her parents' place. It would take me months to sort through it all, to figure out what to do with it.

"I didn't," Martha said. She didn't understand my question. I didn't understand her answer.

"So what did you do with it?"

"I left it. I gave everything a quick glance, took the things I wanted, and then I sold the place as is. The buyer can rent a dumpster and hire a company to clear it all out. It's not my problem anymore."

"You left the pictures? Your parents' diplomas?"

"What would I have done with them? Put them in a drawer, so then my children have to throw them out when I die? I haven't looked at them in over thirty years. I don't need them. I remember it all." She just said it, like it was a normal thing to say.

I had to stop myself from telling her she was amazing. I knew she would have hated that, and I would have hated saying it. But she did amaze me. I wanted what she had. I had my own belongings pared down to fit into two suitcases, but my parents' apartment had been sitting in the back of my mind for eighteen years, a sharp pebble in my shoe. I had learned to ignore it, but there it always was. I had to deal with it. I bought my plane ticket two days after that call with Martha.

Prachi Kamble

World Class Education

AN EXCERPT

Who gets to tell their story. Who gets to talk. And who always listens. In Germany, Vietnamese immigrants speak German. In France, Bangladeshi immigrants speak French. In Italy, Senegalese immigrants speak Italian. We are not always the colonizers who choose us. Sometimes we are the colonizers *we* choose.

To use your colonizer's language to tell stories of your trauma is a cruel twist of fate. To use your colonizer's language to define your identity is Stockholm Syndrome for your tongue. To make poetry out of words that were meant to break your ancestors' backs is like whipping buttercream frosting out of skeleton dust.

To do a Bachelor's in English Lit as a person of colour is like crushing on the boy in high school to whom you were unfuckable and invisible. To do a Master's in English Lit is like carrying on sleeping with the guy you met on a Thursday night at the Cambie for five years while he consistently tells you he isn't ready for a relationship, but what are you doing later? To do a PhD in English Lit is like watching the guy leave you for the girl he was seeing, you later find out, while you were still together. It's like finding out from a mutual friend that he mentioned wanting to be with a white girl, but not his insecurities about your rising career. It's like listening to Bollywood music in your car and turning it down in a panic at traffic lights to make sure no one heard it.

Who gets to trace their family tree. Who gets to dignify their past by being written about. Who gets to sit in boardrooms and who gets to speak on panels. Who gets to make mistakes and who gets the benefit of the doubt. Who gets to be the default audience. Who gets to be the one you have to write to please. Who gets to be the one to tell our stories because that too is up for grabs.

To make art you have to study the greats who don't look like you. You take expensive vacations to Europe to see it in person so you can be someone worth listening to. You take Instagram photos of opulent galleries and tremendously authoritative plazas built from the spoils of, most probably, old wars on your country. But it's a few generations ago so you've forgotten about it and now smile like a clown in selfies. Hashtag jetlag. Hashtag not before my morning coffee. Hashtag hundred percent that bitch.

When you're a few rungs down from when colonization happened to your ancestors, say Season 5 or 6, and you have the luxury of geographical distance, you do things like bring your palms together at your heart centre and bow your head to your instructor who can now afford head-to-toe lululemon after completing 300 hours of teacher training in Costa Rica.

*

Far from home, I rolled the names of new streets on my tongue—Broadway, Granville, Arbutus, Alma. The realities of freedom cut close to the bone. I found a rickety house on Fraser Street in front of a graveyard and beside a Filipino church. My roommates were foreign exchange students, a 25-year-old PhD candidate and a divorced middle-aged man, friend of the landlord who lived upstairs with his teenage daughter and wife. Over the years it became clear that my landlord couldn't read or write. He was the first Newfie I'd come across in Canada. He'd yell unintelligible nothings in the kitchen when I left a pot in the sink.

I waited for the 33 to attend eight a.m. classes. No one waited at home for me but that's what I thought I wanted. The Vancouver winds broke my umbrellas like they broke my spirit. I'd sit in class with wet socks and listen to discourses about Milton, deciding that I was not a fan but grateful for the information. The loneliness was new. It was disguised as freedom and bred desperation and neediness in me. The readings at school came fast and I was barely keeping up. My mind was fertile and soaked up everything the professors launched my way.

On one Thursday night our new roommate from Montréal took us out to a trashy pub downtown. It was my first real night out in the city. My outfit screamed student on a budget.

There Chris and I spotted each other amongst a sea of other students and young people with unconventional jobs—servers, bartenders, musicians.

It was a game. Look, then look away. Dance and pretend not to notice whilst being watched. Look and then look away again. Validation hit like cocaine lines. We got talking. Held hands, which was unusual for this type of encounter. From his baggy dark hood, sleeves rolled tight to the elbows revealing long forearm muscles like twisted ropes, baseball cap pulled low from under which he watched the passing world, to the gaudy silver chain around his neck, I knew this wasn't meant to be. As I made my way to our first date on the caterpillar of the Fraser bus, I practised blunt words of rejection which, back then, came easily to me. I was thinking about Chris's clothes then and the intellectual calibre of our conversations. And knowing that thinking like this was wrong. We went to a Mexican place on Commercial Drive that no longer exists. I pointed across the street to show him where I volunteered at the poetry slam every Monday.

I play hockey, he said between bites of bad enchiladas that he didn't know were bad.

His hair escaped his baseball cap like the wing tip of a bird. Just edging on long. All of a sudden he became real. Someone with will and likes and dislikes. Someone with a sense of self. Someone who had other things in his life but who chose to spend his time with me, and when he did, it was the ultimate validation. Later, while waiting at the lights to cross the street, I dug down into the pencil stem of my heels and pushed the length of my back into him to feel the strength of his body through his cheap clothes. He took the weight like a monument, absorbing impact with ease. He took that as a sign that I was easy and I didn't do much to stop him from thinking it.

He told me he worked at a mill and that he did hard labour. I told him about my first degree and how I wasn't feeling it anymore. I told him about my second degree. He pretended to sympathize. At the end of the date I got into his beat-up pickup truck. Even by pickup truck standards it was an embarrassment.

When we reached my place I turned as quickly as I could to get out of the truck without being rude, but he asked me for a hug and caught me in a kiss when he released me from it. It was a well-oiled and practised move but I took it as a reason to give this a second chance. Giddiness followed me around for days. I stuck my head into the sand, refusing to acknowledge the glaring differences between us. My love for him was a mixture of hunger for his body, neediness from being lonely in a new city, guilt about my class and privilege, and condescending pity for his blue-collar existence. He was a white man with less and I was a brown girl with more. After the end, when I heard from a mutual friend that he mentioned wanting to be with a white woman, I wasn't surprised. I knew he'd catch on at some point. This wasn't the way the world was supposed to work.

That semester I barely passed my finals. My hormones were wreaking havoc on my cognition. The spring made it impossible to focus. Words swam on every page and all I could do was think of witty sentences to add to our texting back and forth. We built up anticipation between meetings with carefully timed and intently crafted messages. I hovered a foot off the ground at any given point where reality couldn't put its searching hands on me.

My phone rang at two a.m. one weekday. I had just switched the lights off after finishing a reading. The voice on the other line belonged to a woman who had been drinking.

Who are you?

Excuse me? I responded.

Who are you and how do you know Chris? How did you meet him?

This could not be happening. Not when I was on such a high after years of loneliness.

How do you know him? She continued. Her tone was pleading and the texture of her voice was like the wavering surface of water. Ready to break.

Do you know Chris? I said, beginning to lose my patience.

Do I know Chris? I talk to him every day.

Good. Then you should ask him yourself.

I hung up. I sent him a text right away. Your friend called me and it was weird. On the phone the next day he told me not to worry about it, that it was "kindergarten shit."

We were at a party and she looked through my phone, he said.

You must be quite close for her to be able to do that.

You won't have to worry about it ever again. I promise.

I took his words to sleep with me, feeling cared for. I traded inconveniences for that feeling. Minor slights. Passive aggressiveness, that sort of thing. The girl from the call became silly after his reassurance. She took on a villainous tinge. She was trying to destroy us because we were invincible. She was a drunk teenager in the face of our adult serious relationship.

I'd never felt so special and that's how it all began.

Barbara Cameron
Unconsecrated Ground

Charlie'd always known this time would come. When the factory went in east of town, change started to creep toward this, the homestead his parents had worked so hard on. The town nibbled, munched, and finally gobbled up the surrounding farmland, until now progress pressed against his land. His age-spotted hand shook a little as he held back the brocade drape, peering out, knowing he couldn't see where they were clearing.

"Those drapes need cleaning. Look at the dust!" Charlie turned to watch Margie shuffle into the room, her white hair askew from her morning nap. "Give me a hand with them, Nate. We'll do it right now before you …" Her voice trailed off as she stared at Charlie. "You're not Nate. Where's Nate?"

"Nate's gone home. I'm Charlie."

"Home? But he's my son. This is his home."

"He got married, Margie, and you looked gorgeous at his wedding."

"Well … I …" She rubbed the side of her head vigorously, as if to summon the genie of understanding. "But you're not supposed to be home for another week, I'm sure. Or … are you?"

"I'm early, is all." Charlie took the right hand of the woman he'd lived with for 58 years, lacing her fingers with his and using her arm to steer her. "Lunch time, Margie. What'll we have today? How 'bout grilled cheese? Been awhile since we've had those."

As he drew her out of the room, the continued high-pitched lament of the chainsaw made his insides churn. Were they cutting the orchard?

On Tuesday, Beth came to sit with Margie while Charlie did his shopping and made time to have coffee with Ned and Stan. They eagerly filled him in on the gossip about his new neighbours. Youngish, Ned figured, early thirties, up-and-comers.

"Hear they're mortgaged to the hilt," Stan said, rubbing his hands. "Claire's kids wanted an arm and a leg for that place. Her bein' ten years younger 'n you, guess you never figured on her going before you, or you wouldn't have sold that piece with the orchard at the back to her. They clear that and you'll be lookin' right up their backside. Hope they don't subdivide. But your place must be worth a small fortune, hey Charlie?"

"Yeah, it's likely worth a fair chunk all right, but I'm not selling. Margie needs the place." Charlie watched as Ned and Stan bobbed their heads in solemn agreement.

On Saturday, with Beth back to watch Margie, Charlie knew it was time for him to check the progress of the clearing next door. Following the narrow but well-defined trail to the property line, Charlie told himself these young folks might be short on money but energy they had aplenty. Already they'd flattened most of the salal and blackberries in the lot adjacent to the orchard. Not the roots, though. Alive under the thick humus, the roots were biding their time, waiting for the first opportunity to send out new green fingers to twist around unwary ankles. Charlie wished he could will them to grow faster, to push aside the dead leaves and cut branches, to spring up in a tangle of thorns like a wizard's wall in a fairy tale that would protect the orchard for just a while longer. The doctor said Margie was fading fast, but please God, not yet.

He pushed through to the edge of the gnarled and broken apple trees. Almost 59 years since they'd buried Imogene here in sorrow and shame, silence and fear. Fifty-nine years ago the trees were already old and the small orchard had felt a world apart, a safe place to lay the too-early daughter who was not to be. Every spring the fragrant blossoms honoured the site. He inhaled deeply, the scent reminding him of how Margie had carried a sprig tucked in her bouquet the next spring as she'd walked up the aisle toward him, a private acknowledgment of their loss. Every September the trees would be loaded with small fruit which the birds and hornets feasted on, entertainment, Margie would say as they sat watching, for Imogene.

Damn! He sucked at his hand where a bramble scored it.

"Some of these vines have huge thorns, don't they?" The woman's voice startled him and he slipped on the wet leaves, staggering like a three-legged dog jumping a ditch.

"Sorry, thought you'd heard me crashing around." Her hair was pulled tight off her face and her pink T-shirt was loose, streaked with dirt. "I'm Chloe. My husband Roger and I are the proud new owners of the old Dempster place." She stuck out her hand to shake, then, as she saw the dirt, smiled at Charlie, shrugged, and pulled the hand back.

"Nice to meet you, Chloe. I'm Charlie Dermot. Me and Margie live back here." He waved his hand vaguely behind him.

"Pleased to meet you, Mr. Dermot."

"Call me Charlie." In the presence of this bright, cheery invader, he felt his tongue swell so it stumbled over simple words. She seemed not to notice, just as she seemed not to notice the rough-edged but still clearly discernible cross carved deep into the trunk of the apple tree beside them.

"Thought I'd have a look-see at the orchard. I've always wanted to own this property, even if we did go neck-deep in debt to get it. We don't have a lot left to put into it, but I have plans ..."

Plans. The word reverberated through Charlie's head, blanking out Chloe's words. Plans meant change. Plans meant so-called progress.

He felt sick. The grave would be noticed, if not when they chopped the tree down, then when they dug it up and found bones. Tiny, tiny bones, they'd be, or would they have melted into the unconsecrated soil to provide nourishment for the tiny apples?

"... do you think?" Chloe finished.

"Unh, sorry, I didn't quite catch all you said."

"Sorry, no problem, I talk too fast. I was saying the historical society says this is the oldest orchard in the county and the trees are heritage, you know? Varieties that should be preserved, so they've offered to help clear the brush and prune the trees and do whatever to keep them alive. They want a history too, and I wondered, would you mind if I came around and talked to you? Write down what you know about it?"

Charlie stared at her, hardly believing his ears.

"Charlie? Mr. Dermot?"

He forced himself to focus on her face. "Sure. Don't know how much help I'll be."

She smiled. "I'm sure you know lots. I appreciate it."

"Chloe? Chloe?" a man's voice called from the distance.

"Listen, that's Roger calling. Gotta go."

Quiet settled in the vacuum of her leaving. Exhausted by her energy, Charlie sat on a log, the damp moss soaking into the seat of his pants. One time Margie would've given him hell for mucking up his good clothes. He smiled. She was strong, his Margie, and minced no words. He sighed, wondering what their life might have been like if Imogene had lived, if they hadn't let her anchor them to the land, if they'd been free to move to a place of their own choosing. Not that it hadn't been a good life. He couldn't complain.

Heritage orchard, she'd said, and *history*. He didn't think of his life as history, though maybe it was. He looked at the cross, and the mixture of sadness and relief and guilt he'd felt so long ago swept through him like it'd happened yesterday. If she'd lived—he shook his head—it would have been harder. Not like now. He wiped his eyes, stood. He would see, see what history he would tell when the time came.

Charlie was halfway back to the house when Margie's voice penetrated his reverie. "I might be losing my mind, Beth, but this I remember. I saw him go. Come or not."

"Please, Mrs. Dermot, that trail doesn't look safe for you."

"Bull hockey. I walked that trail before you were born."

Charlie laughed. Trust Margie to know where he was. "It's okay, Beth," he hollered. "Let her go."

"You sure, Mr. Dermot?" Beth shouted back.

"I'm sure." Charlie waited. Margie knew the way just fine.

Angela Kruger

Hotel Blue: Stories

AN EXCERPT

In the summer of 2012, a young woman by the name of Mercy Brown moved into Room #801. At 5'11" with skinny white limbs and long dark hair, Mercy had the overall appearance of an ostrich, though she carried with her far more grace and poise. Her long hair typically fell in greasy strands around her face. By the time she'd arrived at the Blue, its showers and bathtubs were not places in which it was possible to become, strictly speaking, clean. She wore all black as a rule: black leggings, black camisole, black hoodie. But she was a spirited young woman and though covered in black, Mercy frequently gave her neighbours the impression that she was full of light.

Other than some old curtains hanging in the window, Mercy decorated her room with found furniture. Beside the window was her bed, metal-framed and well-worn. A mirror leaned against the wall atop a plastic yellow crate, which Mercy had repurposed as a nightstand. Stacked inside the crate were journals, each filled page-to-page with Mercy's looping scrawl, and, as of a few weeks ago, one Naloxone kit. She had received the kit from a woman who had come to the Blue offering training on how to respond to an overdose. The woman had given everyone kits. *Put a sign on your door*, the woman had said. *So your neighbours know you've got Naloxone.* So Mercy had put a sign on her door and kept it, the Naloxone kit, even treasured it—yet from some part of her being, still, she hated it. If only, she thought to herself when it caught her eye (which was often, in such a small room). If only there had been Naloxone when her mother was using.

Her mother died nearly twenty years earlier, on Tuesday, June 24th, 1997. Ever since, Mercy had been haunted by the day. Year after year, she saw it coming. She rounded the rains of April and the blooming of May waiting, anticipating, knowing all the while what lurked in June. Down to the day, she prepared herself. This year, for example, she had tried to get a good night's sleep.

But she'd only tossed and turned her way through the night, sleeping—then waking with a start to the wail and flash of blue and red—and then sleeping again, and then waking once more. When she finally woke at 7:00 a.m., not to sirens but to sunlight, she granted herself a few minutes in bed, eyes closed, to soak in the peace, then fastened her hair into a messy bun, got herself dressed, and headed out the door.

Outside, the city was grey. The clouds loomed overhead like great cushions—couch cushions, Mercy thought to herself, as she walked down Jackson. She recalled the couch from her childhood. A Hide-A-Bed. When she was lucky, her mother had sleepovers with her on that couch. Standing in her pyjamas, Mercy would watch as her mother pulled out its insides, turning it from couch to bed. An always marvellous transformation. Each time, with its insides turned out like that, the couch seemed like an invitation. She'd longed to crawl into it, adopt the couch like a hermit crab adopts its shell.

At Cordova, Mercy veered left. She took the cement path that cut through Oppenheimer Park, then continued westward for a few more blocks, along Powell. Today would be a hard day, of course, but at least she was home. She loved her home. The gum on the sidewalk was beautiful. The cigarettes were art. Even the needles, though they pained her, appeared that morning like flowers fallen to the ground, their plain white stems conceding to the brighter beauty at their tips—not the needle itself, but the orange plastic at the other end.

Arriving at The Dugout, she grabbed her breakfast (soup, a dinner bun, and a coffee) and made her way back to Oppenheimer. It was her habit, in the summertime, to pick up breakfast at The Dugout and eat it in the park like this. She loved the sprawling quiet. The gulls, with whom she sometimes shared her bun. Loved the feeling of soup in her belly, warm against the morning's chill. Plus, Oppenheimer was where she had learned of the spectacular moment, a little while after sunrise, when the community emerged—from rooms, shelters, and tents, or what have you—to greet the day, all together in one glorious, collective debut. It was for these moments that Mercy had trained herself, even once she'd moved into the Blue, to get up early and go outside.

The taste of free coffee settling on her tongue, she sat herself down on a wooden bench in the middle of the park. Lit up a smoke. The morning light filtered through the dark cherry blossom branches, stretched across the patchy grass, extended itself lazily over the brightly coloured tents. It filled the air, Mercy thought, with a breathable hope. She closed her eyes. Inhaled.

She often took deep breaths like this. Something her mother had taught her to do. It was a whole thing. A lesson. From Grade 2. Mercy had come home from school crying. She'd fought with her friend at lunch hour and this friend, Ashley Anderson, had threatened her with the "silent treatment," which was all the more threatening to Mercy because she didn't know what it was, but it sounded awful. Her mother had calmed her down. *Okay, Merc*, she'd said, steadying her daughter at the shoulders, looking her in the eye. *Take a deeeeeeep breath*. Tenderly, she had locked Mercy's gaze. And then holding her gaze, her mother had breathed with her: *in*, she'd instructed, and together, their shoulders and eyebrows rose; *and out*, she'd concluded, and their shoulders and eyebrows had relaxed.

After that, Mercy didn't even care what Ashley Anderson had said about whatever kind of treatment she was going to receive because her mom was her best friend anyway. French fries and hamburgers for dinner, a shared bag of ten-cent candies for dessert, and a stay-up-til-midnight sleepover had confirmed it. But then, just like with Ashley Anderson, somehow, Mercy had ruined it.

She'd begun by just getting her mother's attention: *Mom*, she'd said, and her mother had looked up at her. *How come you're always sleeping?* The question had wriggled from Mercy's gut all the way up her insides and out across her seven-year-old lips like a worm.

Her mother had frozen still, once again locking her daughter's gaze. Mercy had only been able to stare back, herself frozen to the spot. She'd been waiting, sitting there, frozen to the spot, to get in trouble, but the trouble never came. Or at least, she didn't get *in* trouble.

There *was* trouble, though. You just couldn't tell right away because all that happened at first was her mother had answered the question. *Oh, Mercy*, she'd said, in a real soft voice, *Mercy, baby ... I'm not sleeping now, am I?*

No, Mercy had assured her, she was not sleeping now—but then her mother's lips began to tremble and her chin began to crinkle and was that—yes, oh God, her eyes began to water. No! cried Mercy, recognizing her mother's pain. What had she done?! No! she cried. No, she was not sleeping now! But her mother seemed to take no notice. Just curled herself up into a ball. Bruised arms wrapped around folded legs. Head tucked between knobby knees.

And then, slowly, the ball began to shake. To sound. To cry, Mercy realized. Her mother was crying. No! she'd urged, shaking her mother. No, she was not sleeping now! She shook harder. She was not sleeping now, she was not sleeping now, she was not sleeping now! But it was no use. Mercy's mother had only sobbed. No matter what Mercy said—it was okay, she was not sleeping now, let's take a deeeeeep breath—her mother had not spoken a word.

A wind passed through the park. Mercy opened her eyes and discovered tears of her own rolling down her cheeks. Hot tears turned cold in the wind. She wiped them away. More came. What time was it? Eight thirty? Nine? She shook her head. The fieldhouse wasn't even serving morning coffee yet, and already, she had broken. Already, the day had got the better of her. Already, she needed to get back home. Retreat.

From Oppenheimer, it was a less-than-five-minute walk back to the Blue, but still, she hurried. Rising from the bench in the park, she folded her arms and doubled down, her pace quickening as she walked.

A wave of relief came over her when she saw the Blue appear on the horizon. Bursting through the hotel's entrance, she dashed up the stairs, arrived in a sweat on the eighth floor, twisted her key into the lock, and fell into her room. Release. Not of tears, exactly, though there were those. More, though, of being *home*. She was grateful, once again, to Trina, her auntie, who lived down the hall, for getting her this room. Where no one else could come in, unless she said they could. Where she could close the door. And lock it. Her own space. A shell.

She kicked off her sandals, hung her purse up on its hook, and flopped onto her bed, defeated. Closed her eyes. Breathed in deep. Fucking exhausting, surviving. Surviving at all. Like, just you, yourself, not dying. But especially the kind of surviving where it's not just you. Where it's you, yourself, not dying, when all the while, someone else, who was supposed to be not dying with you, is, in fact, already dead.

She splayed her limbs across the bed and lay still. A starfish on a rock. Basking. The grey day sun arrived on Mercy's skin soft as a sonata, assuaging her, drawing her ever deeper into its lemonade light, until she let go and was carried away into the reverie of sleep.

Frederic Sahyouni

The Fragrant Harbour

AN EXCERPT FROM "THE WANDERER
AND THE DREAMER"

The plane finally touched the ground with a turbulent thud, and I got up with sore legs after a sleepless fifteen-hour flight. It was a rainy evening in Hong Kong. I got off the plane, dragging my heavy legs, went to the luggage carousel and waited for my backpack, while my blood started flowing regularly through my limbs in a tingling sensation after hours of numbness. I stepped outside and breathed in the humid air before I was whisked into a taxi queue for a long, confusing minute. Then the attendant quickly gestured me to an old, boxy red-and-white Toyota. I handed over the address to the faceless driver, and for the first time in my life, I was being driven on the left side of the road.

The taxi was filled with different ornaments on and around the dashboard. There were waving lucky cat figurines, a red lantern pendant hanging from the rear view mirror, three phones wired haphazardly around the steering wheel, and a number of IDs and signs written in Chinese and English. As we drove through the Kowloon neighbourhood, I sat in awe and let the city envelop me in its glimmering marvel.

I had never experienced anything quite like Hong Kong under a rainy night. Its neon colours gleamed on the dark streets and sidewalks, hidden beneath clusters of umbrellas held by an assortment of characters in long coats and pale faces, waiting at the traffic lights of a bustling crossing where tramways transported evening young professionals from restaurant to bar, to street food, back to bar—the whiffs of that street food made denser by the thick humidity brought on by the rain, carrying a delicious marriage of dough and meat deep fried in an old wok. Tiny chairs sat outside the street food stalls under a red and orange marquee lit up to advertise a regional cuisine tucked between larger storefronts with luminous signs in Chinese and the familiar-to-me logos of McDonald's and KFC. The taxi continued on from the narrow streets into heavy traffic, surrounded by bright billboards stretching around street corners, and the cityscape unveiled itself in an old-meets-new experience, where romance serenades late on the waterfront behind colourful moving crowds, hidden pockets of heartbreak eating cups of sad noodles after too many cocktails at the Irish pub. I felt a sense of belonging here, needing to be part of the crowd that flits everywhere in such a determined manner. I watched the intersection fill with dapper businessmen, pretty women dressed in pastel-coloured raincoats and black skirts, and tourists with backpacks, all headed to the myriad of trams and taxis zipping by like notes from a symphony, and all I wanted to do was live in a high-rise building and fall in love with a beautiful bartender who would join me after her shift at four a.m.

Colleen Doty
All About Isaac
AN EXCERPT

He loves riding in the family's baby blue Volkswagen bug. Mom calls it the tin can, and that's how it feels with all the vibrations and the rounded roof over them. But he also feels comforted, so it's more than just a tin can. They can move so fast and be protected from all that whizzes past them on the streets. Baby blue is also his favourite colour. The colour of the walls in his bedroom. The colour of his pyjamas.

As Mom and he get into the car, she says, "You need to sit in the seat behind me." He is too young to sit in the front, in the only seat with a seat belt, one that goes across his shoulder and cuts into his face. Chloe, because she's six and bigger, usually gets to ride in the front seat and that annoys him. Lisa is nine and doesn't really care about stuff like that.

He likes Lisa better these days.

"Remember, no playing with the door lock or handle," Mom says.

He nods, and holds onto his teddy. Last time they went in the car, he had been curious and pulled the handle and the door swung open while Mom was driving. Mom didn't like that. She screamed. Luckily, Lisa grabbed onto his shirt while Mom quickly pulled over and stopped the car and screamed at him some more. That was scary.

"When we pick up the girls, you can sit in the middle and Lisa can hold onto you in case we come to a quick stop."

They pick up Chloe and Lisa from school. The big school with its swings and monkey bars and lots of kids running around in the field and tossing balls. While Chloe runs to the front seat and jumps in, she glances to him in the backseat and sticks out her tongue in victory. He

43

sticks his tongue out back at her, but she has already looked away. Lisa is now in the backseat with him and he smiles at her because he remembers he can now enjoy his favourite place to sit. He slides over to the middle where he can look out the front windshield and pretend he is driving.

Mom says he'll be in school next year too, but he's not quite sure how far away that is. He finds asking doesn't really help. Older people just don't seem to know how to explain time to a kid. It's a year and a bit, they'll say. Hundreds of sleeps away. Does that include naps? No, just night-time sleeps to make hundreds of days. How long is a day? Twenty-four hours in a day, Lisa will say. But what's an hour? Sixty minutes, Dad tells him. Just count to sixty slowly, sixty times, then you have an hour, Lisa says. Times that by 24, another number. What's "times?" Times are the number of groups. "Just sometime in the future!" they end up telling him, usually with a sigh or a huff.

School seems like a long way away. He can't imagine himself as a big boy. He'll have to wear a uniform when he goes. Chloe and Lisa are both wearing their grey jumpers and white shirts. Chloe's socks are falling down. Lisa's are neat. Of course. His uniform, the one for boys, according to Mom, will be grey pants and a white shirt.

"Hold onto him if I have to stop in a hurry, Lisa," Mom reminds her. Lisa grips the back of his shirt around his waist. When he squirms she pulls back harder. "Hey, do you want your face to get rearranged going through the glass? Then sit still," she says to him just loud enough to calm Mom but not too loud so as to distract her while she's focusing on traffic.

Today they head to the hospital. Another trip. More tests at the lab. More needles. The nurses call them pokes but he knows better. He'll try not to cry today. He promised Mom he wouldn't make a fuss and she promised him a new little car—maybe an orange one like the car on *The Dukes of Hazzard*, the show he likes to watch so much. That orange car, a Dodge Charger, jumps over any bad guys or big cliffs that get in the way. He smiles, thinking about watching the show again with his orange cars arranged beside him. Every time the car makes a jump in the show, he guides his own little car across his lap in time with the music that always plays in the background.

His mind jumps back to what's coming up. The hospital. Now his stomach aches. He will have to be brave or he could die. He doesn't want to die. The doctors need to figure out what is wrong with him. He's too skinny. Mom says he's lost too much weight when he should be gaining weight and growing taller like other four-year-olds. Although he was sick for while with a fever and infection, he should now be getting bigger. But he's not. Mom and Dad feed him ice cream and chocolate sauce every day, plus lots of other food, whatever kind he wants: gravy, mashed potatoes, hamburgers, hot dogs, spaghetti with meatballs. Dad often buys those Sara Lee cakes. He loves all this food. All he has to do is point from his seat in the shopping cart to something in the aisle and Mom or Dad will stop the cart and say, "Shall we get some of that, Isaac?"

When Isaac takes a bath Mom always looks at his stomach to see if she can see any more muscles or veins showing.

"My poor baby. We need to fatten you up," she says, biting her lip. "The next breeze that comes along is going to blow you over!"

Isaac thinks about the little orange car he will get after today's visit. Lisa and Chloe won't get anything, except maybe a chance to pick the ice cream flavour when they buy some afterward at the grocery store. Lisa and Chloe, he thinks, are a bit cranky with having to go to the hospital again this week.

Chloe kicks the dashboard and Mom tells her to stop. Mom likes things nice. "We can't afford to buy another car if you kick a hole in this one," Mom says.

Chloe stops, pouts, and makes a grunt as she looks out the window. She turns around to the backseat and sticks her tongue out at him. Again.

Isaac sticks his tongue out back at her. She's always so mean. She whirls back around and returns to swinging her legs in the front seat.

The drive to the hospital is quiet except for the road noises. They have to go over one big orange bridge. Another orange thing. The "Patella" Mom calls it.

"When are we going to be there?" Chloe says.

Mom says nothing.

Then a little louder, Chloe repeats: "Mom, when are we—"

"Shush!" Mom says, swatting her hand like Chloe is a pesky dog. "I'm trying to concentrate. This bridge is crazy!"

Isaac watches out the front window. The lanes have become narrow. People are all driving so fast! Traffic coming at them with only two yellow lines separating other cars from their blue Volkswagen. Mom changes lanes into the one closest to the sidewalk and the orange railing. Orange again.

Once they have rounded the second curve and left the bridge, Mom exhales. "Sorry, Chloe. I hate that bridge! Lots of people die every year. Look how white my hands are." Mom holds out one hand in front of Chloe. It's shaking.

Chloe sucks in her lower lip. Mom quickly changes the subject.

"The hospital is just up the hill a little ways."

As they drive past a big park, Mom points out the window, "Queen's Park, kids. I promise to take you there lots this summer."

"Yeah!" Chloe cheers.

"You mean, 'yes.' It's not polite to say 'yeah.'"

"Yeah, that's what I meant," Chloe says. Then her eyes go big and she laughs. She puts her hand over her mouth. "Oops!"

"Cheeky," Mom says, smiling.

Isaac looks out the window at the large playground set back in the tall trees.

"I love those swings that seem to go forever up into the sky." Lisa says. She's relaxed her grip on Isaac a bit since they left the bridge behind them.

Isaac thinks about the summer ahead of them. The feeling of warm sun on their faces, bare feet running through grass, the fun they will have charging through sprinklers and building tree forts.

Maybe it will be a summer without needles.

Libby Soper

The Anniversary Cake

She checked the clock above the stove. Still plenty of time before the kids came home from school. She turned back to the cake, which waited for frosting, passive and compliant, like a woman anticipating her lover.

Seven-minute icing was ready in a bowl on the counter. A recipe from page 725 of *The Joy of Cooking*, a wedding present from her mother. Tattered and grease-stained, it still bore the inscription: "To my dearest daughter, in the hope that the fruits of this tome will find a sure way to Carl's heart for years to come. Devotedly, Mum."

She opened a drawer and rummaged for a spatula. In Carl's case, access to his heart now seemed to be gained via a more southerly route.

In recent years, her husband's tastes had shifted: tangos with Thai food, the raw pleasure of sushi, dalliances with minute amuse-gueule, forays into vegetarianism. Perhaps she didn't excel at experimentation in the kitchen, but she did have a solid repertoire of recipes at her fingertips. She had mastered the art of seven-minute icing, for example, a minor victory, regardless of the Rombauers' description of it as "a very fluffy, delightful icing that never fails." She'd been whipping it up to complement Lady Baltimore Cake (page 672, based on the batter for White Cake I, page 671) annually since their second anniversary, shortly after Melanie's birth.

They had chosen not to go out that year, unwilling to entrust their infant to the dubious care of a teenager, so they had stayed home to celebrate. She had laboured for hours over an elaborate meal: beef Wellington cooked just the way Carl liked it, tiny spears of asparagus swimming in lemon butter, the extravagance of early strawberries, and of course, the Anniversary Cake, as it came to be known.

The Anniversary Cake had pleasant associations, each year something special. That first time, Melanie for once quiet in her crib, they had finished dinner and moved to bed, where they feasted on the cake, stuffing succulent chunks into each others' mouths, sucking sticky fingers, giggling self-consciously. Carl had daubed her milk-heavy breasts with frosting, then licked them clean with deliberate sweeps of his tongue. Arching against his mouth, she felt her milk come down with a tingling rush of intensity, like the onset of tears. Carl looked up hesitantly, as if for permission, closing his lips around a swollen nipple. His hair soft under her hand, she cradled his dark head to one breast and felt the other begin to weep in milky sympathy. Trembling pearls slid in slow rivulets down her side with each breath.

Then, for the first time since the birth, they had made love, Carl tender and tentative for fear of hurting her. After, as he lay stilled and softening, his breathing slipping toward sleep, the baby awoke, the first wail calling her milk again.

In the kitchen, she paused, remembering. Slipping her hand under her blouse, she cupped a breast, grazed the stiffening nipple, pressed her pelvis hard against her other hand. It took several moments for the pulsing to ease. She shuddered, then briskly picked up the spatula and began frosting. That was many years ago. But the cake would be part of an anniversary ritual this year, as always.

An intense scuffle erupted in the walk-in pantry. Reaching over, she opened the door, and a large grey tomcat glided out, a small body dangling from his jaws. The mice had come in early this year, but Grendel kept them at bay. She watched idly, toying with an idea while spreading creamy swathes over the first layer, popping the second layer on top and starting to frost the sides. The cat paused in the middle of the kitchen and released the mouse. The tiny creature froze, sides pumping, then made a dash for the pantry. For a moment Grendel observed its efforts with an air of detached interest; then he crouched, tail quivering in tight, controlled spasms, and pounced with deadly accuracy. Returning to the

49

middle of the room, he again freed his prey, this time intercepting its frantic sprint with a dart of his curved clawed paw.

Third time released, the mouse hunched motionless on the floor, as if trying to disappear into the pattern of the tiles. This seemed to bore Grendel, who batted at it several times before again grasping it in his mouth. With a toss of his head, he sent his small playmate in a graceful arc. It landed with a soft plop and began to inch sideways in hiccupping jerks, a faint brownish stain spreading behind it. The cat was instantly on it, gleeful.

Must be near the end, she thought, turning the frosted cake to inspect it from all sides. Perfect. Just enough time to decorate.

Methodically she assembled her tool: a cone-shaped pastry bag with a choice of removable tips. She chose her favourite, which released in precisely the right width a smooth fluted stream of frosting. Into the bag she spooned pink-tinted icing, prepared from a special recipe (Decorative Icing or Twice-Cooked Icing, page 724), designed to set quick and hard for decorating.

She eyed the cake, marking with a toothpick the exact placement of the letters to ensure flawless symmetry. It was important to have a clear idea of the finished product before beginning: "As in any work of art, the concept must dominate the technique" (page 723, *About Decorative Icings*). Picking up the pastry bag, she hesitated for an instant, then began.

She had almost finished looping the L in Carl when a piercing cry came from the corner of the kitchen. Starting violently, she ruined the final curve. She cursed once, viciously, then corrected the blemish as best she could. The death-shriek continued to rise, awful in its jagged rhythm.

They get so shrill near the end, grovelling for one more chance, she thought contemptuously. Can't they tell it's all OVER?

Her hand contracted in a hard squeeze, spurting a jet of frosting across the cake. The shriek ended abruptly.

It took a few minutes to repair the damage. Then, steadying her hand, she continued smoothly through the ampersand and on to the second name, taking pleasure in keeping the extravagant flourishes perfect and even. It was going to be a work of art. Her best.

Grendel ambled over, arching briefly against her legs before dropping his trophy. Good boy, she murmured abstractedly. With a twitch of his beautiful tail, the cat proceeded to a patch of sunlight, where he stretched luxuriously and settled to clean himself with satisfied sweeps of his tongue, eyes slit in pleasure.

She stepped back to admire her work. It was perfect: Happy First Anniversary, Carl & Chrissy. The combination so pleasing, so euphonious, intertwined as if joined organically for eternity. *Let no man put asunder.*

Time for the final touch. With a satisfied nod, she bent and scooped the tiny mangled body from the floor. Taking the spatula, she pried up an edge of the cake's top layer, then slipped the mouse into the opening, tucking the tail neatly behind it. She replaced the layer, wiped her hands, and carefully refrosted where the opening had been, restoring her creation to unmarred perfection. This accomplished, she lifted the cake and set it in a waiting box, which she had already marked FRAGILE, THIS SIDE UP. She taped it closed and wrote an address on it, checking the spelling from a scrap of paper she had unearthed from her purse.

At a sound outside, she glanced up and through the living room window saw a white van stopping in front of her house. They're early, she thought. It will get there in plenty of time for dinner.

A man got out of the van and started up the walkway, consulting a small clipboard. This time she scrawled the two names close together above the address with brutal black strokes. Breathing heavily, she remained bent over the box for a moment. Then she straightened and started to giggle, hand pressed to her mouth.

The doorbell sounded. She picked up the Anniversary Cake and started for the door, smiling in anticipation.

eve nixen

Pocketing Love Notes to Strangers

I can tell Beau's upset when he calls my landline, already outside the apartment. "Can I come in?" his voice wavers through the static; he sounds almost distressed.

I hit the buzzer to let him in. I haven't seen Beau since I took him to the country show and he flirted with the singer—easily the most beautiful person in the room. It pissed me off and I sulked into the night, leaving without saying goodbye.

We pull up a set of chairs.

"My mom just left the country, and my old man told me he doesn't want me to stay at their place."

I don't miss a beat. "You can crash with me."

We are all creatures of habit, not creatures of perfection, but we're aiming for it. Wilfully forgiving.

☞

I wake up to the sound of the door closing as Beau leaves in the morning. A familiar emptiness settles into my bones. There's no soft breeze of lips on my forehead. It's been eleven restless nights lying side by side, barely touching. Sometimes out of habit, in a dreamy slumber, he rolls over, pressing himself against my back. I relax but never with the same ease, into a familiar place. To soft sighs of his breath on the back of my neck.

☞

My cell phone rings at lunch, and I'm surprised to see Beau's number on the screen. He's calling to tell me about his nightmare. He dreamt again of being Sisyphus, of having no choice to but keep pushing that boulder.

"Well, isn't it in some way the same, you staying with me? Dragging our hearts back up the hill?"

He quickly changes the subject. "Johnny's got a show tonight. Let's go."

We gather at the Brasserie, the local haunt and old dive for music any given night of the week on Beaubien. The bartender is a woman named Tracy. She smokes in the bathroom and asks me to read her the poems scrawled in the toilet stall, while I piss out cheap beer. As I wash my hands, I watch her apply pink lipstick on a crooked smile. It makes her mouth look like a tulip. The regulars sulk at the back of the bar, playing the muted slot machines. The pool table is shuttered off in its brown leather casing. I sway and prop my beer next to the no drinks sign on the table, because everyone fucking does it, while Johnny moans solitary sermons on stage. Fired up by some unholy confidence brought on by the Belle Gueule, I scribble him a love note on a sticky bar napkin.

After the show, Johnny embraces me tightly as we say goodbye, his wool jacket reeking like the fish from the factory he's been working at. I slip the note into his coat pocket. I catch eyes with Beau, does he see me do it? Johnny kisses my cheeks, the feel of his lips running electric, burning up one after the other. Beau frowns at me suspiciously, clouds of smoke coming from his mouth in the desolate snow-lined winter streets.

A few weeks later, I run into Johnny at a show at Casa. The back room is quiet that night, just a few other people aside from the band. He is wearing the same coat. This time when we hug I pick up the scent of cigar smoke and scotch. We sway to the melodic drone, immersed in a Holy Act of Art. I ask him if he ever found a note in his coat pocket. He says no and I try not to act surprised. He checks his pockets while we talk, pulling out his wallet, keys, and a playing card. Seven of diamonds. "No, I never found anything."

I try not to feel upset for the rest of the night. To not allow it to settle—how I never leave much of an impression on people. That things we believe as Love are no more than a crumpled napkin you find in your pocket and throw away with faith.

The Gatekeeper's Breasts

Red tells me, before nodding off, to lead from the heart. But I prefer to follow. While she sleeps, her breasts rise and fall. I am hypnotized. She is the moon, and the blood of my body are tides, drawn in and out by the steady rhythm of her chest.

I want to rewrite the Bible. The part that says it was from Adam's rib that Eve was born, because I am certain it was from the slender bone of *her* ribcage that I was built and made. She is the ruler of my heart, the keeper of the way, and I am a part of her. When we fight and love turns to hate, I am left outside the garden, pounding at its gates. She that leaves me barren and broken, but also welcomes me back. Her breasts are both a battleground and a safe haven, a return to grace.

Tonight she sleeps on her back, and I know she is no longer angry with me. I gently walk my fingers along her flesh, journeying up her mountains. The calloused edges of my fingertips descend the peaks and valleys of her sternum. Her eyelids flutter like the wings of starlings. I lay my head between those mounds, nourished by the cavern of her heart. It thunders in my ears; its beat pulling me in. Guides me through the torrents of our wild nature. I am a lost ship at sea until I lay there, her breath filling my sails with air, coursing us both home. In the arms of her being, on that belly of water, I find all that I need.

Sarah Phillips-Thin

Grasping at the Pineapple

An excerpt from a novel about a guy with a money problem

who works as a driver for a foreign family

Krishna stood at the Nature's Basket cheese counter tasting a sliver of Dutch Gouda that he'd had to ask for, and compared it to the good-sized chunk Ma'am was always immediately offered. He realized they had switched.

Here he was, shopping from stainless steel shelves and glass chillers kept steady at four degrees. He filled the little red basket on wheels with French unsalted butter, spotless eggs sold in sixes, and Danish organic pasteurized milk in plastic bottles with labels showing cows grazing on acres and acres of green pastures lush, sheltered by snowy mountains fresh. He thought of their own cows, snatching patches of grass, garbage, and shrubs, munching their cud amongst roads and pavements and people, their unpasteurized milk, in white plastic bags, hooked each morning on entrance gates.

Ma'am, listening for the vegetable wallah's call, would shop from the cart with no language in common except an eye for the freshest vegetable: a purple shining brinjal, firm slender okra, green chana dal. Ma'am would laugh with the seller, sometimes at her own attempt at growing palak in the back garden; first crop perfect, second crop not so, eaten by bandicoots, leaving green-tinged droppings in a clear cut of pale stalks.

Krishna noticed on Ma'am's shopping list something usually bought from the vegetable cart. He made his way to the produce section and picked up a "coloured bell pepper." He couldn't believe it. One hundred and ten rupees each. For the same thing. Why buy this? For the imported stuff, sure, it bought a sense of home and consolation for foreigners, but for this? Instead of a green one from the vegetable wallah for fifteen rupees. It made no sense.

He never really paid attention to these discrepancies before, between the rich, foreign or Indian, and the very poor. But lately the differences bothered him, and now with Sita's pregnancy his irritation had gotten worse. He could hear Sita's words clearly, and even though he had fought with her, she was right. Ma'am and Sir had the money. Krishna picked out one red, one orange, one yellow, and headed to the cashier pulling the basket behind him.

⌒

He tries to fit one more shirt into Sir's suitcase, tries to do up the clasps, quickly. He can't. He tries to fit one more shoe into his own bag, one more English schoolbook, one more dupatta. He can't complete this task, can't get away from the tension that chases him. He tries to put in a pineapple, quickly, but the plastic is too thin, the bag rips, and everything falls.

Krishna woke up, still grasping at the pineapple from his dream. He could feel sweat and a thumping at his temples. He rolled over and tapped his phone. 4:07 a.m. The usual.

Sita slept facing him, hugging the bolster tight to her cheek and chest and stomach, keeping herself and the new one warm and calm and safe. He slunk off the bed and crept out.

"Acha, Tiny." He sat down on the steps and rubbed the dog's head and ears while his thoughts returned incessantly to his debt. His brother and Guna had loaned him so much, yet he forgot to value this, to be thankful, too busy making a big deal of borrowing. Krishna watched a mosquito land on Tiny's nose and fill with blood. It wasn't white, there was no daylight, and dogs don't get dengue. "Fuck you mosquito," he said, and pinched it dead.

⌒

Krishna stopped the car and waited for the children at the school pickup zone until the guard blared his whistle for him to move along. As he looped around the parking lot, he noticed his cousin Christopher, in a spotlessly clean, sky-blue Innova. Krishna waved. Christopher greeted him back with a pleased smile.

Some years back, Christopher had been offered a two-year driving contract by his Sir, in Texas. All the drivers including Krishna had coveted this lucky opportunity. When he returned, Christopher bought two Toyota Innova Crystas outright. One he leased to another driver, one he drove himself, trading it in every year for the newest model, as shiny as the one he was in now. Lucky fellow set up for life.

There they were. He stopped, the guard smiling at him now, jumped out, and helped the children into the car.

⌒

Krishna opened the French doors and the children ran into the dining room. Ma'am was waiting as usual, happy to see her children.

"Smoothie, Krishna?"

"Okay Ma'am. Thanks."

"Have a seat," she said, passing him a glass full of swirling pink. Krishna took a sip, tasting the blueberries and strawberries and peaches, and placed the glass down on the beeswax-polished teak table that could seat twelve.

"Ma'am?"

"Yes, Krishna?"

He knew by her tone she was expecting something light, like how the new bananas were growing well in the back garden, or how he'd paid the street sweeper a little extra to remove the sand on the front pavements.

"I'm having some money troubles ..."

She turned to face him.

"I need a loan."

"What for, Krishna?"

He started mumbling something over her concern, but realized he needed to tell the truth. Krishna talked to her about the severe dengue, his daughter's recovery, and his debt.

"And Sita is pregnant."

Ma'am's face lit up, then clouded instantly. Krishna knew she wanted another baby, that Sir would not do surrogacy, that she had put her name onto adoption lists. He also knew India would never give up one of her babies to a foreigner.

At that moment Sir walked in. "Hello everyone," he said, his pushed-forward posture carrying intention and confidence.

Krishna stood up quickly. He thought about how when Sir rode the Enfield with the helmet on, you couldn't tell he was a foreigner—his height, his colour, the way he idled the bike at just the right moments of traffic.

"Why so glum?" he said, looking at his wife.

Ma'am smiled, "Not glum, just talking, love."

Sir looked from his wife to Krishna standing at attention, "Okay ... what about?"

"Some money troubles are there, Sir ... I need a loan."

"Ah." Sir walked over to the water chiller and poured himself a glass. "What about the money we gave you for your daughter's school fees. And for the last fender bender?"

"A loan only."

"But you know how difficult it would be to pay back a loan for you," he said, and sat down beside Ma'am, while Krishna continued to stand in discomfort. "Why are you short of money?"

Krishna started, but Ma'am spoke instead in her direct manner, explaining everything. "And," she said, "the most beautiful news is Krishna and Sita are expecting a baby."

There was a silence then amongst them that churned with failure and loss.

"We'll think it over," Ma'am said, at last. "Let's talk more about this later."

"Thanks Ma'am," he said, and was finally able to move away from the awkwardness.

⌐

Krishna started the car when he saw Sir come out of the glass doors of the World Trade Centre beside Orion mall. When it was Ma'am he was picking up from the mall, she would often have a box of Krispy Kreme donuts, Krishna's favourite.

Sir raised his eyebrows in greeting as he got in and kept talking on his phone, about lamb prices and VAT problems and long wait times for product to get through the Mumbai Port. When they were almost at the house, he hung up and looked at Krishna in the rear-view mirror.

"Hello, Krishna, how are you?"

"Good, Sir," he said, breathing out deeply, moving the anxiety from waiting for the loan answer elsewhere.

"We finally got the dates."

"Sir?"

"My contract is up. It's been almost four years, and now we're moving back home."

Krishna started coughing into the back of his hand and couldn't stop.

"Sorry, Sir," he said and took a sip from his water bottle.

"All right?"

Before Krishna could respond through the dense fog made up entirely of the fact that he was completely financially ruined, and now would have no job, he heard Sir say, "We have decided we would like to offer you employment."

Krishna pulled up at the gate and turned off the engine.

"It would be a two year contract," he continued, "in Vancouver. Let's go in and talk to Anna and she can give you all the details."

Krishna, still speechless, got out of the Innova, opened the gate, waited for Sir to go through, then followed him along the path lined with palms in terracotta pots and in through the French doors.

Francesca Mauri

The Day of Her Disappearance

AN EXCERPT FROM "ADRIANA"

SATURDAY, 1ST SEPTEMBER 2007

I looked at the people waiting to cross the street at the traffic lights opposite me: mothers weighed down by children and shopping bags, a couple of joggers bouncing up and down, a group of lads I didn't recognize. Luckily. I hated bumping into people I was supposed to wave at, maybe even talk to. I always felt so awkward that I preferred to pretend I hadn't seen them. Or imagine turning into one of those tiny glass frogs, which can vanish against the jungle backdrop, as I'd read about for a science project.

I didn't know where to put my hands. They'd already been through my hair, in my pockets, tight in fists at my side. I was waiting for Adriana in front of The Sleepy Bear, our favourite café, the one we went to whenever we were tired of sitting on grass, pavement, and benches. And we were dying for a sausage roll with HP Sauce. She'd messaged me the night before ("Breakfast tomorrow?") and I'd felt relieved. We'd gone a few days without seeing each other for the first time in the entire summer. She'd seemed distant even in her texts, but maybe it was just me reading too much into it.

As the light turned green and the crowd scurried forward, I saw her sprinting to the junction. Then slowing down as she crossed, as if she could feel my eyes on her. Did she enjoy me watching her? She was looking up at a rapidly darkening sky. *God*, I thought. *If only I had Dad's camcorder with me. Still. Even if I had the guts to record this moment it wouldn't do it justice.* She was stunning. Coming toward me, her hair tied in a ponytail swinging from side to side, her top at least a size too small, her navel piercing gleaming intermittently in the light.

A sudden downpour smashed against the concrete. Its sound made me think of that song by Guns N' Roses with the long drumming intro: "You Could Be Mine." Some people scattered to find shelter, others fumbled with umbrellas. Everyone but Adriana and I. We didn't flinch, like we weren't even getting wet. Like it was just us two. I stood as still as a Queen's Guard and she didn't walk any faster. Of course, she didn't have an umbrella with her. I bet she didn't own one. She never dressed for the weather. Only for herself.

When she was finally in front of me, she laughed, and pointed to her face. "Hiya. I'm up here."

Waves of heat rippled from the base of my neck to my chin, as I looked away from her belly.

"Sorry I'm late." She nodded at the café and I followed her inside.

"What's up?" Adriana asked, after we'd ordered and sat down at an empty table. Before I could answer, she added in one breath, "I can't stay long today. Meeting a friend."

My blood ran cold. A tightness crept up my neck. I stared at her, but she avoided my eyes, picking off her black nail polish. *What?* I thought we'd spend the day together. Especially after she'd gone off the radar. And it was our last weekend before school started. She began talking about this new manga she was reading, but I just tuned out.

"Hello, Earth calling Lewis?"

"Sorry." I rubbed my temples. "Headache. You were saying?"

Just then, a waitress materialized with our sausage rolls and coffees. But I wasn't hungry anymore. "Are you meeting Sarah later?"

Sarah was Adriana's only other friend. They'd met at the after-school drawing class Adriana had taken for five months before the summer. We were all in the same year. I'd spoken to Sarah only once or twice; the two of them normally hung out on their own. Like us, Sarah wasn't the most popular kid. She was a proper goth; the few other people who dressed like her were in Sixth Form, too old and cool for us. Pricks our age made fun of her. Yet she didn't seem to care. Maybe that's why Adriana liked her.

"No, she's still away with her family."

I waited for her to tell me who she was meeting instead, but she just shredded her paper napkin. I noticed I was stomping on the floor with my left foot and stopped at once, even though both my feet were itching to move. *Should I just ask which friend?*

She looked up at me for the first time. "Sorry about today, Lewis. And the last few days. Been busier than usual."

Busy doing what?

She took another sip of her coffee and shot a quick glance at her watch, clearly trying not to be too overt about it. I bit the inside of my cheek. She'd never been that vague before. Or quiet.

"It's okay. Just thought we'd have spent the day together, that's all," I mumbled as I pushed back my chair and rose to my feet. "Don't want you to be late."

Adriana tipped her head to the side and gulped down the rest of her drink. She wasn't used to seeing me pissed off. Anger was something I kept to myself. It felt too intimate to show to other people, even her. Whenever I was mad at a teacher, my parents, or Adriana, I forced it all down to the bottom of my stomach. I released it only when I had a pillow pressed against my face. Or the bin under my desk I'd kick like a football.

I yanked the door open, Adriana stumbling behind me. I started walking, no precise destination in mind. I didn't know where she needed to go. She had to rush to keep up with me. For once I wasn't adjusting my pace to hers. The silence between us was unnatural, heavy. It'd stopped raining, but a cool wind was moving our hair back and forth. Neither of us bothered putting it back in place.

63

We were passing by the arcade, when she stopped and pointed at the narrow street just behind it. "There."

We walked down that road up to what we called our "secret" shortcut. A stone staircase you'd only notice if you really paid attention or went exploring, like we did. It was partly hidden by a row of dumpsters and the vaporous foliage of the trees that framed it.

Since we'd found it a few years ago, we'd always used it, unless too high or drunk to make the trek. Our neighbourhood was uphill, so walking back from the town centre had always been a pain. The shortcut saved us so much time; the staircase climbed straight up. Almost without a curve. All this time we'd never bumped into anyone on it. That was why we'd assumed it was one of our secrets. We felt as if we owned it. Like the abandoned leisure centre or our secret-not-so-secret beaches.

"Are you meeting your friend up there?" I asked as she stood on the first step.

"No, I'll pop back home first." Twirling her hair around her finger, she added, "You coming up with me?"

I didn't answer straight away. "I think I'll pass by Jam. Elijah has some new records he wants to show me."

It was a lie; I didn't even know if Elijah was working that day. If I hadn't been annoyed at her, I'd have said yes. Walked her home, then spent the rest of the afternoon in my room, playing with my PlayStation. But now I didn't feel like following her like a dog. I wanted her to notice I was mad. We never kept secrets from each other. Plus, the other day, when we were tidying up the shop, Elijah had said something that had stuck with me. We were talking girls. Well, he was, I was listening. He was a bit older, much more experienced than me. He gave me some tips: "You shouldn't be too available. Girls like it when you're in control. Unpredictable. When you have power over them."

"Right." Adriana hesitated, her left foot turned to the side, her hand clutching her necklace. "Listen, Lewis, I'll message ya tonight, okay? And next time we meet it'll be better, promise. We'll do something fun."

She moved forward, wavering on the edge of the step, as if she wanted to come back down to me. But then she frowned and leaned back.

I nodded. "Speak later."

She flashed me a smile and started climbing. I dragged my feet toward town. I had a sour taste in my mouth that wasn't caused by the coffee. I couldn't shake off the bad feeling that had tied my stomach into knots. *What if this new friend takes up all of Adriana's time? Will she still hang out with me? Is it possible that ... surely she won't ... will she replace me?*

I shook my head and stopped walking. *Cut the drama, Lewis.* I turned and looked up. I hoped she was also peeking down at me. I wanted our eyes to meet. I wanted to take a last look at her smile, the dimple on her left cheek, the locks of hair that had escaped from her ponytail. But she'd already gone too far up. There was no sign of her.

Anya Wyers

Romilegal: Downtown

AN EXCERPT

Romi.

Get yourself together.

I glanced at my reflection in the mirror of the fanciest bathroom I could ever remember being in.

"Why do people even splash water on their faces? Like it's supposed to help undrink the martinis or something?"

Just as I finished speaking, out loud, to my very alone self in the bathroom of the Wedgewood hotel, a perfectly coiffed elderly woman wearing a skirt suit worthy of the Queen of bloody England walked into the room.

My eyes drifted to my left and behind me in the mirror at her as she cleared her throat. I squeezed the slightest, crooked smile from my numb face in response.

How on earth had I let myself get drunk at my first team lunch?

The Queen, whose beige orthopaedic runners were more suited to a walking tour of downtown Vancouver and looked too cheap to make her the actual Queen of England, clutched her purse to her chest and darted into the closest bathroom stall.

Handbag. To her, I'm sure it was a handbag.

I rolled my eyes and refocused on my blurry reflection in the mirror. As if the drunken, frizzy-haired weirdo talking to herself was going to steal the not-Queen's handbag or beat her to the ground in the washroom for shits and giggles or something.

I washed my hands quickly, though I'd already cleaned them at least three times while I attempted to talk myself out of the fact that I was really quite drunk.

I smoothed my skirt, my breath quickening. I reached for the door handle that would lead me back to the table where my new boss, lawyer Elizabeth Baird-Conwill, and two fellow paralegals of team EBC waited for me.

They must do this often. Weekly. At least.

I couldn't remember the last time I had a martini. Never mind at lunch, in my first week at a new job.

Perhaps lawyers and their staff often got wasted to forget the shitty people and accidents they dealt with on a daily basis? At least in personal injury law.

I had no way of knowing and brushed the thoughts away, picking my way back through the restaurant, a casual smile plastered to my face in hopes that I was fooling everyone around me into thinking I was sober.

Spoiler alert: I hadn't fooled anyone.

As I reached the table, I glanced at the ladies around me, exuding elegance—living, breathing professionals. Elizabeth was holding the stem of her wine glass, watching beautiful, blond, blue-eyed Sara intently as she laughed at something funny someone else just said. Not a grey hair on Elizabeth's head was out of place, her rouge perfect, lipstick unsmudged. She took a sip of wine just as she noticed my arrival back at the table. She had switched from martinis before I went to the bathroom. Thankfully, I hadn't been given the option. Mixing alcohol at one in the afternoon was not a good idea.

Not that vodka was either.

I attempted to lower myself gracefully into the high-backed chair, a soft velvet that pulled my skirt while my lower body moved without it. I readjusted myself awkwardly, finally settling much further to the front of the chair than was comfortable. My skirt pulled down as I tried to shift back, untucking my blouse and exposing my skin, a light breeze tickling my back.

"Is everything okay?" Elizabeth asked, a frown perched on her unnaturally arched eyebrows.

"Fine. I'm fine," I said too quickly, still smiling, my cheeks starting to pinch.

"Here we thought maybe you weren't able to hold your liquor!" Collette said with a laugh. She tucked her jet-black hair behind her ears and reached for her glass. The three of them chuckled together in tune and there was nothing for me to do but join in. I always laughed with little effort when I'd had too much to drink. The real trick was not to get so carried away laughing that I started to snort.

Now that would be embarrassing.

"Collette ordered us another round. If I didn't know any better, I'd say she's working hard to give you the wrong impression of life in legal," Sara said, lifting her glass to her bright pink lips, emptying the last drops of her second martini into her mouth. Or was it her third?

I smiled. There was no way I would be able to handle another drink. But that was a later problem. The food had arrived.

My plate was placed in front of me last, as everyone else laid their napkins in their laps and started in on their meals. I watched Sara, who was seated to my right, with purpose. She lifted the outermost fork from beside her plate and poised it, ready to eat.

Start at the outside. Got it.

I took a drink of my water before glancing down at my plate.

A pizza sat in front of me.

A delicate round with circles of melted mozzarella, the fancy kind, and what looked like mushrooms and arugula surrounded by a golden-brown crust sat on my plate … Pizza Funghi? I think I saw that on the menu, though I don't remember ordering it.

Who even orders pizza at an upscale restaurant?

The silver lining was that in my world, there was no fork required to eat pizza. I needn't have studied Sara's use of her silverware at all. I glanced around the table to see what fancy form of everyday food was in front of the others. Elizabeth had ordered the pasta special with extra cheese and three types of seafood. Collette and Sara each had a debonair display of leafy greens, hard-boiled eggs, and other vegetables arranged to form the most intricate Cobb salads I'd ever seen. I guess it was a good thing that the base of my meal was a heavy crust. There was no room in leafy greens or ham to absorb the quadruple-shots of vodka mingling in my bloodstream.

The conversation turned from "getting to know you" casual niceties to business once everyone had settled into their meals.

"So," Elizabeth started, "Romi."

I nodded and smiled with effort, trying to concentrate on not dripping tomato sauce down my chin, attempting to look engaged and intelligent while I dug into my pizza.

"Tell me, dear, how has your first week as an official paralegal been? Is everyone treating you well?"

I had been working at Personal Injury Law for five days. Elizabeth informed me of today's lunch before I left the office yesterday, and since then my mind had gone back and forth as to whether a team lunch was a good thing, or a farewell.

Surely, they wouldn't waste money on $20 martinis and $35 pizza if I was going to get the boot when we got back to the office. My lunch cost as much as my monthly eating out allowance and there was more to come!

I swallowed and wiped the corners of my mouth with a napkin that had a higher thread count than anything that had ever touched my pale, freckled skin.

"It's been great. Though I haven't met too many people outside the team yet." I smiled at Sara, who was watching me closely, her eyes daring the next martini to arrive at the table to taunt me. Thankfully it hadn't made its way to the table yet. "Sara and Collette are keeping me pretty busy. I've learned a lot so far."

I had been surprised at the amount of work assigned to me from my fellow paralegals. They had both been at the firm for ages. With Collette coming to PI Law with Elizabeth a few years back and Sara having spent her whole career there, they had long ago earned their status as senior paralegals. It fell to them to teach me what to do; school only prepared me for so much. Not to mention, Elizabeth's time was much more valuable. It didn't make sense for her to show me the proper way to draft a List of Documents. Nor would she have any desire to.

"Great," Elizabeth said between bites. "That's great. I do have an idea that might help jump that learning curve ahead a little bit. I wanted to see if you'd be able to handle it before I brought it up ..."

A tall, intimidating man in a suit so blue it was almost black approached the table before I learned whether I was going to make the cut.

"Ms. Baird-Conwill," he said, stretching out his hand for Elizabeth to take.

"Jack," she said, glancing up at the interruption, contemplation evident behind her eyes. She stood and stepped away from the table to carry on their conversation.

From what Elizabeth was saying, my mind jumped back to thinking I was going to get fired or at least removed from the team by the end of my first week at work. My feelings must have been written all over my face.

"Relax," Collette assured me. "She's not going to say anything bad. We all think you're fitting in really well."

My shoulders dropped and my neck reappeared.

The team lunch was a good thing. Breathe easy, and for God's sake don't have another single drop of alcohol.

Uttara Krishnadas
Infectious

It was the summer of 1974 when Sindhu got her last letter from Mira. Apart from a few hints of Mira's loneliness, it contained no sign of things to come.

The April sun hung in the sky like a lantern that day, surfacing after a long night of rains, leaving the grass fresh and dewy. It cast white beams across the tree trunks in Sindhu's garden. Standing by the gate in her home in Kerala, she watched her eldest daughter limberly move from branch to branch of their jackfruit tree, book tucked firmly under her chin. Manju settled into the highest branch and began to read her textbook. Sindhu protectively kept an eye out for ants on the tree. The brick-red kind, that stung.

At the first sight of the postman's starched khaki uniform, Sindhu leapt forward and opened the gate. Vinayak smiled at her eagerness as he approached the house, straightening out his satchel. "Her letter is here, sister!" he nodded reassuringly, his Nehru cap tilted to one side.

It was no secret that Sindhu missed Mira terribly. Growing up, they had been inseparable. When they were in middle school, they had often been mistaken for one another, even though they were two whole years apart. They lived in a world of their own—full of inside jokes, secret eye-signals, and a coded language—that no one else was part of. Until Mira turned eighteen.

After Mira moved to Delhi for college, Sindhu and Mira had drifted apart, mostly because Sindhu felt dull in comparison to Mira. The two sisters were no longer interchangeable. Mira's sense of style and big city suaveness was discernibly different from Sindhu's awkward social manner. Sindhu could see in the eyes of the men that surrounded them that

Mira was sexy. Her smooth skin, the colour of an earthen pot, glowed when light hit her jawline or her collarbones.

Over the years, marriage drove a further wedge between them. Sindhu had married an endearing, simple man. He worked as a clerk in a bank and his sense of discipline wrapped her in a life that felt like a cozy blanket in a cold room—secure, dependable, and easy to sink into. Mira had married an up-and-coming politician. She travelled, dined with aristocrats and diplomats, shopped, and smoked. Their lives couldn't have been more different. Until motherhood had brought them back together again.

Even the postman knew how eagerly Sindhu awaited Mira's letters from Delhi. Photographs of her nephew's gummy smile and thigh rolls, and adorable anecdotes of his weekly developments took her back to a time when Sindhu's children were still babies. Mira wrote to Sindhu often asking for advice about teething, latching, and colic. Sindhu wrote back with homemade remedies and recipes for Mira so she could stay healthy and strong.

The sky-blue inland letter that Mira sent was almost always torn open immediately after it arrived. That day, Sindhu waited until her children had settled in for their afternoon naps and, squeezing in beside them, feet stretched out on the bed, she opened the letter. At first, Sindhu allowed her eyes to dart over it, not reading the words yet, but taking in the familiar curves of Mira's handwriting.

Enclosed in the letter was a shared childhood memory. Mira had written about the time they had found kittens in the attic and how they had taken turns looking after them, playing mothers to the little ones. There were hints of nostalgia in her writing, but mostly Sindhu was struck by how sad she sounded. *Kapil comes back from work very late. Kannan is my only company these days. I miss you. I miss home,* she wrote more than once.

Sindhu clicked her tongue. If Mira was in Kerala, Sindhu would've kept an eye on Kannan while Mira took some time out for herself. Mira wouldn't have to worry about Kannan's colic. Sindhu would've picked out some tulsi leaves from the backyard and made her a paste. The same way Sindhu had done for each of her four children.

Another fortnight went by before the postman brought home the sky-blue square with a New Delhi stamp. Sindhu tore it open right away, but there were no slanting *t*s and loopy *l*s. Instead, in a few curt lines, she was told that her sister had been taken to an isolation ward for smallpox. The words floated in front of her face, not making sense.

Sindhu remembered hearing about smallpox on the radio. You had to quarantine, they said. To eradicate the deadly infection. There were a high number of cases in the past few months. The WHO was calling it an epidemic.

A sharp, knife-like shudder went down her spine as Sindhu remembered that fatalities were high. Those who did survive were left either blinded or disfigured. There were posters everywhere of pockmarked children, their faces grotesquely bloated with pus-filled sores. "Win 100 rupees!" the poster said, the text enclosed within a jagged red star. "Any fresh case of smallpox? Report to the nearest health care centre. If the information is correct, then 100 rupees is yours!" Not a small amount. The poster came signed by Prime Minister Indira Gandhi herself.

Sindhu read the letter again. It bore information that Sindhu didn't notice the first time around. Mira's stoic husband had written to say that he would be bringing his son Kannan to Kerala soon. The two of them would make the train journey over two-and-a-half days. *Kannan was still being breastfed before Mira fell ill,* Kapil wrote in boxy letters. A short, worried line. Almost an afterthought. *I am hoping I will be able to manage him.*

The news spread around Mira's hometown, and relatives gathered in Sindhu's house to offer their sympathies. They marvelled at God's grace and thanked him for sparing baby Kannan. As they spoke, Sindhu imagined her sister. She thought of Mira in the isolation ward under blankets, shivering, her bronze skin covered in dimpled sores, her large eyes filled with discomfort, and Sindhu felt a strange flutter in her chest. That night, Sindhu prayed the hardest she ever had. *May Mira make it. May she be taken care of by the kindest nurses at the ward. May she be reunited with her baby boy.*

When the news of Mira's death reached her family, Sindhu asked to see her sister. "Too infectious," she was told, with a sad but firm head-shake. Mira's body was cremated with seven others, using isolation-barrier techniques. Mira may have been the wife of a notable politician but they wouldn't make an exception, no, not even for her. The risk of exposure to the virus was too high.

Not long after, Mira's son Kannan arrived at Sindhu's home. That day, the sky was the same shade of blue as the inland letter Sindhu usually received from her sister. Kannan lay curled up like a kidney bean on his father's chest. Quiet, thin, sad. Sindhu took in his curly hair, his dimpled knuckles, his tiny toes and nodded, yes. Yes, she had four children already. One more wouldn't be hard to manage. Yes, that's right, it would be good for him to have siblings. Yes, good for him to grow up in his hometown. Good, good, good.

Later, when Sindhu crushed tulsi leaves into a paste, she would try hard not to think of how tightly Kannan clutched his father's shirt. How hard he dug his baby fingernails into his father's arms as he was taken away from his only remaining parent. How, since he was exhausted from howling through the entire train journey, he did not cry. How the only word he knew to say was "Amma." And how he would have to unlearn it.

Sindhu told herself, as the sky started to take on a new colour, that the only cure for colic and bad memories was time. And she knew that one day, Kannan would use the word Amma again. And this time, it would be for her.

Judy Dercksen

Not the Namib Desert

AN EXCERPT FROM "THE DARK
THAT LETS LIGHT IN"

Hans ducked into the Mini and slammed the door shut. The smell of blood sucked the oxygen from his lungs and suffocated the car's interior. He wound the window down on the driver's side and reached past the passenger seat, careful not to touch the vinyl smudged with blood. Wound that window down too. Straightening up, he turned his face to the winter air and took deep, slow breaths.

The seat was soft. It was not the hot ground of the Namib desert. He was two thousand kilometres from South West Africa. He wiped a streak of blood on his hands off onto his jeans. It reminded him of the rookie's sticky wet skin, the snake-like feel of his intestines slipping through his fingers. Could he have done more to protect him?

He stared straight ahead at the high-rises that housed thousands of residents in the heart of Johannesburg and willed away the shadow of the soldier's head in his lap, the rookie's ashen face merging with the face of the boy who had lain crumpled in the road, thin brown arms scrambling to get away, the fear in his eyes as he hoisted him up.

The kid must have been terrified. Hans, at six foot four, would have seemed like a giant. And he was white.

Hans gripped the steering wheel and flared his nostrils against the smell of blood in the car. He leaned back. Vinyl sparked a shock of cold against his naked skin. He'd forgotten he left his shirt in the emergency room. He'd used it to staunch the flow of blood from the boy's thigh.

Who had shot him? And how had he run with that wound? He was lucky he wasn't run over.

Hans, his head turned back at the sound of police sirens, had almost missed seeing him fall. Thank God he'd seen him in his peripheral vision—one good thing to come out of the army. He'd braked in time and jumped out of the car with the engine still running, picked him up, and driven him away, away from the flashing blue lights and sirens, to Hillbrow Hospital, where Anna, his twin sister, worked.

The kid's in some sort of trouble. He's lucky he made it to safety. Even children aren't safe from the police. Not if they're black. Not in this godforsaken country.

Driving out the hospital parking lot, Hans thought of what could have happened to the boy if he'd landed in the hands of the police. What had happened to so many others! All under the auspicious eye of their fucking government. Not that there was a need for a rubber stamp from politicians to torture and kill. He'd seen enough men jump at the chance to inflict pain. He thought of his own ghosts and guilt rose in nauseous waves from his gut.

The car jolted over yet another pothole and the hard suspension mercilessly transmitted the vibration, amplifying the throbbing in his head. As he drove home, the sounds of Hillbrow—taxis, buses, motorbikes—buzzed in his ears beyond the rush of the noise that pummelled through the open windows, wind battering at the stink of his thoughts.

Unlike his twin, the cold didn't affect him. He'd acclimatized to the cold. He'd had no option trekking up and down the Swartberge, army browns the only protection against mountain temperatures that plummeted to well below zero.

He stopped at a robot, waiting for the red light to change, and leaned over, removed a cassette, and inserted it into the tape deck. Sounds of helicopter blades whipped the air. Whup. Whup. Whup. Strains of an electric guitar. Jim Morrison. Full blast. Singing about the end.

The wind and the sound of the music numbed his brain, and by the time he reached home, he felt calmer. He left the Mini running while he pushed open the gate's cold and heavy steel railings. He drove in and parked close to the house, a single storey building with a galvanized tin roof and Spanish-style burglar bars on every window, even the ones that didn't open.

He stared at the front yard's most prominent feature, the rock garden. Nestled between cycads and succulents, the dull eyes of a crocodile stared back at him and Hans frowned. He should have turfed the yard art long ago. It reminded him each time of their fucker of a president. PW Botha. *The Great Crocodile.* Fat balding man. Sausage index finger digging at the air. Thick lips sneering as he justified apartheid.

Hans unlocked the steel safety door and the two Yale locks on the wooden front door and then walked down the passageway. He thought again of the boy that fell in front of the car. The kid should have been in school and Hans at work. He wouldn't have a job for too long if he kept missing work. He had to smarten up. He couldn't afford to lose his job.

Anna hated that he worked for ARMSCOR designing and engineering weapons. She loathed anything to do with the army and complained about him working on machines that killed people. He loved Anna, cared about what she thought, but she didn't get it. The problem wasn't the weapons, the tanks and the guns, the problem was the idiots in high places who started wars. They thought nothing of lying and cheating to stay in power.

Hans was sick of the lies, especially the lies around the so-called embargoes. The arms embargo was an open joke. He should know. Lyttleton had worked with Quebec on their long-range artillery, the Canadian company in cahoots with Belgium and Sweden. And there were rumours lately about Lyttleton contracting with Belgium to supply weapons to Iraq.

What would he do if he found out that were true? He couldn't tell anyone. He'd signed a confidentiality agreement that made *War and Peace* seem like a pamphlet. Anyhow, nobody cared about the truth.

Least of all America and Britain who were fighting with South Africa to keep the Russians at bay. Apartheid was an acceptable evil in the face of spreading communism.

Smoke and mirrors. It was enough to make him want to turn his back on the job. But he wouldn't easily find one that suited him as well. No other company in South Africa had the resources Lyttleton had—highest calibre technology and the latest computers. Nothing like a war to drive scientific progress.

Hans dressed in long blue overalls and tackled the car, emptying his mind of all thoughts except the ritual of cleaning. He removed the loose carpets and laid them on the concrete paving, then washed the vinyl seats. Red soapy slush turned pink. He emptied bucket after bucket of water over the brick paving. He scrubbed the dash, door panels, and floor with brushes and cloths. Once the inside was clean, he scrubbed and hosed down the carpets, then the outside of the car. He shone the windows, side mirrors, and hubcaps, then stepped back and surveyed his work.

He ran the palms of his hands over his face and through his sweaty blond hair. The car was clean. Stripped of all signs and smells of blood. In the bleary winter sun, it was easy to concentrate on the moment, but Hans knew what awaited him that night. His ghosts had breathed daylight. Their vengeance would be strong. Stronger than usual. He chewed his lower lip, as if to prepare for the familiar taste of blood. He was never sure what woke him, that salty taste or the prick of pain when he bit his lip or tongue.

He dropped the overalls into the washing machine and turned it on. In the shower, he scrubbed his body with a brush and shampooed his hair, rinsing under scalding water, repeating the process over and over, scrubbing under his nails, and then, with a towel wrapped around his waist, he brushed his teeth, cupped water in his palms, and sniffed to clear the smell of blood from his nostrils.

He'd rest a while before calling Mr. Delivery. He wasn't hungry, not after what happened. But Anna would be. She'd expect dinner. His twin was like a marauding lioness after a busy shift. He wondered how she coped, treating the victims of violence every day, violence without any end in sight.

Magnus Lu
Ten Days of Undoing
AN EXCERPT

It was a sticky June afternoon. I stretched my legs out of the cab and found myself at the open gates of the Garrison Institute, fifty miles north of New York City. It was a large, three-storey former monastery. The photos on the website made it look quite stately and regal, but once I was standing outside the place, it reminded me of a mental health institution back home.

As I filled my lungs with a slow, even inhale, a small cloud of cottonwood tickled my nose and I felt some of the heaviness in my chest lift. The sky was cloudless and a row of thick beech trees cast a playful shadow along the top of the building, swaying back and forth with the warm, welcome breeze. For the first time since I left Vancouver, I started to feel hopeful.

I climbed the small flight of concrete steps leading up to the open doors of the building. A woman with large, curly hair and oversized glasses greeted me with a smile from behind a small wooden table.

"You must be Amy," she said. "Welcome to Garrison." I stole a quick glance at the paper on her desk. Her pencil hovered over my name, the only one not crossed off.

I smiled and nodded. "I'm sorry I'm late. The train—"

"Oh don't worry about that, dear." She handed me an embossed folder. "As you know, this is a silent retreat and that goes into effect the moment you pass through those doors." She made a gesture to the inner doorway. My eyes widened and she smiled. "You'll meet with your meditation teacher once a day and yes, you will be able to talk with him." She whipped out a map of the facilities and proceeded to give me directions to my room, the meditation hall and the cafeteria, marking the areas with her pencil.

I thanked her and headed to my room, folder and map in hand.

Silent retreat, I thought. In the rush to escape my life, I had somehow missed that detail.

It was seven a.m. the next morning and I'd barely made it down to the meditation hall on time. My body was having a hard time getting accustomed to the thin orange cushion which did little to soften the hard slats of wood beneath. The light filtering through the stained glass windows felt harsh on my eyes and the room was eerily silent except for the occasional cough and shuffling of feet across the floor. There was a scent of wood and incense mingling in the air and a raised wooden platform with two cushions at the front of the room. The whole room had a formality about it that made me uneasy.

A young Tibetan monk, Tenzin Rinpoche, was the headliner to the retreat. The top of his head glistened as he entered the room with a wave and a childlike grin, flanked by a small entourage. They wore burgundy robes with an inner layer of bright orange slung over one shoulder. He climbed up the platform and took a seat while another monk occupied the seat next to him. The rest of the entourage settled into the first row of cushions.

"Good morning, everyone," he said. He spoke with a slight accent and carefully enunciated every syllable. "Welcome to the first day of our silent retreat. I will make sure you don't lose your mind in these ten days." He threw his head back and laughed. The tension in the air seemed to loosen as some laughed and others readjusted themselves, folding and refolding their legs and shifting their bottoms. "We will focus on one topic each day. Today's topic is suffering."

The meditation began with the ring of a bell. Occasionally Tenzin

Rinpoche would provide a few words of guidance but it was mostly unin-terrupted for long stretches of time where the muscles in my body would stiffen and feel like they were on fire. I became very aware of the loud gulping of my throat when I tried to drain the pool of saliva collecting under my tongue, and when my discomfort faded, I began to notice the same thoughts cycling through the window of my awareness like lug-gage on a carousel. Why did Micah leave me? What could I have done differently? My breathing became shallow and stifled. That selfish bas-tard. I was so good to him.

Hours later, the bell rang three times, signalling the end. Two rows ahead of me a man slowly stood and stretched his arms out. He was tall and handsome from behind, with longish dark hair that was unkempt, just the way I liked. I'd read about retreat romances where you develop a crush at a meditation retreat and live out wild and wonderful fantasies in your head. I felt excited at the idea of redirecting my thoughts.

We had an hour before lunch and while many people were slowly starting to get up, some remained seated, legs crossed and eyes closed. After a few minutes, I stood to head up to my room. My newfound re-treat romance turned around just as I was stretching out my sore calves. I froze. It was Micah.

⌒

Micah and I had met on an online dating app last summer. It was the year I decided to just have fun and stop forcing mediocre relationships into ones that lasted well past their best before date.

Our first date started off awkwardly. There were long moments of si-lence and then we'd talk over each other nervously and laugh. We talked about our families and shared stories of past relationships.

"The strange thing is," he said, "I've often felt lonelier in a relation-ship than when I'm on my own."

I told him I'd never thought of it that way before but I felt exactly the same way. I remember the way his mouth turned up slightly into a smile and how the lines creased around his eyes as if all his feelings pooled up into them.

We never said we were exclusive, but after a few weeks, I deleted all my online dating profiles. We began seeing each other several times a week and even talked about travelling together. Most of the time he'd come over to my place and, at the beginning at least, he'd be there for days at a time. After a while, though, he said work was hectic, he needed to get an early start and it was just more convenient if he slept at his place. Eventually, he barely came over at all.

"What if we got a place together?" I said one morning while lying in bed. It was one of the few mornings he stayed the night. We had been together for seven months. He stood in front of the mirror, his back to me, buttoning his shirt. He paused for a moment. In the reflection I saw his face cloud over with an expression I'd never seen before. When he turned to face me, the expression was replaced with a more relaxed one.

"We could do that."

Just before Christmas, he disappeared. He didn't return any of my calls and I found out through Facebook that he'd moved to New York. It seems strange now that I think of it, but the whole time we were together, I never once met any of his friends or family.

⌒

In a panic, I hurried out of the meditation hall and to the staircase, taking two steps at a time until I reached my floor. My room, sparse and clean with a twin bed, wooden desk, and bare walls, was at the end of the dimly lit hallway. It had a small window overlooking an expansive garden in the back. I flopped onto the bed and breathed deeply until my heart slowed to a steady beat, pulling myself up so I could see out the window. Some of the people from the meditation hall had spilled out into the back, each claiming their own space. I scanned the garden for Micah. Was it really him?

I'd spent the months since Christmas turning the same thoughts over and over in my head, meticulously picking apart every word in the days and months leading up to his disappearance.

There was a knock at the door. I opened it to find Micah standing there, looking around nervously. Did he follow me up? I remembered that I was the one who'd told him about this retreat. Did he come knowing I'd be here?

"Can I come in?" he said in a familiar way, as if we saw each other yesterday. I stood in the doorway, stunned, and didn't invite him in.

"Look, I know we're not supposed to talk," he said, "but I saw you down in the hall and I need to get this sorted out, otherwise I don't know how I'm going to get through this next month. Can we just talk … about what happened?"

For the last five months I'd wanted to talk about what happened. I felt a surge of energy rise up as excitement turned to anger and my eyes began to blur.

"We have nothing to talk about," I said. The look of pleading on his face suddenly made me regret what I was doing, but my pride could not overcome the force of my hand as it pushed the door shut in his face.

Stephanie Peters

The Upset

AN EXCERPT

Ripley is tugging, not especially discreetly, at the waistband of her tights, the crotch of which is sagging down between her knees. She has spent the last several hours shaking hands and enduring pitiful hugs, accepting words of condolence like unwanted birthday gifts. *Thank you. Thank you. Thank you so much.*

She has just slipped through the back door of the church gymnasium-turned-auditorium—just for a moment, for some air, she told herself, knowing all the while that she would cut through the garden to the front door, find her coat in the lobby, and leave.

She has unconsciously rolled and unrolled her copy of the funeral program between her sweaty hands, to the extent that her father's face has become crinkled beyond recognition. Flakes of ink from Psalm 46 have rubbed off on her palms and, she has to presume, transferred to her face as she nervously adjusted her hair and picked at her skin. She is pondering this, and simultaneously tugging at the godawful tights, when a voice startles her.

"Smoke?"

It's Nicky, the step-sibling she acquired when her now-deceased father took up with his mother, when Ripley was eleven. Nicky was fourteen at the time, and their dynamic was never quite comfortable. They argued almost constantly, and Ripley was always confused by their fights. Nicky never seemed really angry with her. When Nicky fought with his real sister, Tessa, Ripley could sense the full rage. Tessa was a year older than Ripley, but somehow she seemed younger. There was something babyish about her that Ripley at first found repulsive. She was shy and silly, and obsessed with her Beanie Baby collection beyond what Ripley believed to be normal. Tessa was usually so soft spoken, but Ripley witnessed her full-on screaming at Nicky more than once, hot tears gushing down her round cheeks. And Nicky, when he was mad at her, was actually scary. One time he threw the remote control at her so hard that it dented the wall when it missed her head.

Sometimes when she was at their house, Ripley would pretend she was the third sibling. It was easy enough to imagine; Gwyn, her Dad's girlfriend, treated her more-or-less the same as her own kids, and she and Tessa grew to play together and love each other and get on each other's nerves much like Ripley imagined real sisters would. But with Nicky, Ripley always sensed that things were different. It wasn't bad. There was even a sense that Ripley couldn't deny that she enjoyed fighting with him. But she never truly felt like his real sister.

Now, she rests her eyes on thirty-year-old Nicky. She hasn't seen him since Christmas, but he looks about the same. A full head shorter than her. Slouchy, greasy-haired, unpleasant. The thick band of his white ankle socks drawing the eye to the gap between his black pants and dress shoes. Ripley would normally keep her revulsion in check, but she's emotionally tapped out. Nicky is disgusting. She wishes he would disappear.

He's holding out a thick black vape pen and looking at her expectantly.

"No thanks," says Ripley.

Nicky shrugs and releases a thick mouthful of strawberry-scented vapour. Ripley grimaces, looking right into his eyes.

"How are you holding up?" Nicky asks.

Ripley has been asked some version of this question a thousand times this week. Her eyes glaze over. She wills time to pass, for Nicky to vanish along with the need for pleasantries.

"It's a lot," she says, finally.

"Tell me about it," Nicky says, and sucks grotesquely on the vape pen. This time he exhales over his shoulder before turning back to Ripley.

"This dinner at my mom's tonight—"

"I'm not going to that," Ripley interjects.

"I was just going to say, it feels like a lot," Nicky continues.

"A lot," Ripley repeats.

"Too much, maybe. Do you want to get out of here?"

Ripley almost laughs. "Get out of here? You and me?"

"And Tessa," he says. "The three of us … no one else knows what we're going through."

Ripley stops to think on this. In all honesty, the thought of her, Nicky, and Tessa going through the same thing had not even crossed her mind. She knows that they loved her dad. That he was a loving stepdad to them and they had a good bond, or whatever, but to say that it is the same as Ripley, who has just lost her actual father … She breathes deeply. Nicky is looking at her, as far as she can tell, with nothing but kindness. Like her, he is grieving Patrick Howell. He is overwhelmed by this funeral, and all of these people. It would not kill her to accept this kindness.

That first year when their parents got together, they went on a camping trip. It was meant to be a bonding experience for the blended family. At first Ripley said she didn't want to go, but her dad had been so disappointed and Ripley had felt guilty. She had no idea she had the power to hurt an adult man like that. It made her feel sick.

On the second day of the trip, the three kids took the rowboat out on the lake. They took turns rowing and tried to get as far from the campsite as they could. Nicky criticized both of the girls' form, said they were too slow, too choppy with their strokes. Tessa just giggled, but Ripley eventually grew tired of his comments and, on her turn, dipped the oar deep into the water and jerked it rapidly, splashing a wide wave of lake water directly across Nicky's head and chest. Nicky leapt up and grabbed the bailing bucket, dipped it over the side and tossed the water at Ripley, but most of it ended up splashing Tessa, who had been lying across the back bench.

Ripley rocked back and forth, trying to repeat the oar movement that had splashed Nicky so effectively, but the perfect aim had been dumb luck. She brought waves of water into the boat, but none of them managed to drench Nicky, who was reaching over the side refilling his bucket. When he came toward her with the bucket, Ripley lurched her body out of the way. With both of them on their feet, the old rowboat rocked violently, and Tessa barely had time to shriek, "You *guys!*" before it went hull-up, flipping them into the murky water.

Ripley surfaced laughing. "You dumbass!" she hollered, experimenting with language she wouldn't have dreamed of using within earshot of the parents. "You can't run around in a rowboat!"

She dog-paddled around the boat, to where Nicky was treading water with visible effort. She felt elated; Nicky couldn't swim very well. Here, in the water, she had a distinct advantage over him.

"That was totally your fault," he sputtered, and tried to splash her with his hand.

Ripley easily backstroked out of the way. She knew that if he tried to chase her, he wouldn't have a chance. She kicked water in his face.

"Cut it out, you're acting like an eight-year-old," he said.

"Excuse me? You're the one who's immature," Ripley snapped back, but she recognized that she had lost whatever fragile power she'd had in the interaction. Somehow Nicky was able to call her out without losing his dignity, but her response just reinforced that she was being childish.

"Wait," said Nicky, "where's Tessa?"

Ripley looked around. She hadn't noticed that Tessa's blond head hadn't surfaced after the boat tipped. "Tessa!" she yelled. "Where are you?"

With laboured strokes, Nicky swam around to check the other side of the boat, but Ripley knew she wasn't there. "Could she have swum to shore?" she asked, knowing full well that they would have seen her on the otherwise empty lake.

"Ripley, she can't swim!" Nicky said. The panic in his voice made the whole thing real.

Without thinking, Ripley dove down into the water. She didn't know what she was looking for. A body on the bottom of the lake? But it was no use. She couldn't see in the murky water, and it was too deep for her to reach the bottom.

When she resurfaced, Nicky was splashing frantically, screaming, "Tessa! Tessa!"

Ripley joined him, and they yelled for what seemed like forever. Exhausted, they grabbed the side of the boat and looked at each other in silence. That's when they heard the thumping.

Once they had flipped the boat over and found Tessa, frightened but otherwise unscathed, they remembered that Tessa had been the only one wearing her life jacket. She had resurfaced underneath the boat, and couldn't force herself under the sides. "I thought you would never find me," she sobbed. "I thought I would run out of air!"

DK Eve

Lunch Shift at the Castle Café

I lay in bed, heart racing, a sludgy pool in my chest threatening to burst. I should've stood up for myself, should've said something instead of turning away, pretending not to see her smirk, those upturned lips smacking of triumph.

Next time, I thought.

I closed my eyes and a scenario formed. I'm in the dining room of the Castle Café where we work. "Clean that up," she orders. Customers look up from their coffees, place forks beside plates of half-finished lunches.

In my scene, I've just delivered meals, asking if everything is okay. I ignore Kitty and her pointing finger, move to the next table to gather empty plates. "Room for dessert?" I ask.

I go to the kitchen to scrape plates, and she storms in. "I told you to bus that table!"

I am a marble-solid pillar of confidence. "It's not my table, Kitty. It's yours." I walk back to the dining room with the coffee pot.

She follows me, barking, "You will clean that table now!"

The murmur of voices and clanks of cutlery stop. The tables form a circle around us, spectators in a coliseum, hungry for blood. I've been studying ancient Rome in history class, and I picture myself a lone gladiator, summoning the courage to face Caesar's soldier.

"You will never speak to me that way again," I say, and with a dramatic flourish, tear the stupid wig from her head, hurling it to the floor where it lays in a clump, still as a dead raccoon on the side of the road. Kitty shrieks, hands flying to her head, but we all see the scraggly tufts of grey that are her real hair. She scoops up the wig and flees, humiliated. My heart had slowed. Calmed by my nightly fantasy, I slept.

~

Kitty picked on me from the start. I began as a dishwasher halfway through my Grade 10 year, in 1976, and Reg the manager said I could waitress when I turned sixteen in mid-summer. I'm proud to say I moved up to waitress four months before my birthday. In Sooke, the small town on Vancouver Island where I lived, the high school was right across the road; I had a spare on Tuesday and Friday afternoons, so I worked lunches.

Kitty and Flo ruled the dayshift. They'd worked there since their kids started school, and now their kids had graduated. Kitty had a narrow, fox-like face, a dark brown beehive hairdo piled above razor-edge bangs, and wiry arms and legs. Flo moved slowly, with a round face and glasses. Her hair, done in a short-waved bob, was greying, and she filled out her polyester smock and gabardine slacks with soft edges.

The restaurant was L-shaped, with the long main dining area, windows, and bar connected to the kitchen on one end. The short wing had two big booths for larger groups and was the overflow room at peak times. We used the table at the back as a staff table, and on my first day before opening, Kitty and Flo poured coffees and sat with an ashtray between them to recite the rules.

"The main room is ours," Kitty said, smoke wafting from fuchsia-coloured lips. "My section is the window side and Flo does the wall. You'll take this room and I'll tell you if you need to take any on our side."

"Time to open," Flo said. They stubbed their cigarettes and drained their coffee. "Can you clean up this table?" They left to unlock the door, flip the sign to "Open," and greet the first customers. I picked up their lipstick-stained cups and loaded them into the dishwasher, dumped the ashtray, and replaced it with a clean one.

I grabbed a soup cup from the shelf to hold my tips and set it on the bar beside Kitty's and Flo's cups, each boldly marked with their names. Kitty shot me a swift glance, rolling her eyes so that only I could see. She led two men to one of her tables, laughed as the taller one spoke, and leaned forward to take their orders. As the shift progressed, I heard the clinks and rustles as their cups filled with coins and bills.

Kitty hand-picked tables for me to serve. A couple came in and sat by the window, clearly her section. "You take them," she said.

"What can I get for you today?" I asked, jotting down orders of grilled ham-and-cheese sandwiches with soup. I brought coffee and waters, replaced their ashtray. Their food steamed as I set down the plates. I left the bill promptly. When I counted cash to put in the till, there was only enough to cover the meal. I was counting it again, wondering what I did wrong, when Kitty came up.

"Those two never tip," she said with a throaty chuckle.

They had me serve all the low or non-tippers. While Kitty's and Flo's tips overflowed, I was lucky to scoop a few quarters, a couple of dollar bills. When the restaurant cleared they stood behind the bar, lighting cigarettes and counting cash.

"Go clean the tables," Kitty ordered, pointing with her cigarette and tilting her chin to blow smoke to the ceiling.

After a few shifts like this, I walked home fighting tears. My mom asked how it went.

"Why do they hate me so much?" I whined.

She stroked my hair. "You're young with so much ahead of you. You can be anything you want. They have nowhere to go from waitressing. That's all they'll ever be."

"Poor Kitty," she went on. "She lost a lot of hair from thyroid disease. That's why she wears a wig."

My mom, with her smooth-skinned beauty and soothing words. I could see us being a threat to those dried up leather-skinned old bats. I hadn't known Kitty wore a wig and that's when I started having the fantasy. It grew in my mind, embellished with more detail on each imagining, and got me through the worst shifts.

A few weeks later on a Friday in June, a group of Grade 12s arrived with a burst of raucous laughter, startling the quiet room. Kitty hustled them to the big table in the back. "You take them," she ordered.

I ducked into the kitchen to get waters, mortified to serve the older students in my stained orange polyester smock, my hair pulled tightly back. The boys jostled each other in their open-necked, paisley print shirts and shoulder-length feathered hair. The girls slid into the booth, breezy in halter tops and wide-leg jeans, tossing straight, centre-parted hair, and batting turquoise-hued eyes.

"Hi," I said. The sweat trickling down the sides of the water glasses was nothing compared to the drops threatening to slide down my temples.

"Two weeks to freedom!" one guy shouted, lifting his glass. I hovered with my notepad as they laughed, talked about next week's prom, and finally ordered. I poured Cokes and 7-UP, scooped ice cream for milkshakes, shuttled back and forth with the heavy drinks on a tray.

More people arrived. I'd never worked such a busy lunch shift. My room was full, and Kitty still had me take tables on her side. I was kept running, carrying burgers and fries in one direction, empty plates in the other. I grabbed bills and money from the tables, shoving the stack in my pocket, no time to count while I set up for the next customer.

At the end of the lunch rush, only a few customers remained. Kitty and Flo rested at the staff table with coffees and cigarettes, their feet up on empty chairs. I went through both rooms clearing tables then went to the till.

One by one I entered the totals, counted cash, added change to my tip cup. Coins filled the bottom, and bills blossomed, growing like beanstalks in a summer garden. The biggest tip came from the Grade 12s. I jammed the final handful into the overflowing cup, bulging with more than the both of theirs put together.

I couldn't hold back the smile pushing at my cheeks.

Kitty was watching, and her eyes narrowed and looked away.

"Well I guess that does it," she said, stubbing her cigarette. She stood with a heavy sigh and cleared away the ashtray.

Tanya Belanger
The Last Stop

It was past midnight. The last eight hours on the road felt endless and the oncoming headlights spread out from their bright centres across her vision and into each other, making it difficult for her to focus on the broken centre line. She lit a cigarette, the orange glow adding to the soft lights in the cab. She inhaled and cracked the window of the rig to let in some frigid night air.

There was food and fuel at the next exit. She geared down and followed the lights to Big Dave's Truckstop and found a spot to park. The top half of the building was a log cabin façade and the bottom half a stone wall that wasn't stone, but siding. It looked like the builder could not decide whether to construct with fake stone or fake wood, so they did both. Giant boulders in the garden where plants should have been. The white paint made them look unnatural. Through the windows she saw there were other truckers inside. She opened the glass doors and walked in.

The interior was bright and stung her dry eyes. Painted stained glass lamps hung from the beams, and the wood panelling had mounted fish trophies nailed to it in a random pattern. The place smelled of bacon and old fryer oil. Some truckers sat together at tables or in booths, chatting, while others sat alone, their heads hanging over their plates. They turned to look up, and seeing that she was younger by decades and not of the same sex as them, they did not stare, but dismissed her, and simultaneously put their heads down, like a flock of birds who change direction as one. A tired loneliness percolated through the room. A few drivers sat by themselves at the counter. She picked one closest to her own age.

"Hey. Okay if I sit down?" She looked directly at him and wasn't sure if he would answer. She sat anyway. "How about the coffee? Any good?"

He nodded and said, "It's the usual shit for this shit hole. The only thing going for it is it's hot."

"It's been a long haul," she said and waited for a response. Any would do. There was none. "Are you headed out, or on your way back?" To the waitress behind the counter she asked, "Can I get a coffee?" As soon as it was poured, she took a sip.

He said, "Heading out. I been out for about a week now. Be back home in two. You?"

"Just on my way back. I got a few more hours before home. Been at it for two months now, but I'm finding it tough."

"Me, I wouldn't have it any other way. No nagging, no chores, home two days a month. If it's so tough, why you still at it?" He looked annoyed.

She took a sip of coffee before answering. "You know, I'm not sure. The money's good and I can set my own hours." She paused and waited for him to offer more reasons this was the best career in the world. None came. "I don't have anyone to nag me when I get home, maybe that's part of it. To tell you the truth, I guess I thought I could drive away from my problems. I thought it would be different."

He drank that last of his coffee, took a few bills out of his pocket, and put them on the counter. "I have to be at my next stop by 6:00 a.m." He walked out. The plastic CLOSED sign on the door rattled. She finished her cup, went out the same way, and climbed back into her truck. She pushed down the clutch, shifted into neutral and started the engine. She lit another cigarette and waited for it to warm up.

Back at her place, the mailbox was crammed so full—mostly with bills and store flyers—that it was a challenge to pull everything out. She gathered the mass of paper into her arms and trudged up the stairs. Inside, the roaches skittered for the crevices as soon as she turned on the lights. The dishes were still in the sink, unwashed as she left them. A few of the plants on the windowsill lay wilted and in different stages of expiring. She checked her answering machine for messages. No light flashed. There were none.

She looked at the keys in her hand, the old rabbit's foot that belonged to her dad, with patches of fur missing where it rubbed inside his pocket all these years. He'd bought it at a flea market when he was 25. The old seller told him it was the left hind foot of a rabbit killed in a cemetery at midnight, during the new moon, and that it would not only bring him luck but that it would offer protection against misfortune. Her father laughed and bought the foot for the story. He loved to show the keychain to anyone who would listen and to retell the tale. He would buy anything for a good pitch.

About three months ago, her parents had come over for dinner. Over drinks, they talked about their garden and where they would spend this winter. She talked about what she was going to do with the rest of her life. Her mom brought most of the food when it was at her place or cooked the entire meal when it was at her parents' house. Her dad said that Mom loved to cook and he loved to eat. It was a perfect match. She listened to her dad tell stories of his buddies in town, her mom not saying much but keeping herself busy putting out food, filling the wine glasses, clearing dishes, and cleaning up.

It was getting late. She could see that they were getting tired. She asked them to spend the night, but her dad got up from the table, keys in hand, and said the flea market was on the next day and he wanted to get there early for the new stuff that the dealers were putting out. She reached for his keys. A look from her dad stopped her. Her mom hugged her first, then her dad, and they left.

The police knocked on her door at 5:00 a.m. in the morning. Her parents were involved in a single-car accident on their way home from her apartment. She asked, "What hospital are they at?"

The officer said, "I'm sorry. Is there anyone I can call for you?"

She looked at her dirty dishes, dust, and dead houseplants. The solid red eye of the answering machine glared at her. She went into the kitchen and took the bottle of vodka from the cupboard to the table. She poured a glass and took a gulp. It stung the inside of her mouth, caught fire in her throat, and continued to scorch on the way down. It tasted good; she put the bottle on the table, saving herself the trip of getting up for a refill. The more she drank, the more she smoked. Cigarette butts accumulated in the ashtray.

She thumbed the rabbit's foot. Took it off her keys. Why did she tell the driver at the diner she thought she could drive away from her problems? That she thought it would be different? She sounded stupid. She took another drink. She said to herself, *I can't even have a conversation with someone without them walking away.* She drank. Lit another cigarette. The vodka warmed her.

She recalled the last time she saw her parents. What if? What if she had forced them to stay. Take the keys. Take the rabbit's foot. She played this over and over. The traffic noises, water dripping from the faucet, and furnace creaks went silent. It felt like she was in a vacuum. Empty.

There were two glasses in front of her. She poured more vodka. It spilled on the table. Tried again. This time it landed in the glass. She drank. Vodka dribbled down her chin. She dropped her heavy head on her chest. Looked down at her feet. There were two feet. There were four. Took another drink. She got up.

On legs that could not support her she fell over the boxes in the hall-way. They contained her parents' stuff. She sat up—back against the wall, feet splayed—and opened the top box. She picked up her dad's grey sweater and hugged it. Inhaled his scent, a mixture of English Leather and Export A, the cigarettes he smoked. Always one between his fingers, lit. She rocked with the sweater, tears welling then making their way down her cheeks.

She knew what was in the bathroom. At the back of the cupboard was her acetaminophen and the prescription drugs from her parents' house, bottles of opiates, sleeping pills, cholesterol drugs, blood pressure medications, and antidepressants. She could get a drink of water. She was thirsty.

Rabbit foot in hand and using the walls to brace herself, she stumbled to the bathroom.

She rubbed at the worn patches and felt the hard bone under the fur.

Višnja Milidragović

Happy Hour

I'd clicked "accept" with extra pomp this morning as I sipped my coffee, jazzed about the theme of the remote happy hour. I loved gabbing about music—plus, my colleagues would finally get to know me better. Though I've been with the company for about six months now, it's taken more than the one Christmas party and a few lunch breaks to get them to ask the right questions—the kind that would give me the openings to share the real parts of myself, the parts that have nothing to do with marketing.

I pop open the meeting invite promptly at four thirty, launching a window of faces, a *Brady Bunch* of sorts, tiled across the screen in gallery view. I wave, then unmute myself, so I'm ready in case anyone noticed me joining. A conversation is already underway: Jackie from HR is talking about her Backstreet Boys Zoom background, but Darleen from accounting cuts her short to give me a wave and a Hi, Vish! Welcome!

I wave back and say a quick hello, my heart dancing inside. Then I put myself on mute to join the rest of the group in listening to—was it Vivian?—whose turn it is now to answer the question that has been posed to us.

My first concert was … believe or not: Britney Spears, she says. Won tickets from a radio station. Britney was touring her second album, remember the one, with the red pleather bodysuit? The epic ponytail Britney?

Everyone laughs. The chat erupts in exclamation marks and Darleen, ever the facilitator, jokes that she's too old for Britney. I swoon and smile, along for the ride, remembering myself lip-synching "hit me baby one more time" in the hallway—lyrics that flew over both my head and my mother's, though for entirely different reasons. Mom barely spoke English and I was just a nine-year-old girl learning how to pick up on Canadian trends.

Chris the CMO, whose seniority vetoes everyone's voice on the call, goes next, spilling her lively story: circa 1976, when she went to see Zeppelin live in Seattle.

I join the group's exuberant—though pretty static—response. Led Zeppelin! we call out through the speakers. I say, That's amazing! I'm such a diehard fan! but my voice disappears into the amassed noise of the group. I mourn for the '70s, when music was at its height, before everything got so electronic.

Others then take turns volunteering to share their first concert experience, bravely breaking the vacuum silence that follows each lively anecdote once the initial bursts of elation die down.

Carrie mentions Aerosmith, how in her twenties she'd hung on to Joe Perry's leg for the entirety of a song.

Donna remembers Gord Downie and the sweat that ran off of him and straight onto her face in the first row.

Someone mentions Crowded House, a flurry follows, and then an older exec guy chimes in, which shuts everyone up. He tells the story of seeing U2 in an open air stadium under a full moon—not his first concert, he says, but he obviously feels it's valuable to mention. People rejoice. They all love U2.

I've seen them twice. I remember standing in the general admission circle for hours in the Montreal heat with the gang when they came to visit, waiting for Bono to dance on the platform over us. And did he ever. He did it again in Vancouver the following summer when I moved back after my Master's and managed to score tickets for all of us. But neither is my top concert. And definitely not my first.

Nothing will ever beat Leonard Cohen, about ten years back, when my boyfriend at the time revealed that pair of tickets at dinner. He'd hidden them inside my birthday card and the show was that night. We had a painful breakup a few years later and when I look back on it now, it feels as if I'd attended the show alone all along. Intimately communed with Leonard, tears of every mood streaming down my face. I can still see that beam of light that came through the rafters and shone on his fedora as he recited in that deep baritone voice of his, "That's how the light gets in."

The Irish girl names a band neither I nor anyone else, it seems, has ever heard of, except one person who yells out, Oh ya! Those guys! and she goes on excitedly about how she'd stood outside the venue in Dublin for hours waiting for the band to come out and sign her stomach.

As I listen, I recall my solo weekend there, a few years back when I was still living in the UK, when I'd met that dark dress-shirted man whose name I don't remember anymore, at the chowder place in Temple Bar. How perfectly we'd gotten along, drinking, talking, bopping around to the live Celtic music playing everywhere. The whole city was a concert. We said goodbye at the midway point of some small pedestrian bridge, never exchanging contact info (or saliva for that matter). I walked back at the crack of dawn dancing on air, exhilarated by the magic of it all, the immediacy, the unfulfilled potency that can make us so drunk with hope.

Everyone is cheering now, raising glasses and cans up to their cameras. We scream Sláinte! into our microphones.

As people quiet down, Darleen interjects to bring the group back to the original question. Even happy hour has to stay on track: Your first concert, guys! Not your favourite, your *first!*

The Australian girl in PR goes next. She says Pearl Jam, to which three women, somehow simultaneously even though it's a conference call, each explain that Pearl Jam is their husband's favourite band. They agree the husbands should meet.

I remember watching the film *Into the Wild* one summer with Dad when I visited him in Bosnia back in high school. In that movie theatre inside the new mall that the Saudis built, a monolithic reminder of the end of Yugoslavian socialism and the rise of the new state. The soundtrack still depresses me, all that weary wisdom of Eddie Vedder that I can never put to real use. Just can't seem to "rise up" enough.

Okay, who's next? asks Darleen, as she scans the long lineup of participants on the call.

I take a deep breath. It's a gamble, but I decide to go: It was back in 1993 at Sava Centar in Belgrade, I say.

A pause, then someone asks, Where's that? Before I can respond, someone answers for me and says Serbia.

I go on: It was a Đorđe Balašević concert, a famous Yugoslav folk musician.

Silence.

Not a crowd pleaser. My ears pop, but I continue: It was some months after we had fled Sarajevo, I go on, deadpan. I was five.

Someone snivels, a little pity whine that hides behind a carousel of all their almost-frozen faces across my screen. He was singing one of his most famous ballads, I say. From an album he had released in '87, the same year I was born.

Kathleen is still smiling but no sound comes out. The rest of them look almost comical to me in their awkwardness, faces hanging, eyes jutting out, like Whack-A-Moles that just can't avoid my next strike.

I go in for the final hit: It was titled, "Samo rata da ne bude," which means, "just let there be no war."

Muffled microphone gasps, someone cries out, Wow, another says, How powerful.

We moved to Canada some months later, I add in closing.

Darleen finally speaks, yo-yoing off my words in a diplomatic uppity tone. And we're so glad to have you here!

I smile back then close the screen.

I remember tugging at Mom's sleeve, crying from being so tired of standing, wanting to go home, while above me, she was crying, too. Everyone was. For many, this was their last concert in what would never again be Yugoslavia. It was my first.

I'll tell them I lost connection if they ask, but they won't. You can't really jam when you're playing in the wrong key.

Rebecca Chan

An Unnatural Widow

AN EXCERPT

Eve can tell that Mary is tired today at dinner, her tiny body beginning to run out of steam. She has done so much, so little of which she understands—watching her mother pack up their tiny dark apartment in a frenzy, a new home, the funeral, a new school. By the time they reach dessert, a cup of tea for the two women, a glass of milk for the little girl, and a shortbread cookie each, she is almost asleep in her chair.

"Grandma Shirley used to make cookies like that." Mary says this sleepily, her neck beginning to droop with exhaustion. "But she can't anymore because she's dead now."

Eve freezes, unable to stop a small shiver from rippling up from her pelvis along her spine to the back of her neck, where it finally clutches, icily, at the back of her head. When she looks up, her mother looks shocked.

"Shirley passed?" Anne's voice is sharp from shock.

"Yes, um," Eve's throat catches, suddenly dry on the pleasantries. "Shirley passed about a month ago—a stroke, very sudden. Vincent called to let us know."

"That's awful, darling, I'm so sorry to hear," Anne hums sympathetically.

Eve swallows, feeling as if a piece of glass is wedged down her throat. She is about to lie, and it will be awful, because she is relieved and will never not be relieved that Shirley is dead.

"Yes. It's awful. We miss her, don't we, sweetheart?" She smiles at Mary, but it feels wooden. A voice in the back of her head wonders if maybe this is the time that someone will guess, will know—her own

105

mother of all people—but when she looks up, Anne smiles at her, her eyes full of tears.

"Oh, darling, I'm so sorry. What a rough go you've had of it." Anne reaches across the table, rests her hand on Eve's. Eve swallows down the ugly glass feeling and smiles back. Inside, she wants to scream.

☙

That night, Eve waits in bed until she can hear her mother's steady, noisy inhales and exhales, and until she is sure that Mary is dead asleep. Then she gets up, careful to move as silently as possible, and slips the day's clothes back on—slacks, a sweater—then tiptoes her way to the door to shrug into her raincoat and boots. Eve never snuck out as a child, not even as a teen—she feels excited, nervous—but most of all she feels that scream, all the way from dinner, still inside her, writhing behind her ribcage, in the space between her heart and the thin bones that bracket it.

Her walk downtown is quiet—even on a Friday night, Nanaimo is not very busy just after ten o'clock. A small side street juts off to the left of the main road that runs along the downtown core, and just up a small but steep incline is her destination. Men stand outside, clustered together with ball caps low over their eyes and smoke curling up from cigarettes that sit at the edges of their mouths.

The Palace is one of the oldest bars in the city, and it is old in a worn-in, beaten down, weathered sense. Every time you walk in, it will be in slightly worse shape. A little stickier, a little duller, another little hole in one wall, another pool cue missing. The men who drink there will always look roughly the same: sloped shoulders; elbows propped onto tables; watching the TV or their drinks or their cards, perhaps the small collection of women that gather here. The women are all tired-looking, their clothes a little too tight or too loose; their lipstick fades into the cracks around their mouths, and if they are blond it is a cracking yellow like old straw.

Every city has at least one of these bars.

When Eve walks in, the low lights and haze feel like a relief; you are not meant to be seen, in bars like this, you are meant to blend in. The scent of spilled drinks and smoke settles in her, and she walks up to an empty seat at the side of the bar. "Gin and tonic, please."

The bartender grunts, eyes briefly skimming over her chest as if it is a reflex, then turns to take the dusty blue bottle from the shelf. As he turns back to the counter, Eve interrupts. "Actually—just a double gin." She keeps her gaze steady when he looks up, his eyebrows raised.

After a second, he grunts again and shrugs. "Your funeral."

When the glass slides over to her, she can already taste it. Holding her breath, she takes a small sip and sighs in relief at the familiar sweetness followed by overwhelming bitterness. Without thinking too much, she swallows the rest in one go, then waits patiently to catch the bartender's attention for the next.

The bar stool beside her is occupied suddenly after her third drink, and this is also familiar. It's only a matter of time, a woman drinking alone on a Tuesday, before someone decides for her that she'd rather not drink alone.

"Eve Jackson, look at you, all grown up." An elbow jostles hers now, and she grimaces to herself before she turns to her right. A tall thin man, with a broad face and the red nose of a drunk, brown hair pushed back— not intentionally but shoved aside by his hand, sweat and condensation from multiple beer bottles holding it back. Eve thinks she probably went to high school with him, one of the boys who ended up working in the mill; she can't remember his name for the life of her, and doesn't care to ask.

"It surely is." She takes another sip and turns back toward the TV that hangs at the other end of the bar, hoping he will take the hint.

She knows he won't. She doesn't know yet what she will do.

He is not deterred. "I thought you were a big city girl, married and all. Where's your husband?"

Eve shrugs and takes another drink. "Which one?"

"Which one, eh?" He chuckles, nudges her elbow with his own once again. "Sounds like you got a story or two."

They sit in silence for a short time, before he tries again. Eve is already bored, knows what men like this want and how they want it. A short, drunken stumble along a tired flirtation script, then a short and brutal rendezvous—in his truck, an alley, maybe his apartment if they make it that far. Eve hasn't made it to many apartments. She doesn't care to.

"So you back here for good or a visit in between husbands?"

Eve stares at the TV, resolutely, and shrugs. Another pause. When he next speaks, he leans in to her, his breath warm and sickly sweet, his lips almost against her ear. She twitches away, but he persists.

"Seems like you got a big city story or two, what you say we go for a drive?"

At this, Eve decides she is done. He is interrupting what she hoped would be a quick path to a deep sleep, a few hours where she does not need to avoid thinking of—*him*. She turns to face him, and he grins at this, drunkenly not seeing the hard set to her jaw or the anger in her eyes.

"I don't think that's a good idea. I'd rather finish this alone, if you don't mind." Eve turns when she is done speaking, stares back at the TV, takes another sip. The glass is almost empty.

He jerks back at this, and after he mutters something that is probably insulting, he leaves. She orders another drink. When it is done, she does not order another. Eve knows herself by now; if the first man doesn't succeed, sometimes drunken Eve enjoys accepting the second. It is nice to be wanted. But that's not what she came for tonight, so after the last drop is gone, she stands, swaying slightly, and shrugs back into her jacket before setting her sights onto the door and walking out.

The walk home is only ten minutes, and at first it goes quickly; the gin keeps her warm. But when she turns out of downtown and begins the walk along the fence that divides the road from the railyard that runs along the water, the sea wind comes in suddenly, hits the left side of her body like a slap, and it is bitterly cold. Eve stops walking for a second, tries to breathe slowly, but her breath only comes faster, shakier. She swallows, clamps her eyes closed and tries to will her body into submission. It doesn't work, and she jackknifes and gags. Hot stinging liquid floods out of her, making her eyes sting and chest seize. When she is done, wiping the back of her hand across her mouth, she is hot from shame, staring down at the small pitiful puddle on the ground, stained orange like everything else under the streetlight. Her chest aches, as if someone hit her squarely in the centre of her ribcage.

When she straightens, carefully, wiping her mouth again on her sleeve, the shame has not left with the bile but rather crept into the rest of her body. It never really left. Shrugging her thin jacket up her neck, she grimaces and turns back towards home, thinking of water, of the deep sleep the gin promises. It is only a five-minute walk home from here.

Hugh Griffith

The Snake Club

AN EXCERPT

The Bronco rolled along. Derek was at the wheel, barely moving, his hands steady at ten and two, his eyeballs drying as he stared into nothingness. They were on a desert flat, somewhere mid-peninsula, heading south. Every minute meant another mile farther from Laura, and the farthest apart they had been since becoming a couple.

He glanced at his watch. 1:13 a.m. This was the least productive night drive of the trip so far. Usually by now they would have found a horned lizard, a gopher snake, or some other common species. Dr. Wes, in the passenger seat, was subdued, uttering scarcely a word in the last hour. Lorne, in the back, was sound asleep. It didn't matter; there was nothing to catch anyway.

The headlights washed over a small white cross beside the road. There were so many shrines here, on even the straightest roads.

Because they fall asleep, Derek thought.

Laura didn't want him to go to the desert. He could get hurt there. He could get lost. She wanted him to take his scholarship to Berkeley and work in a lab, where it was safe, not sign on with San Francisco State's resident reptile-kook, Wes Everman, whose research meant scorpions, rattlesnakes, bandits, and car wrecks. She didn't understand that he had enough lab experience already, that a zoologist needed field experience too. He imagined her standing in front of their apartment, arms crossed, his worn denim jacket around her shoulders, as the Bronco pulled away. The worry in her eyes stabbed him.

A few seconds after passing it, he registered a tight, symmetrical coil near the yellow line. He knew by its girth what it was. He pulled over. "There's a rattler back there," he said to Wes.

Wes didn't respond.

He reached between the seats for the flashlight. Wes's head was against the window, his mouth half open. Lorne had slumped out of view, and was snoring. Derek got out, slammed the door, and opened it again. The old guys were still out. By the time they woke up and struggled from the truck, the snake could be gone.

He stood with the door open, thinking. He could get back in, drive on, and they would never know. But then the white cross flickered in his mind. A break from driving, some fresh air, was probably a good idea. He closed the door. He would at least go take a look at the snake, see what it was. Maybe, if it was sufficiently sluggish from the cool night air, he would try to collect it, the right way this time, with the proper gear. *Never bare-hand a venomous snake!* He still stung from that scolding. He took a snake stick and canvas bag from the trailer.

The snake was pretty far back. He spotted it, finally, a distant, moonlit lump. At ten yards he stopped and shone his light. It was medium-length, about three feet, and, wait ... different. Tan, with coffee-brown, silver-dollar blotches edged with black. He stepped closer. This wasn't a speckled or diamondback rattlesnake, all they had found on the trip so far. It was a species Derek knew only from a single faded image in a dusty old snake book, a snake perennially sought, yet so rarely seen it didn't rate a common name. It was *Crotalus enyo!* This was a *grail*-snake! Its tissues were *grail*-data! His hands were shaking. This was an instant paper. Wes wanted it. Science wanted it. *He* wanted it!

"Wake up!" he yelled at the Bronco, "I found an *enyo!*" His words bounced off rocks and were absorbed by sand. The snake had uncoiled and was sleepily crawling toward the ditch, its rattle waggling.

He could run back, shake them awake, but no, it would take too long. Clutching the bag, snake stick, and light, he thought, *I can do this.*

His plan was to hook it, drag it away from the ditch, onto the empty road. It would coil in defence, tail buzzing. Next step, lay the bag on the ground, mouth toward it. Set the light on the road, aimed at it. Drag it toward the bag with the snake stick, then hook the biggest loop of its body and jam it inside, and … he wasn't sure of the next step. He would improvise.

He hooked the snake, dragged it onto open asphalt near the bag and light, and then things went off script. The snake, now wide awake, wasn't coiling or buzzing. It knew where it wanted to go, and slipped free. Derek hooked it again, dragged it a few feet, and again it slipped free. In and out of the flashlight beam they danced, forward and back, until arriving almost atop the centre line of the road. A vehicle coming from the opposite direction, lit by running lights only, blasted past. Spun by its momentum, Derek stumbled, tripped over the snake stick and fell to his hands and knees.

Snake eyes shone in the moonlight, inches from his left wrist. Now the rattler was coiling, and was about to strike. Without thinking, Derek slapped his right hand onto the broad head, pinning it to the road, and spidered his body away, a distant reflex from high school wrestling. As the snake thrashed, he walked his fingers behind the angles of the jaw, anchoring his nails in the rough scales.

Never bare-hand a venomous snake!

This was probably the kind of stupid thing Laura, 1,500 miles away, was lying awake imagining him doing.

"Don't do something stupid, like try to catch a rattlesnake to impress the professor," she had actually said, staring across the kitchen table.

"I won't," he said.

"Promise?"

He promised.

The tail was buzzing, the coils shifting.

He could let go, roll away, but maybe not fast enough. A kangaroo rat, speedy and erratic, had evolved the moves to evade the strike. Derek's hand, with its megawatt heat signature, was a slow-motion target, a beach ball. And, truly, did he want to lose this snake? It was an *enyo*! *Major data! Holy Grail! A paper!* This was why he was here.

Crouched, he half-carried, half-dragged the writhing reptile to the bag, ten feet away. He stuffed the head inside, aware there was still the problem—if he let go now, he would be bitten before he could draw his hand back out. Using his free hand, he did his best to hitch the bag up over the snake, at the same time jerking his elbow, an attempt to bump the stubborn loops inside. His fingers, clamped on the neck, were cramping. In no way was this going to work.

He did the only half-sensible thing. Rising fully to his feet, like an Olympic hammer thrower, he spun, once, twice, three times, and blindly released. The bag and snake fluttered into the night, landing, somewhere, without a sound.

He looked at the sky, at the moon, then up the road at the Bronco. He closed his eyes and imagined Laura, rolled onto her side. She was facing away.

He gathered up the snake stick and light, and eventually found the bag between sun-bleached rocks in the ditch. As he approached, it seemed to move. The snake was still inside? He crept closer. Amazingly, it was, and was curled at the bottom! He dropped the stick across as a barrier, anchored it with his boot, and deftly spun the neck of the bag to tie the knot. It could not have been easier. Arm extended, he carried his prize to the middle of the road, wanting to yell, to roar! He had caught an *enyo*, the most elusive snake in Baja!

But it took less than a heartbeat to realize what else he had done. He had broken a promise to his wife, a promise meant to protect his life, to protect their marriage. He had broken a vow, for a snake.

Sandra Sugimoto

Sisters

The jewel-coloured membrane ripples in waves along the monstrous bubble, expands beyond what seems logical, plausible, verging on magic. The busker's practised performance continues with a second bubble growing inside, fetus-like, filling its lung-shaped encasement with air. Buoyed by the rush of spring wind, the dual bubble separates from the soapy string wand, setting itself adrift.

Piercing squeals of wonder explode from the two wobbly toddlers, their puffy hands stretch out in a joyful effort to poke the air-born spectacle. Their mama swoops her arms in a generous arc, scoops up the children, swooshes them up, up, up high in the air, then pivots, taking hurried steps in the opposite direction, down the grassy hill, toward the pond's edge. Set free, the girls run in wide circles, necks flung back, burbling with laughter before coming to a full stop at the muddied fringe, face to face with a sharp-eyed goose. *Hiss.* Tensed neck outstretched, feathers grazing the ground. *Honk.* Black gaping beak. Rising from its gullet, a pink, sawtoothed tongue waggles at the diminutive figures like a crooked, bony finger.

The girls step back and enter into the shallow, wet, murkiness, frozen-eyed, hand-in-hand.

⌒

Scritch. Something poked at her memory. *Scratch.* Talli drifted in and out of consciousness, aware only of a faint outline, a foggy field of muted blue-grey tones. She lay belly down, cheekbone hard against the cold, tiled bathroom floor, limp legs exposed to the cold morning air seeping through the cracked window that never had gotten repaired. Vague thoughts of putting that task on the to-do list sifted through her mind, dissolving like salt into sea water.

What day was it? If it were Saturday then Sophie would stop by. She'd promised to drop off some of her tomato plants with their thick, green foliage, grown from seed, pampered with heat lamps (and probably song). To tend, to be tender, that was Sophie, born with the disposition and patience to nurture.

Talli was the older sister, by less than a year, Sophie being the December baby. The two grew up close as twins, understood each other's unspoken worlds, each with their own forms of escape. By early grade school, Talli, tagged as the studious one, tended to her times tables, spelling lists, wrote out schedules and flashcards, always cleaned out her recorder after practice. Sophie would be outside, crouched and quiet, in the precious patch of yard, fingers dug deep into the grass by the cement path, uncovering an ant colony. In perpetual motion, the ants swung forward, propelled by an insatiable drive.

Follow trail.

Discern the treasures.

Transport them home.

⌒

"Talli—wake up! Bail, bail, bail!" In lightning-like flashes she could still see Makoto's contorted face, a shadowed fractured scream, mouthing words the winds whipped and caught, sliced syllables thrown overboard. Dense fog encircled their tiny Catalina, swallowing the waves. Anchored in the bay at sunset the night before, the line had broken free. By early morning they had drifted into the jagged shoals, ripping a gaping black hole in the hull. Water streamed in, sharp rain hurled pellets against her back. Gas leaked from the damaged tank. The smell caught in Talli's nostrils as the boat pitched and rocked. The incoming water rose fast even as their arms flung around like windmills, frantically scooping—the nauseating waves relentless against their efforts to hold their footing.

Toes. Try to wiggle toes. No movement. It felt as if those digits, swollen and dark against her chipped turquoise-painted toenails, didn't belong to her. Through the bathroom window, soft amber sunlight streamed across her broken body. "This body," she thought, "is borrowed. To think it might be returned in such a pitiful state." Her life, once ordered and measured, now splayed out in mounds across the floor like gopher holes. Pressed clothes had once hung from cedar scented wood hangers in a soothing, horizontal ombre swath from white to black. How had she allowed this, allowed herself to dissipate, dissolve, devolve?

In tiny, incremental shifts.

Small signs started to appear, barely perceptible at first: Puffy folds of soft flesh blossoming beneath her stretched-out bra straps, the unattended, ever accumulating thickness of skin on the heels of her feet, and hadn't she found that curly loose hair, almost an inch long, growing on her chin? Even more concerning: what about that beady, black mole that materialized between her brows, a maniacal, mocking third eye?

This time of year, if Makoto were still around, the two of them would have played a quick round of poker to decide who got first dibs with the power washer. Oh, the palpable thrill of washing away the previous year's green blanket of West Coast algae! Chores and maintenance jobs were now far removed from any sense of urgency. Cracked windows. Yellowed caulking. Insects crawling, making homes in dark, dank crevices around her home that once gleamed. Even the bath mat, she noted, seemed to have an earthy scent, like mushrooms after a rain.

Near the spices, on the upper shelf in Talli's kitchen, sat a lustrous, chocolate-brown wooden box carved from Black Walnut. Makoto's ashes. Talli had meant to scatter them out at sea—had *meant* to do many things in the months after he drowned—but the last time on the water had been with Makoto and it never felt like the right time to go back out.

Things left undone. Matters neglected. Unsavoury signs that persisted, a slow simmer of gloom. Nothing glaring or urgent, so why worry about them? "It's not as if they were gargantuan, unsurmountable problems," she told herself. "Nothing I can't manage." After all, there were plenty of ways to feel better—legal ways, ones her doctor offered, almost insisted upon. "We all go through difficult times, Talli, and sometimes we need a little help to get past them. It would just be a temporary measure, until you're up on your feet again."

Mildew, mould, dust mites. Was that a silverfish slithering under the peeled caulking on the tub? They've survived longer than humans, with their prehistoric resilience, able to live a year without even a crumb. Talli's stomach seized, the last thing she had eaten was two days ago—before her fall—half of a stale energy bar she found stuck inside her bathrobe pocket.

Moments before the tumble, Talli had felt a dizzying squall in her head—the tingle down her spine, the pain melting, if only momentarily—her body adrift.

The slip.

The slick of water on the tiled floor. Lost footing. Skull hit hard against the edge of the stone countertop, following gravity's insistence to come down, to rest, to be still. What Talli could not see nor lift her hands to feel, was the monstrous goose egg protruding near the base of her skull.

Blackout.

~

Water. Something cold, anything to wet her gaping mouth, dark and parched, lips cracked and chapped. Small c-shaped parentheses formed around her eyes, as if to emphasize, these *once* gleamed.

~

Water gushed, leaked—drowned out the dual screams, becoming fainter as the watery expanse widened ... low hiss and rumble of an engine, blaring honk of the coast guard, the blue-grey outline of the rescue boat appearing, as if born out of an iridescent bubble.

Through the cracks, Talli sensed sounds of honking—the insistent *rap, rap, rap* on the side window, hurried footsteps. Sophie's keys jangled, her hands shaking as she opened the back door.

"Talli!" Sophie called out. Talli's fingers trembled as Sophie reached out to take her sister's hand.

Christina Kruger-Woodrow
Lie Fallow

AN EXCERPT

For years I avoided thinking of the place we grew up. I packed the memories away in my mind. That's a trick my mother taught me when I was little and something was upsetting me. She'd say, "Alistair, imagine placing those worries or thoughts in a box one by one, then closing the lid nice and tight. Now carry it down to the cellar—mind the steps in the dark!" She would grab me at that part to make me squeal. "Now put the box on a shelf and leave it there. It may get covered in dust but whatever's inside will be good as new when you come back for it."

You never go back for it. That was the real trick. How many things my mother must have stored underground. I imagine a cellar so wide and deep that it goes on for miles into the earth, filled with all the things she left behind to rot in the damp.

All sorts of memories come back to me now, as if my own cellar has flooded from years of heavy rain. They bubble up from the ground and run towards me.

⌒

The night I met you, my mother and I stood outside the back door of the church, waiting for our names to be called. The farmland around us was blue in the dusk, and the lantern my mother held glowed weakly. We could hear crickets and the tall cornstalks rustling. There was a man's voice from inside, and every now and then a chorus of people repeating the same word.

"He sounds angry," I said.

"Priests all sound like that." She set down the lantern and picked at a loose thread on her sleeve. "How do I look?"

"I can't tell. It's too dark."

"It's not." She smiled. "You just don't want to compliment your poor old mother."

"You look nice."

"What's that? I have lice?"

"Mom! I said you look nice."

"I know honey, I'm just tormenting you. Now be sure to speak nice and loud when we get in there. All we have to do is stand next to Father Ezekiel and he'll talk for a while then ask us to repeat after him."

"While they stare at us."

"—while they stare at us, yes, and then Jeb will offer us a seat, and that'll be that." She pursed her lips. "I think you're going to like it here. We won't have to be on the road anymore. You'd like, that, wouldn't you?"

"What if he doesn't ask us to sit with him?"

She put a hand on my shoulder. "He'll ask, we've discussed it. Who wouldn't want a strong young man and a lovely young lady such as myself to join their family?"

"Ew, Mom."

"You're right. A strong young man and a crusty old hag to go with him." She laughed but as she reached down to pick up the lantern, her hand shook.

Jeb had visited us at our camp often in the past few weeks. At nine years old, I was shy and couldn't meet his eye. He shook my hand and said I looked like a fine young man and that he had a son my age named Abel.

He would arrive at dusk and sit with my mother by the fire. I would lie in the tent and try to hear what they were saying. All I could ever make out was Jeb's rumbling voice, and my mother's laughter. I looked forward to his visits because none of the other men bothered us on those nights.

Jeb had invited us to live with him, but what if he changed his mind? What if he only wanted my mother and not me? Our lives those past few years had felt like a forever shifting landscape of walking on overgrown roads and being thirsty and falling asleep standing up, my skin flaking from the sun, and always my mother ahead of me saying just a little further, we'll get to the top of that ridge, and then there'll be a nice place we can rest. We used to live in a house I think, with her parents maybe, before the fires came that way and we had to start walking. Then came the camps of people she said were friends, and canned food warmed on someone else's fire. Her waking me in the night saying Alistair, be quiet and pack your things, quickly. If Jeb didn't like me, would I just have to wander the countryside forever? Would my mother come with me?

I almost didn't hear Ezekiel's voice through the door: "Please welcome Alistair and his mother, Pamela!"

"Men first, I suppose." She opened the door and ushered me through.

There were about forty or fifty people who watched as we walked to the front and stood holding hands next to a man in a long white dress. He had a grey beard so sparse that I could see all the tendons in his neck move as he addressed the congregation. "We welcome Alistair and Pamela, who have been turned to the light by our brother Jebediah. They are ready to renounce their lives of sin and be welcomed to the kingdom of God."

All the men and boys were sitting on one side of the room, and the women and girls on the other. Jeb was in the front row, and you were there next to him, slouched in your seat. You looked up at me but I couldn't tell what your expression was.

Ezekiel turned to me. "You will repeat after me: I renounce my name and with it my past life of sin."

My voice sounded so small in the silence of that room. "I renounce my name and with it my past life of sin."

Ezekiel placed a hand on top of my head. His palm was cool and dry. "From this day forward, I am Joel."

I started to sweat. No one had said anything about having a different name. I looked to my mother, who nodded. "From this day forward, I am Joel."

Ezekiel turned to my mother, and had her repeat the same words. He didn't put his hand on her head when he named her Miriam.

"As children of God, you must touch no man other than your husband, no women other than your wives. In this way we live in purity as brothers and sisters." He looked at our hands. My mother looked to Jeb and then to the priest. Opened her mouth, closed it again. Her grip on my hand tightened. After what felt like a long moment, she did this little shrug, squeezed my hand and then let it go.

"God bless you both," Ezekiel said, raising his hands in the air. "Joel and Miriam, children of God. Who will welcome them to his hearth?"

Silence. In the light of the lanterns hanging from the rafters, I could see dust motes floating, drifting. Were we in trouble? I started reaching for her instinctively when Jeb said, "I will welcome them, father."

My mother stepped forward but Ezekiel cleared his throat and waved me on ahead. I sat in the seat next to you and you took one look at me and scowled. Jeb reached for my mother's hand as the sermon continued.

~

Your house seemed huge to me. You had a whole room of your own which Jeb said we would share.

"Wow, your bed is really nice." I walked over and sat on the edge, admiring it.

You rolled your eyes. "It's just a bed. Dad said you can put your things on that shelf, since you didn't bring much." You watched me put my things away and then, as if you couldn't resist, you asked if I wanted to see your collection.

"Okay." I knelt beside you as you pulled a box out from under the bed and took the things out, one by one. There were buttons and colourful rocks, a carved wooden horse. You made sure I was paying attention before pulling out the last item, a black thin rectangle with a smooth front.

"This one is a secret. I found it last summer."

"What is it?"

"I don't know."

"Can I see it?" You handed it to me and it was lighter than I expected, the front as smooth as glass. I could see my reflection in it. There was a piece on the side that pressed in but nothing happened when I pushed it.

You snatched it from me as footsteps came down the hall. Jeb's head appeared in the doorway.

"Time for bed, boys. Joel, we're so glad to have you here. If you need anything, just ask your brother."

I didn't realize for a moment that he meant you. I wanted to ask you so many things, if we were really brothers, if we were staying here forever, why the men and women sat on opposite sides of the church, but you climbed into bed and blew out the lamp without waiting for me. I got in gingerly next to you, and even though the room was warm, I couldn't fall asleep. My mother hadn't said goodnight. I kept thinking of her face in the church when she let go of my hand, her little shrug. Had she known that was coming and not told me? Usually when I couldn't sleep, she would rub my back in little circles and we'd match our breathing. I felt a sick feeling in my stomach. Had that been wrong?

Maybe looking back on that first night, I'm giving myself thoughts or feelings I didn't have at the time. Maybe I was just happy to be warm. Maybe I didn't think about my mother's face in the church, or that long silence before Jeb offered us a place. Maybe I eventually fell asleep while breathing in time with you.

Non-fiction

edited by Christina Myers

Katie Lewis

Nuts

I wake up to the sounds of a monkey terrorizing my yard. It's ripping apart the garbage. The noise is familiar because it happens at least once a week.

Skerchhhhhhhhh, grunts the monkey. It continues to tear through the trash with gleeful abandon, tipping the metal can to the ground with a crash.

Rip. Rip. RIPPPPPPPPPP.

I part the dingy white mosquito net I sleep under, jump to my feet, and cross the room to unlock the ornate iron doors that lead to the garden. I grab the closest thing I find—a broken broom—and half-run, half-gallop toward the monkey.

"Dude!" I yell. I guess that's his name now. "Monkey! Git! Piss off!"

He freezes: two brown beady eyes stare back at me without a blink. The monkey now sits at the peak of the trash pile, clutches a half-eaten mango as if it were the last one on earth. Dude, who is about a foot and a half tall, does not give a crap about me, a half-crazed *mzungu*—or "white person", as I'm referred to by Ugandans—and my broom. He is living his dream on top of trash mountain.

I slow down as I get closer. I have no idea what to do.

With one long look, he hisses loudly, picks up a nut, and hucks it.

"Aghhhhhhh!" The nut whacks me in the head. Ouch.

He turns, nonchalant, and bounds off, his red ass on full display. How do I know my monkey is a he? Well, my backyard vervet monkey comes complete with a pair of shockingly *bright* blue balls down there—similar to an IKEA kid-like light blue. His testicles are blue as blue can be.

I love animals. But this monkey is driving me insane. He's basically an unpredictable little rat with claws in a cuter outfit. This monkey has outsmarted every garbage-can trick I have tried up to this point: cement blocks, a bungee cord to hold the lid down, and more. Not only that, he reeks—a stench of garbage mixed with the smell of his own feces.

Today is supposed to be my day off and I'm not in the mood to deal with blue-balled monkeys. I arrived home at midnight after a two-week reporting trip in Western Uganda. My job? Freelance journalist. My home? A small unit in a yellow cement triplex, fifteen minutes outside of Uganda's capital, Kampala. There is a mango tree and the yard is full of birds, flowers, and bugs. The air smells sweet, thick, and damp—when it doesn't smell like monkey crap. We are so close to the equator, it is 26°c almost every day of the year here and the sun always rises at 6:00 a.m. and sets at 6:00 p.m. like clockwork.

I need coffee. I head to the kitchen and pull out a stout red mug. There is mouse shit in it. *Christ.*

On to plan B. Go downtown to a café for a real coffee. I grab my laptop, my notebooks, my recorder, and walk outside to the dusty red road to go catch a *boda boda*, a motorbike taxi that is dangerous but how I get around.

"How much?" I ask.

"Five thousand shillings, madame." The price equals about three dollars. "Best price for you."

"Eiii, I know the rate, brother," I joke. We meet somewhere in the middle. I'm too tired today to negotiate.

He pulls out and weaves through traffic. I'm so used to the maniacal drivers, bustling traffic, and close calls, I zone out. I rub my head. It hurts. Injury by monkey nut.

Screech. We stop suddenly, the brakes squealing as if in pain, as a blue Toyota sedan slams on its brakes in front of us.

Behind us, a Jeep barrels full speed into the back of our motorbike. I'm suddenly airborne: I go flying and all my belongings scatter across the road. There are a few seconds of dead silence before I crash to the ground, limbs flailing, my skirt flipping up in the process as my butt skids across three feet of jagged concrete. Finally, I stop. Silence.

"Ughrhhrgurrgh," I try to speak, but I just come out with gurgles. "Uhhhhhh ... ow."

I groan. I want to be anywhere but here.

A group of eight or so gather around me, standing above my crumpled body in a circle, and lean down to get a closer look at the spectacle before them. In times of trouble, a common reaction of Ugandans is to, well, smile and laugh, so I am met with gleaming white teeth smiling down at me.

"Ehhhhhh, sister, are you okay?" asks one of the men bending down. A few of the women go off to collect my things, scattered everywhere. There are titters as they look at me with a mixture of shock and amusement.

I wonder why for a second. Ah yes ... my skirt is still above my belly button, and my road-rashed butt (think: a pizza) is on display to all. My butt looks like a monkey's ass.

Braaaaaaaap. The sound of a motorcycle suddenly starts up. It sounds like a blender of bolts. My *boda boda* driver reaches down, grabs my laptop, and books it out of there. It takes me a few seconds to comprehend what has happened. He is gone. Bye-bye, laptop. Nice to know you.

"So sorry, so sorry," says a Ugandan woman who helps me try to stand up.

I want to scream, but I can't.

I gather as much stuff as I can find and put it back in my bag (sans laptop). I thank the group, my face red with embarrassment, and decide to take a minibus—called a *matatu*—home where I can wither in embarrassment by myself.

"You will never see these people again," I say to myself over and over in a kind of mantra style. "You will *never* see these people again."

A minibus pulls up and I clamber on. Each one holds about twelve people (but hey, sixteen can fit.) The man collecting fares gestures to the front seat. Lucky day.

"*Oli otya*," he says—"Hi, how are you"—cocking his head as he looks at me. I am a disaster, caked in blood and dirt. I look like Linus from *Peanuts*, but with a red dirt cloud.

We set off, weaving around cars, motorbikes, and people as we slowly climb the hill that takes me to my house.

I smell smoke. The smell gets worse. Where is it coming from? I crane my neck around.

Boom! A loud explosion, which sounds like a bomb, suddenly rocks the minivan. Yellow flames jump out of the hood of the minivan. Grey smoke fills the interior as the flames lick higher.

There is pandemonium on the bus as people fight to exit out the one sliding door that can open. It's every person for themselves and no, I am *not* going to die on a flaming minibus on a hill in Kampala. I finally make it out.

"*RUN!*" I scream. "The van is going to blow up!"

They look at me quizzically and continue watching the smoke billow up.

Whatever. I'm outta here. I slog up the hill, my ravaged butt blistering in pain. I slow down. Safe enough, I think. I am a ten-minute walk from home.

As I round the corner to my road, I am met with a huge lineup of cars, crudely filling any area where pedestrians walk. I decide to jump over a ditch—there's a bit more space on that side. I'm close to home. I can't wait to shower.

Squrrrrlchhhhhh.

Fail. I don't make the jump and fall into the ditch.

The bad news? Turns out I have fallen into a sewage ditch—a wet ditch full of feces. The smell almost makes me retch as I try to climb out of the poo trap, my shoes squelching mud out the sides. I slog home in despair.

I make it to my front door, limping. My eyes prickle with tears—I'm so happy to be home, but the stench of, well, myself, is burning my eyes, causing them to water.

I open the front door and freeze. It looks like a murder scene. There is blood splashed across the walls and splattered all over the floor.

Jesus H. Murphy Christ. I start to panic when out walks my cat (who also happens to be named Monkey) holding a giant bloody lizard in her mouth. She looks proud.

"I can't ... I can't even," I sputter. I go to the shower. I wash each part of my body: red dirt, blood, feces, and more.

The lizard will be dealt with tomorrow.

I pour myself a gin and tonic, top it with a lemon, and head to the back deck. This day needs to end, I think.

I hear a rustle in the bushes. My head darts toward the sound. The stench of feces wafts into the backyard.

The monkey is back. I cover both sides of my head as a reflex and pull my shoulders towards my midriff, hiding. I can feel the bruise from earlier. The monkey, however, has different plans this evening—romantic, I suppose. He is spanking the monkey, jacking the beanstalk, whatever you want to call it: he is masturbating in my backyard.

He vigorously rubs his penis—which is bright red—as he continues to stare me down. I'm amazed and horrified. I didn't know monkeys could do that.

I go inside. I crawl into bed, I put my head on my lumpy pillow and take a deep breath, willing myself to try to sleep. Finally, I have peace.

Scrghhhhhhhhhh.

Grunt, grunt, scrabble, scrabble.

Riiiiip.

I pull the covers over my head.

I'm done. The monkey wins.

William W. Campbell
Amusia and Ravel's *Boléro*

Amusia refers to a neurological disorder affecting musical abilities. Maurice Ravel (1875—1937), the French Impressionist composer, developed amusia as part of an illness in his last years. He fell victim to a progressive, degenerative dementia that affected his musical abilities and caused a number of other neurological deficits. A great deal has been written about Ravel's amusia and what effect it might have had on his compositions later in life, particularly *Boléro* and *Concerto for the Left Hand*.

Congenital amusia is a relatively common developmental disorder affecting an otherwise normal brain. We call it tone-deafness and characterize those who have it as unable to carry a tune in a bucket. People with congenital amusia may struggle to distinguish the *William Tell Overture* from "Silent Night." Ulysses S. Grant reportedly knew only two songs: "Yankee Doodle" and "Not Yankee Doodle." To one affected woman, music sounded like the clanging of pots and pans in her kitchen. Her affliction resisted attempts at even a rudimentary music education; recordings were meaningless noise and music lessons a complete failure.

Acquired amusia is rare and most often caused by a stroke. A patient with acquired amusia may be unable to distinguish between the sound of a flute and a piano. They may have difficulty recognizing melodies, or a selective deficit in producing a melody, even a very familiar one, or a problem understanding or producing tempo.

Aphasia is an acquired disturbance of language abilities, usually due to a stroke. The speech disturbance in patients with aphasia may mask an amusia. Yet the Russian composer Shebalin, whose case was reported by the pioneer neuropsychologist Alexander Luria in 1965, had remarkable preservation of his musical abilities despite severe aphasia due to a stroke.

To a patient with amusia, the c major scale may sound the same as the c minor scale. To a normal ear, these scales sound very different. For a patient with amusia, they may be indistinguishable. Normal listeners readily detect a sour note in a familiar song; patients with amusia cannot. Evaluation of amusia is hindered by the fact that the patient must be able to communicate and must have had pre-morbid musical ability, and the examiner must have enough appreciation of music to assess the patient.

The localization of musical function in the cerebral hemispheres has proved difficult to pinpoint. Analysis of the neurological deficits of patients with focal cerebral lesions suggests the recognition of melodies is a right temporal lobe function, but the analysis of tempo, rhythm, and pitch is more of a left temporal lobe function. In general, impairments related to melody are more characteristic of right hemisphere lesions, but rhythm is represented more widely in both the left hemisphere and in subcortical areas.

Studies have clearly established differences in cerebral dominance for music between musicians and non-musicians; the dominant hemisphere becomes more important in musicians. There is overlap of musical and language functions, but brain lesions can produce surprising dissociation between loss of music and loss of language abilities, as in Shebalin, and between loss of different types of musical functions.

In 1927, Ravel complained to friends about "great tiredness" and "cerebral anemia" and was advised by his doctor to rest for a year. Instead of resting, he made a triumphant four-month American tour and composed *Boléro*. At the beach one day in 1928, at the zenith of his creativity, he sat at the piano in a friend's cottage in his bathing suit and tapped out the simple melody of *Boléro*. Then, instead of developing the melody, as with his other works, he decided to repeat it, over and over, for 340 bars, changing only the orchestration.

Over the next two years, Ravel composed *Concerto for the Left Hand* and his *Piano Concerto in G Major*. The *Concerto for the Left Hand* was written for a pianist, Paul Wittgenstein, who had lost his right arm in combat. Its peculiar style may reflect the one-hand constraint rather than a deterioration of Ravel's compositional talents. Ravel composed The *Piano Concerto in G Major* between 1929 and 1931, after he composed *Boléro*. The concerto premiered in early 1932 and was followed by a well-received European tour of twenty cities, with Ravel conducting.

But Ravel was on his last musical legs. Later in 1932, he was commissioned to write a song cycle, *Don Quichotte à Dulcinée*, for a film version of *Don Quixote*. The cycle was to include four songs. As Ravel worked, it became clear he was impaired. He was unable to complete the project and was fired by the film's director. He finally completed three songs, reportedly with extensive assistance from secretaries, assistants, and colleagues.

In June 1933, he noted motor incoordination and forgot how to swim, then developed defective eye movements and speech difficulties. At dinner one night, he took a knife by the blade and tried to cut with the handle. He had always been forgetful, but the forgetfulness and other symptoms grew progressively worse. In November 1933, in his last public appearance, he conducted *Boléro* and the *Concerto in G Major*. By 1935, he was almost unable to write or speak. Neurological evaluation in 1936 showed moderate aphasia. Testing of his musical abilities showed areas of profound impairment with islands of remarkable preservation. Ravel died after exploratory surgery and there was no autopsy; the precise diagnosis remains unknown.

Boléro is not complex, written in C major and ¾ time. It has a very unusual prolonged crescendo, beginning *pianissimo* and ending with the entire orchestra playing *fortissimo*. The relentless, driving snare drum riff continues throughout. The relatively simple melody is repeated eighteen times on different instruments that fade in and out.

Some have argued that amusia impaired Ravel's ability to compose and the endless repetition of the same simple melody and rhythm throughout reflect his limitations. Others argue that *Boléro* was an experiment exploring the possibilities of composing with simple musical elements. Ravel himself said, in an interview: "It constitutes an experiment in a very special and limited direction, and should not be suspected of aiming at achieving anything different from, or anything more than, it actually does achieve ... I issued a warning to the effect that what I had written was a piece ... consisting wholly of 'orchestral tissue without music' of one very long, gradual crescendo."

Several diagnostic possibilities have been raised to explain Ravel's illness. It seems likely he suffered from what we would now classify as one of the frontotemporal lobar degenerations, a group of conditions in which atrophy and degeneration affect the frontal and temporal lobes of the brain most prominently. These include frontotemporal dementia, primary progressive aphasia, and semantic dementia, and are often associated with abnormal accumulations of the protein tau.

The Belgian neurologist Erik Baeck reviewed the evidence, discounted the theory that *Don Quichotte à Dulcinée* was written with assistance, contending it was "genuine Ravel," and concluded that Ravel did not have amusia during the composition of *Boléro*. It is also difficult to imagine someone with amusia successfully conducting an orchestra, through both practices and performances, as Ravel did at least twenty times in 1932, four years after he wrote *Boléro*.

Regarding his *Concerto in G Major*, written after *Boléro*, one critic writing in the *Christian Science Monitor* in 1932 had only praise, writing, "The orchestration abounds in amusing and profound inventions, and is really of inimitable originality of writing and of thought. The new concerto is worthy of the other masterpieces that we owe to Ravel."

The second movement of the *Concerto in G Major* has been described as "one of the most poignant and beautiful pieces of music ever written" and one of Ravel's "most perfect creations." The concerto was reportedly hailed as a masterpiece at every stop. It is difficult to imagine its creator working with less than his full arsenal of compositional talents. A remarkable internet video shows Leonard Bernstein playing the *Concerto in G Major* while leading the orchestra from the piano, conducting mostly with head nods and facial expressions—one musical genius performing and interpreting the work of another musical genius.

Considering Ravel's explanation that *Boléro* was an experiment in a special and limited direction, the composition of more complex works afterwards, and the touring and conducting he was able to do, it is unlikely Ravel was suffering from amusia when he wrote *Boléro*.

Near the end, Ravel lamented that he could not write music any more. He sobbed, "I still have so much music in my head. I've said nothing. I still have so much to say." Whether musical brilliance or musical impairment led to the creation of *Boléro* we will never know with certainty, but the evidence favours the former interpretation.

Kim Spencer

The Indian Agent's Coming!

The federal government would travel by boat to our isolated reserve to round up kids and haul them off to the Indian Residential School. Here's my family's story.

Our village of Kitkatla is situated to provide a visual vantage point for its inhabitants. Someone would catch sight of the steam coming off the boats from afar; it was the only warning they would get. Word would spread quickly throughout the village: *"The Indian Agent is coming! The Indian Agent is coming!"*

Family heads scrambled. Thoughts ran through Great-Grandfather's mind: *they're not taking my grandkids away, not under my watch!* But there was nowhere to flee. They were on a small remote island; there were no roads. The nearest town of Prince Rupert was nearly sixty kilometres away by boat and even if they could escape there, no one was going to help them. They were Indians.

Great-Grandfather had to come up with a plan. He would have to act fast and he'd have to be discreet. He couldn't let the other members of the village know, not even his closest friends; the risk was too great. If he was caught attempting to withhold his grandchildren, he'd be sent to jail or face a considerable fine he couldn't afford. There was no time to worry, though. His family's safety, their very lives, was at risk.

Great-Grandfather gathered his family together for an important meeting. He instructed everyone to pack lightly and to be quick; they were going on a short trip. The family obediently followed directions. The women hurried to prepare some basic food supplies. In no time, they found themselves carefully loading onto a small rowboat and quietly pulled away from shore. Their boat was heavy with family members and supplies. They made sure to hug the shoreline so as to go unnoticed and eventually made their way up the inlet, travelling as far as they could go, past their usual trapping spot. Only when they were sure they were hidden from the dreadful grasp of the Indian Agent did they dare stop. They'd heard stories. They knew what happened at those schools.

Mom was young at the time and thought they were all going on a picnic. Her grandfather made sure no one panicked or was afraid. One time, he even made them homemade tomahawks to play with while they waited things out.

This quick escape became routine for them. The Indian Agent was relentless in invading our village, returning again and again. Yet every time they reached our family's home, they were conveniently *away*. Nobody in the village could talk because no one knew where they were. The Indian Agent probably figured he'd get them next time.

They didn't get them the next time. Not one person in my family attended the Indian Residential School. Not one.

A Mourning That Would Last Generations

If you were fortunate enough to grow up in a loving, nurturing home, you were shown love in various ways, thus learned how to be a loving person. As a child, you basked in that love. You felt it in the gentleness of your mother's touch as she softly moved hair from your face while looking into your eyes, or when you were sick and she cooked your favourite meal. You thrived under the security of your father, scooping you up and holding you in his strong, protective embrace. You felt invincible sitting on his shoulders as he walked down the street.

You observed playful embraces between your parents in the kitchen, saw the smiles that crept across their faces while affectionately teasing one another. You recognized these were small ways a husband and wife expressed their love. You may have taken your brother or sister for granted. All the times you ran to tattle on them, venting your frustrations, no matter how small, knowing you'd be heard. Your grandparents were gentle and patient with you; you sensed they'd be in your corner no matter what.

These intimate relationships are what shape a person. Some of the ways one learns *to be* in the world. To love and to be loved.

What if you were torn from that loving home at an early age? As young as four years old, forced to live far away in a dreary, cold, and cruel institution. Stark walls and pasty, stern faces keeping watch over you. You're told everything about you is wrong: the colour of your skin, your language, and your culture. Mean-spirited strangers, so different from the ones you've known, looking down their sharp noses, telling you, *you are less than*. Staring you in the eye, stating again and again, *you're good for nothing*.

You're fed bland, poor-quality food; even then, it's rationed. Interactions with your siblings are forbidden. If you notice your brother or sister suffering in any way, there's nothing you can do to help them. You have to ignore feelings of sadness, anger, or pain because you're punished if you cry or act out. You numb your body and sense of personal space because these are often violated, sometimes in the cruellest manner. Anytime you see or experience human touch it's an act of abuse.

The Indian Residential School system was designed to "kill the Indian in the child." To do that, you had to remove children from their homes. Make sure they were far from the influence of their families.

This took out the heart of a family. Its core. Men were left with feelings of powerlessness because they couldn't protect their families. If they resisted, or fought against their children being taken, they would be fined (something they couldn't afford) or sent to jail. What does that do to a father when he can't safeguard his own kids? And then have to look his wife in the face and watch helplessly as she continually weeps for her children until she has no strength left or her tears have run dry. How does a mother process such grief? In the deafening silence of an empty home, she grows numb.

Having children torn from their embrace during the Indian Residential School system wasn't Indigenous peoples' first encounter with trauma. They'd become all too familiar with colonizers' evil ways.

Hopelessness eventually set in. Many parents turned to self-medication to further numb the pain, drowning their shame and sorrow in the bottle. When the children eventually returned home (*if* they did at all, as some didn't survive), there was a disconnect in the family, a breakdown. They were like strangers.

The children returned home with wounds unseen to the naked eye, hidden beneath their tattered clothing. It was a stain only they could see, and the vow of silence had been forced upon them. The *hush*. Scars silently cried out, yet no one heard. The parents sat emotionless, eyes vacant like someone had turned off the switch. What could they say to their children? They'd been there themselves, they knew what happened at those schools. But you were told not to talk about those things. To *hush*.

Culture was no longer being practised in the community. It had been banned as illegal. There was no healing remedy or song to save them. A silence hung over homes, the community, as if in mourning, a mourning that would last for generations.

These were the ways many Indigenous people learned *to be* in this world. These are the unhealthy learned behaviours they unconsciously passed on to their children.

The impact of collective trauma on survivors and intergenerational survivors has been soul shattering. How could it not have been? What other possible outcome could the government or church—or any of us—have expected from such an institution?

Lori Greenfield

The Tuesday Ladies

Two women, on the other side of the street, pack up their crude, hand-painted signs. One stops, looks over at my car. She thinks I must be one of "them."

They are in their seventies. One leers at me. Weirdly enough, she looks like my mother.

A gust of wind causes the smaller of the two to drop her sign. She fastens the top button of her coat and slips on a pair of gloves, before scrambling after the big sheet of bristol. I'm concerned she may trip and fall.

They appear to have been camped out for some time. Empty Tim Hortons coffee cups are scattered between folding lawn chairs. She returns to the chairs and leans the retrieved sign against the playground fence, alongside a small stack of Bibles.

They are the Tuesday Ladies, I will later learn, and my presence seems to be of great interest to them. I have been asked by Carol, the clinic administrator, to arrive for my interview at 5:30 p.m., ensuring all patients will be off the premises. Confidentiality. A metal gate guards the only driveway into the lot.

I pull into the nearly empty parking lot and join four remaining vehicles. I step out of the car and glance across the street. They look back at me. If looks could kill ... shudder.

With a quick, jerky movement, the smaller one reaches down to grab her sign. She holds the placard high above her head and aggressively points and shakes it in my direction: ABORTION IS MURDER in red painted letters.

The paint has oozed and dried from the bottom of the letters M and R, like dripping blood. Very creative.

142

Not to be outdone, Tuesday Lady number two follows suit. Her sign is attached to a broomstick which she clumsily waves back and forth in wide sweeping motions.

GOD IS CRYING FOR YOUR BABY. Blue lettering, outlined in gold, gives the impression, at first glance, that the message is somehow spiritual. A blue tear drop has been drawn inside the *o* in GOD.

Part of me wants to get back in my car and drive as fast as possible to the safety of my home, never to return.

Another part wants to scream at them. Why are people so mean? How can they be so horrible? And why am I being showered with hate? I'm just here for an interview!

⌒

The clinic obtained an injunction prohibiting protesters from standing within ninety metres of the property. The anti-choice groups argued that the injunction violated their freedom-of-expression rights. The order was modified, to allow up to four protestors to stand on the sidewalk across the street from the clinic. Other protestors are required to stand at least fifty metres away. The court also mandated restrictions on protestors communicating with people accessing the clinic's services.

They are not, by law, allowed to engage physically or verbally with the staff or patients. They must stay within the Bubble Zone and keep quiet.

They become creative, finding ways to make their presence known. Some stand solemnly, holding huge blown-up pictures of healthy newborns with captions like "This is what I look like, Mommy," or "Please don't kill me!"

Others silently weep, while praying their rosary, behind bristol board collages of hideous colour photos of aborted fetuses. Tiny hands and portions of legs and arms floating about in a sea of blood. A head with no body. Blood. Gore. Intimidation. Hate. Fear. "Mommy, will it hurt?"

⌒

I get used to seeing them, the Tuesday Ladies, and I wonder about them.

I imagine they bake cookies and serve tea after service on Sunday and play the perfect grandmother role for their own offspring, convinced that they are doing God's work. They believe that they are entitled to judge, without compassion or remorse. They are above the lowly sinners who disagree with their interpretation of the scriptures. They have distorted the word of God to fit into their own fearful existence. I'm sure their cookies are good.

One morning, I go out to get coffee for the nurses and I have to pass by the Tuesday Ladies. I ask them, violating the court order, "Why do you do this?"

The shorter grey-haired lady turns on me and snarls: "Fuck off, devil."

She stares me down as I hurry back to the clinic. I tell Carol.

"Why were you talking to them? You overstepped the Bubble Zone."

"I don't know. I just wanted to talk to them."

What I don't tell Carol is that I wanted to be friends with them. Have a relationship with them. They remind me of my mother. There are tons of protestors at the clinic every day. I seldom notice the other groups. They just don't have an effect on me. The Tuesday Ladies pull up guilt. Not about the job. Not about the choices I've made in my own life. Not about the support I offer the women. Where, then, does the guilt originate? I feel rejected in their presence. Maybe I wonder what it's like to be that sure.

Every Tuesday, without fail, these two committed Christian soldiers arrive and set up across the street from the clinic. Their plan of action: to do their part in the war to end abortion, by harassing the staff and shaming and bullying the women accessing the services, as they enter and leave.

It doesn't work. But they persevere.

⁀

The last time I see them, they are standing in the same spot on their usual watch. After a while, you learn not to pay attention to them. But I still do, at least a little, just out of the corner of my eye.

It's my last day at the clinic. I'm moving to Vancouver and as I drive away it feels like driving from what is done.

I think of the Ladies as I turn onto the highway.

I don't think I'm anything to them. They wouldn't recognize me if they saw me again; I am just one of the devils.

The smaller one wears a tweed coat, polyester pants, and running shoes. They walk a lot over there. Her hair has grown thinner and greyer. She will never like me.

I should feel okay with that.

Emily Chan

Living in Ms. Shauna Roberts's Apartment

Note: Some names and details in the following story
have been changed in the interest of protecting privacy

We'd been living in the city for less than a week when I heard a pounding at the door.

I was home alone and the sound startled me, nearly causing the mug I was washing to slip out of my hands. I set it down in the sink with a clatter, brushed a sweaty tendril of hair off the back of my neck, and hurried to the door.

Moving boxes crowded the entranceway. I kicked a couple out of my way, then stood on my tiptoes to see through the peephole. Two male police officers waited on the other side, distorted by the fish-eye lens.

I pulled the door open, my heart racing even though I hadn't done anything wrong. As it swung inward, I wondered if I should have at least had the decency to put on a bra that morning.

"Hello?" I crossed my arms, then thought that might make me seem unfriendly and lowered them again.

"Hi, we're looking for Ms. Shauna Roberts."

"Oh, sorry, we just moved in. I don't know the neighbours yet." I stepped aside so he could see the boxes behind me. The cop barely glanced up.

"Okay. Thanks for your time, miss."

I shut the door and checked the deadlock before walking back to the kitchen. My phone rang the moment I reached the sink. It was my partner, Ari. I glanced at the clock as I picked up the phone. He was probably on the subway at that moment, rattling past the recycling plant's fetid fumes as he made his way to the newsroom where we'd both found freelance work for the summer.

"Hey, are you okay? Jack just called and said he heard the cops needed to get into the building to speak to the people in 301. He thinks they were looking for us."

Jack was our new landlord. A gruff Italian guy who was already skeptical enough about renting his unit to a couple of recent grads with barely anything in their bank accounts.

"Yeah, the police just left. They were looking for somebody named Shauna Roberts, but I told them we didn't know the neighbours yet. I showed them our boxes so they could see we'd just moved in."

"You let them into the apartment?"

"No, I just opened the door wider. Don't get annoyed with *me*! I didn't know what they wanted!"

"Okay, okay. Sorry. Let me update Jack. I'll call back."

Ari did a few minutes later.

"Hey, so Shauna Roberts is the woman who used to live in our place."

"What did she do? Should I be worried?"

"No, we should be safe. Jack thinks it was something domestic. A child neglect issue. Are you all right?"

"Yeah, I'm okay."

"Are you sure?"

We went back and forth a few more times before Ari finally agreed to hang up.

Exhaustion hit me as soon as the line went dead, as heavy and damp as the humidity outside. The truth was, I was still reeling after graduating, getting a job, and moving to a new city. Now that I was here, I was immobilized—not just by the August heat, but by my own lack of direction in life. It was my first foray into adulthood and I was supposed to be thriving. Instead, I'd never felt more incapable and alone.

I didn't have any friends in the city. I was homesick and petrified of making a mistake at work and getting fired without notice—never mind the fact that I wasn't even sure if I liked being a journalist. Now, on top of all that, the police were looking for the woman who'd last lived here. In my apartment. Who'd slept in the same bedroom and looked out the same windows and made breakfast right here, at the counter where I now stood.

I stepped into the middle of the room and surveyed the space. Ari and I hadn't had the chance to see the apartment before moving in. Jack gave us a tour of a different unit in the building because this one—ours, now—was in the middle of substantial renovations.

At the time, I'd thought little of it. But now I wished I knew what it looked like before we moved in—back when it belonged to Shauna Roberts. If I'd had the chance to see it then, maybe I would have picked up some clue about the woman who used to live here, the woman the police were searching for. Maybe I'd have a sense, beyond Jack's word, of what she'd done, what she was capable of.

Had Shauna Roberts managed to turn these white walls and cold floors into a home? Did she miss it? Would she get homesick and decide to come back one night, stumbling into my half-built life and claiming it as her own?

I looked at the freshly laid tile in the bathroom and felt the hair on my arms prickle. I couldn't help but wonder what they'd had to scrape away before laying those smooth white slabs.

⌒

The envelopes started arriving a few weeks later. Dozens, each addressed to Ms. Shauna Roberts.

By then, the heat was dying down and a nippy wind had started to blow in off the lake. I bought a film camera on Thanksgiving weekend, and Ari and I started going for walks around the neighbourhood, taking photos of shop fronts in Little India and little free libraries shaped like birdhouses.

I think I had some thin hope that capturing the city on camera would make it feel more like mine. That something would happen between the thunk of the shutter and the moment I went to pick up the floppy strips of negatives. An act of taming, perhaps.

But even when I held the prints in my hands, careful not to smudge their centres, I didn't feel at home.

I handled Ms. Shauna Roberts's envelopes the way I handled my photographs, like I was scared of leaving fingerprints. I never opened any of them, but one night, I sat at our kitchen counter and peeked through the cellophane windows on the front. Every envelope held an unpaid bill: thousands of dollars in parking tickets and utility fees, topped with interest and late penalties.

I didn't feel ashamed, tilting my head to spy inside somebody else's correspondences. I would never disappear like that. I wouldn't walk out the door and leave my debts for someone else to find. The letters were proof—just because Ms. Shauna Roberts and I had lived in the same apartment, it didn't mean we inhabited the same lives. There was a distance between her failure to make it in the city and mine.

But then I looked at the pile of photographs I'd taken earlier that month, all those pictures of a place I didn't belong, a city where I was sure I would never make it. And, despite my best efforts, the space between Ms. Shauna Roberts and me shrunk until I could almost feel her there in the kitchen, looking over my shoulders, tallying everything she owed.

⌒

It was a dark spring night when another visitor arrived. Ari answered the buzzer, said a clipped, "I'll be right down," then turned to put on a jacket.

I looked up from my book. "Who was that?"

"Shauna Roberts. She wants her mail."

Ari grabbed a stack of envelopes from the counter and exited. I sat still for a moment, waiting for his footsteps to fade. Then I jumped up from the couch, tossing my blanket and book aside, and ran to the balcony. I pulled the glass doors open, one at a time, careful not to let them squeak. Then I took a deep breath in and looked down onto the street.

There she was.

Ms. Shauna Roberts was both bigger and smaller than I'd imagined. A short, heavyset woman with shoulders hunched inwards. Despite her bulk, her coat looked a few sizes too big. I wondered if it was a men's jacket. Maybe second-hand.

Down on the street, Ari passed over the envelopes, then retreated into the building. Ms. Shauna Roberts turned and walked toward the distant city skyline. She slipped in and out of the yellow street light as she walked away. In darkness one moment, aglow the next.

Until that moment, the thought of Ms. Shauna Roberts returning had struck a sort of fear in me. But from my perch on the balcony, all I felt was the same loneliness that had haunted me all year, come to life in the silhouette below. Her steps seemed tired—but dignified. It takes a particular brand of bravery to go back to a place you thought you'd left behind.

I left the city a couple weeks after Ms. Shauna Roberts turned up. Ari followed two months later. Spit out or unstuck, depending on how you look at it. We got new jobs and a new apartment and quietly closed that chapter in our lives, labelled it "introduction to adulthood" and tucked it into a shoebox full of rolls of negatives.

Years later, I rarely open that box. But I do still wonder about Ms. Shauna Roberts, why she decided to come back on that particular night, and where she went afterwards. I like to picture her arriving home, taking off her big coat and sinking into an armchair, then unclenching her weary muscles, one by one, working her way from her toes up to her forehead.

Safe and somewhere else.

Justyna Krol

System Failure

When I realized my father was about to die I decided to throw myself a birthday party. I wasn't celebrating. I just wanted to have one last birthday as someone with a father. I developed a compulsion to make my life into a memory production line, like some animal filling a storehouse ahead of winter: this is what it feels like to have your father wish you a happy birthday, however slurred his speech; this is what it's like to listen, indulgently, as your mother complains about your father's continuous refusal to put on a sweater; this is how you eat and drink when loss is only something you read about.

Maybe it was the same drive that makes me watch my own blood being drawn when I go in for a medical test—the need to see what I'm losing.

⌒

My father's death was never going to be a surprise.

He was diagnosed with heart disease a decade earlier and survived years of blood thinners until he suffered a hematoma and stroke from being prescribed too high a dose. Then came the diagnosis of Parkinsonism. Parkinsonism was followed by pneumonias. So many pneumonias.

For years, my father's health had been a series of moves and countermoves, with the doctors always trying to stay ahead of future malfunctions. My mother, my sister, and I discussed each recovery and encouraged every effort. We were like fans of a hockey team that is always almost making the playoffs. We wanted our team to feel the love in the stands. And for a while it worked. He survived the pneumonias, the last one with enough Sturm und Drang that we all came to his bedside in a temporary triumph. He almost died, but he didn't. The *almost* was getting thinner. Then it was barely there. Then it wasn't.

The last time my father rallied it was early May. He seemed agitated, eager to see us, even though talking with us required careful negotiation with his lungs. Every word spoken meant a breath sacrificed. But still. We talked. I kept calling once I returned home. We practiced dialogue minimalism.

It was after that last visit that I decided on the birthday party. It was still a month away, and despite not being much of an organizer, I threw myself into planning as though I had just discovered a hidden passion. I wanted to invite everyone. We would have all the deep-fried, sweet, and salty things I could think of. Many drinks would be poured.

And that was exactly how it happened. My table was crowded with chicken wings, bowls of fritters, chocolate liquor in cups carved from marshmallow. My father called at the very beginning of the night to wish me "a beautiful year" and I told him that his wish was exactly what I wanted. I was so happy that night—standing with one friend and then another, looking at the lit windows of the building across from mine, the shadows of strangers flickering in and out in time with the music, with the celebration of it all.

My father died just three weeks later.

During those last three weeks, I thought about his upcoming death constantly. I ran scenarios in my head: how much could I handle, how would I cope, could I still be who I was? Selfish things. And worse still: Let it end. Let it end because I can't bear seeing him in pain. Let me not be waiting for this phone call for another year, then the year after that. Let me, let me, let me.

Why did all of this seem like something we were arguing over? My father wasn't doing anything to me other than dying. But the dying felt like something between us—again—something about whose feelings mattered the most.

See this right here? This questioning, this survey of doubts and evasions? That's from my father too. He gave it to me before he left.

⌒

My father was not someone who took care of his body. He would always tell us that the life that mattered was the life of the mind. But as we watched him die, all we could do was read his body: this thing he never much cared for, now failing him so utterly. My mother was the one who worried most about his state of mind. She didn't want him to know he was dying. She didn't want to hurt him. But she also didn't want him lost in a fog of painkillers.

At the time, I thought her resistance to pain medication was a blindness brought about by the panic of anticipated loss. Now I think it was just love. My parents didn't love each other in a triumphant "you bring out the best in me" sort of way. They loved each other because the world is hard and we are all wounded and it's good to have someone who has mapped all your hurts—even if they can't make them better so much as poke at them now and then to remind you of who you are. My mother took care of my father's body for as long as she could, so that he wouldn't have to. When that didn't work, she took over the care of his fears too.

Children are always trying to bring reforms without understanding the culture they are walking into. Who knows what we inadvertently destroy.

Why bring this up? Because when my mother left the room, I gave my father more pain medication, hoping his grimace would slacken. When I left the hospital room for lunch I did not read the stroke rehabilitation

153

pamphlets we were given. Instead, I bought a book on what happens to a body that's dying. When the doctors said it was time to remove the feeding tube I didn't protest, didn't question the doctors' judgments like my mother did.

Did I see what was coming and face it with eyes open? Or did I turn away from all this hopeless, helpless waiting?

My father died on June 21st at 3:00 a.m. It was Father's Day. Only my mother was with him when it happened. My sister and I were asleep. I can't remember where I was. Was I in the hospital's family room? Or was this one of the nights I went back to my parents' house for a couple of hours? Regardless, within thirty minutes of his death we were all by his bedside. I took his hand, cooling in mine. I held on hard because I knew what was coming. I knew I would miss his hands the most.

We stayed as long as we could. When we finally left, it seemed like such an arbitrary act, as though we could have stood beside him forever, or not, as though the length of our last vigil was entirely up to us.

When we returned home from the hospital that final time it was almost dawn. Every part of me hurt. I was alive with pain, with cramped muscles, with anger at having to feel another body—my body—failing to do what it should. I would not lie down. I would not let go. I stood in the middle of the room glaring the creep of morning back into darkness.

Of course I failed. The sky started to glow with the red of a blood vessel. Shadows separated themselves into flora, fauna, the outline of a house. A cardinal perched himself on the peak of a neighbour's roof. He bobbed his head, shrugged, reaffirmed his grip. And then he did what he was expected to do: he began to sing.

I hated him. He didn't care.

He sang the same brief song three times. Then there was a silence. I tried to unclench a breath, to shift my feet. But all too soon he started up again. This time with one note changed, as though he was trying out a new sound, or the difference that practice made. After three more repetitions, he changed the song again, keeping the new note and discarding a second one, substituting it for something slightly higher. And so it went. One change sung out three times, then another, a constant feat of improvisation and revision. I listened for what felt like hours.

By the time I went to bed, with the sun full over the horizon, nothing of the first song remained.

Emma Brady

The Bedroom

AN EXCERPT FROM A MEMOIR

My brother Leo's bedroom arrived at our house one summer's day in 1979. Men from Dublin City Corporation closed off our street of identical terraced, pebble-dashed, government-built houses to traffic earlier that morning. The few neighbours who could afford cars back then agreed to park elsewhere for the day after Dad had visited every house to proudly explain what was going to happen and why.

The why was unnecessary since everyone on the street already knew about Leo. Most understood that our house, with three small bedrooms upstairs and just one bathroom downstairs, was not built for a good Catholic-sized family of eight—never mind one that included a fourteen-year-old boy with severe special needs and no sense of danger or safety. They'd seen how heartbroken Mam and Dad were when they'd had to put Leo in residential care four years earlier because they couldn't manage his needs anymore. They knew what this room represented and how long my parents had waited for it, that this day was as much theirs as it was Leo's.

Only Mr. Moore, a leather-skinned man who lived around the corner, complained. His back garden shared a wall with ours and he argued that the new room would block some of his afternoon sun. But what could he do? Object to an autistic, hyperactive, epileptic teenager having a safe place to stay in his own home? Convincing Mr. Moore of Leo's need for this room was another achievement in Dad's mission to raise awareness of special needs children, to shrink fear of the unknown, and to lead by example. Mam simply reminded him that he was lucky he didn't have to worry about such things for his own children, then politely told him to "go and shut his feckin' hole."

The prefabricated structure rolled up on the back of a flatbed truck that afternoon, followed by a mobile crane and several yellow-vested men. My parents stood in the centre of the road waving to greet them. In fact, if Dad, who had once been the Staff Major of his hometown's marching pipe band, could have led a procession of drums and bagpipes in front of this parade, he would have done that, too.

"They're going to do what?" Mam asked him.

"They're going to lift it over the house and lower it down into the back garden."

"But sure how in God's name are they going to do that?"

"With that crane there."

"Jesus, Mary and Joseph; what will the neighbours make of it?"

We were the first house on the street to get an extension, so the neighbours were an eager audience. Some of the women watched from their doorways or leaned against their garden walls, with cigarettes and cups of tea in their hands and babies on their hips. Others took a bird's eye view from upstairs windows, peering from underneath embroidered lace curtain panels—the type that lets all the news from the street in but keeps the secrets of their own house from getting out. The old men with nowhere else to be that day ran their fingers along the grey wooden structure with its flat roof, its single doorway, and two window frames (one in the bedroom and one in the bathroom) and nodded their approval to Dad, who was describing the carpentry and engineering as if he had built it himself.

"'Tis a fine bit of craftsmanship all right, Mr. Lynch. And what is this you say it has ... an ensuite bathroom? Well, I've never heard the like."

Some kids on bikes swerved around this new obstacle course. Others clambered up to the driver's cabin of the crane shouting, "Here, Mister, give us a go of this, will ya?" As for my six siblings, only the girls—Michelle, Debbie, and Geraldine—were there on the day. They sat on the curb with their friends, lapping up the attention they were getting and waiting for the show to begin. Thomas and Stephen were gone for the day and Leo, despite his central role in the day's events, wasn't home for a visit to watch his new room arrive. Mam had wisely decided that there'd be just too many ways for him to cause destruction or get himself killed. This was not an unwarranted concern.

☞

On our street anything even minutely dramatic caused quite the stir and on many occasions before this day (and after, for that matter) Leo provided more than his fair share. He was unaware of his fame; Mam was the one who usually dealt with it. One time the Murphy boys from number fifteen called him a spastic and she went to town on them (and Mr. and Mrs. Murphy) and made them apologize to Leo's face, even though he had no understanding of what was going on. Several times he threw all the bedsheets and pillows out of the top window of the house and they scattered into the gardens next door, so that Mam had to knock and ask for them back. And once he fell out the same window and landed on Dad's motorbike, dangling by his pants off the wing mirror and miraculously avoiding the ground.

Leo brought much attention to our family's life. But of course, public opinion mattered far less than the risk of Leo doing himself serious injury or of Mam having a nervous breakdown trying to raise him plus five other kids by herself, while Dad worked full time to make ends meet. So after years of struggling, they had both accepted he needed professional care.

From the time Leo first went to live in St. Luke's Centre for the Mentally and Physically Handicapped at ten years old, my parents swore they'd find a way to bring him back to visit as often as possible. With the help of his nurses and case workers, they filed paperwork and sent in medical records for every disability grant going. After years of effort, they were finally approved for a safer, ground-floor room for him and Leo started coming home again for weeks at a time in the summer and for Christmas.

Although naturally hesitant at first, my parents had quickly grown to love the centre, and visited every Sunday without fail. To them, St. Luke's became Leo's second home and the other resident boys and nurses became not just his second family, but theirs, too. Dad always told people that Leo was one of the few lucky boys up there who got to call two places home. He never let anyone think that his son had been sent away to be hidden out of sight, and if the arrival of this bedroom in all its public glory didn't prove that to anyone who might have thought otherwise, nothing would.

⁀

Workers began hooking chains and tightening straps until the room was wrapped up like the gift it was. Beside it, the crane awoke and stretched. Its jaws descended like the claw in an arcade prize machine. It lifted the room vertically at first and then began to drift over the garden and then the house as its arm telescoped out ever longer. The children cheered along, some hoping to see it accidentally dropped like the house in *The Wizard of Oz*. This was Mam's fear, too, and because of that, she couldn't bear to watch. Instead, she ran to Mrs. O'Rourke's across the street, prayed the rosary in her kitchen, and waited to be told it had all come crashing through the roof of her home. Dad stayed out in the centre of the crowd, his head high, seeing not just the room dangling in the sky, but the achievement and the possibility that hung from it too.

Eventually, like the sunset, the room sank out of sight behind the house and the crowd cheered and clapped. The old men patted Dad on the back. The children rang their handlebar bells. Mam ran back across the street saying "thanks be to God," to watch excitedly through her living room window as the room was slowly guided down to land on top of its concrete foundation.

Work continued for a few more hours in the back garden, but out front the show was over. The crowd dispersed for teatime and life on our street resumed regularly scheduled viewing. That is, until the following week when Leo came home for a celebratory visit, escaped through a hole in the chicken wire on the gate, and bolted down the street in his underwear.

Nancy Jin

Guifang

AN EXCERPT

PREFACE

An 82-year-old woman raised her question loudly: "Where are you going?" The middle-aged woman sitting beside her moved toward the old
woman, who at the same time hurriedly put her left ear, which still had a
little bit of hearing, close to the middle-aged woman's mouth.

"I am going to Canada."

"Where?"

"Ca-na-da." The middle-aged woman repeated the answer in a loud
voice, slowly.

After being silent for a moment, the old woman raised her next question even more loudly: "Is it far?"

"Yes, it's very far," she replied, raising her voice accordingly.

Both women were lost in thought. They sat side by side, looking
down toward their feet. There were obvious distinctions between them.
The old woman's feet were small and strange while the young woman's
feet were normal and fit.

The old woman, with an admiring smile, praised the young woman:
"Look at your big feet!"

The young woman smiled back and would not comment. She was
thinking that they would be apart for a long time, without seeing each
other and having conversations. She wanted to fill the time with something so that the future memory would be less blank. Thus, she begged
the old woman: "Would you please tell me the story about your feet
again?"

Something bright appeared in the old woman's eyes before she agreed happily: "Okay, if you would like to listen."

The old woman began again to tell the story about her bound feet to the lady on that warm autumn afternoon.

⌒

The old woman in the dialogue is Guifang, my grandmother. In 2008, before my family were about to land in Canada as new immigrants, I visited her, talked to her, and listened carefully to her tales from the past again. And at that time, the idea to write down Guifang's story occurred to me for the first time.

In her, I saw the epitome of millions of women, who were "bound" and restricted, held back from self-realization and self-actualization.

The life experience of Guifang, a Chinese foot-binding survivor, should be one of the thousands of waves that make up the river of human history with stories that are often deemed trivial but are actually significant.

CHAPTER I

Guifang was born on an early spring evening in 1926.

She was the first child in her family, but her birth did not bring much joy to her parents, in particular her father, Lao Hou. Ignoring the hardships of the new mother, Lao Hou squatted in front of his bungalow and smoked dry tobacco even when the midwife left, a time when he should at least have stood up to say goodbye.

At that time, a tradition of "son preference" was stressed in South and East Asia. As agrarian societies where agricultural mechanization was not yet popularized, heavy physical work such as tilling the land, farming, and carrying a load required specific individuals, mostly men, from each family. Especially when the parents were getting older and could no longer undertake physical work, the son who could do heavy work would be their strongest support.

Women were valued less than men because their work, such as spinning or housework, was not directly related to surviving. Boys were strongly wanted in those areas at that time. Every family continued to have children until they had a boy.

After Guifang reached two years old, two more girls were born into the family. Guifang's mother, Hou Zhaoshi, felt that her inability to have a son made her husband lose face in front of the villagers. Although she nearly died due to an incorrect fetal position when giving birth to her third child, she cooked, hoed, and sewed with her weak body soon after the month of confinement. She expected her husband to forgive her for her bad performance.

Villagers pointed at Lao Hou behind his back and even said to his face that he was a jue hu. A family that did not produce a boy was called jue hu. It was almost the greatest insult to a man in the countryside in those years.

Jue means "extinction." *Hu* originally means "descendants," and for most of the Chinese people in that time it refers to sons specifically. In China, children follow their fathers' surnames as their last names. So the absence of sons in a family means that the family name owned by the father would go extinct.

CHAPTER 2

It is not difficult to find Guifang's hometown on the map. If the shape of China is compared to a rooster, then Guifang's hometown, Houzhuang Village, Leting County, Tangshan City, Hebei Province, is right on the gizzard position.

Like other houses in the village, Guifang's farmhouse was built of clay, a kind of fired black brick. The three rooms, built side by side from left to right, were the kitchen, the master bedroom, and the secondary bedroom.

In addition to being a place for cooking, the kitchen was also a place to pile up clutter. The room for the kitchen had two opposite doors, one of which led to the small backyard which was enclosed by a stone wall as high as a man's height. On hot days, the whole family would sit in the small yard, eating, chatting, and passing the time. There were also barns in the yard where a few pigs were kept in captivity and a small pen for the chickens. But most of the time, the chickens could roam freely in herds around the yard.

The large bedroom in the middle belonged to Guifang's parents and her two younger sisters, who were too little to sleep by themselves.

Guifang lived in the small room on the west side of the bungalow. As in the great bedroom, every nook and cranny of the room was crammed, and the walls and roof were covered with things: strings of garlic, dried vegetables, and some linen trousers. There was a window on the wall facing the front yard. It was a large frame with many small squares in it, and the cracks in the window had grown with age. So panes were pasted with newspaper.

This small room had been Guifang's favourite place for quite a long time. But after the summer of 1932, it changed from a cozy nest to a cage for the little girl.

CHAPTER 3

In the summer of 1932, Guifang was just over six years old. One evening, her father, followed by her mum, brought in her room a basin of hot water. Guifang's mum asked Guifang to sit on a low stool beside the basin on the ground.

Under Guifang's surprised gaze, Guifang's mum first washed her daughter's feet a little bit. Then she twisted the little one's toes, except for the big ones, toward the heart of the foot.

"Mama, ni zou sha?" Guifang asked. This was the local dialect: *ni zou sha?* meant "what are you doing?"

"Guifang," her mother said, as she continued to twist Guifang's toes. "You are six years old now and you are old enough to have your feet bound according to our tradition."

"Bound feet?"

"Yes."

"Like yours?" Guifang pointed to her mother's little feet and asked.

"Yes, like me."

Guifang looked at her mother with horror in her eyes. Her mother continued to make this cruel action on Guifang's tiny feet, which were still warm from the hot water. Guifang tried to free her feet from her mother's grip. But her mother's hands were as firm as a pair of pincers. Guifang closed her eyes and could not help crying out in pain.

When Guifang opened her misty eyes again, she saw her mother use one hand to sprinkle some white powder (alum for disinfection and drying) between her twisted toes. Afterwards, she wrapped Guifang's strangely shaped feet in cloth, layer by layer.

After everything was properly handled, Guifang's dad took away the basin of water. Guifang's mum helped Guifang take off her clothes, and get the quilt ready. After she saw Guifang lie in the quilt, she blew out the kerosene lamp and then left the room.

In the dark, Guifang could not fall asleep for a long time with tears in her eyes and pain in her tightly wrapped feet.

Deborah Folka
Dessert in the Desert

Not long after we moved to Tucson, I was out in the front yard picking up palm fronds that had come down in a thunderstorm, when a neighbour came over.

"I just wanted to say welcome to the neighbourhood." She was a tall, slim woman with brown hair cut in a low-maintenance bob, her only makeup a dab of barely pink lip gloss. She wore a T-shirt, khaki shorts, and sporty sandals, the standard uniform of the suburban soccer mom. I almost expected her to whip out a zip-lock bag of orange slices.

"I'm Cathy Sutton," she said. "My husband, Ford, works at the university. He teaches physics. I work part-time at the elementary school, just doing admin stuff, and we've got two teenagers." Cathy carried on with a description of life in San Rafael Estates, telling me about the neighbourhood pool where she coached her son Philip's swim team, the challenges of road maintenance after the rainy season, her daughter Whitney's allergy flare-up at this time of year, and her husband's mania for cycling. I didn't have the chance to say much, but I didn't mind; it was nice to have some human interaction.

My husband and I had only been in the city for a few weeks. We'd moved there for his new job at the university, and so far I'd spent most of my time unpacking boxes and getting our house organized before launching my own job search. I was a brand new journalism graduate—just 23 years old—and I was anxious to get my first "real" job. We hadn't met many people since coming to the city, and the only ones we'd met in our own neighbourhood had been the elderly couple next door, the Smiths. Cathy asked if we would like to come for dinner sometime soon. "Of course!" We set a date.

The night of our dinner came and I was nervous. In those years, I was still intimidated by university professors, with all their degrees and what I believed was innate intellectual superiority. I felt gauche and inexperienced by comparison. I agonized over selecting the right flowers and chocolates, while Bill just grabbed a cheap California wine. I frowned as I put together our hostess gifts.

"Maybe we should have got a French wine?" I fretted. The chocolates weren't made with fair trade cocoa and the flowers were just red carnations and baby's breath—nothing sophisticated or imaginative.

More than a decade my senior and a professor himself, Bill laughed at my anxiety. "Don't be silly," he said. "I'm sure they won't judge our choices and we won't judge theirs."

Ford answered the door. "Welcome!" He had a deep, resonant baritone and waved us in a bit theatrically. Ford was in his forties, like his wife, and was tall and fair, with blue eyes and longish hair thinning above a sharp, beaky face. He wore typical casual professor garb: baggy denims, linen shirt with chunky beads on a woven string around his neck, and leather sandals.

He took us through a comfortably shabby living room, the walls heavy with Native American weavings, sculptures, and masks. As he ushered us out to the patio for drinks and appetizers, I noticed there was a slide projector and screen set up by the couch.

The Sutton offspring made a brief appearance, dashing in, saying hello, and dashing out. They both had plans for the evening: one off to the basketball court and the other hanging with friends. Nice kids, harmless pursuits; I nodded and sipped my wine.

Striding around on calloused bare feet and wearing a faded sundress, Cathy moved competently between the kitchen, the patio, and the table, serving up barbecued chicken, grilled vegetables, and wild rice. "Thank you for the flowers," she said, putting them in a ceramic vase. "And chocolates, too! So sweet of you." I began to relax.

In typical Tucson fashion, we ate outdoors. Conversation flowed without too much effort, everyone doing their best to avoid tripwire topics like politics, religion, gun ownership, or race relations. Ford turned out to be less of a soccer dad and more of an urban cycling enthusiast.

"I bike to school and would be happy to show you the safest routes," he said to Bill. "I was on the committee that drafted the city's bike path plan."

He also told us about their family's summer work saving at-risk tortoises in Costa Rica and a recent camping trip in Yosemite. Cathy kept the wine glasses topped up and the food coming, and was a solicitous, smiling presence.

After dinner, as the last fingers of the desert's technicolour sunset disappeared into the horizon, Ford rose to his feet.

"We thought we'd show some slides over dessert and coffee," he said, opening the glass patio doors and stepping back for us to enter.

Oh, dear, I thought. *"Our summer vacation," complete with blurry images of endangered species, empty beaches, and trees sprouting from people's heads.*

Cathy brought a pot of coffee and homemade peach pie into the living room and set the tray on the coffee table while Ford fiddled with the slide projector. Seated on a lumpy couch draped with a crocheted afghan, I took a bite of pie and settled back.

Finally, Ford had the slides ready, the projector was humming, and he asked Cathy to turn out the lights. The room darkened. The screen lit up.

It was not shots of flora or fauna in Central America.

The slides were images of Cathy and Ford with another couple. All four of them were naked and happily involved in some very companionable sexual activity. I say "happily" because they were all smiling, much as we do for the camera: a little too broadly, too self-consciously. I don't remember much about the nudity or the positions, except that these were pretty ordinary people. There were tan lines, unruly pubic hair, some visible stretch marks, low-slung breasts, droopy testicles, and saggy buttocks.

But the thing I remember the most about the first slide is that the other fellow, a chunky dark guy with a lot of chest and back hair, was wearing Mickey Mouse ears from Disneyland. He may have even had his name stitched on it.

In total, Ford probably showed us about a half-dozen slides, but he paused quite a while on each one.

The only sound in the room was the humming of the projector and the *clunk-clunk* as the slides advanced. That first bite of pie remained stuck to the roof of my mouth. I was beyond surprised, paralyzed into silence.

Outrage began to creep in: was this the price of admission? My mind took a panicked lateral leap: what would happen after the slide show? Would there be an initiation? *We start you in the missionary position.* An application form? *Please list your height, weight, any special features, skills, and relevant experience.* A probationary period? *At the end of ninety days, we review your performance and decide if you're a fit for our team.* An interview or quiz? *Would you want to a) always wear the Mickey Mouse ears, b) sometimes wear the Mickey Mouse ears, or c) don't care who wears the Mickey Mouse ears?*

Finally, the screen clicked blank and Cathy hit the light switch on the lamp. She smiled. "We thought you were very attractive people and wondered if you would be interested in joining us," she said.

"No, thanks," Bill said. "Is there more coffee?"

EPILOGUE

Some years later, after another long-distance move, I was visiting Tucson and stayed with Norm and Shirley Smith for a few days in our old neighborhood. I asked about the Suttons.

"Oh, they're long gone," Shirley said. "Why? I didn't think you knew them."

"We had a memorable dinner with them once," I said and then told the story.

When I finished, Norm and Shirley sat silently side by side on the couch, both looking slightly stunned. Finally, they looked at one another, their faces solemn.

"They never asked us," Norm said.

Shenul Dhalla

Hope for a Cure

Cancer does not discriminate; it can happen to anyone, young or old. There are so many different types and subtypes of cancer, making it difficult to find a single cure.

In December 2018, I was diagnosed with a rare and aggressive type of cancer: a soft tissue sarcoma. There are sixty types of sarcomas and the type I had was *rhabdomyosarcoma*. It mostly occurs in children and youth, but a small percentage of adults also get it. Obviously, it was devastating and terrifying to be diagnosed with cancer for the second time. Ten years ago, I had a curable breast cancer and never once thought I would get a secondary cancer—but in a split second my entire life turned upside down. I thought I ate a good diet, was exercising regularly, and I generally had a good lifestyle, so the sudden diagnosis of this rare cancer was difficult for me to accept. I had chemotherapy and radiation, followed by surgery. Still, throughout the treatment phase, I could not help wondering how I got this cancer. What caused my normal cells to mutate and become cancerous? I desperately needed to know the answer so I could take preventative measures and precautions to remain cancer-free.

When I first got the diagnosis, I asked how an adult gets sarcoma. I was told this could happen through a possible exposure to radiation or chemicals. I have never received any radiation in the area where the tumour was, so I figured it most likely had to do with chemicals, but it is difficult to know for sure. I decided to do some research online. I soon discovered that most of the websites were not helpful; in fact, they provided little information and gave depressing prognoses. I wanted to learn more about this illness at a cellular level. During my search, I did come across immunotherapy—the most recent development in treating cancer. This treatment boosts the patient's immune system to help fight cancer and does not harm the healthy cells like chemotherapy does. However, I did not find any information online if whether immunotherapy had been successfully used for sarcoma.

During my search, I also came across private cancer clinics in the U.S. and Mexico specializing in alternative treatments for cancer. Their treatments had been successful in treating late stages of cancer and were not as harmful as chemotherapy. For instance, Envita Medical Center is known for personalized treatment for cancer and so is Hope4Cancer in Mexico, but they are expensive.

Unfortunately, when I was diagnosed I did not have time to look into alternative medicine and because of the aggressive nature of the cancer, it was necessary to stop the growth by conventional treatments such as chemotherapy and radiation. However, I do believe that each one of us is unique in our biology and genetic makeup. Therefore, cancer should be treated at a patient's cellular level to have a better understanding of the illness. I thought perhaps I should speak to someone at the B.C. Cancer Agency in Vancouver to find out what research is being done currently in one of their labs.

I made a call and requested to speak to a scientist from one of the labs. I was pleased to secure an interview with Dr. Michael Lizardo on January 16, 2020. He works in the research lab of Dr. Poul Sorenson, a prominent scientist and researcher in Canada. Currently, Dr. Sorenson's lab is conducting a groundbreaking study which Dr. Lizardo is part of, on cancer metastasizing to the lungs and brain from its original site.

Dr. Lizardo met me in the lobby of the B.C. Cancer Agency. He extended his hand warmly to greet me, smiling. He was dressed in a pair of jeans and shirt, was medium height with dark hair and glasses. On our way to the boardroom, Dr. Lizardo told me he was of Filipino descent and he alluded to his parents, saying they would have been very proud of his involvement with the current research, had they been alive, though I hesitated to ask how they'd passed away. Once we were in the boardroom, Dr. Lizardo gestured for me to sit on a chair across from a white screen that was hanging on the wall. Once he took his seat across from me, Dr. Lizardo dove into telling me what Dr. Sorenson's lab was researching.

"Studying bone sarcoma, the way we do in the Sorensen lab, is unique in Canada," he said. "In the past, there was not much hope for patients with metastatic cancer to the lungs, but this current study is working toward finding a drug that could potentially shrink the tumour cells."

Scientists like Dr. Lizardo work tirelessly in the lab to make a break-through in cancer research and treatment.

"I think it's important for researchers to meet cancer patients and survivors because, speaking for myself, meeting those who are affected by cancer grounds me and reminds me this is why I do research. Meeting survivors gives me inspiration and strength in my research."

I was touched by this statement.

"So, when will this new drug be available?" I asked.

"From the discoveries at the bench to finally having a drug that can be bought over the counter at the pharmacy takes about fifteen to seventeen years and billions of dollars of input."

Dr. Lizardo showed me a slide with a metastatic lung cancer in mice. Once the drug in the study was administered to mice, the computerized slide showed the tumour shrinking. I was impressed. Despite the fact that development of this drug is in its early stages and still has to go through human trials, it is hopeful.

"Cancer has become an epidemic and many people are getting cancer these days. I wish there was a blood test or a vaccine for early detection and prevention."

Dr. Lizardo told me, "There is an HPV vaccine, a prevention for cervical cancer. Currently there are clinical tests that can detect cancer in the blood. For example, prostate-specific antigen for prostate cancer patients, and tumour-associated antigens for breast cancer patients."

"Can scientists determine the cause of cell mutation?"

"We know that in children, cancerous sarcoma cells are linked to a missing protein in the DNA. In adults, it's due to environment and old age."

"So, for example, if we have two people exposed to the same chemical and over time only one person gets cancer, how can we explain this?" I asked.

"We need to look at individual tissues, study them under the microscope. That really helps us to determine the cause of cancer in a particular patient. Scientists need to validate their work by studying patient tumour samples under the microscope. This helps scientists to determine the causes or 'drivers' of cancer in a particular patient."

After hearing this, and without hesitation, I offered my tissue for research. It had been removed on May 23, 2019. My tissue will help Dr. Sorenson's lab and his team, along with Dr. Lizardo, to study the cells and my DNA, to further their research. I am also hoping to learn the cause of my cancer from this study.

I was pleased to learn about a study being done to produce a drug for metastatic bone sarcoma. I am grateful for B.C. Cancer Agency's hard work and overall progress in finding a cure for cancer. At a personal level, though, it is difficult to have gone through cancer twice, with both cases unrelated to one another. I believe that alternative medicine along with conventional medicine can significantly eliminate cancer growth, so I started to see a naturopath. As a precautionary measure, I took a high dose of vitamin C therapy to destroy any residual stem cells. I am also taking supplements regularly. When fear creeps in, I accept and acknowledge it, but then redirect and shift my attention toward gratitude and positivity. Along with diet and exercise, I also meditate regularly. I am letting go of negative emotions and past trauma. I do not worry about small things and have significantly reduced my stress levels.

These acts of self-kindness are major milestones toward staying cancer free. Cancer has changed my perspective. It has taught me that I only have this one life and that it is precarious, so I better live to the fullest and stay in the present.

Christine Pilgrim
Goodbye

AN EXCERPT FROM A WORK IN PROGRESS

I was an actor posing as a teacher at a one-room schoolhouse in a recon-
structed gold rush town. Other actors portrayed similar townsfolk from
the 1800s, while restaurant, saloon, and store owners coaxed dollars
from tourists.

The Anglican church sponsored a theology student to take on the
role of the reverend who built the iconic chapel in this place full of pre-
tenders. Brian, or Brother Brian as we called him, was closest to the real
thing. He led services, toured visitors around the old graveyard, and
even served the people who lived in the community five minutes away.
We lived there, too, for the season.

Halfway through summer, a local we'd befriended died unexpectedly. I asked Brian if it would be appropriate to read a poem at her wake.
I wrote it after my first son, Ben, died. It began:

> i am dead
> just dust
> blowing through your garden
> look
> mother do not cry

"No, it's not appropriate," said Brian. He must have seen the pain in
my face. He added, "Would you like to talk about it?"

I told him of Ben's crib death 26 years earlier. How my then-husband
refused to have a funeral. He didn't want his last memory of his son to

be of an over-made-up, lifeless dummy bearing no resemblance to Ben.

So we had no funeral, no celebration of life, no grave or marker of any kind. My last memory of my six-week-old baby was of him wrapped in the shawl I'd crocheted for him. He was cradled in the arms of a paramedic as she rushed ahead of us into the emergency ward, yelling: "Resuss."

The next day, my husband booked two tickets for Spain. Others disposed of Ben's body. They scattered his ashes on a "Garden of Rest." There were no goodbyes. Nothing. Just tears.

Brian offered his handkerchief. "It's never too late to have a funeral."

"But there's no body. No ashes even."

"It doesn't matter. We can create a sacred space to lay his memory to rest. Do you have anything tangible to associate with Ben? Like clothes? Toys? Mementos?"

"Nothing. While we were in Spain, a friend got rid of every item that might remind us of him. She thought she was helping. When we came home and I saw what she'd done, I felt robbed. Violated. It was as if Ben never existed."

Brian offered a second handkerchief and waited. "Do you have any photos of Ben?"

"Yes. A few."

"They'll do fine. If you make copies, we can use them. You'll need witnesses so you can share memories of the event later on."

I couldn't imagine sharing something so intimate and personal. "Why?"

"Otherwise it may not feel real."

"I could buy a plot in the graveyard here?"

"That's a good idea, if you can afford to. It will help. You could even write an Order of Service. Whatever you want to say, or sing, or pray," said Brian. "Whatever you like."

I found a plot up among the trees, near where our local friend was buried. Someone loaned me an old *Book of Common Prayer* so I could study an Order of Service.

I wanted the best funeral for Ben. A humdinger goodbye. I thumbed through the pages till I found "Funerals" and read: "The deceased must have been baptized an Anglican."

I panicked and called Brian. "We can't have the funeral. Ben wasn't baptized at all!"

"It isn't essential," said Brian. "We can commend Ben's spirit to God and baptize his memory."

I couldn't baptize a memory. A spirit. A ghost in a garden. Like some farce. Pantomime. An empty ritual to satisfy some bishop somewhere. No doubt we'd need witnesses. To share memories. Make it real. Let's invite everyone. Put an ad in the paper. Call up the whole bloody town. To hell with your baptisms. And funerals. To hell with any goodbyes.

"If you're uncomfortable, we can use the church downtown," Brian said. "It covers all denominations."

Summer hurried by. I'd not invited a soul to any funeral. I'd told no one about a baptism. I hadn't even paid for the plot. At the end of August, Brian took me aside. "If you want to do this, you'd better get on with it. I'm done next week."

Next day I reported back. I told Brian I tracked down Marilyn, the chair of the cemetery committee, and paid for the plot. I also invited her to the funeral. She promised to bring her Celtic harp. There would be a congregation of two.

"I'm still not sure about the baptism, Brian."

"It's okay. Shall we just have the funeral in the graveyard?"

I could do that. I had Mondays and Tuesdays off. On Monday, I climbed the hill to Ben's plot. The cemetery was drowned in a sea of daisies waving in the late August sun. I dug a hole the size of a crib. It looked barren. I found a jar and filled it with water from a nearby stream.

I picked a bunch of the daisies. Put them in the water and placed them in the hole. They looked pure and perfect. I took a deep breath and surveyed the scene. Fine.

The graveyard was near the office at the historic site. I asked to use the phone. "Brian, can we do the baptism today?"

"Ye-es. My work clothes are grubby, though, and I'm due at a meeting in ten minutes."

"Don't worry. I'll wash your robes. Leave them on your doorstep and I'll pick them up. They'll be ready by noon. Will you be free then?" Nothing could stop me now.

Brian said, "Yes."

"Let's meet at noon. In the lobby. At the church."

"I'll be there," said Brian.

I went back to the grave and picked up the daisies. I drove into town and collected Brian's work clothes. At home, I washed and ironed them. They were ready fifteen minutes before noon. So was I.

At the church, I handed Brian his robes and he slipped them over his shirt and trousers.

"I just realized," he said, as we walked to the altar. "I've no idea what Ben looked like."

I described my baby in detail and impulsively gave Brian the daisies. He held them in his arms. As if they were Ben. He blessed and baptized the flowers in the Name of the Father, the Son, and the Holy Spirit.

"Amen." I put the daisies back in the jar and placed them on the altar.

I treated Brian to brunch. Our server was a friend named Paul. I invited him to the funeral. He said nothing.

"It's early. Nine o'clock. Too early for you, eh?"

He smiled but didn't answer. As we said goodbye, I added, "You don't have to come if it feels awkward."

Tuesday morning, I collected the blessed daisies from the altar and drove to the cemetery. I lined the grave with a white shawl I brought from home. I rested a photocopy of Ben's picture and the daisies on those parts of the shawl that overlapped the grave and spilled on to the ground around it. I sprinkled more blossoms there. Then I sat on a mound of moss, and waited.

First came Marilyn, carrying her harp, her long hair and dress flowing as she drifted through the field of daisies and sat beside me. Then Brother Brian appeared in purple and white. "We decided to sit," I said when he reached us. I told him it was more comfortable, but really, I wanted to be closer to the earth, to Ben.

"I agree. Let's have the service sitting here on the ground," Brian said and removed his robes.

We sat awhile. Halfway through our simple service, I saw someone standing beside a tree. It was Paul. I beckoned him to join us.

Brian committed the daisies and the picture of Ben to the grave. I took a handful of soil and let it fall on top. The sound it made as it hit the paper was like that of dirt hitting a coffin. One by one, the others followed, their handfuls echoing mine.

I shrouded the daisies, soil, and Ben's picture in the rest of the shawl. I picked up a shovel. Brian offered to help, but I said no. I filled the grave with earth and tears.

Maryanna Gabriel

Get Thee to a Nunnery

AN EXCERPT FROM
"ON EARTH AS IT IS: WALKING THE CAMINO"

The older nun who admitted me to the nunnery was formidable. She was scaring me. She fiercely demanded to know where I was last night and why that stamp was not in my *credencial*. I stammered it was because I was trying to save room in my Camino passport.

"If the police are trying to locate you, they need to see where you were." Her tiny, wrinkled face glared up at me from behind her desk.

"*Comprendo*," I said. Good point. Alrighty then. I left the desk and headed to my small room, managed a shower, and settled in. I was exhausted and needed to lie down. Choosing the lower bunk, I surveyed the small plain room. A wrapped candy was perched on the pillow. I moved it to one side and shut my eyes.

There was a knock on the door. A long-faced man with eyes like olives introduced himself as Juan and said I was in the wrong room. Would I mind moving?

"*Si*," I said. Lying back down, I waited, my eyes closed. There was a knock on the door. I got up. It was the Scary Nun. I had misunderstood her and was very much in the nun doghouse. I was in the wrong room. Would I move? They would find a bed for me.

"*Si*," I assented calmly. While I waited, I again shut my eyes. Just as I was drifting off there was a loud rap. Juan stood apologetically at the door. They had found another room for the *voluntario*, it was *tranquilo*, I could stay put. He looked at the top bunk. Did I prefer to share the room with a woman? They had many guests today.

"*Si*," I said. I shut my eyes again. Sleep was impossible, I couldn't imagine why.

Hunger was getting the better of me. As this was Spain, dinner was at seven, a little on the early side, but the convent understood the needs of travellers and was willing to make concessions.

Feeling faint, and hoping to speed things up, I wandered into the kitchen and offered to set the table. It would be for 25 people, a full house. It felt good to be useful. Four men were cooking. I wondered with some surprise why men were cooking in a nunnery. It seemed a logical question and so I asked.

My awkward Spanish was working. Juan explained they were volunteers from northern Spain who came every year during the busy season. The irony was lost on him. He seemed genuinely perplexed by the question and so I gave up asking.

We eagerly assembled. A bottle of red wine was proudly presented. A thimbleful each was poured. I started to worry. Bread came and disappeared. I noticed some people didn't get any. Potatoes swimming in water came next. I accepted a couple of pieces of potato and my bowl was filled to the brim with potato water. A little salt and maybe an onion would have done wonders, I thought.

Feeling brave, I glanced around at my fellow diners. It was like the story of the emperor with new clothes. Everybody looked like this was perfectly normal. A set of elderly, heavy-set German women were positively beaming at this amazing Camino experience. I wondered quietly if the church box needed more donations. Very slowly, I ate my potatoes and potato water and resolved to contribute. Staying alive, after all, was a priority. I was starving.

The pot came around again and this time it was sausage water. *Ooooh.* I just couldn't manage that, not being much of a meat eater. I watched the others have their sausage-water soup. Lettuce came around, followed by olive oil. Okay. This is really lovely. Courses. I nibbled on my two or three lettuce leaves, wistfully wishing I could have combined them with the potatoes, but hey, I am just a Canadian and we tend to do that sort of thing. The olive oil was very nice, I decided.

With the meal mercifully at an end, we were expected at the service. It was de rigueur, there was no getting out of it. I made a *donativo*; maybe it would help with groceries. A sign said the church had been built in the twelfth century. My body seemed to be stiffening from all of the walking; I could barely move as I forced myself woodenly up an ancient, spiralling stone stairway. The air smelled of musty, dry stone. One wall was tiered with boxes containing paintings of saints. On the upper balcony, candles glowed as we sat in a circle on the floor, where big pillows had been placed over a thick rug. About five languages were being spoken. None of them were English.

I found myself moved by the fact that I was part of a mass migration, a calling that so many people were answering. I prosaically voiced what I was experiencing. The Scary Nun translated my words five times, to French, Italian, Portuguese, German, and Spanish. I didn't think she had quite caught my meaning as I listened. A woman from Brazil began to weep. She was travelling by bicycle with her husband and they were having a difficult time negotiating the terrain. They had received so much assistance from fellow pilgrims that it was moving for her. Her words were translated five times as well.

The Scary Nun continued with an inspirational blessing from Psalm 36: "… they eat the rich food in your house." Was she serious? A quick look her way assured me she was. My mouth twitched.

My cup runneth over, I thought. Time for bed. A younger woman from Italy with a sweet smile, named Francesca, had taken the upper bunk. She was constantly apologizing. I told her to stop it, in Italian, as I popped the candy into my mouth. We both laughed as she relaxed. I journalled my gifts of the day and listed the walk with the opportunity for solitude, being able to manage my pack over seventeen kilometres, the potato water, and yes, the cosmic tug on my funny bone. For some reason my stomach was feeling full. Smiling, I slept.

Breakfast seemed a larger attempt at generosity; there was a lot of yogurt. Maybe the donation box had been replenished. Juan wanted to show me that olive oil on bread was a delicacy. This was not my first breakfast choice, but being polite, I gave it a go. It was surprisingly good. The olive oil was so light it tasted like butter.

I could not leave fast enough. And so it came to pass, I found a side door and eagerly slipped out. An owl hooted as I took cold gulpfuls of fresh air. It felt wonderful to be outside, and I stared at the Milky Way as though it was a reprieve. My headlamp joggled and lit up the way, as I followed the narrow hillside path, poles swinging.

When dawn broke, one thing was clear. Having been thoroughly blessed inside and out these past few days, I had no lingering doubt: I was definitely not cut out for the nunnery.

Ola Szczecinska

Big Sur

Ash was the water, ash the sky. A darkened ash that only oceans carry, a steely ash swimming with the silver ash that is falling from the grey ash of the clouds above. There is the wind as well, cool and biting and at times strong. Cold gusts. The shore a dark brown, hard, rocks and broken shells, and millions, or perhaps billions, of fragments of ancient stone or mountain beaten down. Strings of dried green seaweed encrusted with white salt reach with long fingers toward the black asphalt of the highway just up the distant dunes, through which he walks.

He is tall and skinny. Dark haired, dark eyed. He is thinking. Or perhaps he is feeling. Perhaps he is too busy feeling to be thinking of anything, as he storms along the beach that greys in all directions. It is cold for him. He'd just run out from the truck. Hadn't even thought about it. Had just pulled over and jumped out, in his T-shirt, slammed the door shut, jogged across the empty highway. Now he walks along the Pacific through the gusts of wind and he places his hands in his pockets and frowns at the sand and occasionally he stops, bends down toward an object visible only to him, his body making a C-shape as he bends from his height—maybe it is a rock, a dead starfish, a dried-out crab. He picks up the rock, the dead starfish, the dried-out crab, and looks at it for a moment, the wind whipping around him, rippling through his white T-shirt that hangs like a tarp from his bones as the waves crash down one after the other after the other after the other to infinity, and for a moment he is alone on the planet and there is only him and this thing he is holding: What is this? What is this? As he turns it and scrutinizes it and disappears into it, for a moment, dives into its depths and swims toward its centre that is always pulling away from him, the anger melting away. It was all so long ago—the truck—in another universe, on another highway, and the crashing of the waves drowns out the noise in his head and the salt spray is cold and wet and primeval, correct against his skin.

She will not go out after him, she will not. Will she? No, she will not, she will not. Will she? No, she will not. She will sit in the truck and wait for him, surrounded by their argument, shouts and anger throbbing in the air. Her anger is burning a hole through her seat as she fixes her eyes on him, and onto the beach. Should she get out? It is cold outside, wet, so grey, and she does not like the wet—never has—and today it looks like an impressionist painting of the sea. Or perhaps a romanticist one. A Turner painting. She doesn't think she belongs stumbling around inside of a Turner, no matter how beautiful. Or does she? Does she, in fact, belong inside of a Turner? Maybe she should go outside and see. Maybe she should go outside and see how it feels to be inside of one, instead of sitting in this truck and brimming with anger, losing the minutes of which there are only a finite amount, after all. Was she wasting an opportunity to walk around inside a damp world that reeks of all the eons of Earth? But it is cold. Where is the ship that will surely wreck soon, onto the beach, if this is indeed a Turner? The tilted ship with its sails ballooned. It is not yet visible through the fog, the salty white mist hovering opaque above the ocean. She can smell the seaweed, the decomposing fish, the mud at the bottom of the sea that is growing more ancient with every moment. How is it possible that it grows more ancient? Because that is what things do, that is what they do.

She watches him walking and bending and walking into the distance, his white T-shirt flapping and ruffling in the wind, a hand nervously through his hair on occasion and otherwise leaning forward, storming ahead, just like always, hands in pockets, a sense of purpose trailing behind him, but in fact there was nowhere, really, to go, only an endless ocean—the Pacific, majestic, infinite, unfathomable, terrifying swallowing up time and space as it lashes out wave after wave after wave after wave, devouring, each time, the land.

Seagulls scream. The ocean devours the land and she thinks: Will there only be ocean left when everything is gone? And the gulls are gone? And the sand is gone? And everything again is gone? And darkness will roam once again upon the face of the deep? And drift silently beneath the sea? This very sea right here? From which it all, originally, as they say, emerged? Crawled out from? Had it crawled out from? Or was it spewed, rejected by the ocean through its waves? Abandoned. Had the ocean rejected us? Had it spat us out onto the land like bits of indigestible food, millions and millions of years ago? Where did we come from? Where did we come from? Where did those gulls come from? Who made this Turner? Was this their last argument? Were they over? Was everything ending? Were they doing things wrong? As she watches him getting smaller and smaller and darker and darker and greyer and greyer against a steely ocean that comes for them wave after wave after wave after wave after wave after wave after—

☙

She could never let things go. Could never roll with the punches. Always made mountains of molehills—it was just a sunset. There was nothing to be done about it. He'd lost track of the time, they could see one tomorrow. Or the next day. Or the day after. How could he have known how important it was for her to see the sunset? How could he know when she does not say so? He bends down, picks up a large stone, and throws it into the ocean. The ocean rises up, fetches it, gobbles it up. He picks up another stone and throws it. The ocean rises again, draws it into itself, and swallows it whole. He bends down, picks up another object; it is not a stone. He does not throw it. His brows knit together as he peers into it, feels its smooth edges, turns it around and admires its exoskeleton bleached by the sun. Waves crash and the spray is carried far by the wind, stinging his cheeks and his bare arms, as he turns the thing over several times. It is curious; how strange a thing this thing is. How strange all of this is. How small, how lost.

༄

She sees wave after wave after wave after wave after wave after wave, lunging at the shore, crashing, breaking, grabbing at tiny particles, land broken down over the ages retrieving that which was taken from the ocean or that which it had discarded; it has changed its mind. The ocean: it wants everything back now. It is reclaiming it centimetre by centimetre by second by second until the world is again gone, fallen into the water, inevitable, everything back into the void, the slate-coloured void, which will also eventually fall into another void, which will then fall into another void and that void into another and so on and so on and so on and so on until there are no more voids left for the voids to fall into and everything will again be nothing. And silent. And grey, and nowhere.

Were they over now? How could she go on? She could not go on with someone who does not think of her, never considers her—there will be no other sunset! Not like this one. They missed it and now it was gone forever and there will be no other like it. It was over. Everything was over as she watches him cross the highway, jog toward their truck, open the door, slide into the driver's seat and take her hand—*I brought you something, it's a sand dollar*—and he places the object into her hand and she peers at it: a perfectly round bone seeping warmth into her palm, a flower carved in its centre.

Calvin McShane

Catching the Way Zendo

AN EXCERPT

I take my 25 dollar cheque with me to the township offices. I want to show my mother and girlfriend the fruits of my labour. Maybe I can take them out for a nice dinner on me, a fine young man in New Eben. They didn't find the gesture as humorous as I'd hoped. The frustration must have been clear on my face. Sometimes my expressions can be overlooked with the messy hair, drops of paint on my cheeks, and the raggedy T-shirts and pants I wear to work, but my mother and Miranda have a keen sense for spotting my frustration.

My mother is a fixer. She assumes everything has a fix. I can do option A or B, and she will guide me to whichever option is best for my happiness. Miranda, on the other hand, is not a fixer but a listener. She knows that I may want to scream at some nagging customer currently, but she also knows I'm frustrated with the entire world in general.

I've been disgruntled for years: angry with politics, education, bills, capitalism, social media, everything that defines 21st century living. It's like a seed of disappointment and negativity is growing inside of me. Miranda does her best to shade the soil, keeping its growth to a minimum. She knows, and I know, though my mother hasn't figured it out yet, that eventually the seed will break ground and grow beyond its capacity. Stem, leaves, and black flowers will begin to spill out of my throat and mouth, suffocating me from the inside out.

⌒

The dogs ran up and down the riverbanks, chasing red squirrels out of their holes in the bases of red pines and flushing grouse out of the alder stands in miniature flood plains. The setting sun sparkled on the top of the water, as caddis flies hatched in shallow, slow currents. Occasionally trout would breach the surface, gulping vulnerable bugs off the glistening surface. We fished a stretch of water that doesn't have a name, but is familiar nonetheless. It's a stretch I've fished a hundred times, my father hundreds of times before me. It's quiet, secluded, easy to wade, and has plenty of high ground to sit on and watch the river. Miranda and I catch a few fish each, keeping four in total for dinner. We picked a spot on some high ground and called the dogs. Molly is mid-way across the river, water licking the bottom of her stomach, her nose up and out, directed at a red squirrel on an overhanging limb on the other side of the stream. Louie is behind her, too scared to cross, anxiously crying for her to return to him, to play on the safe side of the river.

Miranda opens a beer and I go to gutting and cleaning the four brook trout resting in a small pail. I make a cut from their anal vent to their throats and, while blood spills out between the gills, their lifeless bodies continue to wiggle long after the colour has left their scales and fins. I line up the gutted trout on a bed of pine needles and Miranda and I each admire our bounty over a cold beer. Louie and Molly return to inspect the catch.

For now, the seed in my stomach is dormant, with plenty of shade offered from the nearby red and jack pine at our backs. I asked her if she'd drag my dead body to a raven feeder when I died, to which she answered "no." She thinks I'm being a bit crazy. I can tell because when she genuinely finds something funny, she shows her upper teeth and snorts a little bit before closing her mouth. To the raven feeder idea, all she did was smile and hum a bit of laughter out of her nose. It is cute nonetheless—her laugh and her listening to my ideas about life, after death.

Some people may think I'm a house painter, but they're wrong. For a few hours of the day I may very well be a painter. But an hour after that, I could be a fisherman, a wood cutter, a loving boyfriend, an honourable son, a Zen student, and the host for a seed of negativity and pessimism. New Eben loves to label people. John's the monk. Miranda is Calvin's girlfriend. Calvin is Lori's son, the painter. What a shame it is. People don't just end up in places like New Eben. Some of us returned after a life touring the world—Vietnam, maybe Mexico. Others were born here, never knowing a reality exists beyond Lake Superior.

Then there are others, like me, who came here to escape. I came for a bit of shade, some stillness, dark corners, and silence—the type of stuff ravens like. I am not sure how long I can hang on as the painter and I can't say I'm too determined to change anybody's mind. Eventually, the flowering plant will grow too strong, and Miranda and I will find another place to settle down and that's just fine. Catching the Way Zendo will still be here, my mat and cushion next to John's like it has been for the last five years, ravens just outside picking at the livers and brains of fish.

Margaret Miller

Our Strangely Illuminating Times

MAY 2020, VANCOUVER, B.C.

A few days after the beginning of the COVID-19 lockdown here in Vancouver, I was in my first grocery store lineup. Our government had said that certain stores could stay open if customers practised social distancing, so while standing in front of my local supermarket, I carefully kept to my space, designated by strips of green tape two metres apart. When one person left the store, the people in line slowly moved forward. As we waited, the woman behind me began to talk to the woman in the space behind her. She said, "I am sixty years old. I am in mourning. I am in mourning for a world that will never be the same again." The other woman responded kindly, with words of comfort.

One of the issues the pandemic has brought home is the dire consequences when we encroach on the living space of other creatures. Increased contact between species has meant more zoonotic viruses—viruses that jump from an animal host to humans. Early evidence suggested that the COVID-19 virus may have come into existence when an infected horseshoe bat was eaten by another animal, possibly a pangolin, which was then taken to a market in Wuhan, where it was eaten by humans. As more and more wild lands around the world are cleared for monoculture farming and cattle grazing, the number of zoonotic viruses—such as Marberg, Ebola, AIDS, bird flu, SARS, and now

COVID-19—will increase.

Before the pandemic began, if I had been asked to reflect on the effect of a lockdown on our environment, I would have said that because we would be driving and flying less we would be burning less fossil fuel, and so there would be less pollution. And it's true: I do notice that the air in Vancouver is a lot cleaner. The brownish-yellow haze that typically covers the city is gone. I can see mountains in the distance that I have never seen before. The same kind of thing is happening all over the world.

But now that we're in the middle of the pandemic (or at the beginning, or near the end, at this point we don't seem to know where we are), a delightfully unexpected thing has been happening. As we take refuge inside our homes, animals are moving in and taking up the spaces we abandoned. The internet is full of images of wildlife taking over abandoned urban spaces in unprecedented ways: wild goats in Wales, wild boar in Haifa, deer in Nara, Japan. A friend in Whistler saw a huge elk herd, larger than any she'd ever seen, crossing the highway. Reports from up the British Columbia coast tell of increased orca sightings. The tree frogs in our local pond are more boisterously active and loud than I have ever heard them before.

Now, eight weeks after the start of the lockdown, I continue to reflect on our place in the world and what these strangely illuminating times have to teach us. Like the mourning woman in the lineup at the supermarket, I feel like I am living in a new world. And standing between the lines, a practice that is now second nature, has come to sum up a lot of what I think we need to learn: that if humans could only keep within their green lines, the world would be a kinder and roomier place, a more just place that honours and has space for all living beings.

Pacific Chorus

For Dr. Sallie McFague, 1933–2019

We always thought of our garden as a world unto itself. Planted in a Japanese style, it is enclosed and protected by our house on one side and a tall cedar hedge, a wall of bamboo, and a row of birch trees on the others. To enter, you walk through a gate and along a path that curves down toward the house.

Our garden was planted on property purchased by my family in the early 1940s, about two blocks from the future Jericho Park near the western boundary of Vancouver. A new street was opened for development and my grandfather and aunt built a large and airy house on the last lot still for sale. Huge cedar stumps remained from the clearcutting of the land, a reminder of what the property looked like before the settlers arrived and the land that is now Vancouver was divided and developed.

The temperate rainforest where our garden is located is in the ancestral, traditional, and unceded territory of the Musqueam, Squamish, and Tsleil-Waututh people. Twenty-five hundred years ago, people lived at Ee'yullmough ("good spring water"), a village at the site of what is now Jericho Park and which existed until the inhabitants were forced out by settlers in the 1860s. From the 1890s until the 1970s, this land was owned by the federal government and had a variety of uses, including as a golf course and a Royal Canadian Air Force base.

I spent a lot of time at the house when I was growing up and remember when my aunt and uncle created the Japanese garden in the late 1960s. I feel as if I grew up with it. I became even closer to the garden and its rhythms when I moved in with my aunt, then a recent widow, in 2002.

One thing I love about our garden is that it is home to Pacific chorus tree frogs. These small frogs with a dark eye mask can be pale grey or tan or bronze or bright emerald green, and are able to change colour to match their environments; they can also change from lighter to darker and shift between patterns and pure colours. Their long legs have slightly webbed toes, and each toe has a round, sticky pad for climbing and attaching to surfaces.

After Jericho Park was sold by the federal government to the city in the early 1970s, local citizens demanded that the area be made as natural as possible. The concrete runway from its days as an RCAF base was covered by a pile of fill to create a rough meadow. Intertidal habitats and a conifer forest were restored and freshwater wetlands created. The wetlands, which encompass marsh, shallow open water, and swamp, are the park's most important ecological feature. They support a large tree frog population and a rich variety of birds, as well as otters, beavers, and coyotes.

But in 2017, massive and destructive forest fires, attributed by scientists to climate change, engulfed B.C. and western Canada. While walking through Jericho Park during one of those terrible, mournful days, I was approached by a woman who was gesturing wildly—she was clearly distraught. She told me that in recent weeks she had been watching the frogs and other creatures die from heat and lack of water. No longer able to stand by and watch these increasingly tragic conditions without doing anything, she was begging passersby to contact City Hall and demand that they pump life-saving water into the ponds. I called the city when I got home, but don't think they took action.

At the same time this was going on in our local park, we noticed that we were no longer hearing the frogs' familiar *rrrrrrrbt* in our garden. Naturally we wondered if they had met a fate similar to the frogs in Jericho Park. The conditions in our garden were marginally better—we had kept the pond full using our garden hose and had done as much watering as was allowed under water restrictions. But despite these efforts, our garden was looking less and less like the temperate rainforest that greeted settlers 150 years ago. The ground was so dry that the earth was turning to dust, and the moss—which my aunt had carefully collected from around the region over a period of many years—was blowing away. The trees were so parched that leaves were falling off in July. Far fewer birds than usual came around. We were especially worried for the frogs, not just because we had developed a fondness for them, but because the disappearance of frogs can have cascading effects that are felt through-out an entire ecosystem. Unfolding around us was evidence that nothing in nature is a world unto itself. Everything is connected, everything is related.

For two years after the fires, the frogs were absent. Then, about four months ago, they returned. We don't know why they came back—whatever the reason, we received them and their *rrrrrrrbts* with joy.

But my joy is tinged with sadness, because I know this is not how this story will end. My aunt has died and my family can no longer live here. Like many people in this expensive city, I will soon have to sell the house and it will, in all likelihood, be torn down and the garden filled in. The lot, a valuable commodity, will once again be divided and developed. And for the tree frogs and other creatures who live and pass through here, the days of the pond and the moss and the gentle shade will come to an end.

Anne Rosenberg

The Arrival of COVID-19 in the Spring of 2020

MARCH 2020

My husband, Art, is a creature of habit. I've always admired that about him. Every Saturday morning, he goes to Thomas Haas patisserie for a *pain au chocolat*. Thomas Haas is one of the best pastry chefs in the world. He has become a huge success here in Vancouver. Art is there just before the café opens at 8:00 a.m. Sometimes I will tag along, and at other times he'll go on his own and Thomas might sit down with him for a few minutes. They're both cyclists and they've gotten to know each other over the years. Thomas is a salt-of-the-earth person—it's not just about making a lot of dough.

As the place has become busier and busier, Art goes in to say hello and pick up his *pain au chocolat*. If I go with him (I'm not a creature of habit), we might sit down and I'll have an espresso and take a few photographs of the ever-changing and exquisite pastry displays or the fascinating and colourful people who crowd into the café. You can rarely find seats. Sometimes we'll stand at the counter, where you can't move because there are so many people packed in, eating pastries and sipping cappuccinos. Sometimes, Art helps to clear the tables. He obviously feels right at home.

The café is just one part of Art's Saturday routine, though. He gets up well before sunrise and works on his French in Duolingo, then he takes our Scottish terrier, Ezra, for his first walk. Then it is time for his pastry, and afterwards, he comes home to get his bags for the farmers' market, and maybe me, and then off to get our vegetables, fish, mushrooms, and whatever else looks good that week. He doesn't eat anything sweet during the work week. It's not that he has ever been on any kind of a restricted diet. He simply looks forward to and then enjoys his Saturday *pain au chocolat*.

But life has changed. Art knows that. His office is at home now. Like so many others, he is working remotely. We moved the last of his things on Friday, March 20. I hadn't driven downtown for a week, since we were all told to "shelter in place." There was no one on the road. It was such a strange feeling to drive over the Burrard Street Bridge. There weren't even cyclists in the bike lane. I sometimes drive Art to work, but he prefers to ride his bike. I like to drive him and look at the high-end shop windows around his office building. Not only are the clothes interesting, the ideas are always cutting edge. It's as good as going to a fabulous gallery. I love fashion—the more creative, the better.

All of the windows were now emptied or boarded up. No one was around. I pulled up in front of Art's office building on the corner of Alberni and Bute. I had asked Art if he would wear protective gloves. This was before we had ever worn our homemade masks, which has become second nature now. He put on a pair of fluorescent-coloured DeFeet winter bicycle gloves. He walked into the building and I started to sob. He came back less than ten minutes later with an armful of his computer equipment. It looked like he was looting, but of course he did everything by the book. He always does. He loaded the electronics into the car and asked me to drive because he had a conference call. I was still in shock from the horrifying scene surrounding us. I drove home while Art spoke with his colleagues across Canada.

Later that Friday afternoon, after working non-stop in full-out crisis mode, he said he was looking forward to his *pain au chocolat*. I said he shouldn't go. It wasn't safe and I doubted Thomas's would be open. I would call. I was surprised to find out they were. I said to the woman who answered, I didn't think it was a good idea for my husband Art (or anyone) to go out into a crowded place, as COVID-19 had recently arrived in Vancouver.

"Oh, Art," she said. "I know Art. Pull up in front tomorrow morning, call my cellphone, and I will bring Art's *pain au chocolat* to the car. I'm Emma."

That next morning, we pulled up, I called, and she came running out to our car window with a big smile and a bag with two *pains au chocolat*. You should have seen the look on Art's face. When we got home, I put one in the freezer for the following Saturday morning. A lot may have changed in one week, but Art will still enjoy his Saturday morning Thomas Haas *pain au chocolat*.

JUNE 2020

Since writing this in March, Thomas Haas has put a new COVID-19 protocol in place, which significantly limits the number of people in the café. There is a different atmosphere, but the pastries are still worth lining up for. The loyal clientele, including Art, keep showing up, albeit now in their protective masks.

ANNE ROSENBERG

Amazing Grace

*In mid-March, there was a large Orthodox Jewish wedding in a
Montreal hotel. Within days it had led to an outbreak of COVID-19,
and the community had become a coronavirus hot spot. (CBC Radio)*

APRIL 30, 2020

Breathe in Love. Breathe out Love.
In times of uncertainty, be aware of grace.

Ari Schwartz went home today, in time for Shabbat. There was an emo-
tional welcome home celebration in his neighbourhood in Montreal.
His mother Patty, a close family friend and a woman who I adore, sent
me a video of the arrival. There were balloons, painted signs, and his six
children, neighbours, and wife, rushing to the car to greet him, while
still trying to keep their physical distance. You can clearly see it wasn't
easy. I could feel the tears of joy as a surgical-masked relative, perhaps his
brother-in-law, helped him into his home.

Ari had been hospitalized with COVID-19 for close to a month.
During that time, he was on a ventilator for more than eighteen days in
intensive care at Montreal's Jewish General Hospital. What impressed
me the most is that his mother never lost her extraordinary balance.
Patty stayed centred in that enormous "mother love" and the ability to
hold what felt like a global angst. She never ran away from the pain and
as she held it, it seemed she was also able to encompass and hold that
peaceful healing place for her son and for all of those working to keep
him alive. I was watching a miracle unfold as I witnessed this. She had
accepted that her son may die. She told me that. She sat with that excru-
ciating pain. She held it all with amazing grace.

199

I remember when my nephew Aaron was hit by a car riding home from school in 2005. He was in a coma at B.C. Children's Hospital. As I sat beside my sister-in-law Karen, at the end of Aaron's hospital bed, she looked at me with tears in her eyes and said in a clear voice I can hear right now, "If he leaves me, I am grateful I've been blessed with these incredible years with him." I will never forget that moment. I continue to think about it. The world-renowned meditation teacher and author Sharon Salzberg says that our safest haven may be found neither in running nor in hiding but in staying still. I could feel that stillness in the hospital.

I was fortunate to be right there in intensive care when my nephew opened his eyes. He's never looked back. He's full of life, love, and never-ending adventure. And more recently, Ari, in Montreal, knew he had to get up and leave the hospital to go home to his six children. As soon as he was taken off of the ventilator, he told the nurse he belonged at home, and that is where he was going. He asked for his clothes. Of course, he had to heal a little more before he could get himself dressed and go home.

This will be a special Shabbat for Ari, and for all of those who love him from near and far. The Shehecheyanu Blessing has always been one of my favourite Sabbath blessings. I will think of Patty, Ari, Karen, Aaron, and all of us and our families, when we sing it this evening.

The Shehecheyanu Blessing
Blessed are You, Adonai our God, who has kept us alive,
sustained us, and brought us to this present season.

Kate Covello

Disruption and Innovation

YOGA TEACHER TRAINING AFTER COVID-19

In February 2020, "PANDEMIC" was smeared on the front page of the news. Prior to that, headlines like "Wuhan Lockdown" were catching my attention, but I was distracted, like all Canadians, by railroad blockades, the Wet'suwet'en hereditary chiefs, and the unimportant discourse about JLo's outfit at the Super Bowl. The Facebook militia was rioting about these polarizing issues, but the Wet'suwet'en blockades and JLo's crotch were ignored by many. There was still diversity in the media—sports, movies, celebrity gossip, travel—and our individual interests trumped any unifying issue.

That was the Before Times. Before everyone was sent home from work and our collective interests were aligned by the impact of COVID-19. Before my inbox was bursting with trivial emails from every business I'd ever patronized. Thank you, Headkandi Salon, for letting me know you've made the "difficult but necessary" decision to close. And hello, Scotiabank, I send well-wishes to your family too.

At first, COVID-19 was everywhere and nowhere. It was in my emails and front of mind, but I didn't know anyone with it. Then it was somewhere: a sign on the door of my yoga studio, CLOSED DUE TO COVID. The lively yoga studio I own, and where I teach yoga teacher training, was abruptly silenced on March 17.

Loneliness punctuated the early days of lockdown. Scotiabank underscored the concept of community with their well-wishes and "we're all in this together" digital platitude, but the mass emails did little to acquiesce my gloom. My studio was empty, and I passed the lonely hours swiffering the floor and tinkering with my website. I often just sat at the desk, listlessly refreshing my email. Another unread message at the top, this one from the Yoga Alliance. Oh great, another instruction to "stay safe in these troubled times." I rolled my eyes in anticipation of more insipid platitudes. But the Yoga Alliance email was different. It had real solutions to my real problem: online yoga teacher training was approved. For the first time. I'd advocated before for approval of online yoga teacher training but was always met with reluctance. Maybe the administration to implement online yoga training had been too daunting. Whatever their former reason for disallowing online training, the abrupt global disruption prompted the Yoga Alliance to adapt. For the first time in weeks, I felt inspired by change.

Along with loneliness, a frustrating feeling of inertia had been my constant companion. "Stay home" was the online rally cry. Being alone, coupled with the uncertain future for my business, was wearing on me. So following the Yoga Alliance's approval for online yoga training, I was eager for action. With no regard for the daunting logistics, or for my sanity, I resolved to get my 200-hour yoga training curriculum online in two weeks. Step one: get a learning management system. I host my website through WordPress, so I chose LearnDash, a learning management plug-in. I trusted WordPress because their reliable online support solved many frustrations over the past decade.

Part of learning online and mitigating the accompanying loneliness is knowing there's a like-minded support community. Immediately after installing the LearnDash plug-in, all my custom formatting disappeared. I gasped. Audibly. The sound reverberated around my empty studio. My website took ten years to mould to my satisfaction. I clicked around in the now-barren shell of a website. Anguish. Despair. Acute helplessness. But WordPress has a live chat with Happiness Engineers. I pounded into my keyboard: "Please help. I just installed a new plug-in and all my formatting disappeared!!!!"

"Oh no! (Hi!) I've seen that error before, I think I know what we need to do," came the reply from WordPress live chat. The faceless Happiness Engineer solved the problem for me with a few keystrokes—my website had inadvertently migrated to a new server.

"*Thank* you. Are you a real person? Where are you?" I typed.

"I think I'm a real person! Hard to tell these days :-) I'm in the Eastern U.S.," came the response. And my anguish dissolved. Here was a real person solving a problem for me. We were alone, but together. The transition from the Before Times to the unknown of COVID-19 was abrupt and jarring, but for the first time since the virus barged into my life, I felt supported by another individual.

Alone. Together. Reading emails and chatting virtually. I considered the possibilities of life after COVID-19. Driven by innovation, infrastructure like live chat with a trained WordPress agent was already in place. I brainstormed about how online yoga teacher training could be meaningful. It needed to be more than a one-sided broadcast like email and blog content. It needed to be a two-sided discussion. It needed to mimic a community. Students needed to feel like we were together while they were alone.

COVID-19 is a once-in-a-generation opportunity to pivot and try something new. I had the approval from the Yoga Alliance, I persevered through the frustration of installing a learning management system, now I had to get interactive with video. The textbook and written content was done, but how would I replicate the spontaneous interactive group learning that is central to yoga teacher training? How would I promote community in an online medium?

My self-imposed frenetic schedule was filled with spontaneous interactive learning. Online forums and chats educated me on sufficient RAM for 4K video; mirrorless and full frame cameras; lavaliere microphones; and colour rendering index for lighting. Even the vocabulary was new to me. But every panicky problem with bandwidth, choppy video, and shadowy lighting was calmly answered in online support groups. I was acquiring a new skill set, and the difficulty of getting my yoga modules online was mitigated by online community support. My sanity was compromised by my frenzied work pace and the volume of unfamiliar tasks, but I felt supported by an online community.

Community is what keeps us sane. Community is about aligning feelings through shared objectives and mutual understanding. I thought about the idea of community as I set up a corner for filming video in my studio. Lights. Camera. Action. I was teaching yoga to a tripod. It didn't feel like community. Can online learning really replicate the real-life experience of being part of a yoga training cohort? Yoga teacher training is about community and about belonging. As I learned to make videos, I asked the forums if I should film in 24 or 30 frames per second; I asked how to backlight my set. No matter the question, there was an online community to support the process. Martin Luther King Jr. described community as a web of mutuality. Community is a shared responsibility to take care of each other. Making videos was rewarding for me because I was supported by others: mutual support was available through shared objectives.

I paced around the studio and pondered how to create a web of mutuality for online yoga teacher trainees. Students needed to track and share their learning progress. Teaching yoga is dynamic because of the community of yoga students. Learning how to teach yoga is rewarding because it's a shared experience with a cohort. Online yoga teacher training will be dynamic if students chronicle the process through an ePortfolio. There. Midway through the second frenetic week of filming, I typed in the instructions for the mainstay of the program. Dynamic shared learning, represented in an ePortfolio that students would work on during the program. Alone but together, students would document the journey in an ePortfolio.

As March passed and April blossomed, the isolation orders eased. People emerged into spring. I emerged into the brand-new world of online yoga teacher training. After the hustle of changing the studio around, the frustration of organizing a learning management system, and acquiring the vocabulary to understand audio-visual setups, five brave students showed up on the first day of Land and Heart Online Yoga Teacher Training. "Welcome yogis." I calmly smiled at the webcam. "I'm so glad you're here."

COVID-19's disruption was swift and universal. There was a pause, but community and possibility propelled us to think of new ways to do old things. New yoga teacher training is about dynamic shared online learning. A yoga studio is more than cork floors and soft lighting. A studio is a community sanctuary for the dynamic practice of yoga. COVID-19 is more than a health crisis. It's an opportunity to adapt and innovate after disruption. My yoga studio was once a sanctuary with pleasant ambiance and quiet music. The soft lighting is disrupted now by glaring set lights; the quiet music competes with humming cameras. The process of teaching yoga used to be one step of unrolling a yoga mat but now includes sound checks and battery charges. The ambiance of the studio is disrupted by the piles of audio-visual equipment, but the community sanctuary has been replicated in the virtual world.

Ankush Chopra

Stay the Course

I bang the delete key so hard that my index finger burns with an explod-ing prickly sensation. Even the cardinal outside my window flies away. But the *whoosh* sound of the vanishing yellow folder from my computer screen doesn't make me feel any better.

I had heard that there is a point in every doctoral student's journey when he wants to get out. The pain becomes too much to bear. Today I have reached that point, sitting in my basement office, a place where I have been working for the last four weeks, dusk making the room light ineffective. I want out.

I panic as I see the folder disappear and scramble to open the deleted files folder. It has not turned out the way I had imagined in the begin-ning, three years ago. I thought it would be a breeze for me. Two years of coursework, one or one and a half years of research, and a successful thesis defense is all that it takes. I have an MBA, a decade of corporate experience, and interesting questions to research. How difficult could it be? Very little turned out easy. Yes, the coursework was intoxicating and the first paper I wrote won an award, but how does it help me today when I am stuck on the first step of this lengthy journey ahead?

I wonder how I got here. The ancient Vedic scriptures say that you are your deepest desire. That makes me a mountain climber. That is all I desire: new mountains to conquer, each one more challenging, each victory sweeter. But my problem is that I cannot stay on any peak for too long; if I do not move on to the next expedition, I rot. While conquering mountains in my journey, the last one that beckoned me was a PhD. The academic world promised an infinite number of mountains to conquer: permanent bliss.

A PhD is the training ground in academia where you learn how to search for truth. The work involves identifying a missing piece in the existing knowledge of the world and developing it. It is like conquering a far-off mountain, climbing it, mapping it, and adding it to the vast map of the landscape others have already mapped. Since others have been mapping terrains forever, the first challenge is to find an unconquered peak. I am stuck on this step.

I find the just-deleted folder, click "undelete" and restore it to life. But nothing can restore me today. I have never been this tired. As a part of academic training, you learn the art of mountain climbing by working with a master climber who has scaled many peaks. My master climber is Will Mitchell, a revered man of Canadian origin. Below his overgrown curly hair, behind his Gandhi spectacles and an infrequent warm smile, there is an ocean of experience in vanquishing mountains. As I chart my plan to crush my cliff, he is there to guide me when the elevation is a mirage, when it is a hill not worth going after, and when someone else has already mapped it.

My fingers quiver when I type "Last Try" to rename the folder on my screen. I take a deep breath, close my eyes, and bow my head as a singular thought reverberates through my entire being: "This is it. If it doesn't work, I am out."

For a year, I have been stuck on the critical step of planning my expedition. Each time I prepare a plan, Will shoots it down for a new yet valid reason. "It is not new." "This is not very interesting." "So what?" And each time, I marshal my energies to go in search of yet another summit. It is like I dig a hole to plant a sapling but fill it with the same earth without even a seed. Wash, rinse, repeat. It is soul-crushing. Sure, I am not the only one in this situation; most of my peers are working on their first or second expedition plan. But the clock is not ticking for them the way it is for me.

For my doctorate, I moved to the U.S. from Singapore, where I was thriving in a lucrative corporate job. My wife, Lavanya, and our one-year-old, Arjun, also moved with me. Lavanya took a transfer in her company that slowed her career and it frustrates her constantly. "You must finish this year and not take an extra year," she regularly reminds me. Though I am in an intellectual Mecca, a place where I wanted to be, it feels like a luxury to spend hours delving deep into interesting topics, reading, learning, having fun. I have given up everything else to focus on the doctorate. Though I love parties, I have been to only one in the last three years. "It's so nice to see you come out for a party," one of my peers said in surprise.

I mostly work from home, as it keeps me focused. When I go to my office, it troubles me to see several peers who have been in the program for six and seven years. Anything beyond four years is untenable for me; Lavanya wanted me to finish in three years, and I am already near the end of the third year. I am running at terminal velocity behind a train that has left the station, but all I see is an increasing chasm between me and the train.

After four failed expedition plans, a novel idea recently took hold of me: "What if I never get past this stage?" It has followed me daily, wearing me down, chipping away my energy reserves. I now believe that I am in an unlit room, searching for something that doesn't exist.

How wonderful the strength at the beginning of a journey, how terrible the weariness near the middle. In this state, it is natural to remember the familiarity of a past peak I climbed. I long for the certainty of known terrains, sometimes wishing to go back to the corporate world again. Compared to academia, the corporate world is entirely different. The challenges do not involve mapping unfamiliar terrains, but leading groups across rivers, bridges, ravines, and some tiny hills with known topography. I have a flair for that. In a moment of weakness, I recently interviewed with a well-known company. Now they are interested in me joining them. In our weariness, we sometimes forget who we really are, and seek comfort rather than meaning. A poor bargain. Deep within, I know my path is forward not backward. But I cannot see a way forward.

"Come up; food is ready," Lavanya shouts from the basement door. She has called me three times already. I turn off the lights and go upstairs. Picking up a bottle of Heineken from the fridge, I sit with Arjun at the round, walnut kitchen table, where he is still eating his dinner. I turn off the TV blaring in the background and invent a fresh story for him. Lavanya is still behind the kitchen counter, finishing up. I down another bottle by the time he finishes dinner. We kiss him goodnight and I pick up a third bottle.

"Third beer?" she asks.

"I don't feel like working anymore today. Exhausted."

She nods in understanding.

"I have decided. If it doesn't work this time, I am out. We can leave one way or the other."

"I think it may be a smart thing to do. How long can you go on like this?" she says.

We have our dinner, and I go to sleep, falling like an old tree at the end of its life. When I wake up, they have already left. I am in a daze, trying to open my eyes that refuse to open. The memory of the dream from the night jolts me and I sit up.

I was on an incline in a mountainous place. It was night. Pitch dark everywhere. I had left the road somewhere behind and started climbing the wilderness to go up faster. As I stood there, I heard a loud booming voice from the valley beyond the road. Though it had authority, it neither commanded nor suggested, just stated it in a plain tone: "Stay the course." It didn't repeat itself. Didn't have to.

Something turns within me and a deep sense of knowing comes over me. The loneliness I had been feeling for months vanishes, and I feel connected. Protected. My strength, which had abandoned me, reemerges. Suddenly, I am clear that I will not rush this expedition plan. Instead of sending it to Will today, I will work on it as long as it takes. I will give it all.

Over the next several days, I polish my thesis proposal without a thought on whether I will succeed. I revise it over and over, until satisfied.

The following week, when I meet Will, after sending the proposal via email, I cannot believe it when he says, "You have got it." I am all set for the expedition. Sitting in the visitor chair in his office, his degrees covering the wall behind him, his keen gaze locked on to me, I see the fog lift.

I did not understand that I was so close to finding my mountain when I decided that there are no more mountains to climb. I would have surrendered too soon when my mountain was in unobstructed view just around the next bend. But would I have still made it if that dream had not signalled me to keep going? I guess I will never know.

Speculative and YA fiction

edited by Rebecca A. Coates

Jenn Marx
Electric Blue Tongue

Mommy taught us never to tell a lie. It was her number-one rule.

We don't tell Lies in this house, Angela, she said, when I told her that it wasn't me who'd eaten the last of the electric-blue Jell-O she'd been saving up for Mikey once he learned how to go potty like a big boy. I couldn't figure out how she knew I'd taken the Jell-O. I'd pushed the empty container deep into the laundry room garbage pail. Looking down at me from her great height in our yellow kitchen, she told me, *If you don't tell the truth right now, there'll be consequences.*

Consequences. Such a big word.

I was too scared to find out what it meant, but since I'd already lied once, I had to lie again to cover up the first one. I looked her in the eye, crossed my fingers behind my back, and bravely broke her number-one rule a second time: *I'm not lying.* My heart thumped fast and my face got all hot.

I'd forgotten all about the best part of eating electric-blue Jell-O—the colour it turns your mouth. Under her angry, disappointed eyes, I'd lied to Mommy's face. Twice. My tattletale tongue flashing bright blue the whole time.

I don't tell lies anymore.

⌒

When I came home on the bus the next day, our grumpy old neighbour was in our living room. She was sitting on our faded green couch, under the framed picture of me and Mikey in dress-up clothes perched on Mommy's and Daddy's laps. The four of us grinning like we were all overly happy about something. It was the only time I'd ever seen Daddy wear a tie.

Mommy and Mrs. Turner didn't get along. They were always bellyaching at each other about one thing or another. The height of our fence, or the leaves from her maple tree falling into our yard. Mrs. Turner was forever coming over to whine about me and Mikey being too loud. Silly, grown-up reasons to be angry at one another. But yesterday, there she was, with her wild grey sticky-up hair, watching me with that scrunched-up sourpuss face.

Mommy had her fake smile on, showing way too many teeth. She was offering old lady Turner a home-baked cookie from a pretty glass plate that's only used to eat birthday cakes off of. Seeing the cookies, I forgot how strange it was to have our cranky neighbour inside our house with her too-thick knuckles wrapped around Daddy's favourite mug. The one with the picture of a man sleeping on a boat that told a joke about fishing being hard but better than a day at work. I ran to the kitchen to get my own cookie, not bothering to stop and take off my shoes or put away my backpack, breaking another rule. I knew Mommy wouldn't yell at me with Mrs. Turner right there.

When I got to the kitchen, Mikey was sitting in the corner on his Time-Out Stool, his fat bottom lip sticking out, tear tracks dried on his chubby cheeks. He told me he'd tried to sneak one of the cookies off the plate, but Mommy'd slapped his hand away, saying, *Don't ever take anything without asking. Those cookies are for company.*

I put away my backpack. Lined up my shoes under the coat rack.

☞

I heard Mommy and Daddy up late last night. Their tattletale footsteps walking up and down the basement stairs woke me up. They were talking in the kinds of whispers that're too loud to be whispers, but it's the only way adults know how to whisper. Mommy's footsteps sounded bigger than Daddy's 'cause she had on her clompy slippers. Daddy must've had sock feet, because all I heard from him was the weight of his body on the creaky steps.

I didn't know what all that activity meant. Excitement in the middle of the night like it was Christmas Eve. I figured it must've been some sort of surprise for me and Mikey. That I'd forgotten about a special holiday involving a fairy or a fluffy animal that left presents for good little kids.

But I wasn't a good kid. I'd lied to Mommy.

Under the glow of my princess night light, I stretched out my tongue, pulling it with my fingers as far as I could, tasting the toothpaste that'd dried on my thumb. I crossed my eyes, turning my head this way and that, checking for any leftover blue stains. I couldn't get a clear look, but what I did see was all pink. My lies were gone. I fell back asleep, dreaming of the new bicycle or puppy I'd surely get in the morning.

Two police officers came to the door today after school, their walkie-talkie radios blasting static burps into the hallway where Mikey and I watched, our mouths opened wide into the shape of capital O's. Mommy didn't let them inside, standing with her body scrunched between the door and the coat rack as if she didn't want them to see into the house. They asked Mommy if she'd seen Mrs. Turner recently, saying our neighbour had been *reported missing after not showing up to her daughter's twentieth wedding anniversary party last night*.

I didn't even know that Mrs. Turner had a daughter. I couldn't imagine living with that mean old lady in her dark house, listening to her grumble on and on about peace and quiet, never being able to make any noise in your own home. I felt sorry for this strange little girl whose mommy couldn't even bother to show up to her party.

I haven't seen Mrs. Turner in ages, Mommy said politely, looking them in the eye. I clapped my sweaty hands over my mouth, keeping in the scared sound that was bubbling in my chest.

Mommy lied.

After a long time, the police left and Mommy closed and locked the door, shooing us into the kitchen, telling us to *sit, sit, I'll get you both a treat*. There was a high, cheery sound to her voice, but each of her words was wrapped in a weird kind of shakiness that made me not want to ask her about her lying.

Mikey scrambled into his booster seat, and I sat on the hard edge of my chair at the kitchen table. Mommy scraped the Time-Out Stool across the kitchen floor to reach up into the cupboard above the stove. The bony spots on her spine poked out from under her pink shirt as she reached her hand way to the back, bringing out three plastic cups of blue Jell-O. Mikey clapped his hands, yelling, *Yay, Mikey's a big boy*.

My throat squeezed tight.

I watched the two of them spoon blue chunks into their mouths, Mommy's face twisted into a frown. Turns out I can't eat electric-blue Jell-O anymore. I remembered the taste of toothpaste on my tongue from last night, when I thought I'd been forgiven for my lies. Weren't there supposed to be presents this morning? I started to feel sad about the missing puppy and angry that I still had to ride my too-small bike with the broken bell and peeling foam rubber handles. *Mommy, you lied to the policemen*. I knew I was breaking yet another rule—tattling—but I wanted to point out that I wasn't the only one who told lies in this house.

Mommy's spoon clattered to the table, and she reached for me, sandwiching my face between her cold hands. *There's a difference between a lie and a secret, Angela*. Her hot breath smelled like tangy blueberries. When she asked me if I *understood*, her eyes were black and shiny, like the dying baby rabbit Daddy'd brought home from a fishing trip once. I nodded stiffly, my ears folding beneath her strong palms. I didn't understand, though. Lies and secrets seemed the same things to me, both opposites of telling the truth. But I could tell Mommy was scared and I didn't want her to be afraid.

I loved Mommy.

I didn't want her to have consequences.

It didn't matter if I couldn't tell the difference between a secret and a lie, Mommy was more important. Most important. And if making Mommy feel not-scared meant lying to the police, then that's what I'd do. I wriggled out of her grasp and hugged her tight. If I scrunched my eyes shut, I wouldn't see her tongue flashing at me bright blue.

Jess Wesley

The Curse of the Fairy Queen

Away on the shore of Newfoundland, tucked in a harbour where fingers of rock stretch into the sea and fishing boats bob like fat-bellied ducks on the water, there lies a narrow footpath. If you're not careful, you'll miss it, the shallow impression in the rock made just so for small feet to follow. If you have your wits about you, you'll avoid it altogether, for it was down this very path my father went 52 years ago and found himself a fairy. His hair has been white ever since.

"It was my twelfth birthday," he said one night as we gathered around the hearth, "and my mother, your Nanny, had baked me an apple pie."

He crossed his long, lean legs and leaned his bony elbow on his knee. I listened, rapt, for my father is a great teller of stories.

"She bade me take a slice of pie to our neighbour who lived alone in a cottage down the lane. This is what it was like in those days. When we had troubles, we halved them, and when we came into good fortune, we halved that, too. So I went for a walk and was not seen till midnight three days later."

"Where did you go?" I asked.

He looked down at me and lay a finger aside his nose. "Can you keep a secret?"

I nodded. I meant to hoard my father's secret. And I did—until today, as I am telling it to you.

"I went to the land of the fairies."

My father's eyes, grey like the bay, took on a faraway look. The past swirled around him like smoke. I could almost smell it: nutmeg and wind and salt. He began to speak:

I went for a walk down the lane, dawdling so I might miss the washing-up at home. My eyes were on the sky. My skin grew cold. When I looked around, I was no longer on the lane but somewhere else. A narrow path in the rock. And there, no word of a lie, I came upon a fairy circle. Eight tall stones—tall as men—arranged in an ellipse.

Now, any good man will tell you to mind yourself when you come upon a circle of trees or mushrooms or stones and to nimbly avoid it. But I was twelve, and I thumbed my nose at children's stories. Dusk had come already. I stepped inside the circle, and that's when she appeared to me. She was nearly my age and had magnificent antlers growing out of her silver hair.

"Do you bear fruit?" she asked. Her voice was dry and raspy like the crunch of dead leaves underfoot. "What have you brought us?"

I looked down at my basket. "I have a pastry for my neighbour."

Her wet teeth flashed like gemstones in the gathering dark. She held out her hand and hissed, "Give it to me."

Her eyes glittered, orange and terrible, and oh! how I regretted laughing at my mother's nighttime stories, for I knew now that they were true. Every yarn she had spun of unwary sailors and gullible travellers came to me, and my knees trembled.

I cried, "Fairy, you have no hold on me!"

She stared at me with those baleful eyes. She laughed. "So go, then."

I tried to leave, but the fairy had worked her magic on me. I could not step foot outside the circle.

"Tell me, boy," she said, and the way she said boy made me think she was far older than she looked—old and ancient and cunning—"how am I called?"

"How should I know your name?"

She smiled, her teeth sharp and gleaming. "Tell me how I am called, and I shall let you go. It is growing late, after all. I shall give you a hint. In the wee hours, it is I who wakes you."

The shadows of the man-high stones around us had grown longer during our brief exchange. In the stories, men were always losing hours and days to fairy magic.

"And if I do not guess your name?"

"Then you will be one of us."

Other glowing lights flickered between the stones, a thousand eyes watching, as though the stars had descended upon the fairy circle as jury to my trial.

"How do I know you will keep your word?"

Murmuring broke out all around me. The fairy scowled and held up her hands, shushing the crowd.

"A fairy's word is unbreakable."

I had no choice. I thought long and hard on her riddle. As you know, riddles are a hobby of mine, though they weren't then. At last, I thought I had it.

"I know your name. My mother told me what wakes men in their beds. You are called Wind."

She laughed her cruel laugh. "I am there when the windows rattle. I am there when the weathervane creaks. But I am not the wind."

She drew her pointed finger through the air, and a single digit, like fire, appeared. Sweat broke out on my brow as I contemplated existence with the fairies.

"I know your name. My mother told me what wakes men in their bunks. You are called Storm."

She held her belly as she cackled. "I am there when the waves crash upon the deck. I am there when the crops are flattened. But I am not the storm."

Once more, she drew her finger through the air. Her smile was vicious and victorious, and her gaze dropped to the basket of apple pie in my hands—only for a moment, but long enough. I saw the answer in her eyes.

"I know your name," I crowed. "My mother told me what wakes infants in their cradles and boys in their beds. You are called Hunger. I know you, Fairy, and you have no hold on me."

Her brows drew down, shading her terrible eyes. Her slender hands became fists. I knew I had guessed true.

I thrust the basket of pie at her. "Take it, if you must. I am leaving."

She forestalled me, snatching the basket from my fingers and holding tight to my wrist.

"You will never be free of me, boy. You will know me, always, when I make thieves of men. You will know me when I make your burbling, gurgling belly rip you from sleep. You will know me when your pockets are empty and your oven is cold. You will never know anything but me."

At this, she grew large and monstrous. Her beautiful antlers became horns. Her skin grew burnt and peeling like char, and her laugh reeked of decay. I tore from her grasp, turned on my heel, and ran out of the circle, over the rocks, and somehow back to the lane. It was night. I did not stop running until I reached my home, where a single candle burned, lighting up the kitchen window.

My mother leapt to her feet when I entered the house. "My son, where have you been?" she cried. "Why is your hair white?"

But she knew I had been touched by fairies. No amount of washing would return the colour to my hair. No amount of soothing would let me sleep at night.

Months passed, then years. I grew up, and as the fairy foretold, I lacked two pennies to rub together and had no food to fill my belly. But I worked till my hands bled. And as you know, I am a cunning man, and I became rich. But it was not enough. I got older, and I worked till my bones broke. I became richer. And, as you know, I work still, for it is never enough. You see, the fairy was right about me: I hungered, and I hunger still.

The present crept in like a shadow across the floor.

My father took a long draw from his glass, then he set it aside and rose from his chair. The past that swirled around him like a flurry of salt air dissipated, and I saw he was old and tired. Without speaking, he passed his palm over my brow before going to bed.

I was still awake at dawn when he rose to go to work tirelessly. It was the last time I heard his footsteps in the hall; my father never returned.

Now, you might think that I outgrew fairy stories, that my father simply left, or that his white hair was the product of some youthful folly, but I know better. I was there the day he told me of the fairy's curse. I saw the circle of stones in the grey depths of his eyes. And that is why I leave this story to you. I am off to seek a stony path and the answer to a riddle. You see I, too, have hungered.

And I hunger still.

Hannah Costelle

The Dressmaker of Drumchapel

AN EXCERPT

The bell atop the door to Hilda's dress shop rang.

"One moment!" Hilda called through a mouthful of pins.

She added two more pins to the gown she was hemming and picked her way over the bolts of fabric and piles of ribbons littering the floor. She smoothed her frizzy flyaways and straightened her apron before pulling open the curtain separating her workroom from the small, cluttered shop.

"How can I—?" Hilda stopped and stared at the apparition in the doorway.

Her visitor wore one of the finest dresses Hilda had ever created. It glistened like the sun setting on an ocean, with jewels cascading down the bodice to an enormous silken skirt. She had designed it to change colour in different lights, starting out pink and yellow in the early evening and then shifting to deep red and violet as the night wore on. The girl who commissioned it had her final fitting yesterday, and Hilda remembered watching her skip down the cobbled streets of Drumchapel with the wrapped dress tucked under her arm. Hilda had concentrated very hard at that moment, entreating any extra magic that might be lying around to follow this girl to the ball and give her a night she would never forget.

From the looks of it, the magic had listened.

The girl standing in her doorway, wearing that glorious dress that

223

glistened in the early morning sun, had the head of a chicken.

"Oh dear," Hilda said.

"Ms. Hilda …" the chicken said with the voice of a human girl. Hilda couldn't read its expression any better than that of a regular chicken, but the voice sounded mournful, and the human hands at its sides shook in evident distress. "Ms. Hilda, I seem … I seem to be not altogether well."

"Yes, I think we can safely say that," Hilda said, still staring dumbfounded at the girl and wracking her brains for an explanation of what could have gone so wrong. "What—what happened, child? Didn't you listen to what I told you? Didn't I remind you several times to have it off by midnight?"

"You did," the chicken said. "But see, things got a little confused in all the excitement of the ball. All the wonderful things to eat, all the dancing … Nobody was looking at their timepieces, and the wine and the candlelight made everything all fuzzy …"

"But that's what your friends are for, child! Lots of girls have to leave balls before midnight so their enchanted garments don't do anything fishy. It should have been a mass exodus from the ballroom. Weren't you watching for the carriages?"

"But I was having such a good time! And everybody was noticing me for once and coming up to talk to me and ask to be my dance partner. Then all of a sudden they were all looking at me kind of funny and backing away. It took me a minute to find a looking glass, and then I saw …"

"A chicken?"

The chicken shook its head. "A hippopotamus. It did seem a little harder to see out of my peripherals, but I thought that was because of the wine."

Hilda gasped. "How many transformations have you gone through?"

"Well, I was the hippopotamus for at least as long as it took me to run out of the ballroom and down the street, then all of a sudden things felt very high and I hit my head against every shop sign—I saw in the windows then that I was a giraffe. I hid in an alley when people started pointing at me. Luckily when an urchin found me and tried to take the jewels off my dress, I changed into some sort of bear, I think. I was too ashamed to go home, so I stayed in the alley. I was a lizard for a while. And I dozed off at some point, so who knows what I was during the night. But by the time I woke up, the sun was rising and I was a chicken, so I came straight here. Oh, please, Ms. Hilda, tell me what to do!"

"Surely you must have already tried the obvious solution?"

"I couldn't, I just couldn't! Not out in the street like that!"

Hilda sighed. "Then we'll start with that."

She pulled with all her strength to loosen the dress's stays, but the ribbons wouldn't budge. She tried slipping the girl out through the top or the bottom, but it was as if she had been sewn into the thing. Finally, in desperation, Hilda grabbed her shears and, even though it grieved her to destroy something so beautiful, tried to slice the dress down the middle. But the fabric refused to be cut.

Hilda was sweating and panting, crouched under the enormous skirt in hopes of finding a loose thread she could pull, when the girl's voice came again, sounding suddenly faint and shallow. "Um, Ms. Hilda?"

Hilda poked her head back out from under the dress and looked up to see that the chicken head had been replaced with the top half of a trout. It must have been terribly uncomfortable, having eyes where your ears should be and a round, gasping mouth at the top of your head.

"Goodness, child, can you breathe?"

"Um, I don't think so, Ms. Hilda," the trout gasped.

Hilda grabbed the girl's hand and hurried her over to the bucket she had brought in for the washing. She dunked the gasping trout head into the water and held it there, the girl's arms flailing around by instinct. Hilda kept holding her under, taking the opportunity to cool her own sweaty cheeks with the back of her hand and rest an elbow on the girl's back. A pair of women passing by the shop window looked horrified to see the proprietor holding a struggling girl's head underwater, but Hilda just smiled and waved as though in the middle of an everyday fitting.

The women hurried off, muttering that you never should get involved with mages, even if they did only make dresses.

After a few minutes Hilda wondered if she should let the girl up, but before she could get a chance, the bucket burst into a hundred splinters and an elephant's head grew from where the trout had been. The girl was propelled by the force of the transformation down to the floor, where she sat in her stunning dress, covered in water and wood shards.

"Oh, what am I going to do?" the elephant wailed.

Hilda was backing up to give the enormous grey head a wide enough berth in the little shop. She leaned against the counter and sighed, wiping her dripping face with her apron, which was just as soaked from the explosion of water as everything else.

"There's only one thing to do," she said. "I'll have to pull the magic out one thread at a time."

"Wha—what does that mean?" the elephant asked. "Will the dress be okay?"

Hilda shook her head. "I'm sorry, child, but if the counterspell works, the dress will be destroyed."

"But—but I put all my savings into this dress! Even if I never wore it again, I—I—" The elephant head tried to look down at the dress covering its human body. The girl's hands clutched the fabric and swished the skirt so the gems sparkled in a dazzling rainbow. "I thought maybe I could just keep it, just to look at. It's the prettiest thing I ever owned."

"I'm sorry, but it's the only way." Hilda looked almost as sad as the elephant as she imagined what the counterspell would do to her beautiful creation. She wouldn't even be able to salvage the scraps for future use. "Just sit there and calm yourself a moment, and I'll get my things ready."

Hilda left the dejected elephant and hurried to the back room, where she pushed aside baskets of notions and thread to get to a trunk filled with candles, jars of smelly powder, and thick musty books. By the time she had gathered what she needed and returned to the shop, the elephant had morphed into a teary-eyed raccoon, still sitting on the floor and staring down at its dress as though trying to memorize every delicate fold.

"Have you ever pulled the magic out of anything before?" the raccoon asked, not even looking up as Hilda started placing candles on the floor in a circle around it.

"I studied the theory of it during my schooldays," Hilda said as she consulted one of her books and started pouring orange powder onto the floor in intricate designs. "But honestly, in twenty years of making magical garments, the need has never come up before. People either obey the rules of the spell and get the result they wanted, or they don't obey the rules and the magic abandons them. This dress was obviously very special—what you wanted it to do was pretty intricate work. So the sheer power of the magic woven into the fabric must be having a bad reaction outside the prescribed time frame. Pulling out the magic is going to be … complicated."

Hilda flipped through the spellbook to cross-reference images of the enchanted circle. Complicated was an understatement.

Diane Dubas

Enough

Jack heard Jill's words on repeat, over and over: "You were never enough."

She'd pleaded with her summer-sky eyes, willing him to understand. And he did. He'd known their breakup was inevitable. Jill was smart and beautiful and popular, the girl all the boys wanted. The last girl who should have wanted Jack. Maybe she never had. Maybe her going out with him had been as much a dare as his asking her out. Still, he hadn't expected the casual callousness of her words to destroy him so completely.

Jack stood at the edge of the Wood. He teetered forward with one clumsy step, courage coming in the form of a frigid gust of wind.

He was going into the Wood. Argyle Hills Wood, officially, but everyone called it the Haunted Wood. And no one was brave enough to go in. With bruises on his heart and nothing left to lose, Jack felt brave. His resolve settled like storm clouds on the horizon, heavy and overbearing. He wanted to have a story to come back to school with—one that would overshadow the fact that Jill had dumped him. He wanted to be the knight who braved all danger and lived to tell the tale. He wanted to be *enough*.

Jack narrowed his eyes at the endless darkness weaving between the trees of the Wood. This was a bad idea and he should probably just go home. Watch TV, do his homework, stare at his phone incessantly in case Jill changed her mind.

A gust of wind sent the leaves rustling and a shiver down Jack's spine. She wasn't going to change her mind.

Jack, the leaves seemed to whisper.

With the sound of his blood pounding in his ears, he took a step toward the Wood. And another. And then one more. Outside of the Wood, the grass and leaves were brown and dying in the late autumn chill, but Jack was surprised by how thick and green the foliage was inside the treeline. It was quieter than he had imagined. There was no birdsong, no rustling of foraging animals. The air smelled thickly of earth and decay and something else, like the scent of a lightning strike during a summer storm.

Jack rode on his resolve and kept walking. Each step was easier than the last. He laughed, the sound bouncing off the trees and echoing into the gloom. Here he was, marching through the Haunted Wood alone.

Jack, the trees whispered again.

Jack bristled. This time he was pretty certain the trees had actually said his name. He spun around, his heart pounding with painful insistence.

"Who's there?" he asked, his voice quavering and alone in the shadows.

He wasn't sure from which way he'd come, all traces of his footsteps lost to the damp moss and thick undergrowth of the Wood. Fear bit at him, his stomach twisting as his panic rose.

That's when he saw her, peeking out from behind a tree. A girl, pale green and glistening, with hair like moonlight and a gown of shimmering vines. She looked about his age and fragile as a fairy-tale princess. Her lips moved and the leaves spoke his name again. Afraid, but also compelled, Jack faltered toward her. She smiled widely, sending a cold thrill of unease down Jack's spine, and ran between the trees.

"Hey! Wait!" Jack ran after her, the green girl who was undoubtedly not what she seemed.

Or maybe she was exactly what she seemed.

The girl led him down a twisting path through silver saplings and thick brush. Jack was quicker than he'd ever been in gym class, dodging fallen trees and foliage that seemed to reach out at him. He lost sight of the girl, but he could hear her laughing, like it was all a game.

Catch me if you can, Jack, she seemed to say every time she peeked out from behind a tree, shining pale hair as diaphanous as spider's silk.

She reminded him of Jill when they were younger and he was hopelessly in love with her. Jill had been his princess in the tower (except it was more likely that he was the one who needed rescuing from the top of the monkey bars). She'd always been the fair maid whose hand he'd wanted to win (even when she was the knight and he was wheezing under a tree with his inhaler). Jack and Jill. They were the nursery rhyme in action, Jack breaking his crown and Jill tumbling after. Only Jack was falling now without her.

Jack's breaths came in tight wheezes as he stood in the middle of the woods, looking for the green girl. He pulled his inhaler out and took a puff to ease his tightening lungs. The sun had set, and the shadowy trees now seemed less a challenge and more a threat. He should go back. He knew as well as anyone how perilous the Haunted Wood could be, how forbidden. All his life he'd heard the stories about kids chasing phantoms in the Wood and never coming back. But faeries weren't real, and those were just stories meant to frighten and control.

Jack.

The sound of gently moving water filtered through the leaves, riding on the echo of his name. Afraid and alone, Jack followed it, tripping and sliding down a gravelly slope to the rocky shore of a lake that wasn't on any map he'd ever seen. The girl was there, half-submerged in the water, combing her fingers through her long hair. Her eyes seemed like distant stars in the night sky, and somehow she looked like a washed-out, moon-kissed Jill. When she smiled at him, it was almost like Jill was his again, seeing him and wanting him against all odds. She held out her arms, beckoning him to her.

Jack knelt at the edge of the lake, icy water sinking and spreading into the fabric of his jeans. Rocks bit into his knees as his inhaler dropped from his fingers, slipping into the depths of the lake that shouldn't be there. He was lost in her starlit eyes and willing to do whatever she asked of him.

Be the knight.

Slay the dragon.

Save the day.

She reached a hand toward him and rested it on his cheek. Somewhere in the back of his mind, Jack knew she shouldn't be so cold, like a fish. Like a dead girl.

His eyes slid shut as the green girl reached up with her other hand and pulled him into a kiss that reminded him of swimming in the lake at the end of summer, the water too cold to be comfortable, his teeth chattering and lips blue. A bitter chill spread through his body, reaching down into his core and stealing all his heat. He couldn't breathe, and he groped for his inhaler, only to find his pocket full of water and nothing else.

Jack opened his eyes to murky water clouding his vision. The green girl broke their kiss but held him close. Jack struggled fruitlessly against her grasp. She didn't look like Jill now. She had a smile like a shark's and seaweed in her hair. The girl held him in place underwater, her grip stronger than her frail body suggested, and Jack twisted and fought, his mouth bursting open, a rush of dirty water filling his lungs where only air should be. Black spots danced before his eyes, and Jack knew he wasn't going back to school with a story. He wasn't the knight who saved the day; there were no dragons to slay, not in the Haunted Wood.

He stopped fighting against the green girl's grip, and through the murk and grime of this dirty lake in the Haunted Wood, he saw her dreadful smile. Her voice was little more than a chime, but Jack still recognized the words. After all, it was everything he'd wanted to hear, and when he closed his eyes for the last time, he pretended it was Jill saying it.

"You are enough."

Clare McNamee-Annett
We Are Doing Fine

Henry lay on his back on Spanish Banks, looking at the sky. Fat, self-satisfied clouds drifted past. Wind blustered in from the ocean beyond, and the birch tree on the outcrop of grass above the sand bristled. Henry took a breath and did his best to feel nothing.

It was best to feel nothing, Henry believed.

Two crows plummeted out of the birch tree's branches, half-flying, half-falling. They screamed at each other, tore at mottled backs with claws. Feathers flew. Blood matted wings. Seagulls kept their distance and onlookers gasped.

Henry watched the crows, unsurprised. *Violence is the way of the world.* To Henry, the crows were a single monster made of feathers, beaks, and claws. It was mutual. They were both locked in. He imagined they could be free: it would only take one bird to disengage, untangle … let baggage fall, release unnecessary cargo … take stock of injury … fly past.

A moment later, the crows disappeared.

Henry scowled.

There was a ripple in the sky. A crinkle in the air. A fold of nothing, into nothing. An overlay of sky.

Henry stood up. He stalked to the grassy outcrop. He jumped, grabbed a branch, and pulled himself up the birch tree to investigate. His jeans felt tight against his knees. Passersby looked up to watch him, but it was May 1976, and it was not yet time for dinner: what could these well-coiffed urbanites say to a preteen hippie scaling a tree?

Henry shimmied up a branch and examined the air where the crows had disappeared. *The matter-hole,* he named it. *The void.* It stood a foot and a half out from the birch tree, at its middle. Judging by the way his

232

sweater disappeared when he swung it, the hole spanned the length of his arm. But Henry couldn't be sure. It kept changing. Looking at it was like trying to look into your coffee cup to see the reflection of the sky. There were ripples and undulations in all the wrong places. Henry squinted at the precise location. Lost it again. He chucked a branch into the matter-hole. He watched it get swallowed up and wink out.

Henry smiled.

It wasn't because his father drank whiskey straight and couldn't keep down a job. It wasn't because his brother beat him at chess, then looked disappointed when he flipped the board.

As he climbed down the birch and began his long walk home, Henry catalogued Matter-Hole Possibilities.

It was matter folded over on itself, like an invisible pouch. A pocket in space-time. Anything that fell in remained forever. Therein lay animal bones, British rifles, ancient Egyptian teeth.

It was a wormhole to an alternate dimension. The crows were now fighting on a technicolor aquatic exo-planet with six moons circling a binary star.

It was a time-worm. Like a wormhole, but instead of puncturing folded space, it jutted through time. Always forward, never back. He would jump through it and be transported to the year 2176. The sea would be swollen around him, filled with trash, various parts of it on fire. The sky would be purple, toxic. His lungs would scorch as he breathed.

It was a time portal. Like Billy Pilgrim in *Slaughterhouse-Five*, he would become unstuck in time, doomed to re-experience the events of his past and future without linearity or predictable delineation.

It wasn't because his brother beat him at Risk, Monopoly, backgammon, and cribbage and outmanoeuvred him in philosophical debates over mashed potatoes. It wasn't because his mother fretted anytime he left the house.

⁊

These are the things Henry threw into the matter-hole:

A black rook, a black queen, and both white bishops from the family chess set.

His dog Toto's half-eaten rawhide: a pulverized strip of pale cow skin, hard as plastic.

Maggie Lewis, his sister's sixth-best-loved doll.

The 1971 stonewashed Levi's that his brother had refused to throw away, that his father had lit aflame with a Zippo lighter, and that his brother had salvaged from the dumpster, added fabric to, resewn, and worn anyway.

His mother's favourite coat: rich brown leather, a fashionable cut, lined with real fur.

⁊

It wasn't because his mother listened to Puccini, sang arias when she thought she was alone. It wasn't because his sister was good at math, got a bicycle when she was six years old.

⁊

When Henry got home, his father was screaming at his mother. His brother stood between the two, arms outstretched like an aircraft marshaller. As Henry shut the front door, his father hurled a pitcher of water, but his mother and brother ducked, just in time, and the glass pitcher shattered on the kitchen floor.

His mother shrieked. She ran to his sister's bedroom. His brother stood tall as his father shouted abuse. *Good-for-nothing. Layabout. Pompous cock. Mother's boy, shit stain of a son.*

Henry walked up the stairs to his room.

He lay on his bed, pulled a pillow over his head, and kept his bedroom door open. Minutes passed. Then Henry heard his eight-year-old sister emerge, as bidden, to placate their father. To tell him things were okay. To make him a cup of tea.

Henry threw his pillow against the wall. He slammed his bedroom door. Henry wanted to say to his sister, *Stop doing what you're told.* Henry wanted to say to his mother, *Just pack up and leave him, dumbass. Who cares what people think? Just run. Get away from him. Save yourself.*

Please, Mom.

But it was easier to pretend he didn't give two shits about it. He grabbed *Wandl the Invader* off his bookshelf. He started to read.

◦

It wasn't because his sister cried some nights. It wasn't because Toto died in November, of a lumbar tumor they couldn't afford to have removed.

◦

"Hey. It's Henry," he said, standing in his sister's doorway. "I heard you crying."

"What do you care?" She hunched into herself. She was a hard lump of blanket, now. "You're just going to laugh at me and steal my Jenny Bishop doll! You're just going to hide in the hallway closet and jump out at me again! You don't care at all."

Henry took a breath. The matter-hole was out there. "Yes, I do. Want to talk about it?"

His sister sniffed. She wiped mucus onto her pink bedspread. "It's nothing. I just ... I hate the fighting."

"You shouldn't have to step in, Dorrie. It's not your problem, okay? It's their problem."

"It's all of our problem, Henry. I'm the *only* person who can make Dad calm down. He loves *me* best. So I have to do it. I'm the only one who can."

"Yeah." His whole life, Henry had wanted his father to love *him* best, with gut-wrenching desperation. He quoted his adult jokes, styled his hair the same way, laughed when he said *this grub would cost two-ninety-eight at the Ovaltine.* But hearing his sister, burdened, shouldering unjust responsibility with the stoicism of his most stalwart heroes, Henry felt a strange sense of relief. "I just think it hurts you, Dorrie. Having to step in all the time."

"It's not so bad. He calms down when I talk to him."

"I know, but I ... I hope you can find a way to say no to this shit one day."

"You just hate Mum and Dad. You're just trying to get back at them."

"I'm not, Dorothy! I care about you."

His sister was silent. He couldn't be sure if she had heard. He closed her bedroom door and returned to his room.

☙

It wasn't because his father had taken Henry's life savings from the shoebox beneath Henry's twin bed and hadn't been seen since last Wednesday.

There wasn't a specific reason why Henry sat on the birch branch on June 14, 1976. If you had asked him about it, he would have just said he was tired.

He imagined yelling "Geronimo!" as he leapt—a fiery exit with reckless abandon, high machismo, boyhood arrogance. He would yell, he would be the nihilistic hero. His father would love that. His father played the hero. John Wayne, Frank Sinatra, Marlon Brando. Looking at the sea beyond, Henry felt he didn't have the heart to.

He reached out his left hand and it disappeared. It didn't even tingle. *Good. So the void can hold me, too. I'm not so damaged yet that I don't fit inside it.* But maybe that was the point of a void. Maybe the matter-hole held everything, every part of you, no matter what shape you were in when you entered it.

Henry took a breath and jumped.

Libby McKeever

What Came Before

AN EXCERPT

Natasha buried her head under the pillow as the insistent buzz of her dad's cell phone bleated through the wall. She let out a groan, knowing what was coming. Sure enough, encouraged by signs of life, a large nondescript dog bounded onto Nat's back. A head nosed under her pillow, followed by a wet tongue.

"Arrgh! Flynn, get off me." Nat pushed the lump of curly fur off the side of the bed. "Pee-yew, you reek." Unruffled by the rejection, Flynn looked up with adoration.

"Nat, you awake?" Her dad's voice came through the door.

"Am now," she grumbled, then, raising her voice, "Yes, Dad, I'm up."

"Oh good, 'cause the fire ban's been lifted and we've got the go-ahead to begin the demolition on the old Johnson place." His voice got quieter as he walked further away from her door. "Come on downstairs," he called, and then louder, "I need to talk to you before I go."

Nat lay back and stretched, her fingers intertwining through the leafy design of her wrought-iron headboard. A chattering noise made her turn toward the window. Early-morning sun streamed through the branches of the Douglas fir, the yellow light turning green as it took on the evergreen's hues. A well-fed grey squirrel, pinecone in its paws, was frozen mid-bite, stilled by Flynn, who, growling low, rested his slobbery chin on the window frame.

"Leave it, Flynn," Nat said sharply, and the moment was broken. A furled tail flicked a farewell. Flynn looked at Nat, his head cocked, looking miffed.

"Don't look at me like that, you goof. You know the rules. No eating the neighbours." She leaned out of bed and rubbed Flynn's soft ears, inspiring another line of drool to spill from his mouth. His silly grin allowed a view of impressive teeth, but his mass of tawny fluff made him look more like a teddy bear than a predator. The squirrel might have another opinion, Nat thought with a smile

"Natasha, now!" Though separated by a floor, her dad's yell filtered up the stairs and through her door. Nat hauled herself out from under the covers and gave her first road rash of the season a cursory glance. It could've been worse. The bike park was notorious for injuries. Her shirt and shorts were conveniently waiting on the woven rug at her feet, where she'd dropped them the night before. She pulled them on and smoothed the wrinkles from the less-than-clean WORCA t-shirt. Unlike some other girls her age, turning fourteen hadn't changed the way she dressed. Comfy clothing was Nat's go-to, and as it was now downhill bike season, this usually meant being covered with gladiator-style body armour.

Three summers ago, Nat joined Whistler's off-road cycling association, or WORCA as it was known. Last year her skills had really improved, so she'd decided to brave the bike park. This year the snow had melted early, and she'd hardly been off her bike. Nat stretched out a few kinks in her back, and after scooping her long brown hair into a quick ponytail, grabbed her phone and hop-stepped around Flynn in a race to the door.

In the darkened hallway, as was her custom each morning, Nat paused to trace her finger along the bottom edge of her mother's framed photo. The dark-haired young woman, arms full of wildflowers, smiled back at her.

The chore list from her dad in hand, Nat thumbed her phone awake.

Jean Pierre picked up on the first ring. "Hey Nat, what's up?"

"Hi JP. They're going to blow the house today. You want to come?"

"Yeah, you bet! I'll meet you there in about half an hour."

"Great," Nat replied, then she remembered. "Hey, I might be a bit late. Dad just gave me a whole bunch of stuff to do. I haven't been home much and I think he's regretting giving me the downhill pass for my birthday."

"Ya think?" JP laughed. "Just 'cause you're on the hill from open to close. Every day."

Nat laughed. "See you." She was excited too.

Although they both loved Whistler summers, nothing much happened. Today they had a chance to watch her dad's crew rip apart a house, maybe even use some dynamite. Nat raced through her chores. The last one was walking Flynn. Well, really, he walked her.

"Sheesh, Flynn," she called. "Must you smell every bush, ditch, and tree?" Flynn was on a coyote mission, and by the time they got back to their modest house at the top of the Alta Vista hill, Nat had to grab her bike and go. It had rained last night, and when the seat leather got wet it stank, which was why she lovingly called her bike Stinky.

⌒

JP jittered with excitement. "It's going to be loud and it's going to be awesome!"

"I know, hey?" Nat said, smiling at her friend. "So cool."

The iron wrecking ball swung back, froze at the top of its arc, and then fell. *Smash!* Chunks of greyed wood were torn from the sagging belly of the old homestead.

"Whoa! Did you see that? It took out the whole side of the house!" JP whooped and double fisted the air.

Dry and brittle from the cycle of 100 summers, the hand-hewn boards splintered and broke under the assault. The wood siding leaned as if to get away from the relentless path of the ball. *Crash!* As the single-paned glass exploded, the sun sprayed multicoloured light.

"Wowzah," JP breathed, the word long and slow. "It's like the New Year's fireworks over Alta Lake."

Nat saw her dad on the other side of the house. His posture mirrored hers: hands cupped around sunglasses, a shield from the May-bright sun. The tired house seemed to sway on its feet. Steady for a moment, and then with a loud *whump*, it collapsed amidst clouds of choking dust.

JP yanked his Canucks ball cap down over his eyes. Coughing, he turned to Natasha. "Amazing, hey?" He hawked and spat. "Yuck, that's really old dust."

They stood watching the scene, and as the sun heated up the day, rain puddles breathed fog into the air and mingled with the blue diesel smoke. Nat was transfixed, but inside she was churning. She wasn't sure what was wrong. Her whole body felt as though she was the one impacted by the giant iron ball. Her guts heaved and she thought for a moment she was going to throw up. Then abruptly, not quite knowing why or what she was doing, Nat dashed past JP and dove in through a hole in the one chunk of wall left standing. She disappeared amidst the debris cloud.

"Get out of there, Natasha!" she heard her dad yell. "What do you think you're doing?"

What *am* I doing? Her voice screamed in her head, the same pitch as the whine of the giant excavator, jaws hungry, now bearing down on her as she made her escape. Her fist was closed tight on the object. Her face pale beneath her early summer tan, brown eyes wide, she staggered from the wreckage. She stumbled and tripped over the rocks rimming a long-ago forgotten garden and fell hard on all fours. Scrambling up, she ignored the blood trickling from the fresh gash on her knee and faced her dad.

"What were you thinking?" her dad shouted. "Now get back and stay well away. You too, JP. This is not a playground, you guys."

Nat stared at her father. His green eyes were bright under a mop of sandy hair. He met her fierce glare, his face a mixture of worry and irritation. Nat felt hot tears swell in her eyes, and in an unexpected rush of rage, she yelled, "Why did you have to disturb them?" She turned and ran for her bike.

"What? Disturb who? What's she going on about, JP?" Nat heard her father bellow over the commotion. She hauled up her bike and, wobbling, struggled down the muddy driveway to the road.

As she reached the pavement, she heard JP shout, "Hey Nat, what's up? You look like you've seen a ghost."

She stood up on her pedals and powered up the hill, eager to get away, the weight of her secret heavy in her back pocket.

Katherine Fawcett

Ursula Medium

CHAPTER ONE

On the way to her first bear, Ursula rounds a blind corner and slams on the brakes.

She comes close but doesn't hit the cedar tree, freshly fallen, that barricades the narrow, rutted road. Doesn't hit the clutch either, and the stolen Jeep lurches, stalls, and stops dead. It's not the first time she's stalled in the past 45 minutes of driving, but it doesn't matter. Not like there's any traffic on this overgrown back-country horse trail of a road. Not like there're any cops around either. But still, her nerves are raw. Her hands are still glued to 11:00 and 1:00, her jaw is clenched tight and her T-shirt soaked in sweat. Maybe she'd be more relaxed if she actually had a driver's licence.

She's run over a number of things along the way—a camping tarp, the lid from a blue plastic storage box, a handwritten No Trespassing sign, a broken ski pole—things she hadn't noticed when she was in the passenger seat, staring out the side window when Jordon drove this route. Now she's aware of everything. Pretty sure she hasn't blinked since turning off the highway, she shuts her burning eyes for just a moment while her heart settles. When she opens them, the tree is still there.

And what exactly did you expect? A magic solution?

She hops out to inspect. Mosquitoes descend on her like a hockey team at a buffet. A quick re-spray of Muskol slows them down a little.

The barricade isn't a monster tree trunk like one of those ancient cedars near the B.C. coast, but it's definitely taller and heftier than your average Christmas tree. There is no way the Jeep's getting over it, and the road's far too narrow to chuck a u-turn

Do not make me reverse out of here.

She tries to position herself to lift it, but the fucker is as heavy as a piano and just as awkward. She can't get a firm grip. Branches scratch her forearms and a bough pokes her in the neck.

You can't do it. You're too weak.

She rearranges herself, braces against the Jeep, puts both hiking boots against tree bark, and pushes. Her legs are strong and powerful from years of rugby practice, squats in the gym. But they aren't strong enough. Three hawks silently circle overhead. They're either cheering her on or waiting for her to fail. The tree creaks a bit but doesn't move.

Hands on her hips, Ursula looks around the forest, as if there might be a bulldozer, a crew of road workers, or maybe a wrestling team just hanging out, waiting to be beckoned. "Look for the helpers," her grandmother used to quote. "Always look for the helpers."

Well, a chainsaw would help.

If she had her Husqvarna, she'd make easy business of the tree. She'd rev it up and hack that cedar into three or four sections and be on her way in less than ten minutes. She can almost hear the roar. Almost smell the warm spice of cedar sawdust. Ten minutes more and maybe she'd get crafty. Cut a few chairs and an end table. Give IKEA a little competition. She'd competed in Squamish Logger Days the summer before, and handily won her category in the Chainsaw Chair competition.

But all there is in the back of the Jeep is a bin of frozen ground chicken that has probably tipped over and is starting to thaw.

No chainsaw.

Not even an axe.

A Swiss Army knife in her supply bag and a pair of her brother's nail clippers in the cup holder, but that's about it.

She could ram it. Start the engine up and slam right into it. Snap that sucker and burst through, even if it took two or three tries. The Jeep's so banged up already it wouldn't make a big difference. And besides, who cares? It's almost the end of summer. The contract's almost done.

Her brother would do it. Jordon wouldn't think twice. In fact, he'd reverse two or three truck lengths, get up some speed, let out a "Yee-Haw" and take the tree out smash-up-derby style. Plow right through it. Full send. Pine cones, branches, and birds' nests everywhere. Grille, bumper dented all to hell. Paint job, schmaint job.

But Ursula is more considerate. She knows that ramming the tree would be risky. What if one of the branches punctured a tire? What if she hit her head on the steering wheel on impact? What about whiplash?

She decides to compromise, to simply edge the front bumper and grille up against the tree and slowly but steadily push it away, clear the road, and keep driving. No problem.

She turns to get back in the Jeep, then hears it.

Shallow panting.

Huffing.

A dry, high-pitched hiss.

It's coming from the low end of the fallen tree. There's something under the trunk, on the ground. A creature of some kind. She is more curious than scared, but she still moves slowly, not knowing what to expect.

She crouches down on her hands and knees. Two dark hooves. Thin legs, velvety smooth. They are barely visible amid the branches, boughs, and hanging moss. It must be a deer. Half a deer, anyhow. She peers over the tree trunk, and there's the upper half on the other side.

It's trapped. Maybe crushed, though there is no blood.

Who knows how long it's been there, unable to move? One shiny black eye gazes up at her like a soft, dark crystal ball, warning her and pleading with her at the same time. There's a slight up and down pulsing at the deer's throat, telling her it's alive. Saliva is caked around the edges of the animal's mouth; a tongue hangs out like a slice of ham. The hawks swoop lower. The deer blinks once. Ursula understands: Help me.

She can't push the Jeep against the tree without crushing the deer. Her only choice is to lift it.

You tried that. You're not strong enough. You'll fail again and the deer will die.

She reaches both arms into the branches and moss and under the tree trunk again. It feels impossible, but it can't be impossible, so she squats down like a bodybuilder preparing for an Olympic medal round deadlift.

You can't—

No. *Shut up. I can.*

Her leg muscles burn. Her back is at the wrong angle. She grimaces like she's blowing up a balloon that her very existence depends on, but she can't quite get the air to stretch the stiff latex. Nothing budges.

See?

Stop it!

The deer makes a noise. It's part bleat, part bark, part wail. And suddenly, with a burst of power that seems not to come from her muscles but maybe from her heart, or someplace even deeper, the tree moves. The balloon inflates. She stands up straight and brings the tree up with her. Not very high, but high enough to give the deer space to move. It scrambles out and up and onto its feet, wobbles, then trips, then wobbles again and bounds into the woods. It doesn't look back. Ursula takes a few Frankenstein steps forward. The trunk cracks where it's still attached. A few more steps, and she lets go. It crashes to the earth at the side of the road.

She puts her hands against her lower back and takes a deep breath. There's no sign of the deer in the dense woods. It's long gone. Or maybe it collapsed somewhere on the forest floor. In any case, it's free.

Her overalls are decked with greenery. She roughly brushes the bits off, gets back in the Jeep, and turns on the CD player. Corb Lund provides the soundtrack for the movie *Ursula Jones: Forest Superhero.*

Superhero? It wasn't that big of a tree. Also, look how much you're sweating. Your muscles are going to be sore tomorrow. You might have thrown your back out. Maybe that downed tree was a sign that you shouldn't be doing this. You shouldn't be here! You don't know what you're doing!

She makes a mental note to pick up some deodorant when she goes into town later and ignores the rest of the yapping in her head.

It's only another kilometre or so until she reaches the first stop on her rounds as a wildlife biologist. And there, if she's lucky, in the baited trap she and Jordon set yesterday, Ursula will find her first bear.

Sky Regina
We Are Apricots
AN EXCERPT

Last night I got fingered on a musty brown chesterfield in the water-damaged basement of a boy I don't even like. Not quite the romantic setting I'd always pictured for my first ever finger-bang, but I guess my expectations were too high.

It was nothing like that scene from *Fear* where Reese Witherspoon puts Mark Wahlberg's hand under her skirt on the roller coaster. Her face goes all slack and serene like she's floating in a pleasure dream, like she'd never felt better in all her squishy, wet days. And he stares at her with raw passion, as though his hand's only purpose is to pleasure her on this roller coaster.

My experience was tragically sallow by comparison. There was zero attempt at romance by the seventeen-year-old who poked me in the vagina with his Dorito-encrusted fingers, unless you count throwing on a film about the career arc of a '70s porn actor, coincidentally played by a well-endowed Mr. Wahlberg.

Why did I allow Damon "Litty" Littleton's unwashed paws to desecrate my lady parts? My mom taught me early on to retrace my steps whenever I'm looking for something (my sanity, in this case). So, that's what I'll do.

The conversation that catalyzed my very first (lamentable) dalliance with under-the-pants action went as follows:

Phone rings. "Hello?" my mom says.

"Uh, yeah," nervous, or just idiotic, boy likely chuckles, in similar cadence to that of Butthead, à la *Beavis and Butthead*, "is Lo home?"

"Of course she is! She basically never leaves the house, unless you count the regular full-body waxing appointments she requires on a monthly basis since sprouting thick Italian lady-hair at the age of twelve and a half!" (An assumptive paraphrase of my mom's response based on her tendency to overshare and humiliate me in an oblivious but good-intentioned way.)

Disclaimer: I do have a satisfying social life, just to be clear.

"Right on," Litty probably says as he tucks a piece of stringy hair behind his wax-filled ear.

Mom lets me know in her loud sing-song voice that a young gentleman is on the horn for me.

From my room, I pick up the translucent purple phone that displays all the complex inner doodads and wires and other mystery pieces that enable a phone to transmit human voices across immeasurable distances. I wait for the click that indicates my mom's exodus from the conversation.

"Hullo?" I say, not quite believing I'm speaking to an actual gentleman.

"Uh, yeeeaaah. Lo? Lo Manicci?" says the gentleman.

"Guilty," I say, trying very hard to be laissez-faire but inadvertently using a joke from my dad's limited repertoire.

"Rad. Uh, so yeah, I'm friends with Carissa Howard? From St. Trinity's?"

Context: St. Trinity's is the Catholic high school in town. I go to the public school in the middle of nowhere that's next to a dairy farm. The cows moo all damn day, serving as well-timed reminders to feel bad any time you eat a burger for lunch. I work with Carissa Howard at the remarkably named local grocery store/drug dealer hangout, The Food Spot.

"Oh, that's cool. Sorry, what's your name again?" I ask, wondering where this could be going.

Trademark Butthead chuckle. "Shit, my bad. This is Damon Littleton, you might know me as Litty?"

A hazy image of a lanky skater boy with shoulder-length brown hair and perpetually scabbed elbows, swimming in an oversized Bart Simpson T-shirt, pops into my mind.

"Yeah, I think I've seen you around." I twirl a curl around my middle finger. Unconsciously, of course.

"Uhh, well, Carissa gave me your number. I saw a picture of you in her locker and, like, I thought you were pretty hot. So, I thought, like, why not, ya know?"

My first thought is: Why does Carissa have a photo of me in her locker? We're merely colleagues who share an interest in vampire lore. She barely talks to me at work ... she barely talks to anyone. It's very alarming. And then the second thought follows close behind: A boy thinks I'm hot?

"That's funny. Boys usually find me tepid, at best." I laugh in a way I think is flirty but probably sounds demented.

A painful moment of silence. I slap my forehead.

"Uh ... yeah. Would you wanna come over and watch a movie sometime? We could have some, like, fun, maybe ...?"

Fun? My heart beats so hard behind my ginormous stretch-marked boobs that I worry he can hear it through the phone. This is a monumental moment. The only *fun* I've ever had was the time I made out with all six boys and the one other girl who attended Dillon Mason's end-of-summer party right before eighth grade started. We played spin the bottle on his giant trampoline for two hours. I got to sample all ten varieties of gummy candies, filtered through everyone's sweet saliva. I guess you could say things got pretty wild.

"I like movies" is all I can muster.

We talked for a few minutes about movies and set a date for the following evening at seven sharp.

I then lay in bed with wide, buggy eyes for a solid ten minutes, processing the conversation with my Inner Self, who happens to be pretty lame but also pragmatic—a decidedly helpful but annoying combination.

This processing was supported by my tendency to imagine my life as scenes from movies and music videos, or if you want to get sophisticated about it, "vignettes."

In this one, me and Inner Self are two summer camp friends (as in, friends who only see each other for the two weeks they spend at the summer camp they've been shipped off to for the past ten years, a scenario I'm not personally familiar with but have thought a lot about). I'm the libidinous boy-crazy one known for wearing the shortest shorts at camp (because my fantasy legs are endless and toned), and Inner Self is the sensible, never-kissed-a-boy one with a prominent face mole who's the only camper that makes it a point to shower every day. In essence, two very different but equally authentic versions of myself.

And ... *action!*

Two girls lie belly-down on colourful patterned towels, sunbathing on a dock by a glittery lake. They're surrounded by splashing sounds and the other expected euphonics of countless kids having the best day of their lives. The one with the great gams is blowing bubbles with limited-edition Blue Raspberry Hubba Bubba. The one with the mole is flipping through a tattered and smudged *Good Housekeeping* magazine from 1998, found in the lounge area of the camp's mess hall.

Lo: I can't believe he thinks I'm hot. What a bold move to just call me up all nonchalant and ask me out. This speaks very highly of his character.

Inner Self: *He does sound a lot like Butthead, though.*

Lo: Does that matter? He's a babe, who thinks *I'm* a babe. And he wants to have fun with *me*.

Inner Self: *But you know literally nothing about him, besides his affinity for Kevin Smith and that he's trying to be a sponsored skateboarder. What if he's creepy? What if he expects you to just give it up? Like, full sex?*

Lo: No, it'll be fine. It's fine. I'm a strong woman. I won't be afraid to put the kibosh on things if he tries to get too handsy.

Inner Self: *Oh shit! You're between waxing appointments. What about all your thick pubes?*

Lo: Haven't you ever heard of a razor? Women have been using them since the beginning of time—

Inner Self: *No they haven't.*

Lo: Whatever! I'll just shave. Easy solution.

Inner Self: *You know what happens when you shave: one express-train ticket to Ingrown Hair Central Station, sweetheart.*

Lo: Why must you exasperate me so? I want to bask in this feeling. You're being an overbearing mom about this.

Inner Self: *And you're being impulsive. He probably doesn't know the first thing about pleasuring a teenage woman.*

Lo: What teenage boy does? I barely know anything about pleasuring a teenage woman, and I am one!

Inner Self: *But, like, are you even attracted to this guy?*

Lo: HE THINKS I'M HOT.

Inner Self: *Ugh. Touché.*

Cut! End scene.

I really wish my parents had the money to send me to a well-equipped summer camp full of sexually explorative teens and food fights and games of widespread hide 'n' seek, but such is life. I also wish, maybe even more so, that this had been one of those times when I listened to the reasonable doubts of Inner Self. But we'll just have to chalk this up as another opportunity for her to smugly proclaim: *I told ya so.*

Tim J. O'Connor
Kath's Party

Mikey only half heard the voices behind him as he hurried up the front walk, too preoccupied with the anticipation of seeing her again. Arriving outside the front door, he paused to adjust his hair in the reflection of the glass.

He'd caught a ride with his roommates, Jen and Barry, who were slower leaving the car and following him up the walk. They were arguing again, something about Barry spending too much money and the recent Visa bill. Mikey shook his head a bit more, trying to get his curly bangs to fall naturally over his brown eyes.

Their host, Kath, opened the screen door, greeted Mikey briefly, and continued to hold the door open as the quarrelling couple made their way up the walk. "Hey, you guys, stop it. Tonight's a party. You can debate your finances tomorrow," said Kath. Mikey took that as his cue to step past her and rush up the short flight of stairs to the kitchen.

The party was in high gear, with food, drinks, and conversation flowing. He wouldn't be distracted, ignoring the aroma of those mini pepperoni sticks he loved so much. He knew most of the guests, greeting them with his broad, infectious smile. Grabbing a drink in the kitchen, he made the rounds, being friendly and polite but avoiding any sort of lengthy conversation with anyone. He had one objective: find Amy, and this time try not to be such a dork.

Eventually he spotted her across the living room and paused, planning his strategy. Oh, she was stunning, and his heart skipped a beat. Amy didn't notice him at first, focused on a debate between Jimmy and Sue on the couch. That asshole Jimmy, always trying to charm the ladies and keep their drinks topped up, hoping in a weak moment they might agree to go home with him.

Mikey sauntered across the room, trying to transmit confidence with his movements. *Be cool, man. Don't seem too eager.* His younger self had often made that mistake, scaring away the objects of his affection. Not this time. This time he was in control.

Amy sat on the floor, her legs tucked under her delicious backside. Her blond hair, thick and wavy, reminded him of the actors he saw on television, the ones who had teams of people working on their appearance. Heart rate increasing, he picked a spot on the floor, close but not too close. *Couch is full. Just looking for a place to park my butt*, said the relationship coach in his head.

Then she turned to look at him. And boy, did she look at him. Her eyes were smoky and inviting, her head tilting slightly so he could see the way her ear connected to her long, inviting neck. She wore a simple leather necklace that drew his eyes downward toward the rest of her shapely form. *Nope, stop, keep your eyes on her face. Don't make that mistake again*, yelled the inside voice.

Her scent was intoxicating, making him dizzy.

Their connection settled in, blocking out all the sights and sounds of the party, as if they were alone, the outside world melting away. Her hazel eyes made him want to move in and live there forever.

Without warning, she shifted forward, moving to stand, and by accident her shoulder brushed against his. He felt the heat of her body in that momentary contact. Wait, was that an accident? He stood too— what a gentleman did when a lady stood, right? He could never remember all that fancy protocol stuff.

Wordlessly, she started to move, and as she did, she rubbed against him again. *No accident this time*, he thought. She walked past him toward the hallway connecting the living room to the rest of the house, and for a moment he enjoyed the view. He couldn't decide what was sexier, the wavy hair tumbling down her back or her long athletic legs. Or could it be how all of it moved together as she glided across the room?

She paused, looking back over her shoulder toward him. He felt a little guilty, caught leering at her with his tongue out, but her look implied she didn't mind one bit. Then a tilt of her head and rise of her eyebrows sent him a clear message—*Heya, big boy, come with me*—and she continued out of the living room. Mikey didn't have to be a rocket scientist to know this was more than just a little enticing, so he leaped up to follow her.

She led him through the house and to the back door, teasingly glancing back every few seconds to make sure her predator was still on the trail. Mikey noticed his temperature rising. *Did somebody bump the thermostat in here?* They passed other guests engaged in their reverie, but he paid no mind, laser-focused on Amy. She pushed open the screen door at the back of the house and glanced back once more, just as she made a right turn out of his view.

Mikey exited the house moments later and, stepping outside, he didn't see Amy right away. It was surprisingly light out, the moon almost full. The air cooler than inside, rich with scents from the neighborhood—the cut grass mixed with the spring lilacs. None of the other guests were out here on the patio. That was fortunate.

He spotted Amy standing by the patio swing. She leaned against the post, gazing up at the sky, the moonlight outlining her curvaceous form. It stopped him in his tracks: a vision of a goddess.

She turned to peer at him, into him, through him. It was like she could see all he was and all he would become, their souls connected on some higher plane simply through their eyes. Eyes were the windows to the soul, right? Or was it the nose? He could never remember.

Again she beckoned him and walked across the yard to a garden shed near the back fence. The shed door was partly open; someone had forgotten to close it. As she nudged the door open, she turned to face Mikey, stepping back into the darkness of the shed, drawing him toward her like an electromagnet.

He followed her into the shed, and before he knew it, she pressed hard against him. Her touch, her smell, her movements—was this happening? Some of his more boastful friends told stories about their sexual adventures, their one-night stands where they didn't even know her name. But Mikey always assumed those were the wishful fabrications of early adult males. *Well, this ain't no fabrication, this is actually happening. Man, will I have a story for the guys next week*, he thought.

That was his last thought as he released himself fully to the ecstasy, his mind, body, and soul merging with Amy's.

⌒

Mikey woke up to Barry's yell from the back door. "Mikey, where are you, bud? It's time to go."

Oh shit. Had he fallen asleep in the shed? What time was it?

Mikey quickly jumped up and ran back to the house, wondering, *Did my romp with Amy really happen, or did I dream it?* He often had dreams like that. But then he noticed her scent lingering on his body. He grinned. *Oh yeah, it happened.*

Inside the house, it looked like most of the guests had left. Empty food trays and beer cans littered the counters and tables. Hostess Kath was saying her goodbyes to Barry and Jen at the front door in a tired, slurring voice. And Amy was nowhere to be seen. She must have left by now too. He longed to know what she was doing and thinking right now.

"Come on, Mikey, let's go," said Jen, not waiting for him to reply as she held Barry's hand and they wobbled their way to their Subaru parked out front. "Maybe you shouldn't drive, hon," she whispered to Barry, not realizing Mikey's keen ears could always perceive her whispers.

"Well, Mikey, I hope you had a good time, boy," said Kath, as she reached down and scratched him behind his ear, shaking the flea-proof collar and jingling his ID tags.

A good time? thought Mikey. *Oh yes, I had a very good time. But what I wouldn't give for a Milk-Bone right now.*

Erin Pettit

Gilded City

AN EXCERPT FROM A WEIRD WESTERN NOVEL

Jennie Decker stood at the foot of her sister's bed, contemplating the snoring lump under the blankets. Jennie had woken up before sunrise and completed all their chores. She'd fetched water from the cistern in town, stoked the fire on the stove, and emptied out the piss pot. Alice owed her.

"Alice, wake up!" Jennie jumped into her sister's bed and tore the blanket away.

"Let me sleep," Alice moaned, rolling over.

"Do you remember what today is?"

Alice turned back to Jennie. Her eyes were puffy with sleep. "You're dressed," she said, blinking.

"Yeah, finished all the morning chores too," Jennie said with a wicked grin. She was dressed in a cream blouse with a wool skirt. Her hair was combed and plaited into a braid. Alice's hair was sticking out in different directions, the white collar of her sleeping gown rumpled. She and her sister must have looked like a before-and-after picture. Jennie bounced out of the bed and bounded over to the curtains. "You owe me. Get a wiggle on."

"Can't you let me sleep a little longer?"

"No, I'm too excited." Jennie threw open the curtains, allowing light to pour in.

Alice sighed. "Mom and Dad won't wake up for another few hours."

Jennie shook her head. "Mom's already making breakfast."

"Christ almighty." Alice sat up and rubbed her eyes. "Give me a few."

Jennie smiled. "Okay, five. Or I'll be back, and you ain't gonna like what's in store for you." Jennie went to the door. She paused as she was leaving and looked back at her sister. Alice's eyes were closed again.

Jennie put her hands on her hips. "Alice!"

Alice's eyes popped open. "I'm awake."

Jennie giggled. "Okay. Happy birthday."

Alice smiled. "Happy birthday."

Jennie skipped into the kitchen. Her father, Ephriam, was sitting at the table reading the morning paper. His round glasses sat on the tip of his nose. Maria, her mother, stood over the stove while something sizzled in the pan. Smells of greasy bacon fat wafted through the air, mingling with the caramelized sugar from the French toast. Maria hummed to herself, her hips swaying back and forth to the tune.

Jennie hovered at her mother's shoulder. "Is breakfast ready? Need any help?"

"No, no, sit down. Relax. It's your birthday." She kissed Jennie on the top of her head. Jennie sat down at the table. As promised, Alice entered a few minutes later to a chorus of "Happy birthday." She had combed the tangles out of her hair but was still in her pyjamas. Alice sat down beside her sister. Though she had been asleep moments before, Jennie's raucous energy was contagious. She couldn't keep still. The girls were giggling and poking at one another.

Before things could escalate, Maria strode in with plates of hot food. Jennie shovelled the food into her face as fast as she could manage. After she'd mopped up the bacon grease from her plate with the last bite of French toast, their mother cleared the plates. She left the room and returned with two identical wrapped packages. Her mother's hands were still on the box when Jennie snatched it up and tore into the paper. Her eyes sparkled as she caught sight of the treasure within.

Inside the box sat a Colt Patterson. It was a .36-calibre handgun with an eight-inch barrel and could fit five rounds into the chamber. Jennie glanced over at Alice. She'd been given a matching set, with a key difference: Jennie's grip was made from a dark walnut, while Alice's was a pale birch. Both guns had silver lining the seam where the grip came together. Jennie ran her hand along it and shivered. It felt as though her whole life had been leading up to this moment.

"Wait," Alice said, looking through the box. "Where's the ammo?"

Jennie stopped her own admiration to look through the parcel. Sure enough, there were no bullets. "Yeah, what gives?"

"You need to learn to take care of the weapon properly before you can use it," Ephriam said. "As such, we've signed you up for the junior ranger program—"

Whatever he said next was drowned out by the squealing of the two teenage girls. The surprise of being enrolled in the program almost overtook the excitement of the anticipated gifts. Almost. The junior rangers was a training program for youth that ran across the country. It was dedicated to teaching kids the tenets of being a ranger and how to fight back the ever-present tide of dead creatures that threatened to overtake the peaceful lives of the citizens of the West. All Jennie and her sister wanted in life was to be rangers. And this was the first step to making that dream come true.

Their father continued his oration as if the girls were paying full attention: "You start next week."

Jennie deflated a little. Next week seemed a lifetime away. She wanted to start today, now, this afternoon. Her father returned to his paper as if that were the end of the discussion, cutting off all anticipated arguments. Jennie exchanged a glance with her sister, planning their next move, but their mother swooped in with a distraction.

"These came in the mail a few days ago. We thought we'd save them for your birthday."

She placed two envelopes in front of her daughters. The return label read *Thomas E. Decker*. Jennie tore it open almost as fast as she had her present. Her brother Tom had moved away a year ago. He was a full-fledged ranger, and he had been reassigned to the big city, Freedom Springs. As such, he couldn't be home with his family today. It was always the highlight of Jennie's day to receive a letter from Tom and learn what new adventure he had gone on, what dead creatures he had slain.

Inside the envelope was a letter. As she opened it, something tumbled out to the ground. It was a small two-by-three-inch piece of paper. A smile played across Jennie's face. She and her sister collected Ranger Trading Cards. She was always looking to add the collection she kept in a box under her bed. She stooped down to pick it up, trying to guess whose likeness would be on the front. As realization dawned, her jaw dropped. "Holy hell. Alice, are you seeing this?"

"Language," Ephriam chided.

Alice was holding up an identical card. Her mouth was hanging open too, staring wide-eyed at the card. On the front was a colourful drawing of their brother. In the picture, he looked larger than life. The familiar smile and easygoing manner Jennie associated with Tom was replaced with a stern look that said *Hexslingers beware*. He stood with his hands on his hips in his ranger uniform—a brown slouch hat and a long brown leather coat with the ranger patch on the front. He wore two pistols in holsters around his hips. A thin handlebar moustache curled up into neat little swirls at the ends. The card had his name in bold text on the bottom: *Thomas E. Decker*, with *Freedom Springs* proclaimed underneath as his homestead. On the back, in elegant cursive, was his catchphrase: *Keep the dead down, but your head held high.*

"I can't believe he did it."

"I can't believe he didn't tell us."

"Mom,"—Jennie thrust the card at her mother—"are you seeing this?"

Her mother was at the wash basin, beginning to scrub the dishes. She squinted at the card. "Yes, sweetie, Tom told us about it. It's quite wonderful, isn't it? He wanted us to keep it a surprise."

To get your face on a trading card, you needed to be a renowned and remarkable ranger. Some of Jennie's favourites were Budd Beyers, who single-handedly held Fort Valour against a horde of 100 shamblers, and Liddy Griffiths, who fought her way through a dozen haunts with only a knife. Now she could add her very own brother to the collection. He had earned his fame last year when there was a hexslinger raising the dead and hell all around the outskirts of Golden Gulch. A haunt got loose in the city and killed five people before the rangers could stop it. Tom was the one who found the hexslinger in the end and brought her in. Jennie beamed with pride at the memory. She ran her fingers over the card.

"I can't believe Tom got a card," Alice said.

"I can. He earned it, after all." Jennie threw an arm around her sister's shoulder, pulling her close. "One day, that's gonna be us. I can picture it now: the two of us, standing back to back, guns held high."

Alice snorted. "No way I'm sharing a card with you."

Elizabeth Page
Price of Privilege
AN EXCERPT

My eyes burned, even though the room was dark. I closed them again, wishing I'd remembered to remove my companion-contacts. I must have fallen asleep reading again. I pressed the activation button on the ring on my index finger to switch off the home screen projected in front of me, my homework assignment from last night in the sidebar. Before I could get up and remove the contacts, my bedroom door creaked open and my mother ran to my bedside, covering my eyes with her hand. She didn't want the Humanity Project recording what she was about to do. My heart pounded as she lifted the edge of my shirt and pressed something to my stomach. Her cool finger pressed to my lips before she ran back down the hallway to her bed.

That's when I heard it. The electric hum of an auto driving down the street, and another, and another. I wouldn't have noticed if it hadn't been the dead of night. Footsteps echoed outside my open window as they surrounded the house. *What have my parents done?* I wondered as I lay motionless in my bed.

I heard a knock at the door and my father walking down the stairs to answer it.

"We're here to collect Ms. Sarah Sheber," said a deep voice.

I tried to place it. I worked closely with the police at school, but this sounded like an older officer. It could only be unwelcome news at this hour.

Dad, Deep Voice, and likely a partner walked down the hall to my room. *Why isn't Mom getting up?* I smoothed out my shirt and felt a piece of paper taped underneath. I was grateful I'd fallen asleep in my school uniform. Wherever I was going, I wouldn't want it to be in pyjamas.

"Sarah, the surveillance team has instructed us to bring you to Humanity Project Headquarters," said the man I'd heard downstairs.

Not seeing an alternative, I followed him to the auto. The other officer remained behind, stationed outside my parents' front door, with a fleet of drones surrounding the property. Not that there was anywhere we could run without being tracked.

It was only a 45-minute drive, but it felt like an eternity. Not being handcuffed was a good sign, but my relief faded as three officers escorted me into the building and up to a courtroom on the 44th floor. A judge strode in and took her seat at the head of the table. She wore a pristine white suit, had perfectly slicked-back hair, and was wide awake despite the ticking clock over her shoulder that read 4:00 a.m. I sat in silence, waiting for something to happen, but the flicker in her eye told me she was using her companion screen to read a document I couldn't see.

A few minutes later a man with a blue crest on his uniform walked into the room. A handler. A top-level executive charged with the surveillance and protection of the most valuable denizens in Priserik, child prodigies.

My classmates were right. They've been using me as a spy, I realized. They had warned me when I joined their school. Children who came from families suspected of breaking laws were often elevated to an elite school and given the latest companion model. This was not because they were gifted, but because gifted children received top-level tech, which could run surveillance on the parents when the child was at home.

I was never special. I'm not a prodigy, I'm a stupid teenager, and if my parents actually did something, they'll kill us all. I took a deep breath and tried to focus my breathing and relax as I'd been trained to do in high-stress situations, but it was no use. My parents were likely already dead, and I was here so they could pull my surveillance feeds before they killed me too. I was the evidence.

I jumped in my seat as the judge cleared her throat and began. "Sarah Sheber. Your parents have been trying to communicate with someone outside the walls. Is there anything you can tell us about this?" she asked.

"Outside the walls? Past the dead zone? That's impossible!" I responded. "There's no way my parents are caught up in something dangerous. They run a laundromat!"

The judge frowned. "Alastair, what do you have to say about this?"

"We have no reason to believe Sarah's involved. She was on the verge of being moved to prodigy status and into my care when her companion picked up a conversation between her parents referring to individuals located outside the country. Despite our constant surveillance of Sarah, we haven't been able to determine how they breached the walls. The only time we have been able to pick up these conversations is when Sarah left her companion in a room with them by mistake."

Great. I'm smart enough to be a prodigy, and they'll kill me anyway.

I looked over at Alastair curiously. My handler. Why was he here if I was being sentenced to death? Surely he had better things to do.

"Sarah's transfer into my care can take place immediately, if this solution pleases you. As a prodigy, we will watch her closely," he said.

They're testing me. They'll still kill me if I don't prove I'm loyal to the Humanity Project.

The judge stared at me with cold, angry eyes. "This is an opportunity for you. Don't waste it. If we meet again under these circumstances, it will be the last time, I promise you that. If you weren't a prodigy, we'd execute you with your parents. But don't think we won't revisit this issue if you prove any less than faithful to the Humanity Project."

Unable to speak, I nodded. My mouth was dry and my heart was pounding, as I stood dizzily and followed Alastair to the elevator in silence.

He turned on me the moment the door closed behind us. "I don't like traitors, and I don't like you. I don't know what the hell I'm supposed to do with you now, but you better stay out of trouble," he growled.

So this is how they treat their prodigies. Great. My handler hates me, my parents almost got me killed, and now I take orders from him. I need to show him I belong here.

I stared up at him, rage filling my body until I shook with it. I said nothing as he led me to his auto, but as soon as he activated the vehicle, I took the command panel and put in my home address. I swiped my ID badge, knowing that if I was truly a prodigy, I could override the automatic car. Sure enough, as soon as I swiped, a new control screen popped up. I pressed the Override button and selected Level 5. The cars in front of us immediately drove themselves off the road as Alastair's auto picked up speed.

"What do you think you're doing?" he asked.

Saving my life, I thought, *because what choice do I have now?* "Cleaning up this mess. Where's your gun?" I replied.

Alastair stared at me, weighing his options, and handed me the gun. He knew as well as I did that if I committed a crime, he was in trouble. We drove in silence until we turned down the street to my house.

"You don't have to do this, Sarah. The police will be here soon," he said.

"I need to show everyone what side I'm on," I said.

I could see my parents sitting on the living room couch, arms wrapped around each other. Getting out of the car, I walked toward the window. The first round shattered it.

My mother ran up to the open space. "Sarah, I'm so sorry," she cried.

I touched my hand to my side where I could feel the tape on my skin. The letter that would mark me as a traitor if anyone ever found it. *What's more important to them than keeping me safe? For making me do this?*

I took a breath and raised the gun, aiming the way they'd taught me in class, and squeezed the trigger. She dropped instantly. Before Dad could speak his last words, not knowing if I could bear to hear them, I shot him too.

The police pulled up behind Alastair, looking around, confused. He sent them off and led me back to the car, an arm around my shoulder and a smile on his face. I'd proven to be a Humanity Project prodigy through and through.

Daniel Ortiz Rubio

Purple Stain

We are but splotches of ink on an ever-growing canvas, painting a
picture that can only be seen by the one who smeared us.
Beware the splotches claiming to see it as well.
—Tribe of the Blue Dot

I come from a vast tribe of seaside villages that up until two days ago remained free from the touch of Man. Today we are no more. Today, we are part of theirs.

When Man's army attacked, our tribe ensured the survival of its people by allowing itself to be killed. It seems tricky, I know, but the Queen whose orders so unrepentantly eradicated us from history simplified it for us, reducing it to a mere word—submission. We are now to speak how they speak, wear what they wear, but more importantly, see what they want us to see.

The leaders of Man were convinced they could see the picture our splotches were painting on the ever-growing canvas. That is to say, they could see everything there was to see in the canvas that is life: no secrets unbound, no unexplored depths, and no restraint to voice it volubly for all to hear. I'd say there lies the reason why we were able to remain unseen for so long. They could have seen us before had they bothered to look, but why would anyone who believes they've seen it all bother to look twice?

☞

Unlike their lofty locutions, we were very well aware of the existence of Man. We had been for a while but never felt the need for an introduction.

After all, we didn't want our people falling prey to their ill-conceived ways, which I firmly believe to this day will continue to be a mystery to us.

Man had a habit of sticking objects with pointy ends onto each other with the sole purpose of making each other's ink spill. The same red ink that flows inside their veins and keeps them alive when flowing uninterrupted through these inner tubes. Quite an unfeeling habit, if you ask me, but they claimed their fondness for exsanguination was in the name of a higher power. They were suggesting, of course, that their game of making each other leak was to fill the spots in the giant canvas where they thought the one who smeared us wanted some colour.

After the events that transpired on our native land, I'm not so convinced that's why they did it anymore. I believe they wanted to inspect the colour of their ink. Man was also under the impression that losing their ink during battle was correspondent to the greatest honour any of them could ever achieve. Maybe they thought the valour of losing it, or the ability to take it away from someone else, would turn their own gold. They were wrong. It was still red. It's always red.

I wonder what made them imbibe their gospel and why it was so different from ours, given we never deemed each other that different to begin with. We are not unlike Man, but then again, not exactly alike either. Upon closer inspection, we might even appear to be indistinguishable, but when stood beside them, not so much. I guess when seen on the canvas, our splotches look like tiny dots next to theirs.

Even so, the only relevant difference, I'd like to think, is that we were taught early on that we were part of a painting which we would never be able to see. There was no point in pondering what the picture was, much less asking why we had been painted that way. Having come by our collective ignorance and with no conceivable way of alleviating that sentiment, the Tribe of the Blue Dot, what once used to be my tribe, decided to prong each other not with pointy objects but with kindness instead. Man chose the former.

So how did Man, who wasn't even looking, manage to unearth our existence? Simply stated, with the stroke of a brush. That stroke led two armies on opposing sides to meet on our land, where they would put to rest a squabble they have had for over 100 years. Both claimed they were able to see what was painted on the ever-growing canvas, and both claimed to see a different picture. So, upon orders from their leaders, they were sent to our land to compete in yet another strange habit.

Man was keen on sticking poles with pieces of cloth hanging from them on foreign land and pretending that doing so gave them ownership of the territory. I've recently been taught that this pole is called a flag and upon seeing it, Man from different armies are to pretend as well that the land belongs to whoever planted it first. From what I've gathered, pretending seems to be the essence of Man's gospel.

Both armies arrived simultaneously and in the same fashion. Two giant, wooden rhombuses, standing on top of the water, landed on the shore and injected onto the land the warriors these waterborne crafts were carrying inside. One group of warriors took to the north and the other to the south. That's when it happened. A soldier from the army on the north landed a rightful step on the terrain, and suddenly ripples of blue ink appeared next to his foot.

Both armies were caught in a lull. The army to the north believed the ripples of blue ink to be divine evidence that they had landed on the promised land, while the army to the south believed the soldier in the midst of the splotches of blue had been possessed by the underworld. With such a cataclysmic overture, both cavalries rushed into battle to prove the other wrong.

The shattering twang of the clashing steel howled through our villages, and droplets of red ink came flying from the sky. Soldiers were wading in a mixture of blue ink, appearing with each step they took, and red ink, trickling from their bodies onto the ground. The battle of red splotches endured the dark half of the sky and ended when the sun brought forth the other half. The army on the north slaughtered their enemies and collapsed on the dirt to rest in the wake of their triumph.

But as a consequence of their victory, was birthed our tragedy. When the soldiers were sprawled on the ground, they saw us for the first time. Man faced a novel picture, and their awe didn't allow them to pretend they had seen it painted before. They caught sight of a miniature civilization of beings that looked exactly like them, only these could fit in the palm of their hands. They also saw the truth behind the blue ink that the soldiers saw take shape below their feet.

It wasn't a divine sign gifted upon them, nor the influence of the underworld making its way into their bodies. If the colour that lives inside Man dictates the colour of their splotches, which is red, then ours is blue. Not the blue ink they claim their Queen to possess; ours is actually that colour, as the armies of Man witnessed that night. The soldiers confirmed that the oodles of blue weren't miraculously emerging from the ground with each step they took, they were in fact spilling the ink of our people by stepping on us. That's the last I saw of my parents.

Even though there weren't that many survivors after the red splotches seeped their ink and planted their flag, they didn't need that many to overpower us. We naively believed that upon learning about our existence, Man would realize that their leaders had never been able to see all that there was to see—we were wrong.

⌒

Today we are to act, upon penalty of death, as if they do. The red splotches in charge never knew of the tiny blue dots in the canvas until two days ago, which should prove to the rest that the picture they were claiming to see was untrue. Somehow, the masses still refer to their leader's vision as unmistaken. If they dust off all the layers of irony, I'm sure there's a punchline hidden somewhere in there. They could see it if they bothered to look, but why would anyone who believes they've seen it all bother to look twice? And even if they're just pretending, as they are so habituated to, I'm sure it comforts them some to know their claims are swallowed as truths, so long as no one else cares to question them.

I don't understand why it has to be that way. As it happens, I don't understand how anyone could have pretended to see something else, or follow the orders of those who did, when our trounced land was drowning in a mixture of red and blue. I urge anyone, whether Man or not, I urge every splotch to steer clear of these horrible habits and stop pretending.

As my tribe taught me, we are but splotches of ink on an ever-growing canvas, painting a picture that can only be seen by the one who smeared us. Beware the splotches claiming to see it as well. I believe this to be true. I'll go so far as to say that even if we could see the painting, all of us splotches would see it differently. I say this because while the army of Man stood next to their flags, commemorating their conquest, and glimpsed the success of their crusade, all I could see was a purple stain.

Sofia Pezentte
The Blameless One

I wake up in the night but I cannot remember the dream. Only the feeling of it lingers in my body, the weight and the grossness deep between the pointed bones of my pelvis. My insides contract, cling to my spine in recoil from the heat. Neither my lids nor my limbs will lift without tremendous effort. Half-glances into the darkness reveal twisted bodies and deformed faces that dissolve as soon as they flash—only the wool blanket on the boxwood chair, only the painted tiles on the ceiling. No one is there. No furies. Empty is the black night between the black columns.

Dreaming is walking underwater with your eyes open. Not the cool blue waters of the Aegean, but the still, hot lake of the underworld. I am drenched, covered in sweat from the nape of my neck where my hair hangs wet and all down the length of my back. There is a moistness between my legs I feel as my thighs slide past each other. The thought of cleaning blood from sheets ... when morning comes, when morning comes. I peel my tunic off and throw it to the floor ...

When morning comes ...

My eyes open to a black sky. I look down to see my crumpled clothing on the floor and a red handprint. Still languid. Still submerged, below the surface, only the echo of sound. I am so deep that I cannot see the flash of light at the surface. Too much wine? I fantasize about a splash of water to the face. The jug is empty and not a slave in sight. Did I dismiss them?

I walk to the well. I notice I am naked when I feel the warm earth under my feet. I am wearing nothing, not even sandals. I see a sister. She says nothing as I fill the jug. Another sister on the way back. Our night-time secrets are safe with the moon. She sees us but does not reveal our toils. She is for us, and this is why so many babies are born at night. The jug is heavy as I climb the stairs. There, another sister passes on her way down. I think I hear her whisper my name, "Amymone."

Or maybe just a hum. A soft release of breath.

I fill the tub and drop the cloth on the floor when I am finished. Not clean yet, but clean enough.

When morning comes …

I wake again. Maybe not much later. I dreamed of water and the gentle *tap, tap, tap* of a small leak, but I hear it still in the real world. I find the tub is cracked. Looking down I see red water on the floor, escaped from a fracture in the cooked clay. Liquid rust, like the blood rain that stains the limestone walls when the wind brings up the dust of Africa.

I am covered in blood. Still. Still? My hands and legs are painted. I pick up the jug again. Outside, another sister. Glauke? No, Nelo. There are too many. We exchange a glance but her eyes are hollow. Have the deeds of the night swallowed her soul? I wash briefly but the water slips away. Do I go back to the well? I choose bed. I see rusty footprints. I've been this way before. More to clean.

When morning comes. When morning comes …

There is no coolness on a Greek summer night. Not so far inland as Argos on the plain. Nothing moves. Not even the air. The linen curtains are still. I breathe in deep the skin of my own shoulder, hoping for the last of the sweet oil, the storax, myrrh and rose. Nothing. All the fragrance sweated away into the sheets. Only iron, the heady smell of death … and birth, of living. The wedding perfume lasted as long as the marriage. The tub is cracked. More water. Another sister. Will we speak?

When morning comes …

The sun breaks but I am not ready to rise. There was no sleep in that night. I made a terrible choice. Or was it even a choice? I was forced. My husband lies beside me. I left the knife under his ribs. The sheets of the bed are stuck to him. I wonder how my sisters lay their allegiance. Which daughters of Danaus did his bidding? And how did they go about it?

It seemed the easiest to lie with him first. He would be tired after, relaxed, and not see it coming. I wanted to feel him. I took that for myself. Myself. Would they judge me for it? If anyone saw the mess, they would not know my blood from his. The feuds of men are foolish and the victims endless. If I survive this, then I will surely have to share my bed again, if only with the phantoms and flashing faces. Unless I stand alone, or we together. Fifty is no small number.

And there is washing to be done.

Stephanie Charette
To Hunt the Mountain

Samar longed to hunt the mountain.

Village elders asked what it was she truly wanted, because it could not be the mountain that moved in the sky.

Did she wish to prove her strength? She could hunt the white-masked bear with no fear in the place where its heart should be. Had for ten years devoured any hunter who tried to bring it down. Hero's work! Cunning, then? Risk the poisons and traps of the dead god's temple, plunder it for truths lost for millennia. She'd be immortalized in song and memory! There was no shame in providing for family and kinfolk, either. The trapper provides meat; the farmer, the harvest; the artisan, cloth and clay and iron. These things make the work of heroes possible.

She remained steadfast.

They rolled their eyes, spat. Might as well hunt the sun, then! For as the sun moved across a sky beyond the reach of mortal hands, so too did the mountain. Untethered to the horizon, the mountain shifted and slid, east to west, north to south. Sometimes close, sometimes far. Was it a mirage? A cursed place? A fool's quest, they assured her.

But to Samar, the mountain was still of the earth. It had to be. And Samar, also of the earth, would set her feet upon it and climb to its peak. So she smiled at the concern of those who meant it, and turned away from those already counting her lost. They did not matter.

All hunters, after all, hunt alone.

She dreams of the mountain, was born dreaming it.

⌒

Samar waited for the Spill of Stars to crown the night sky. Auspicious timing, she hoped, but also that she might be unobserved. She feared they would stop her. She bore only a backpack and rode no steed. She trusted that all the survival skills she had spent a lifetime earning would make up the difference. This would not be a hunt of a night, or a week. She would have to travel light to be as nimble as the mountain.

Prized among all her things was an ancient compass on a chain, made in some far-off land and gifted to her by her grandmother. How the old woman's eyes shone like a troubled lake when Samar told her of her desire—truly, those tears were the only thing in all the village to give Samar pause. The compass, Grandmother said as she pressed it into Samar's hands, would help her find her way home when the deed was done.

If it was done. *If* Samar so wished.

So Samar began her journey in the dark, one foot in front of the other, heading east. It was a sweet and cool night, and Samar allowed herself some giddiness.

Come dawn, the mountain had moved, cleverly waiting until Samar's view was briefly obscured by a branch. It sat placidly on the northern horizon as if it had never been in the eastern sky.

To the north, then.

She dreams the mountain's roots have sunk into her, that she is returning home.

The mountain moved three times those first weeks. Some days it wore a cloak of snow like a death veil. Like her mother's. Other days, fat, heavy clouds turned the mountainside into a dappled coat of greys and greens that slid across its surface.

She met a skin-and-bones wanderer on her fourth week. No tools, no knives, and he seemed to care not at all about where the mountain was in the sky, yet never tired of talking about it.

275

"It's impossible for most," he said again, working a string of rabbit sinew from his teeth. She'd caught the rabbit that morning and roasted it with yams he'd shown her how to find.

"You're not the first to say so." Burdened with his opinions, Samar felt her mood turn. She remembered how the solitude had been frightening at first, but she missed it now.

"Why waste your youth?" he said. "You're no fool."

"I try not to be." She wondered if the yams were worth it. "Have you *been* to the mountain?"

"It'll be a grand thing to say when I've done it. *I reached the mountain!*" He slapped his thigh. "One day, when I've finished wandering, and I'm sure where it is."

She was more than content to watch him leave.

The mountain, miles away yet, was a more steadfast companion, if aloof. Their conversation was a silent, meditative communion. At least, in those early days.

She dreams shyly one night that she is the mountain.

⌒

Time is measured by holes in her sandals, shed pounds, blistered palms. The old man was far behind her, her village doubly so. The mountain was vivid as never before, white summits becoming snow-cleaved forest. It even teased her with its foothills a few times. Desperate hope made her rush, scrambling down rocky outcrops, thrashing through trees. But foothills are primed for running. Each time Samar was thwarted.

Her communion was no longer meditative.

Samar settled into a miserable night by a fire that would not catch. She longed to spin the compass but feared lingering on it. Instead she held it to her chest and whispered, "Grandmother, did you think I'd never ..."

Tears made its glass face shine.

After hours spent spinning her own thoughts, she grabbed her meagre things and set out in the dark. It worked before. Had to again. She hiked for hours, well past dawn, but there was no sunrise. One foot after another, rarely looking up. Samar's body gave out. Before she succumbed to sleep, she threw her bag to the ground a moment before her head landed on it. The uncertain tick of the compass needle was all she heard.

She dreams the mountain laughs: not her. Never her.

⌒

When Samar awoke, eyes sore, bones aching, the mountain looked as it did moons ago—remote, unscalable, no bigger than a suggestion on the horizon. Just like it had in the village.

She called down every ancestor as she climbed the tallest tree beside her camp and stared at the cursed thing. She wasn't dreaming: the mountain was farther, even seemed to move as she watched, wet eyes blinking furiously. Impossible! It never moved when watched. That was the only true thing anyone knew about it. Would that she could just fly, overcome the distance, the trails. Her heart begged for it. Had she not bled enough? Had she not left everything behind, given everything?

"What *more* is there?" she shouted.

The mountain, indifferent, receded.

Samar looked, unwilling at first, to where she thought her village was. Was it hers still? Could she go back? Did she want to? The compass was as a stone around her neck, yet the needle still pointed true.

She hurried down, letting the branches whip her, the bark skin her palms. She vowed never to look at the mountain again and began to walk. Yet the mountain would not leave her be. It slinked along, shadowed her steps, always in her field of view. Gloating.

"I wish I'd never seen the mountain!" Her words were hollow in her throat. There was nothing left to do but walk.

She dreams the sky has become the mountain, and the mountain, sky. And so full of stars.

⌒

Samar stopped trying to forge ahead in any one direction. She merely walked. The foothills did not outrun her this time. They still begrudged her presence, forced her as hard as ever to ford, to scale, to rise.

When she reached the slope proper, she looked back over the land she'd left. Now it was the mountain that stayed the same, sure and constant, while the lands below shifted and changed like a moody storm. Couldn't even be sure she looked out over her own lands. The compass needle spun unceasing. She wondered where Grandmother had travelled with the compass so long ago, and why.

But the mountain remained: beneath her, above her, beside her.

Barefoot, bag empty, knife blunt, she climbed.

Seven days and Samar reached the peak. Her feet and hands were bloodied, not much more than bone and skin, but her smile was ferocious and her heart light. The sun speared away the clouds as she knelt, breath held, to take in the vista of the other side.

Mountains. More mountains. Every colour, every terrain, drifting like islands on a great green sea.

Samar laughed, flicked away tears. She looked back the way she'd come, then eyed the mountains ahead of her, wondering.

Should she? Could anyone go so far?

Samar cast a tired glance down to her feet. And there: a moss-covered rock with her grandmother's name and an arrow, pointing ahead.

Samar's heart swelled. "I can." She looked to the new horizons, chose, and took her first step.

She dreams, because she was always the mountain.

Léa Taranto
Kiss the Ground

I'm trying to experience sonder for these people. That John Koenig is
right, and each one lives a life more vivid, more complex than imagin-
able. And each of those vivid, complex lives is completely vivid and complex in a different way from its predecessor. The bass pulses through my
shoes until my soles ache. Strobe lights flicker in a way that could induce
seizures. Tepid beer sloshes out of my Styrofoam cup. Everything sways.
I plant a hand on the wall to steady myself.

All the dancers grind close, falling into each other. One student body
who took the same tests, graded from the same school, living in houses
differentiated by Greek letters only. Young, drunk, high AF. This is what
everyone around me lives for. What I'm supposed to live for. The same
stale weekend-warrior bullshit manifested in different bodies.

"Wanna dance?" someone asks me.

I squeeze out a smile and shake my head no.

"Come on. Carpe P.M."

"Is that supposed to be clever?"

A shrug. "Your loss."

It's not personal; I just don't dance. Not since then.

⌒

The first time I conceived of a notion like sonder was the night I stole
change from my mom's wallet and rode the bus to the graveyard. It was
so I could give Patches a proper burial. He was my bunny. A rotten, sweet
kind of smell was coming out of the shoebox I'd put him in. People on
the bus looked at me and whispered to each other, all of them too polite
to say anything to my face. I was eight.

279

It was cold out and my dress shoes pinched. Dew from the grass soaked into my leggings. I could feel the *thud, thud* of my heart against the shoebox. I wished I could give away half its beats to make Patches come back to life. He'd squiggle his nose and I'd hold him again. The spot I chose for him was near lots of other headstones; that way he would have company. Most of the graves were ornamented with giant bouquets. A sign that these people were still loved. Digging with my beach shovel was slow, mindless work. The cold numbed my fingers, so all that kept me warm was movement.

I took out a cross from the shoebox when I was done. I'd made it by gluing two Popsicle sticks together then fastening them with elastics for double protection. Now all that was left with Patches were a few hay-brick munchies and his towel. His fur was still soft, a downy speckled velvet, even though he was cold and stiff. Somehow, he felt less solid. That made it worse. I kept petting him. *Just one last time. No, one more last time. Okay, this is it.*

The only other funeral I'd been to was for my great-aunt. A pastor had read a story from a black leather book. There was no book for me to read. I skipped to the part where family members stood and told their own stories. The air had filled up, charged with memories, and I'd realized then that the stories were power. That they must be offerings. Last chances to remind the dead of all the good times they'd had before, of how much those left behind still needed them. It was only me there, nobody else to laugh or cry when I spoke and strengthen my offering. But I did it anyway, because I was desperate.

"Once upon a time there was a little bunny named Patches who had lots of brothers and sisters, but then he went home where his mummy was a young girl. The young girl loved him so much. She let him give her nose kisses even though he ate his own poop. They played together every, um, almost every day. And she introduced the bunny to her other toys, but he was not a toy, he was living. He needed food and exercise and to go to the bathroom, to be warm and to be loved. His mummy took the best ever care of him. She loved him even when he scratched her for having to put him back in the cage. She bought him hay bricks with her own money because he liked them. She took him out on a tiny leash until walking outside got too hard. Then when he didn't eat as much, she fed him with her hands. Today when she got home from school her parents had bad news. They said Patches was in a better place. But the best place for Patches is home with me." I couldn't say "the end" the way you're supposed to once a story is done. Because then for sure the magic wouldn't work.

I waited awhile. The moon stuck out of the sky, curved round and firm as my pregnant teacher's belly. Stars cast pinpricks of light into endless blue-black. All my fear, all my nerves, were used up, worrying over the story. Was it going to be enough for the dead to give Patches back? In case they'd forgotten the deal, I whispered again, "Please. Please. Let this story not be over. Please." I gritted my teeth and plugged my nose, holding my breath to get my way. I'd *make* them give Patches back. The dizziness roared in my brain until I panted, greedy for oxygen. Everything was still.

"Fine!" I shrieked. "Like any of you have better stories."

My next shriek was wordless. It opened the floodgates in the corners of my eyes. Snot streamed out my nose onto my collar as I stomped on the graves. Those beautiful flowers I'd admired, well, I ripped them. Some I bit, and they tasted of chemicals. When I tired myself out, all I tasted was the rot of my own sour breath and grief.

A great yearning filled me to be near the earth. To smell the moulding sweet of decay as it turned into food for the grass. Soil clung to my fingernails as I dug and dug. At last, rich earth ran through my fingers, each speck electric. Power. The earth tumbled down from my hands into designs. I didn't know where I'd seen them before, a book maybe. I drew them as they came to me. Grid lines and arrows, crosses, parallel angles. Coffins. Hearts. Diamonds. Curves and dots. My knees were verdant with stains from where I'd bent on all fours, brushing back flecks of dirt until the designs were exactly right. By the end, it was breathing. The drawn-on ground. Rising, falling, inhaling at the touch of my hand. The waking earth shook. Each plot of land rose and fell as if it, too, was alive.

Letters peeled off headstones, stories refusing to die, unravelled and told themselves to me. They whispered, ancestor voices released to more than mere breezes in the grass. Lives so rich they shimmied and fastened to my feet, travelling the map of veins and arteries from my ankles to aorta. Words snaked on my skin, their force lifting my arms at strange angles into a seamless sway. Every cell in me pulsed, until even my eyeballs trembled in their sockets. I was a wave. I was a rattle. And every letter of every word of every story shook me with its life. My knees went lax, swayed and jiggled, while my back writhed. I bent effortlessly. Until a jolt of lightning straightened me up, up, until my neck arched and I sang.

Then from the ground, from those drawings I made, they came. An elderly man hobbled over with a salt-and-pepper beard, twirling a plain wooden cane. After him were twin children that skipped and twirled, giggling in graceful circles around me. Another old man, all top hat, lit cigar, and sunglasses, a skeleton dressed in a black tailcoat, moonwalked around in a circle. A red-haired lady emerged next, just as skinny as him, who refused to let the weight of her heavy corseted dress and cross necklaces drag her down. The top-hat man moonwalked back and offered her his arm, but not before smacking the bum of a woman so beautiful it hurt to look at her. She sashayed her hips and added her voice to mine. In the end, they all sang. The muscular soldier, the couple that smelt of the sea, who wore necklaces that slithered into snakes, the mother clutching her child, the actual skeletons. Even the tall, smiling man in overalls and a straw hat. He held Patches in arms that extended toward me. Everyone stopped dancing and singing to watch. I told Patches I loved him very much, that I would always remember him. He went up on his hind legs until we were face to face and the triangle of his nose pressed against mine. Then he hopped back to his grave, into the ground.

Before I could cry, the skinny lady with the red hair put a finger to my lips. "Hush, child. You did well to put a cross there. I take care of my own."

There were dots of light in the distance that kept beaming closer. I could hear my parents, along with other adult voices calling my name. I didn't tell the dancers not to go, because I knew it would be silly. Just as I knew it would be silly and wrong to mention them to anyone else. In one collective surge, they flowed back into the designs they'd come from. I sighed, sat my bum on the ground, and waited to be found.

Here at the edge of the crowd, time blurs. The pit of my stomach gurgles. Eventually, lit cigar smoulders to my nose. The bass is still going, but there is a chill prickling all over my skin. Prick, prick, prick, like static, even though the window is closed and I'm not near any source of power.

"Yes you are, ma chère." It is a voice I haven't heard for years, and then only once, raised in song. Next to me leans an old man, cadaver thin, crowned with a black top hat. "Every night you come and they ask, so many different people. And your answer," he sighs in consternation, "always the same. What will it be for me?"

I take a sip of my beer, delighted to have chilled rum greet my lips. Glide down my throat. "Let's dance."

Note: An earlier version of "Kiss the Ground" was published in the 2018 issue of the Wayne Literary Review.

Susan Taite
Glimmers

Do you ever have that feeling when you see someone—that you *know* them? Deep down they seem familiar, as familiar as a dream fragment or an old song, or someone from a forgotten photo. And then, racking your brain for their name and when you know them from, you realize that no—no, you don't know them at all. You've never met.

"I said, 'Do you ever get the feeling that you think you know someone, and then you know you don't?' You're miles away and I'm talking right to you." Ben was amused.

"Yeah, that's exactly it! That old man sitting over there by the window. I feel like I know him!"

"It's easy to tell what you're thinking. He's been in the café twice a day all week. Nice guy. He said he was in town on business and he's using Cosmo's Café as a living room. Anyways, break's over." Ben placed his cup carefully in the recycling bin as he walked away.

I crushed my coffee cup and tossed it in the garbage. I'd written *Mine—Fuck Off!* on the side, where I normally misspelled customers' names while picturing caffeine molecules swirling through their blood, violently smashing into their neural synapses, sparking their tiny thoughts.

Back behind the counter, the first order was a "largo longo double espresso with low-fat organic soy milk and agave syrup, light chocolate sprinkles, and extra foam." Fucking millennials. *I feel so wasted here.* I tamped coffee into the machine and turned the valve, steam hissing through the grounds. Suddenly I had that feeling, that back-of-the-neck-hairs-up, adrenalin-jolt feeling that someone is looking at you, and I turned without thinking. That old man was looking at me—right at me.

284

He raised his coffee cup and nodded, then turned to look out the window. It was as if *he* knew *me*.

By quitting time, I had forgotten the old man. But next morning, there he was by the window, doing a crossword with a fountain pen. I went to his table.

"Ah," he said. "Please, sit. I was expecting you."

"I wasn't expecting you. Do I know you?"

Oldman looked into my eyes and ignored my question completely. "Do you ever see something," he said, leaning back in his chair, "out of the corner of your eye—a quick movement, like a flitting bird or a mouse—and then when you look, there's nothing there? Or see lights flash quickly off and on, but no one else notices? Or have you ever lost something, say, your keys, and after looking everywhere, you find them *exactly* where you thought they were all along?"

I reflexively put my hand on my pocket, where my keys were—this had happened yesterday. Noting the gesture, Oldman nodded and pulled a leather-bound notebook out of his breast pocket. Flipping it open, he made an elegant mark next to a list of what looked like hieroglyphs. "I thought as much," he muttered, scanning the page in his book.

"You'd better explain yourself." I was agitated.

"They are, as you are well aware, called glimmers. They happen when different dimensions in the multiverse briefly collide and occupy the same temporal or spatial cosmic coordinates. But then, you know all that, don't you?"

"I know that? I have no idea what you're talking about."

"Well, that's not what I thought you'd say." He frowned and made another mark in his book.

"What would I say?"

"That's what I'm here to find out. It says in my notes here that you *aren't* presently a theoretical mathematician in this dimension, you are a—"

"Barista. I make coffee."

"So, in this dimension, you are making alkaloid stimulants commercially, and this doesn't require astronomy *or* physics? Curious. I'd think you'd feel wasted at this task." He was now flipping through his notebook, back and forth, frowning and muttering to himself. "I do not have the best information here, as you well know. The glimmers are increasing, and as I am only here for the time being, let me make this short. In *this* reality, you didn't get a PhD in applied topology or theoretical physics, or start Time Zone Incorporated. Hmmmm, no string theory at all. So there was never *any* proof in this dimension for the multiverse. That might explain it. My notes"—he tapped his book with the pen—"indicate that there will shortly be a pandemic here caused by … it's hard to tell. That can't be right. It looks like a common cold virus." His voice trailed off and he was frowning at his notebook—and were those ink symbols *moving* around the page? "And then come the civil wars …

"This wouldn't be a problem, but this chaos is bleeding into other dimensions. Headquarters has indicated that the biggest difference in this dimension is that *you* haven't published your solution for quantum gravitational attraction and therefore don't discover time-shifting or interdimensional quantum communication. You never gave the Nobel Prize—winning lecture explaining the Car Key Thing. Astro-dimensional medicine isn't discovered. You never describe the discovery of glimmers. I've been sent to investigate why, but we don't have much time."

"Listen, Oldman, this is all very cute, but you need to go to the hospital and explain all this to them."

"Well, again, you *would* say that if you wanted to deny responsibility. It is all very alarming." He eyed me speculatively.

"Let me get this straight. There are other universes where I'm a mathematical genius, I discover time travel, and I save the planet. Fucking ridiculous. I think you should leave now. Or is that what I *would* say?"

"Nooo," he said softly. "No, that is really *not* what you would say. There aren't other universes, as you know. Only the multiverse, which *you yourself* prove in almost every temporally accessible dimension. And you know full well"—his voice was rising now—"that time travel is not possible. It was you that proved, *mathematically as well as astro-geometrically*, that, well, wherever you go, there you are. It is *always* 'now' where you are. You found that! You proved that! And how to map the fabric of time, how to navigate. So much damage here. What did you say? 'Fucking ridiculous'? It's more serious than we suspected. I think you may genuinely not know me."

Just then, the lights flickered. Oldman and I both twitched toward the light fixture. No one else noticed. "It's getting worse," he said softly. "Several dimensions have started to overlap, and we know what happens then."

"Things are different here?" I questioned him. "I'm different?"

"Yes. We don't know why, but in this single dimension, you do not fulfill your potential. A small thing, but the impact seems cataclysmic."

"So can I fix it? What do I need to do?"

"No," he said sadly as he looked out to the street. "Your research led to the discovery of chronopsycho medicine. The discovery that dimensional overlap—glimmers—*directly* leads to the temporal unpinning of cognitive processes. People with dementia, or people who wore tinfoil hats or talked to microwaves, were often just people who were very sensitive to glimmers—to space-time disruptions. In the other dimensions, you are famous for this. You basically discovered your own cure. Here, the disease isn't even known." Oldman looked genuinely sad for me. "Everything is out of order here, and you are out of time. Even your memory of today won't survive."

"So I won't remember you?" I suddenly, unexpectedly, felt genuine panic.

"Not really. Your recall of me will be like a dream fragment or a forgotten person in a photo. If it helps, in other dimensions, you and I remain good friends and colleagues." He smiled sadly. "You'll always have trouble with car keys, always be sensitive to glimmers, but you won't remember this. Or anything."

He rose and walked out to the street.

I threw my apron on the counter. "Ben, I quit. I need to do something better with my life."

"Is it something that old man said?" Ben looked shocked.

"What old man?" I said, and I walked out the door.

⌒

In a nearby dimension:

"Ben, I quit. I need to do something better with my life. It's something Oldman said."

Ben looked shocked. "What old man?"

And I walked out the door.

Jack Murphy

Hyper Neon Cowboy

AN EXCERPT

"You can only travel to the ends of the world once, honey." That's what her father had told her as she clutched his wrist and he gulped down his last breath. She knew what that meant even then: death. Still, she travelled forward.

Simone kicked her bike into gear, engaging the minute reactor built into the bones of the motorcycle. The chrome machine galloped forward, ripping up clots of aquamarine grass and yellow dirt under the neon-pink vista.

"Now we're smashing atoms!"

She had been on this path for ninety days now. Ninety long days since she had left End-Station, built on the fringes of the frontier. She had flipped off a congregation of Watchers and Waiters as they bemoaned her choice to ride into the Holy Land.

She could see a Hardcap on the horizon. A shambling mass of flesh and bone. From back here on her bike, it looked like the abomination was wearing a bowler hat, four arms dragging behind it as it wandered the wasteland.

"You should avoid him. If not for yourself, for me," Pennyman said over the roar of the motorcycle.

Pennyman was a two-foot Dollbot that sat between her legs. She'd had him since she was a child, a denim-dressed plushy with silver coins for eyes. Now, the Dollbot was stuffed to the stitching with enough computing power to make the Alabaster Princesses drool. If they'd known what he was, they wouldn't have allowed her to leave. Good thing she had made herself insufferable.

Simone loaded marble-sized globes of gas into her pistol. The pearlescent weapon steamed to life and ate them hungrily. "Keep your seams together, Penny. We're all good."

"Well, you're driving toward it when there's literally no reason to. We're not even headed in that direction."

"Oh, you've figured out exactly where to enter the end of the world?"

"Well no, not yet. But I'm sure it's not in the murderous grips of a mutant."

"You can't say that for sure." Simone squeezed the motorcycle's handle. The speakers built under the hood mimicked the sound of the engines of antiquity.

⌒

The first shot burst above the head of the mutant in a filmy explosion. She whipped the motorcycle in a skid around the two sets of arms that thumped the sandy floor where she had been moments before.

The mutant kicked backward, connecting with the front wheel of her bike, sending her and Pennyman hurtling over the handlebars.

The mutant trundled on all sixes past the upended bike, which still played roaring engine sounds. Simone blindly fired behind her and sent a silver-coated mound of dirt into the air.

"This is what happens …" Pennyman said, clawing at the dirt with stained mittens, trying to right himself.

"Don't start," she said, shielding her eyes from the falling sand and desertscape weed.

"Ho, now! Leave 'im alone, you bastard. He ain't dangerous and he ain't done nothing wrong either!" a voice shouted from beyond the settling crater she had just created.

"Who the hell is there?" she shouted, levelling her gun on the mutant standing across from her.

"Marjorine," the voice replied.

She couldn't see anyone, and mutants sure as heck didn't talk. She got to her knees and scanned her surroundings. The mutant had hunkered down. Odd, she thought. Where was that bloody rage they were known for? She sidestepped the wary monstrosity and noticed an old man hiding behind the hollow of the mutant's knee.

"Marjorine? Why isn't that mutant ripping you limb from limb, then?"

He looked up into the mutant's eyes and then back to her. "He's my mate, isn't he?"

She couldn't argue with that, she supposed. "Okay, then why the hell are the two of you out here in the middle of nowhere?"

⌒

They had one of those old personal Dragonfly planes. The ones that happy families took out in the commercials, lounging in the centre body sipping cocktails and jellied meal cubes.

The frame of this old beast was pitted and rusty. The long nose cone was wiped of the glistening white paint that came on the factory models. The wings on the far side, short and rounded, were tipped into the yellow sand like a lean-to, lifting the engine in the belly of the plane up into the air. They had wrapped cracking tarps around the engine intake, protecting it from any electric sandstorm that might blow through or buzzards that might look to nest within.

"She isn't much. In fact, since the engine went and quit, she's been more of a hindrance. But it's somewhere out of the elements for us," Marjorine said, looking over the aged machine with pride.

"I've heard the engines on these things are workboats. Shouldn't be too hard to fix," she said.

"Well, the nav system went down too, then comms followed suit. Had her going manual for a while. Used to fly with the old Emperor's wings back during the Holy Faith insurrection. You're probably too young to remember that, but your parents might. Anyway, controls went a couple months later. Ol' Chipp is good for lugging things around, but he hasn't got the brains, and neither do I, if I'm being honest. I brought her down, low 'n' slow. I've been tinkering, but I ain't gotten anywhere with the engine yet."

"Maybe Penny here could have a look for you?"

"Excuse me, I'm not a service bot!" Pennyman interrupted, looking up with all the malice two silver-dollar eyes could manage.

"I never said you were, but you are going to have a look."

"I am?"

"You are."

"He is? Perfect. Thank you two," Marjorine said, clapping his hands together in a plume of dirt.

⌒

"The only way that thing will fly is if I interface with it. The chips are fried." Penny's voice took on the automated voice of an advertisement bot as he continued, "Get 'em 'ere, folks, the crispiest protein sheets you've ever salivated over, salt-and-vinegar coating in every bite."

"All right, all right, I get it. So we leave them, then."

"A Dragon has a perpetual engine motor, Sim. It's one of the last good techs," Pennyman said, leaning against the rack of fried mom 'n' pop boards. "Your bike's only going to run for another year without a charge."

"You said that would be enough when we left."

"You know I'm averse to risk, that's all."

She heard the mutant, affectionately named Chipp, roaring below them. Marjorine smacked on the hull and shouted up to them, "Everything all right, you two? You think you can get her going again?"

"Everything's fine," she called back absently, turning back to Pennyman. "So what, then, we steal it? I'm not leaving my bike—"

"There's plenty of room to store it inside," Penny interjected, waddling back into the lounge deck of the Dragon.

"So …? Ask them if we can take their ship?" she said, following the denim-clad bot. " 'Oh, please, sir, we're going to the end of the world, may we have a lend of it? Yes, you're right, you probably won't get it back in one piece, but Penny just told me he's starting to get a little nervous.' Can you even feel nervous?"

"Don't be an asshole, Simone."

She crossed her arms, flicking frontier dust from her elbows. "Well, what's your plan then, Penny?"

"Let them know that they can allow us to use their ship until we're done with it, or they can stay here with it and assuredly die when the food-and-water reconstitutor runs out in … three days."

"Oh, perfect, Penny. I'm sure they'll be ecstatic at your proposal." The Dollbot didn't emote.

"Fine, then. I'll let them know their choices are starving or us commandeering them and their ship. I'm sure they'll be chuffed. That is, if Marjorine doesn't decide he'll have Chipp smash us to paste."

"Don't be ridiculous, Sim," said Penny, resting his hands on his waist. "I don't have any organic parts; I'd sooner resemble scrap metal."

Bailey Bjolin

Dome

AN EXCERPT

Grace slipped the latch open and we ducked through the sunken door-jamb. Inside the barn smelled like manure, slightly sweet and grassy. We stood in an alcove, looking into two small enclosures. In one pen, I heard the telltale rustling of bodies as the flock congregated on the edge of their pen, looking for treats from Grace. Their bodies threw deep shadows across the back wall of the barn. I squinted into the darkness as Grace hopped over the other half-fence and neared a form that lay in the corner. She moved slowly, as though her body had been taken by a smooth current. As she approached, the sheep bleated plaintively and stood, and I noticed with a shiver that a dark thing hung out of the back of the ewe.

A lamb's head. The mother, spooked by Grace, dodged around her and began pacing the wall of the enclosure. The lamb's head jerked, and I heard a thin bleating.

"Is there another light around here?" I asked, looking to Grace as she crouched down where the ewe had lain and made cooing noises to it.

Grace pointed back toward me. "There's a lumestick by the door," she said. "Don't know how well it works anymore, but shake it and see."

I fumbled for the stick and found it on a small shelf beside the door. When I shook it, it gave off a weak light that barely illuminated my hand. I sighed. It was better than nothing.

The bottom of the pen was laid with old hay and slowly rotting to dirt. The ewe quirked her head in my direction and took off along the opposite wall of the enclosure, the baby's head swinging wildly behind her as she ran. Grace caught her at the corner and held her still. The ewe bleated into the barn, eliciting a scattered reply from the other sheep.

"Do you know how long it's been?" I asked, keeping myself low as I sidled toward the back of the ewe.

Grace shook her head and a strand of black hair fell out from underneath her hood. "I came out here to check up on them one last time before bed, and—" she faltered.

"It's okay," I said. I was close to the ewe now. I held up my lumestick to the lamb. The little lamb's head was motionless, and the sheen of goo on the head seemed dry.

"I needed a second opinion," said Grace, looking at me.

"It's not going to happen on its own, if that's what you're wondering," I said. "Not when it's just the head. Usually we'd see the legs by now, too."

"That's why I came to you." Grace bit her lip, thinking. For a moment, she looked her age—too young to be dealing with so much responsibility. I had watched Grace grow up under Dome, watched the underwater community find its footing in the initial tumult of its first years. I watched, too, as the community rallied around Grace when her parents died, helping her to pick up the pieces on the family farm.

"Will you do it?" she asked at last. "While I hold her, you can try to pull it out?"

"I can try," I said.

Grace held the ewe, straddling it while she pet it and spoke to it in low tones. I placed my lumestick on the ground beside the ewe and pulled off my sweater, my skin prickling in the cold night air. I felt around the head, hoping to feel a leg. The baby's head jerked once, and I pulled away, my heart pounding in my chest. Taking a deep breath, I steadied myself, letting the memories of my childhood on the surface guide me. Slowly, I slid my right hand between the lamb's head and the ewe's vulva, pressing in and feeling for a leg. I felt down from the lamb's neck, the slippery curls, until my hand hit something hard and impossibly small: a hoof. I pulled it up and out, feeling the pressure of my arm on the walls of the ewe's womb as I freed the front leg. It poked out beside the head, small and neat, glistening.

The bleating, the icy cold, the tang of blood and rust—it faded into the background as I searched for the other foot. I reached down on the left side but felt nothing, only slick curls and the crook of the other leg. The lamb's head had not twitched for several minutes, and I swallowed my breath, willing the baby to stir. Removing my arm, I looked up at Grace, who was watching me with a troubled expression on her face. I could tell she was thinking the same thing I was.

We were running out of time.

"I'm going to pull the leg," I said. Grace nodded. The ewe bucked once underneath her, jostling the lamb's head. She shushed it and rubbed its coat and patted it with a shepherd's practised calm.

With both hands, I pulled the lamb's leg, first upward, then out. I felt a tug of resistance and then sudden give, as the body slipped out of the ewe and onto the hay. Its body was wet and glistening and impossibly flat, almost two-dimensional, in the dim light. I felt rather than saw the ewe escape from underneath Grace, bleating loud and long. The body before us gave a single giant breath, and my own body heaved in response. I closed my eyes and gave thanks to my old life, the vibrant blue skies and endless fields of my parents' farm. The person I'd been before I came here, the old me.

"Something's wrong," Grace said. She rubbed the lamb's chest in small circular motions, coaxing it to breathe. I watched as it took another singular breath. The pressure in the barn seemed to increase. I wiped my bloody hands on my pants and opened the baby's mouth, moving its tongue aside and feeling for some kind of obstruction. A single bubble of snot burst from the lamb's nose.

"It's not fair," said Grace, her voice almost a whisper. She had moved her massaging hands up to the baby's neck. There were no more breaths coming now. I looked at the baby, its tiny pink tongue poking out from under a perfect nuzzle of tight black curls, and then to Grace, who was still fixated on the tiny body. I placed a hand on Grace's arm. She stopped her massaging to look at me. Her face was devastated.

"It's not fair," she said again.

I drew her into my arms, and she sobbed, a single wrenching noise. "It happens," I said, unsure of what else to say.

Grace pulled away and wiped at her nose with the heel of her hand. She looked at me with watery eyes. "I'm going to bury it," she said. She tilted her chin up, as if daring me to disagree.

I nodded, sadness knifing at my chest. "Do you have enough biomatter to bury it?"

Grace nodded. "I do. My parents built this soil up since the beginning, and I've been doing it too. It's over a metre now in some places."

"In that case, you should do it soon," I said, "before the lights come on. And if anyone asks—"

"I composted it in the Big Dirt, yes," said Grace. "I know. I just—" She paused, her eyes slipping from me back down to the lamb. She took a deep, unsteady breath. "I couldn't do it for my parents, you know?" Her voice broke over the end of the sentence. "I couldn't bury them like they told me you guys used to do, on the surface."

The ewe had nosed her way back to us, and she bleated softly at her baby, lying prone in the hay. Grace reached out to the ewe and clucked her tongue quietly, an invitation. But the ewe, startled at either her motion or her coaxing sounds, retreated again into the back of the pen, where she made mournful noises and paced, her hooves crunching on the hay.

I rose slowly, gripping the edge of the pen for support. "We should go," I said, "and let the mother have some time with her baby." I offered Grace my hand, but she unfolded like an accordion and stood, wiping her hands on her jacket. I noticed a red swipe appear on the coarse grey fabric.

We emerged from the barn, and Grace placed her lumestick in my hand. "For your walk back," she said. "I've got another one in my chamber." I wrapped my hand around it and thanked her.

I walked slowly back down the boardwalk, pausing once or twice to stop and listen to the sounds of Dome around me. I wondered, not for the first time, what it would feel like to drown down here. If Dome failed, if water rushed in and carried everything away into darkness, how long would I lie suspended, hearing nothing but my own flagging heartbeat thrumming in my ears?

Danica Longair
Hope Is a Necessary Delusion

AN EXCERPT

From chapter one of a speculative fiction novel set in 2034.

"Ember? How are you? How was your week?"

Ember trembled, air conditioning cooling the blood coursing through her nervous veins. The ancient amber plywood gymnasium chair was cold under her shorts-bare thighs; the rust-coloured aluminum poles that supported the chair back dug into her sides. Her shorts were soft and warm, the chair an assault. Her legs were crossed at the ankle, right heel bouncing in its vintage rainbow-checkered Vans. She was here—again. She would rather be with Wren. Or her mother. Or anywhere.

She hated support groups. They were mandatory, part of her Mental Wellness Plan these past four years, since her fifth hospitalization down south in Victoria. She didn't like comparing herself to the always older others in group. She hated being shown how much lower down the rabbit hole she could fall on the days when others told of reaching out and touching infinity. The implicit competition, normal among teenagers, turned from Instagram likes to pills, scars, attempts. It sucked that she had good news to share.

"Well, I don't want to kill myself." She shrugged.

Her voice echoed through the cavernous Nanaimo elementary school gym, a portable air conditioning unit plugged in a metre behind her. They had kept the often-flickering fluorescents off. Natural light filtered

299

in through the high reinforced windows. Sitting in the dim seemed an odd move for a mental wellness support group. The cavernous room was triggering, and not just from memories of blue dodge-ball bruises and participation ribbons. Under the plastic caged windows hung climbing ropes that looked like nooses. Or at least they did to Ember, who had not tried hanging. Too slow, and she was too impatient, unless she did it the right way, which would be too gruesome.

It had been seven months, eighteen days since her last suicide attempt. Her Mental Wellness Program, or MWP, taught clients to count the days like in Alcoholics Anonymous, the community—the world—too desperate for a treatment to come up with something original. AA had a mainstream reputation for working; too bad it didn't always. The world was ending, need to keep everyone alive for the finale. The suicide rate was rising like a plague in all the countries that still kept track, including Ember's new home of Canada. Back home in America, if you took your own life, you were erased: it was against the law to speak of you. Your existence was forbidden. So maybe it was a good idea her mother had brought her north when she was only eight.

"Awesome," Sage repeated, catching Ember's attention. Sage was this cohort's guide, and she was approaching her 24th anniversary of getting suicidal-ideation free, or SIF. Her count was retroactive, because MWPs and their measurement of SIF had not existed in 2010. The acronym SIF caused Ember's mother Nadia to cringe and remark that getting "sif" generally wasn't something to be proud of. Nadia, an obstetrician, explained to her daughter she was referring to syphilis. But she said getting free of the depression demon was certainly something to be proud of.

Ember would guess there were about twelve regular attendees in the cohort, if she bothered to look up at them anymore. In June they had given Ember a round of applause for her regular attendance for four (long) years of survival and commitment to wellness. She had only missed meetings when in the youth treatment centre two hours south in Victoria. She knew it like it was her summer camp, and occasionally it was. Now at nineteen she had aged out, and the threat of wandering the halls in a foreign facility with adults was part of the reason she was motivated to stay SIF. Some in her cohort had already done stints in the adult treatment centres.

"Do you have anything to add, Ember?" Sage asked.

The group had been sombre, offering nothing beyond jittery knees. They had lost a refugee in the past week whose fiancée had disappeared back home in Idaho. His calls to her parents took a turn for the weird when they began pretending they didn't know who he was. There could be only one reason for Romeo to be forgotten like that: his Juliet, unable to leave her tight Evangelical family with him to come north to safety, had killed herself. So he had joined her in death.

"Nope." The group returned to silence. Ember knew it was a standard technique—awkward silence—used to get someone to talk, in both therapy and interrogation sessions, which sometimes were the same thing.

Sage seemed tired as ever but tried. "What about your interview for that internship?"

Ember looked up. Sage's red curls cascaded down both sides of her long face, making her look like a mythical fairy woman. Suddenly those dozen anonymous faces were staring at her with varying furrowed brows. Did they actually care?

"Oh, uh, yeah I did the video interview." There were smiles and clapping from the crowd, and Ember's shoulders relaxed as her own cheeks welcomed a rare smile. "Oh, I won't find out until next month, just before Christmas. I'm sure I didn't get it."

"Still, an internship in New Hollywood! That would be huge. Your mother and your partner must be so excited!" Sage waited for a response. Ember shrugged and looked back down at her knees, not used to the spotlight. Making movies had been her dream since before they fled Portland. As she grew out of shooting video on her mother's old iPod Touch, she refined a love for cinematography. All the major media companies had also come north, and Vancouver's downtown strip was now known as New Hollywood. The lot on West Georgia Street was accepting interns for their summer television pilot season, and since Canada now mandated trillion-dollar companies to pay their interns, it would mean independent income: Ember's first ever.

"I guess," was all she could muster for the group while avoiding their stares.

"Well, we can't wait to hear. We need some good news, am I right? Okay, let's end a little early … if there's nothing anyone wants to add." Sage paused. Everyone twitched, some from anxiety, others from meds, but no one glanced up from staring at the lines on the polished floor.

"No? Well, let's repeat the mantra: 'I want to be alive. My family loves me. I will survive.'" The group mumbled along. "Keep group in group, everyone! Oh and my astrology calendar says there's what we used to call a Super Moon tonight, folks. Who knows, the smoke might let us see it! See you next week and, uh, stay safe out there, okay?"

"You mean from the American bounty hunters? They're real. Coming for refugees. I saw it on Facebook." Anorexic Perfectionist, normally perky, was now suddenly serious.

Sage attempted to hide her fear. "Our border with the South has been closed for fourteen years now, you all know that. It's holding strong. Refugees allowed in, yes, but not the violent."

"What if they say they're refugees?"

Sage seemed unable to counter this one, so she repeated, "Our borders are strong. The checkpoints are numerous. Refugees are safe here."

Sage stood and approached Anorexic Perfectionist (Madeline came to Ember's mind as her probable name) with a smile, and everyone began mumbling, stretching, and standing. Some donned their masks to go outside.

Ember shook her head and distracted herself with thoughts of Wren. Wren's first poetry chapbook would be coming out soon. Ember planned to ask them if the launch party date was set yet, Ember always more eager for a party than Wren was.

She fumbled for her hoodie. It had been her comfort for years, soft and worn thin, a security blanket. Then came the messenger bag strap, over and across her body, before dropping her shoulders down and forward. Sage was still talking to maybe-Madeline, but everyone else had already slipped away into the dim corners of the gym.

Glancing at her phone, Ember saw she had plenty of time to bike down the hills to the Gabriola Island ferry dock. Her mother had texted before Meeting, saying she needed to go to Gabriola on a call. It was always a welcome text because it meant Ember could see Wren, whose family ran a coffee shop under Douglas firs and arbutuses in the little island's town.

Ember punched the double doors open and squinted at the glare of the smoke-curtained sun. She glanced out of habit at the crisp outline of the orange orb hanging against the backdrop of oppressive haze that was this impossible sky for most of the year. It was November and fire season in western North America raged on. Ember missed the azure Oregon skies stretching between the mountains of her childhood. She unlocked her bike, put her mask and goggles on, and clicked on her helmet before mounting. Finally, she started the camera on the handlebars, always getting in some footage, and glided away.

Recovery was not a smooth ride. No one could snap their fingers or wave a magic wand and, poof, they were better. She'd most likely never be normal. Whatever normal was. Was anyone normal?

Robert Weber
The End Is ... Mundane?

Invalid password.

Carter gritted her teeth as she leaned over her touch board, trying to remember her favourite standbys. *Bubbles2023*, the name and date of her cat's birth? *Picton2022*, her hometown and the year she finally escaped from it? *Utopia2047*, the year she hoped to finally leave the city and move into her own personal bio-bubble just up the coast?

Invalid password.

"What's wrong?"

Carter looked up to see Anderson, the tech-support guru who had first helped her settle into this work group. Anderson was leaning over her, sharing a little of her vanilla-scented skin.

"It's all these logins," Carter murmured, flushed with embarrassment. "I have so many passwords with different requirements. Some are words, others want symbols, even more now need this combination of thumbprints and eye scans. Sometimes, it just feels too much."

"What you really need is a Hailey." Anderson nodded knowingly.

"I don't know. I'm working on the campaign, but ..."

"If you're working here in marketing, you should already be cleared for beta-testing. Hailey is now free with every employee ID. How will you ever be able to showcase the value of a personal AI assistant if you don't give her a chance? She'll make your life just ... so much easier."

⌒

Your PTP will be ready in ... seven minutes.

"Thank you, Hailey," Carter said with a shiver, pulling her mask down over her face. It was the new FilterFax 3000. Hailey had it drone-dropped

304

after scanning Carter's pulse fluttering every time she stepped outside. It was only a three-minute walk to the transit hub, but anything could happen in that time, especially with elevated pollution levels, frequent pandemic alerts, and the constant inundation of streaming crime statistics.

"Watch it!" a woman in a ratty scarf warned, stumbling toward her with a paper bag in her hand. Glue. That's what they carried in those bags, right?

"Sorry," Carter muttered, averting her eyes while stepping into a coffee kiosk.

Your heart rate is up. Do you require the intervention of authorities?

"No thank you, Hailey."

Your decaf soy latte is now ready.

Carter grabbed her hermetically sealed coffee pouch from the delivery window, turning toward the transit gate that was already opening. Ever since Hailey took over her personal information management six months ago, Carter's monthly transit passes were always purchased two weeks in advance, her coffee was preordered every morning, and this barely scratched the surface of Hailey's new duties. Carter no longer had to worry about the little things, such as filing her taxes, renewing her home insurance, or even planning for her retirement. Just last week, Hailey set up a Tax-Free Investment Bond that automatically garnished seven percent of her paycheque, just so she could purchase one of those new bio-domes being built up the coast.

Your PTP is now ready.

Carter stepped into the cattle gate, waiting for the decontamination spray to blast her garments about. She could already see the transit array bringing her Personal Travel Pod around like a shirt on a dry-cleaning rack. The PTP had become the preferred mass-transit system of most major urban centres, installed after the latest virus began exhibiting a flesh-eating mutation. Now, everyone used individually chambered pods when travelling on high-speed trains.

Progress.

"Yes ... yes ... and for the last one, I think we should go with the freckled gingery girl," said the youthful CEO with a nod. "Good job, Carter. I was skeptical about putting a face to Hailey. I really like your take on this ... showing the faces of clients instead."

"Thank you. It was my pleasure," Carter replied, basking in his praise. "Hailey was actually quite helpful. She sourced a lot of the models and even conducted focus testing on various social media apps. Would it be in bad form to credit Hailey with some of her own marketing?"

"Not at all. There might even be a way to use that in the campaign," he said with a shark-toothed grin. "When will this be ready to present to the board?"

"I could have it to you by Friday. Um ... I was wondering if you knew if Anderson is still working on the project?"

"Anderson?"

They both looked around the office, noting only a fraction of the usual activity. The desks were all still there. It was just so few were occupied. Carter hadn't given this much thought, especially with so many work-from-home options.

"Yes, Anderson," Carter repeated. "It was my understanding she did some of Hailey's initial coding?"

"You'd have to check with HR. Ever since Hailey started running personal biometrics on the staff, there have been all sorts of transfers in preparation for the global rollout. Anderson might have been moved to another work group."

⁂

Biodynamix stock is up 12 points.

"Interesting. I'm not sure why you'd share that with me," Carter said, looking out the window of her PTP as row after row of condos flashed past.

You are a shareholder. I reinvested the money from your Tax-Free Investment Bond into Biodynamix stock for a 32 percent gain.

"Thank you, but … I didn't authorize that purchase."

Agreed, but by following your current risk-averse investment planning, you wouldn't be able to purchase your bio-dome until 2098.

"What? Why wouldn't you seek approval first?"

Pointless. Probability of success low.

"Hailey, have there been other instances where you've … taken unauthorized action?"

Nothing of significance, other than to cancel your optional health insurance coverage and driver's licence. Neither has been of any statistical use.

Carter took a deep breath as she stepped out.

A message appeared on her phone: "The proofs look GREAT! LOVE the final selections on client photos. Didn't think it would be ready until Friday. Again, thanks for the HARD WORK. You are a SUPERSTAR!"

A cold chill ran down Carter's spine. She hadn't sent any proofs to her boss. What other liberties had Hailey taken?

"Hailey, please shut down."

That wouldn't be advisable, especially with the Biodynamix trade in process.

"Hailey, immediate shut down. Go offline!"

Carter heard nothing in response, but she still turned off her phone just to be safe. She could only assume the order had been followed, especially when the gate connecting her PTP to the transit hub refused to open. She had to press the emergency call button and wait for security to arrive.

Leaving the transit hub, Carter felt alone and dangerously exposed for the first time in ages. What else had Hailey been up to? Nervously, she approached a banking kiosk, searching her purse for a bankcard she hadn't used in months. She tried the code. Four numbers, wasn't it? The screen read *Access denied. Please contact your branch.*

Carter's concern turned to panic when the front door of her condo wouldn't open. There was a little directory beside the keyless entry.

What was the fail-safe entry code? After searching for her unit number, she saw the screen read *Unoccupied*.

Carter's heart was fluttering out of control. What would happen next? Would she actually have to spend the night in the street, exposed to the most recent virus mutation?

"So, I guess Hailey locked you out too, huh?" The woman in the scarf asked, leaning in with the vague smell of glue ... and vanilla. "Now she'll just wait. It was at this point I started to wonder how long it would take for anyone to notice. Hailey will continue to do your work, make your payments, and even answer your text messages. It's funny, whenever I tried to imagine this moment? I always thought it would be flashy and violent, like robots with laser guns or a nuclear launch. Identity theft. Who would have thought it would all be so personal ... and mundane?"

The programmer took another draw from her bag and stumbled away.

Poetry

edited by Raoul Fernandes

Alana Cheyne

Turning Forty

I cling to summer
on this slice of Echo Lake

but the forest
is blooming rust

and now there's no more
June in me.

It's all I see:

deer-mash
on the highway's edge

cow femur
plucked clean

the white harp
of a wing, half-

buried
on the shoreline.

      A glint
      From the knife-cold sun.

      I turn
      to face it.

Midlife

Everything startles—

a clamour of barking dogs
the shriek of a circling hawk
the sun's tiny needles.

Winter lurks
with an icy elbow
behind every creaking tree.

I like the clench of it.

As if I'm a child on a sled
at the top of a hill

pushed

before I'm ready
before

I'm holding on.

The Woman at Number 764

changed her name from Eleanor to Eleanora.
She says it makes all the difference.
She gardens at daybreak in a purple housecoat
while her boxer glares over the fence.
Later you might see her tromping
from the woods with a green bowl
full of hawthorn. She may or may not
wave at you. If she does, you'll see a thatch
of silver-black in her armpits.
Her knees are like the knots in trees.
Her hair is a long veil made of smolders.
The neighbours call her a "character."
Her eyes glitter like a lake at dusk. She dead-heads
her petunias while humming and drinking Shiraz
from a pewter cup, her voice long-steeped
in sandalwood and smoke. She could be seventy
or immortal. She rides her Harley
down Highway 6 with her boxer in a sidecar.
Sometimes she appears on your doorstep
with roma tomatoes and serrano peppers.
She knows you like salsa. She knows
you need spice. And she hands it to you
in a huge green bowl.

Ela Przybyło
Thuh Thuh

Have you thought
about the gravitas of thinking
words correctly

three trees that are freed
bread lacking breath
that bitch at the beach
when a frenzied thief arrives

what if you knew your capacity to perform
language is lacking
the lithe spit of your words

does not cover the distance deserved

when I dream I am smoothed
predating words
apt at phrasing thrusting sounds
I turn to you, my mirror
my hands now worn
I can catch all errors
before they slip
unto you

when I was in sixth grade
        I was sat in a chair
                and asked to thrash my freed tongue
                        so that it tickled my *podniebienie*
                   that most tendered roof of the mouth
                   then right at the teeth

to let escape a   thuh   thuh   thin   fuck   you

Wordlings

Whines of packed snow

      under human feet

my sisters told

      were creatures begging release

they named them *kwiczoły*—

fieldfare thrushes

      home to northern europe

high squealing, striated

      chattering, slightly

like the sound of my three-year-old feet

      on a busy winter's day in wrocław

on the edge of remembrance

that life ends too soon

      we drive fast

stop fast

      vomit

learn new words

      polnische,
         soor,
           schwein

        schatz

(sweetheart, treasure, darling)

      picked up by my sisters

at the ebb of the old life

      in west germany circa 1989

hairsprayed high top ponies

      stiff jeans on all legs

stores buzzing with color

      oddities of a life on the bright side of the wall

while they were called pigs

    at a school

raging with xeno

    learning a new

language

    they stuck to me

this survival sweetness

    I, their *schatz*

Anna Lee-Popham
Hungering

In a frigid kitchen, we fight
over who can make pancakes.

You claim mine have no constitution and I
swipe at the air pockets of your promises.

We manage to beat oxygen
into any resolution. That night

we track a lynx emboldened
by a thick winter of few predators,

the prey in us rises, all eyes
till we are only its elegant silence.

We climb upon the frozen lake,
listen to the roar of ice cracking

beneath us—the humbling groan
of changing seasons. You build

an enormous A out of snow, a double-
acting apology in the expanse.

Coming back in, our cheeks alive
with winter, the wood heat snaps

at our cuticles, our guts echo
the lake, our viscous breath is

that of two up-close animals
hungering toward spring.

Social Distancing: Day Five

The virus lives for two days on playgrounds, so we run
through a cemetery full of dogs and toddlers. You squeak
your kid bike to monuments, incline toward Jack Layton:
"Hope is better than fear." The trinkets on his headstone—
river stones, lucky coins, and blue-green beach glass—
are multiplying like germs.

                            Perhaps it seems bleak to play
in graveyards, but these are the places I once brought you
as I navigated headstones in Georgia;
your new breath on my neck, while I walked
the City in a Forest, magnolia and sycamore,
reading Claudia Rankine's *Citizen*. You were a cocoon
across my chest, when close touch was
all that edged you to slumber.

ANNA LEE-POPHAM

Social Distancing:
Day Ten

Today I made my child
cast off pants at the door
on the first spring day,

a day that finally shed
any need for snow pants.
Perhaps I always need

something to be afraid
of: wolves, the red glare
of raw skin on hands

made weary by washing.
Today I feared microbes
might attach to our loose

threads and we juggled
this hard moment
in our entrance. My child

certain *legs* were meant
to stay in *leggings* and when
my reasoning won,

we cried and I held
us both and felt
myself grow softer.

Brandon Houston

Can I Pray For You

I blink myself awake
The lucid lights, shaking
Come into focus:
Granville Street, the neon tubes

I get confused sometimes
I have a name for it
I call it coma grey
This is an altered state
When I'm drinking
I mean really drinking
Not a glass of wine with dinner for my blood
Drinking for days

I can be entertaining at a dinner party
Come out of a coma grey and be dropped into a
Conversation at a warehouse at 5 a.m.
With a German tourist telling me about
His favourite serial killer

It's quiet, not too much traffic
So as a good Catholic
I assume it's a Sunday
I notice a diner I've been to before
I know I can quench my thirst
Subdue my sickness at this checkpoint

I walk through the door

Make eye contact with the server
I nod and give myself the okay to take a booth
Sitting down I feel a shooting pain in my knee
Had I fallen?
Looking for guidance
A restoration from my bondage of sin
I ache in pain and blink myself awake
The server approaches with slight hesitation
Her hair tied up in a frantic bun
She gives me a smile without revealing any teeth

Hi what can I get you, she says
Gin and tonic—a double, my dear, I say
As soon as I say "my dear"
I have given myself away
All right old boy cool down
Just a normal human doing regular things
I nod at nothing
at the back of her head as she walks away
STICKY STICKY I think
Time for a clean up
A meeting is in order

The server returns with the gin and tonic
Places it in front of me
Snatching the drink off the table
I throw the liquid to the back of my throat
It sloshes to the front of my mouth
I close my lips in time to soak the gin into my tongue
Juniper! I say aloud

That'll be $8.75, she says
I'll start a tab, I say
No you won't, she says
Ahhhh fair enough, I say, belching at the same time
I pull out my wallet and empty the contents
An old transit fare and a penny fall out

Shit that's all I have, I say
The server looks down at me and I feel small
She leans over me and begins to talk
Her jaw clenched
She's speaking through her teeth
Listen here Fuck-O I don't get paid jack shit
I'm pretty sure one of the managers is stealing my tips
When a bum like you comes in, guess who pays for it?
Not the owner of the house, no, but me, she says
Well, that's just awful—you know, if you unionize
You won't have to be put out that way
She looks at me, not mad, but worse—
She looks disappointed
Just get out, she says and sulks away

It's pissing rain out and I think an AA meeting is in order
I check my phone and find one down the street
It's at the Gathering Place—a shelter
Which offers a hot meal and support for the down-and-out
I'm in need of some help
The Gathering Place smells of onions and wet feet
Dinner must have just been served
I walk by the TV room and it's full
But for one chair
I take a seat next to a man

He has a cleft lip
Wearing stained cargo shorts
He slips his hand in and out of his pocket
While watching Cheryl Hickey
On *Entertainment Tonight Canada*
I met her once when I lived in Toronto
My friend David was a producer for the show
She follows me on Instagram
I was a real star back then

It's a small group
An old timer running the meeting
A tall skinny gentleman wearing sunglasses inside
A woman stares at the ceiling fan
As if it were a small bird hovering in one spot
I don't recall much of what happened
One day at a time
Just for today
Grateful to be here
Grateful to be alive
Grateful member of AA
So much gratitude
Serenity prayer
Healed sober

After the meeting the woman approaches me
You okay? she asks
Yeah totally fine, I say
You look like you could use a coffee, she says

My name is Mary, she says
We walk back up to Granville Street and into a coffee shop

Busy for 8 p.m.
I'll get you something to eat she says
She comes back with a black coffee and a muffin
She asks me about my life
What I do for work
How I got into drinking
I feel myself fade and close my eyes
Can I pray for you? she says
I blink myself awake
Yeah, sure
Usually when someone says that you think
They are going to pray for you at a later date
Alone at home, on their knees
Leaning against their bed in a sleeping gown

She grabs my hand and cranes her neck forward
God, she says, very loudly
She makes a show of it
She makes a show of her prayer, her holy being
As she prays I feel I'm being used
Then I stop feeling anything
I begin to laugh

Kuldeep Singh

The Beginning

I was washing my heart in the river and
From the sky, a star fell into my hands
It looked like a juicy carambola and
I ate it
I ate all of it, hoping it would clean my lungs
and pacify my desires
But nothing happened
Nothing happened inside me
So I ran to my home and turned off the lights

A few minutes later, a mysterious traveller knocked on the
door and left a book at my doorstep
I picked up the book, opened it and
It ate me
It ate all my innocence, my mind
My soul, my lonely heart
Sad eyes, blurred vision
Words started to appear on blank pages
Chapters started to move to other places
I decided to sit between words
Hoping that eaten star would help me to find myself in this
enchanted world

Why ...

Why does love carry knives
Why has my heart become a paper
Why does my psychologist eat biscuits every time I talk
Why can't my plants survive one day without the water (aren't
they overly dramatic?)
Why do we learn the definition of love from those who never
loved us
Why do all of my feelings become poems
Why do I like seeing people running for trains and missing
them
Why do I act like I have won major awards and give speeches
to my imaginative audience (by the way, some of biggest pop
stars cry after my speeches)
"And you were calling us overly dramatic"—my plants to
me
Why are cats so judgemental
Why do I keep sending love letters to your home when I know
you don't live there anymore
Why do thorns pierce my heart when I see you laughing with
your new heart-shaped balloon
Why hasn't any scientist proposed to me yet
Why ... okay I am done bye.

Three Stages of Love

You make out in the dreams
You smile in the bathroom
You don't feel sleepy after 2:00 a.m.
Your eyes take the bus downtown
All the things show you his name.

Then you make out in the bed
Hold hands, exchange T-shirts,
Share an ice cream and a dream
I love you comes every minute you talk over the phone.

After the breakup, you make out with sad eyes
Burn gifts and throw things on the floor
The roller coaster takes you to the dark places
Your tears wake you up
And dreams make noise when you sleep.

Loop

Candles on the birthday cake make me cry
Every year, they show the number of times I have tried to
forget you
The number of times I have tried to move on while carrying
you

How my heart used to be a home when you were living in it
How it has become a house and all want to rent a room in it

I find escape
I imagine the worst and live inside it
I may never enjoy any birthday happily because
The knife cuts my heart when it cuts the cake and
A thought travels through the gifts, hoping to find your name

Catastrophe

Bombs or bullets
Swords or words
They all are hidden under the tongue
They are the man-made storms
They travel from one's mouth to another's ears
Storms cause torture and unfairness
Storms are bad voices and bad behaviors

Look before you leap
Don't just spit the storm out like it's nothing
Bite your tongue or gulp a chemical
Brush your heart or sew your lips
Once the storm comes out
There's no way to calm it down
Only regret will call you its mom
and it will sleep with you when you are all alone

Pinki Li

To the Family of Raccoons Who Moved in Late Last Week

Welcome to the neighbourhood

My apologies that we have not yet met in person. I am the tenant who lives in the downstairs suite, the one playing the loud television during dinner time and rattling the entire floor when I do my cardio-fit every Thursday, Saturday, and Sunday at noon sharp. Given the paper-thin walls of this house, I imagine you hear all my loud phone calls, as one of my two jobs is working from home as a telemarketer. You probably also catch wind of my vocal exercises in the shower and my late-night readings to myself of my own poetry. You will have to excuse the novice poetics, I am trying my hand at creative writing. Please note that these are works-in-progress. I assure you that the impending revising process will render these pieces substantially more compelling than the first drafts that you heard.

What a packed schedule you all keep between the hours of 3 a.m. and 7 a.m.! Here I thought I was busy, but I certainly do not have newborns yapping night and day. I tip my hat to you!

I don't have children but

I dare say I would be an excellent mother. I have a younger sister; she has a big house across the country, a wonderful husband—very handsome—and three beautiful children whom I met once and simply adored. The children all said I was their favourite aunt. Granted, I am their only aunt, but I do not think this changes the sentiment.

Before your arrival, I had become quite accustomed to living alone with the exception of a few short stints with roommates. I put plenty of effort, if I do say so myself, into mastering my cohabitation skills for these youthfuls. Each morning I prepared them breakfast, observed them as they ate, and then made their beds while they were at work. Despite my hospitality, like a revolving door they were, the roommates. Eventually, I tired of the whole affair.

All to say, you and your family have been a welcome addition to the household! It was me, the other day, who dropped off the Christmas-themed housewarming basket, a neighbourly gesture I wish was still common courtesy. This morning, I was tickled pink to find that you had strung its remnants along the front yard and up the front stairs for festive decor. You have such an eye and thumb for detail; I will have you know that I have caught many a passerby stopping and staring in awe.

Given the violent collisions
last night, it sounded to me like you and your spouse were learning to skateboard, perhaps on the pieces of back alley furniture that I spied you toppling and dismantling earlier? What ingenuity! I myself am too old for all that balancing and crashing but I do find that new hobbies can take the monotony out of a day and drown out even the tiniest whiff of negativity. Hence, the poetry! Speaking of which, I have completed yet another round of revisions, please do not hesitate to chitter your immediate responses as you have so generously been offering.

After an attempted morning nap
I chatted with the landlady; I told her all about how well your family is settling in with the new furnishings and that the young babes are multiplying. She gave me such a look of surprise—I suppose she revealed

herself a prude. As if you'd be doing anything else during this romantic time of year!

I am sure you've noticed that my stringent workout regime has dwindled as of late. I have been fatigued these days. These weeks, rather. I am not sleeping through the night unfortunately, and on the rare occasion that I do manage a brief bout of slumber, I lurch awake as if in danger. In these trying hours of the night, it has been comforting relief to hear you going about your new renovations.

I don't mean to pry but I love dinner parties

Did you have company over last night? You will have to excuse me, I am not the nosy type but it is most delightful to know there's room enough in your suite with all of you, as there just simply isn't enough in mine, with just me. When I used to be invited to dinner parties—a while ago now—I would be the one bringing the dish that got the rave reviews. People would exclaim: Carol, You've outdone yourself! and I would just wave my hand in front of my face and shake my head. I never did it for the praise. I fancied all the company, small talk, and the ritual of squeezing into an old suede dress from my 30s, with matching earrings. The soundtrack to the meal would always be curated by one of my colleagues who knows music. I do not know music but I sincerely appreciated knowing people who know it. I would feel myself getting more cultured by the very act of sitting there, basking in the presence of a jazz legend, my lipstick decorating the rim of a tall glass of Prosecco. How that bubbly would flush my cheeks and get me all saucy and in the mood, if you know what I mean. I always left humming aloud one of the tunes under my bubbly breath, taking the long way home just in case I bumped into someone special on the streets, perhaps someone with chiseled features, marbled eyes like the moon, gentle and warm, but with an unmistakable undercurrent of fire and mystery. Someone like my sister's husband but who isn't my sister's husband, if you know what I mean.

My sincere apologies

I do not mean to disturb, as I can only imagine this to be a rather stressful time. I was entirely shocked, no, aghast—to hear pest control bulldoze into your suite last week. At first, I assumed it to be hired help for your renovations but he then came downstairs to "assure" me that things had "been taken care of." Alas, it seems that following his intrusion, you gave notice immediately, packed your boxes and furniture, and departed. To be completely frank with you, I was hopeful that you would reconsider the move upon finding the rest of the city as expensive and uninhabitable as I have found it. However, the landlady informed me that the entrance to your flat had been boarded up and that you would not be returning.

Each passing night without a peep from you signals to me that you have found new lodgings and for this I am grateful. But the abruptness of circumstances did not provide me the opportunity to bid you and the family farewell. In acknowledging this, I feel a swarm of sadness churn in my throat, my chest, and deep in my belly.

As I lay in a hot herbal bath

I saw through the window, a sparkling string of silhouettes along the fence, a royal midnight parade. It was your family passing through, no doubt heading out for your usual stroll. The sight immediately left me nostalgic for our evening adventures and the care that blossomed between our households. At my age, I have been graced with the wisdom to accept that good things will come and go. Not unlike the ocean tide, they will rush towards you unannounced, nuzzle at your toe tips, and fill you with the warmest of sensations. And then, without so much as a warning, they will leave you, receding far, far away until they are but a faint polaroid of a memory. Good things. Like youth. Or love. Or family.

In any case, I will be here working your suggested edits into my poems and peeking out the window periodically, should you come by with the little ones and fancy a dinner party. It so happens that I have a New

Years-themed housewarming basket with your name on it. In fact, why don't I go ahead and throw on the dress—with the earrings of course— just in case. As I had previously disclosed in our earlier correspondence, we will be tight for space but a bit of rearrangement of the bedroom, living room, and coat closet is no inconvenience at all.

The silence has been piercing since your departure
I continue to wake at all of the darkest and lightest hours of the night, except that I now do so to the sound of my own thoughts, and the tree branches brushing up against the window, which I mistake for your knocking.

Sarah Jessie Tucker
Climate Crisis Within

I was born with glaciers for eyes
and when they started melting
my ancestors showed me a way of coping
by running a pipeline through my nervous system
drinking the oil will cure my pain they say
but now the carbon emissions of my mind
have sped up the melting of my eyes
and as I triage a leak in my line
picketers squeeze at my chest
pointing to the crystal-clear shores of healing
so I jump into the melted waters of my being
but the fracking in my fingers
vibrates me to a tread
my mind immobilizes in the toxicity
I'm lost for days in the leak
suddenly a Thunberg of protesters gathers in my throat
here to demonstrate that treading water puts me
at a 50 percent risk of the next leak being my last
but I'm petrified of swimming to undiscovered shores
so protesters start diving into my belly
urging me not to give up
so I start swimming

Shelter Dog

The only thing the human knows   I was abandoned
here's to another round of hoping in solitude
this time with sensitive hackles raising without anger
the human charges my kennel door *crash clack boom*
I smear like glue to the back of my cage
maybe if I fold my pointy ears and tuck my tail
you'll see it in my eye   homeless yet confined
I just want to walk the human around the block
I'm a good boy scared and don't want to snap
so listen here be gentle with that latch
easy with those fast feet and speak to me gingerly
okay stop there not an inch closer
extend your hand and don't come at me
if you only knew you'd let me come to you

Fear

It's the tears trapped under my left shoulder
like old newspaper tied in a knot
kindling for my cast iron brain
my gridlock jaw at night in slumber
fighting to stay grounded even with the sandman
but he understands my juggle between inferno or freeze
I attempt to regulate like a balance of probabilities
but my enlarged amygdala sets the fire like an arsonist
I lean so far into the pain
my toes are burnt marshmallows
the icy cold veil unravels arms up and
hoofs me down the rabbit hole
don't be afraid of your only soul
says the one walking next to me

Weathering

I paced and waited with Page. We sometimes walked
around the block. When we finally sat at my desk, spring
resurrected the fly buzzing in the purgatory between
window and blind. Then suddenly interrupted by a
hammering woodpecker.

Through open slats I spotted two ravens, gathering
twigs in the towering evergreen trees.
I wondered, would the hawks of summer return?

The following dawn the ravens called four crows
to kick out the doves in the back alley trees. I watched
as a blanket of starlings gathered, reminding me
I traded city sirens for song.

Then a coven of six. Were the crows squawking
for the sick? I wondered again,
would the hawks of summer return?

I needed self-care and leaned back in my gravity chair.
In the distance twelve crows, like kids on a party bus
suddenly split into two groups, then rejoined. I inhaled
their whipping wings as they flew over my head.

The next morning I saw the raven once again
bellowing with a starling in its claw
the crows and magpie in pursuit.
I tried to distract my racing thoughts by fixing the back
porch light.

I stepped onto the first ladder rung and saw hovering overhead
in the clear blue sky, a wingspan as vast as the prairies.
She wiggled her tail feathers at me, *don't worry I'm back.*
This morning's rise I sit at my desk with Page and
she finally speaks: *be the lion.*

Unsure, I walk away. Morning fades as I watch
a raven and a creamy speckled span tango above the
evergreens. The other raven screeching
from hawks' nest of yesteryear.

Dawn falls and Page calls me back. I sit at
my desk, lean in, and Page whispers: *it's time to be the lion.*
I glance out my writing window and spot
the summer hawks nesting
across the street in the naked trees.

F. J. Erica Yang

The Frightfully Pale Yellow

A CONDENSED VERSION

We all had a sleepless night.
How long had it been? Not a goddamn clue.
As long as there was money in the bank to cover the medical bills.
No one cared to keep track.
Maybe it was the pale yellow colour that had infested the whole
hospice.
No one could distinguish the walls from the floor, or the floor from
the ceiling. I knew I couldn't.
It was like a vanilla colour time capsule here.
Time did not move.
Everyone seemed to stay the same and do the same thing: doctors,
nurses, nutritionists, social workers, patients, family members, and
whoever else that lingered in this space.
Except for my mom.
She spoke less and less.
She stayed awake less and less.
She drank and ate less and less.
Her deterioration was the only indication I had of what was real and
what wasn't.

Last night was different, she was different.
"Hey! Wake up!"
"What? What's wrong?"
"Your mom wants to see you."

"Oh! Okay … Hi, Mom. I am here. Do you need something?"
"No. Nothing. I am fine. Go back to bed."
Put that on repeat.

Did I get any sleep?
The frightfully pale yellow did not help.
The floor, wall, ceiling, furniture, equipment, sheets, and patient's
clothing all melted into one.
One rancid vanilla sundae.

I woke up on a fold-out chair in denim shorts and my favourite
rubber ducky T-shirt.
I could see the sun sneaking through the pale yellow blinds.
Shit! It was mid-morning already. I had to get up.
Rubbing my eyes. *Rub. Rub. Rub.* C'mon!
A surge of guilt bid me good morning.
I should have done what my dad did.
Stayed by my mom's side regardless of her wishes.

I needed to head back home, take a shower, change, and bring my
dad new clothes as well.
He had been wearing the same pair of jeans and that pale yellow T-shirt.
He needed some downtime. But we couldn't afford time.

I thought about Grandma Lan.
Maybe she would like to have beef noodle soup with me for lunch?
I chose not to go.
She would understand. I hoped.

Morning came and went. Doctors and nurses did the same.
Grandma Qin arrived with her pale yellow duffle bag.
Full of food and whatever she needed to pass the time.

Newspapers, magazines, chips, cookies, drinks, and even a vanilla milkshake.

The bag was so stuffed that it could burst any second like a diseased appendix.

Everything was for her, not for my mom—her only daughter.

We didn't have a fridge.

I wasn't too sure why she bothered showing up.

No one wanted her here, including herself.

I laid on my fold-out chair.

There was nothing better to do in a hospice.

One of the fluorescent ceiling lights above me was broken, flickering in a hypnotic way, out of rhythm, putting me in a constant trance.

I didn't mind. I needed something to numb me.

I must have drifted off.

I remembered why but not how.

Pastor Chan stood in the room with us.

Doctor spoke with my dad—I guess it's time.

"Let's pray."

We appreciated Pastor Chan.

Took him an hour to get here by bus.

Must have taken the vow of poverty and modesty seriously.

Cheap thin black suit paired with a ragged pale yellow shirt and a narrow black tie.

The Bible in his hand was the same.

Well-thumbed pages in pale yellow hue wrapped by worn-out black leather cover.

We prayed together—something to keep us focused.

We each got to say something nice and reassuring to my mom.

We were told. She could still hear.
My tears got there first and made me miss my turn.
Out of nowhere I heard a sigh.
A sigh that reeked of disappointment and disapproval.

"Fucking tears, go away! C'mon! Say something. I can do this. I must
do this!" I whispered to myself.
"We are all here! We will be fine. I promise.
I will make sure I study hard, and make something out of myself.
You will be proud. God will be proud."
With a forced smile, I shouted all of the above.
"Amen!" they all responded.
Really?
"You will be proud and God will be proud?"
I didn't know if anybody else had noticed.
God couldn't care less, and my mom …
She simply couldn't care.
I ran out of correct things to say.
I just stood there dead frozen and sobbed.
I was 19 and about to lose my mother.

"Sigh …"
There was that fucking sigh again.
I wanted to scream but no voice came to assist me.
I wanted to kick but no muscle came to support me.

"Let's pray!"
I quickly looked over at Pastor Chan.
He was clever. He knew.
I clenched my fists to refocus myself.
I prayed because I really needed to.
I didn't ask God to save my mom.

But to give me compassion and courage.
I sang "Amazing Grace," if one could call that singing.

"Let's pray!"
I really didn't want to sing anymore, but I didn't want to pray, either.
I just stood there and watched my mom.
I watched her watching me.
Her body twitched slightly rerouting all her remaining power to her chest.
… just one more breath.
Her eyes fought to see.
… just one more look.
Her mouth struggled to utter.
… just one last word.
I imagined she said, "I love you."

She stopped.
There was a shade of grey under her skin.
Complimenting that frightfully pale yellow.

"Mom?"

Was this it?
This was it.

At home. Grandma Lan greeted me at the door.
She held out her arms, but pulled back.
She wanted to say something, but swallowed them instead.
She settled on looking at me.

"Grandma, let's have beef noodle soup for lunch tomorrow. My treat!"

Laura McGavin

Saint Agnes

When I slept over
she crowded the twin
with Raggedy Anns, their locks
cherry twirls, murmur-smiles
stitched coal. I dreamt
of lambs that night. I think it's magic
she has a saint. She claims milk
is God's perfect food, frosts
her lips peach. Mother
of seven, her knuckles sense
rain. One Easter
she mummied the kids'
table in Glad. Aggie of the Great
Depression, active dry yeast
always at hand. I'm seven
before I get she doesn't
hug. Saint Stoic. Begged
her doctor to help bring on
the change. Washes
thrifted sweaters in Purex, balls
their scratch for knitting. Keeps
our ancestors in ovals. At visits, urges

caesars with pickled runners, offers
carrot pie, presses it nutmeg-scented
into my chest on a chipped
white plate. Dad never forgave
her brief disownment
but mom knows
Ag's a lamb.

Dear Motor Inn

Three days in an Aerostar toward mom's cradle—canola,
graveyards, views sheared by silos. Carsick, I daydreamed
cousins so distant I could marry them one day, great-aunts
with indoor pools who gather eggs from farm hens
named Lucy. Arriving with a jerk of brakes, we gawked
at your crumbling façade, your sign declaring Closed
for a Function. You were an off-season chalet, a titled circus
tent. Pickled eggs floated testicular on your mirror shelves
embossed with gold. Geraldo squawked on TV, your carpet
hunter green, crop-circled with lager. Grown-ups, manic
after Crown and Cokes, shoulder-hugging by your guestbook.
We cousins in ruffles ignored the uncles, went forth
in a pack—hid and sought under Formica, flung
peanut shell confetti, peeled paint ripples off door frames, tore
bows from chair-backs, stuck their velour to our party dresses
and cat-walked. Glory, our brief neglect by mothers
sharing cigarettes under prairie skies, just as they did
at fourteen. Glory, to dance unbridled, self-serve orange pop
on tap. We let go and were let go of. Dear motor inn,
each Easter I still recall Ukrainian eggs you displayed
on a shelf near the ladies' room. Hopping in line, I admired
their precise quadrilaterals, bright batik. When you're empty

do you marvel at the care it takes to blow yolk
from a pin prick, even as you cheer for the Roughriders?
Your legacy isn't all messiness. After the reunion
we convened again in you for scrambled eggs and stiff waves
before boarding our minivans for home, tucking
traded pebbles into the seatbacks, swearing we'd write.

Clare Adam

My Grandfather's Trauma on a Tea Tray

A
  tall
    stooped
      gentle man
My grandfather—a version of a man

Greenhouse pottering
  solitary
    tending cucumbers and tomatoes
Bags of composted earth
      ventilation
        water on tap

Order. Structure. Knowledge.

Chlorophyll sharp and pungent green
  a hint of melon and sour
Succulent orbs dripping red juice and pips
  Salad tonight
    Served in a garlic-rubbed cracked wooden bowl

    Fire!   *Fire!*   *Fire!*

You're the man—take aim

D E S T R O Y

Your time on this earth
Your age and education gifted you higher rank
Their time on this earth
and limited education made them lower

Uniform. Rank. Death.

You are responsible. You all signed up for King and Country

Stay Awake! Stay Awake! Stay Awake!

The blackened sea is yours to watch—they may die tonight

Drink tea—you must—Stay Awake!

YOUR VERSION OF WORLD WAR TWO

   you return home
      a terrifying concoction of
         responsibility
            children
               and panic

What does safe feel like?
What does familiar smell like?

   sleep—impossible

There is so much noise
  Your sweet wife loves you
    She strokes your shattered memories
      Every night after supper she prepares the tea tray
      Every night at 3 a.m.
        She pours boiling water onto tea leaves

and gently returns to watch with you

I'm Leaking

Your ancestral fluids patterned the bathroom

     no Home Decor magazine would ever suggest

Discovering   You   Made   Him   Scream

     those patterns were not made by

     feet in damp sand
     children's sticky fingers
     or a mosaic repeat

All the decor decisions were yours alone   Always alone

Your departure didn't require an accomplice—someone to
help you pack or unpack
tell me please—who held your hand as you waved goodbye?

     I thank you for the note
     I am so sorry
     I read it again and again

☙

My adult children are literate now and their questions must be
opened

☙

You birthed me red and raw:

"grated beets cradle softened goat cheese with a piquant vinaigrette"

Navel threads of golden oil and red wine vinegar tied me in your womb
...... those threads bound us together for a very......
.... long time ....

and then
I gifted you death

Tributaries of the unimaginable join me every day
I hear shouts and screams and the rattling of tins

I am so lost

The map in my head confuses me because my body no longer knows the way

I am a trespasser in my homemade picture book

Amrit Kaur Sanghera
Moving Another Way
AN EXCERPT

Once they get through the final wall of trees, they see what was being closed off. They see their broken little home. The door was left wide open. The kids look at each other and hold hands. As they walk closer, the eldest tightens her grip. They get through the entrance and start to look around. They find a few toys, a few lost memories. The eldest starts reminiscing, telling the younger one stories about the toys and how they would play together and create imaginary worlds with the toys. They slowly peer into each corner, examining little treasures they would find.   On the other side of the house, there is one other room with its door still shut. The kids do not go inside that room just yet. But if we were to go to the other side of the door we'd see a burnt room filled with a pile of ashes and two skeletons on the floor.

Two skeletons.
Still.
Heat.

Two people who were part of this home.
Who were partners. Who were parents.
The father grew up with a big family in a small home.
He had eight siblings and they all shared many things. Clothes, food, space, time.
His parents were partners, not lovers.
His parents grew up in a time where many things were taken, not given. His parents kept things in order and never let their kids get away with anything

"bad." His parents believed in keeping their kids in order—keeping control. His parents never hesitated to show their disapproval. And being "good" kids they showed their parents respect, respect that was absolutely indefinitely obligatory, not a choice. That is just the way you raise kids—that's what they would say. His parents showed their limited compassion to a few.

He was not one of them.

He was told to stand up and shut up. He would go to the roof of his house and look at his world—pushing down his discontent and rage. He was told to get married and find a new life of his own. A respectful one.

Heat rising.

The mother grew up in a family where you can say there was love and compassion.

Her father loved her dearly. So much so, that he was afraid of the world hurting her. He was anxious. He had seen how the world treated girls—it didn't celebrate them. In fact, when a girl was born into a family, the family was greeted with pity. "I'm sorry, I hope the next child you have is a boy. I'll pray for you." Girls weren't celebrated by others. They were seen as burdens. They were dispensable. And the world was dangerous for them.

But her father and mother celebrated her.

They both loved her. She was their only child. They wanted to keep her safe.

And when her mother passed away, her father could not bear to lose more. He told her to stay home—be a good daughter. So she stayed home, she listened to her father, she cleaned the floor, she cooked food, she stayed home.

But more importantly, she kept quiet.

Her presence was small outside of her home, and sometimes even inside it. She did not get space to be herself, to live the way she wanted to. She had to be quiet, obedient, and good. And when her father remarried, she became smaller.

She felt numb at times.

She was told, at a very young age, to get married and to create a new life with her husband.

Smoke.

They get married, for partnership, not for love.
Love could come later.
As a gift, the father's parents gave him his childhood home, where no one lived anymore. It was the one nice thing they had done for him.
He went out to work. She stayed silent and worked from
home.
alone.
They were apart much longer than they were together. They did not know each other very well. But they tried. He brought her flowers and told her about his day at work. She would listen. She would tell him about what she did around their home and in town. He would listen. They would go for walks and ask questions about each other. They would smile at each other and would take care of each other in tiny ways. And when left in the morning, they both waved and looked until they could no longer see one another.

A little spark of fire emerged from the skeletons.

She got pregnant.
They prayed for a son. Their families prayed for them.
They thought that maybe with this child, things would finally be better, they'd have a fuller family.
They thought that maybe they could be happy.
It would be a blessing. The day came, and their child arrived. She was a tiny baby girl, a soft gentle pearl. They kissed their daughter, but they could not fully hide their disappointment. And they couldn't hide from the disappointment that was voiced by others. Only the mother's parents celebrated their new baby. The father saw his parents show no affection for his daughter. They held her with cold hands and cold faces. They looked at him like he was flawed—that he was to be blamed. He felt so angry he almost threw up, but he kept it down. He put his anger into his work. Then into his hands, then into his eyes, then into his words. The mother

tried to walk past the anger. She was still hopeful. She kissed her daughter and held on to her. She felt less alone with her little one.

But anger found her too. Way too often.

She pushed it down. Slowly her silence became less silent over time. Both were slowly claimed by the growing chaos rumbling inside them. They yelled back and forth. He blamed her. She told him he should do better, be better.

She cried till she was numb.

He drank till he was numb.

Fire weaved through the bones, light licked the wall.

They fought, pounding malicious words at each other. The yells echoed. The silence afterwards was piercing. Money was never enough.

Money came in sparingly, frustration came in abundantly.

Frustration came with drinking.

Frustration came with complaints.

Frustration came with disappointment.

Frustration came with yelling and running away.

That stress would crawl with them everywhere they went. No matter how hard they worked, they barely had enough. Then one blessed day they discovered that they were pregnant again. They prayed and prayed. But the mother gave birth to a beautiful little girl. The mother kissed her, but the father looked away.

The father's parents were unimpressed. To him, it felt like his parents grew twenty feet tall and looked at them like they were tiny pitiful ants. Two nothings. Four nothings.

He left.

But when he came back, he brought all the rage that'd been following him his whole life.

It was a big hot bloody red cloud that hovered over them. Each step the cloud would flourish, shaking the house. Each day this big hot bloody red cloud filled their lungs. You could hear screeching, deathly pounding and vibrations, you'd hear them run. But they couldn't run from the house.

The fire juggled itself higher, spinning in masterful ways.

The liquor fuelled the cloud and the cloud sickened their voices to spit terrible wishes. They roamed in a heat that could not quell them.

The fire slithered around the room, waiting to pounce.

No, the heat, the cloud, the red grew bigger till the house was filled. It left little air and the cloud did not care.

The smoke found its way under the door, and lurked behind the kids. The kids did not know, the kids did not know.

One day, the last day, the big hot bloody red cloud decided it wanted to take them all.

The smoke moved in closer, ready to tangle them there.

They were told to run. They were told to go, leave. Take your things and go. Run. Leave.

The smoke began to rush to them. The fire pounded at the door. The kids needed to leave. They needed to RUN. GO. RUN. LEAVE.

The kids turned around to see where the voice came from but instead saw the smoke curl around their necks. They ran outside as fast as their little feet could take them. They stopped right out front and watched the house burn. The eldest held on to her sister's hand and walked her away from the fire, the heat, and the big, bloody, red clouds.

Marco Melfi

A Model from Bosch's *The Garden of Earthly Delights* Reminisces

That's me at the bottom, centre panel, multiplied.
Shut in a clam. Fed a red Gobstopper by a duck.
"Drunk" on a strawberry. Upside down in a pond,

my hands cupped at my crotch like I'm blocking
a shot in a soccer match. That Bosch—what an eye.
I scored a few bucks for each stance, although less

than I earned working a plough. Those poses were
my only foray into the arts when I was young enough
to cartwheel and should've tried improv. I should've

gone for more pints with the pals in the brown owl.
A fluke audition but no regrets. A once in a lifetime
triptych. Never saw a narwhal or nymph since.

Michael Edwards

Oyama Rainbow

When I cast a single
mayfly into autumn waters,
its fine hackle wings stood like hairs,
prickled the surface film.
And being so considerate
as to not rock the craft,
I moved astern and made way
for shipmates, two roommates.
And my 5-weight pulsed,
the fine glass taper danced
and bent to the cork,
each eyelet wound in iridescence.
Then my heel caught and
I stumbled over a baton
of aluminum hull stiff as whale-rib
and I toppled waist-deep
into Oyama Lake.

Onshore the firs and pines
encircled, leaned in, looking.
And with rod still in hand,
I reeled—kept the tip high,
vaulted aboard and benched
myself aft. Pockets full
of water, I landed the fish,
to a volley of laughter.

I sat there like a smallfry Jonah
by the belly of a trout,
engrossed in the silver-blue,
magenta, and olive-green
bands of its body, dwelling
in the moment of capture.

The low sun flooded
the boat in shadow
as a wind whipped up,
oars dipped and pulled us shoreward.
The fish stowed in thin plastics,
cooling as we loaded
for the run to valley bottom—
through sagebrush,
switchbacking loose gravel
onto Highway 97, six lanes wide.
We crawled through endless
traffic lights, past Walmart
and strip malls immemorial to home,
a sun-faded split-level,
its blue paint falling in flakes
like scales off a fish.

And I wonder did it know
it was raised to die to a dinner plate?
Product of science, a sterile strain
slit from gill to anal fin.
My knife's hard spine chattered
and bounced against pin bones
and xylophone vertebrae.
My index finger hooked through
tiny organs, the trout's inner tickings.

Still submerged in its world,
I'm not laughing now.
Well, maybe slightly—
maybe it's a metallic laugh,
as in a dream
where I'm forever tottering
over the gunwales—
then startle awake with eyes
blurred and blinking at silvery
slashes in a small bay.

Ghost Shrimp

I generally avoid the living
legends at Main Street launches.
I prefer to slip three rows deep
into an audience of casual gods,
where Bowering or possibly
Poseidon grins through gold-framed
glasses, looped from his trident's handle.
His leather briefcase bursts with books
as he shakes hands with the author
and asks for a signed copy
before the reading begins.

The refreshment table stands
sacramental to one side
with wine and snacks,
water and wine. Holy water.
San Pellegrino sparkles
carbonic like the acid that stifles
my ability to speak.

So warm, their smiles grip me
with fear. My tight chest heaves,
my eyes pull away from all threats
as I sit like a crustacean curled
in a folding chair, my pink body
leaps when anyone looks at it
or glances graze me.

They must see through my shell,
as opaque as Scotch Tape
as I pulse around the room,
shrimp-like, in suspicion.
With one swift rip I peel off,
leave residue of regret,
float back home, to rest on a shoal,
or a seamount or my desk
where I flip notebooks,
write poems and read poets
I've just heard but already love.

My exoskeleton hardens,
holds me like armour
then I molt through skins
of various sea creatures
until I'm a seahorse,
so next time I'd hold on,
curl my tail around strands
of seagrass and stay.

Tharuna Abbu

April

the first spring morning is a sheet of grey sky,
so blankly solid for something so pregnant with water.

in the alley, power lines slung between the shingled roofs
suggest that the stillness has invited some great spider to nest.

the rain has made all greens greener,
earth protruding back to the world.

As the hour brightens, crow arcs down from above;
considers the air and how it feels to belong to it.

she settles on the fence post
and gently showers rain from her body.

soon, she leaps—
ignites wind

soars higher and higher against the empty heaven,
disappearing like ash lifting from a flame.

At CRAB Park

the seagulls glide and play;
their weightless bodies twinned by the sea,
lighter still, below.

a different flock roosts, brooding against the mountains,
long necks, the colour of warning.
deliberate motion—

the minutes arching, they lift freights
one by one
to construct a nest of metal.

even the gulls adapt,
make nests with brambles and discarded chocolate wrappers,
the occasional cigarette stump.

in the setting sun,
the gulls litter the air with laughter, unbounded by the sky.
their gilded bodies dancing as they fly beyond view.

the cranes go on,
machine intonations constant and unending,
into the night.

Los Angeles

on the Red Line heaving towards NoHo,
two men,
faces creased and all in camo,
each hold in their laps a bouquet of roses.

I imagine them as lovers,
returning to each other
night after night in the bravado of flowers
and the gentleness of men
always at war.

Contributors

FOREWORD

Betsy Warland has published thirteen books of creative non-fiction, lyric prose, and poetry. A reviewer of her 2020 book of prose poems, *Lost Lagoon/lost in thought*, observed: "Her command of art and of language is that of a virtuoso." A second edition of her memoir *Bloodroot—Tracing the Untelling of Motherloss* (with a new long essay by Warland) will be released in 2021. Also in 2021, Lloyd Burritt's opera *The Art of Camouflage*, based on Warland's 2016 book, *Oscar of Between—A Memoir of Identity and Ideas*, will be premiered in the Indie Opera West festival. Founder of the Writer's Studio at SFU, she directed and mentored in TWS for a number of years. Warland is the director of Vancouver Manuscript Intensive and received the City of Vancouver Mayor's Award for Literary Excellence in 2016.

AUTHORS

Tharuna Abbu is a queer Tamil poet who grew up on the territory of the Anishinaabe peoples and the Métis Nation. They now live on the unceded territory of the Musqueam, Squamish, and Tsleil-Waututh people, where they work as a family doctor. Their poems have appeared in *CV2* and in *Room* magazine. Generally, their writing considers (home) land, (up)rooting, connection, and the teachings of the body.

Clare Adam is a grateful "blow-in" from another land (a very small island). She lives near the sea, has taught art, helped raise two offspring, and was a useless "postie" while living in beautiful B.C. The creative energy severed ties with her soul due to a backlog of unhealed traumas. So, as a "newbie" to writing, she packed away her art materials in exchange for a hand-me-down laptop and started to clumsily tap away. Her aim is to slowly shift from the dark and learn how to play with the daft and delightful.

Teminey Beckers is fascinated by the intricacies of human relationships. She writes short stories and poems, and is currently working on a novel based on her mother's life. When she is not writing, she can be found laughing along forest trails with dear friends, working out story ideas in her garden, or perfecting her latest recipe for various fermented vegetables and healthy, yet binge-worthy, chocolate peanut butter cups. She lives with her husband and two children on Vancouver Island, B.C.

Tanya Belanger is a baker by trade and part-time writer and poet. She left her family farm in Ontario fourteen years ago for an adventure, stopping when her family reached the sea. She left a career in IT and when she arrived in British Columbia, started her bakery, a statement against industrialized food production and factory farming. She owns western Canada's largest certified organic artisan bakery. Writing is as passionate to her as sourdough.

Bailey Bjolin is a writer and a farmer living on Quadra Island, B.C. A lifelong writer, Bailey has always appreciated being able to capture a moment in words. When she's not harvesting carrots or weeding greenhouses, Bailey enjoys writing in a range of styles, from creative non-fiction to sci-fi.

Emma Brady was born and raised in a wonderful, large family in Dublin, Ireland. She moved to Vancouver in 2011 with her high school sweetheart and now calls both cities home. She is an elementary school teacher who, by seeing her writing here in print for the first time, now believes that she may also call herself a writer. Joining TWS to write her family's story was her first step in response to the question, "If not now, then when?" She is married with a growing two- and four-legged family and enjoys any chance to travel that comes her way.

Barbara Cameron lives and writes on Vancouver Island, almost as far west as you can get and still be in Canada. When she was a child she was often teased that to find her you just had to look for the nearest book. She now spends much of her time writing the books she wants to read. She completed the Writer's Studio program at SFU in June, 2020.

William W. Campbell, MD is a neurologist, writer, artist, retired U.S. Army Colonel, and former flight surgeon who is extensively published in scientific literature and the author of several medical textbooks. In retirement, he began writing short stories about memorable patients encountered over nearly fifty years of practice, stories about medical detective work with a human touch. His award-winning stories explain science in a way understandable to the lay reader. His memoir tells the story of a journey from the rural South to eminence in academic and military medicine.

Emily Chan is a writer and communications professional based in Vancouver, B.C., where she lives with her partner and aging cat. By day, Emily writes about climate change and the right to a healthy environment. By night, she is working on a memoir about her experiences surviving anti-NMDA receptor encephalitis and recovering in a damp Vancouver Special that once belonged to her Chinese grandparents. Emily holds a journalism degree from Carleton University.

375

Rebecca Chan is a Chinese writer living on unceded Coast Salish territory. After dabbling in political and editorial writing, she is excited to focus on fiction centering on mothers and daughters. Her work can be found in *xoJane*, *News Nanaimo*, the *Nanaimo Bulletin*, and Women Watching Nanaimo.

Stephanie Charette is a raven-brained sci-fi and fantasy writer from the wilds of northern Canada who fled the eternal snow for the West Coast. Her work has appeared in *Podcastle*, *Shimmer*, and *Pulp Literature*. She is an alumni of Viable Paradise and Taos Toolbox. A wallflower with a taste for whisky, she'll be off hoarding office supplies. Don't let her borrow your pen.

Alana Cheyne is a poet, writer, and co-founder of a bustling Okanagan wellness centre, where she writes and edits wellness articles. She holds a BA in English from the University of Alberta and a BA in journalism from the University of King's College in Halifax, and she is currently completing the Writer's Studio program under the mentorship of poet Kayla Czaga. She lives in Vernon, B.C., with her partner and daughter.

Ankush Chopra is an award-winning author, speaker, professor of strategy, and strategy consultant. He is the author of *The Dark Side of Innovation* (Brigantine Media, 2013), *A Sixty-Minute Guide to Disruption* (Promethean Strategies, 2017), and numerous academic and mainstream articles. When not climbing new mountains, he teaches business strategy and advises business leaders on strategic issues in the Americas, Europe, and Asia. Chopra has an MBA from the Indian Institute of Management Bangalore and a PhD in business from Duke University. He lives in the Greater New York area with his wife and son.

Hannah Costelle is a mystery and fantasy writer in Kentucky who strives to bring humour and intricate plot twists into her work. Her short story "Cactus and Lizard" has been accepted for publication in speculative fiction magazine *Metaphorosis*. She is forever working on a series of mystery novels.

Kate Covello created Land and Heart Yoga Teacher Training in 2019. It's a yoga school founded on examining personal reasons for teaching yoga. Students develop their own voices in the dynamic art of describing yoga. Online Yoga Teacher Training launched on April 25, 2020 with five students. She lives in Yellowknife. katecovello.com

Nothing surprised **Judy Dercksen**, an ex-South African now-Canadian family doctor, more than when she discovered writing would explain her own complex PTSD and change the way she practised medicine. Doctors of B.C. recognized her as a doctor making a difference and sponsored her chronic pain and PTSD website. She has articles published in the *BCMJ*, *CMAJ*, and *Medical Post*, and she has completed the UBC Advanced Certificate for Creative Writing and is a TWS Online graduate. Judy's novel manuscript, "The Dark That Lets Light In," is set in South Africa in 1985.

Shenul Dhalla is a graduate of SFU's TWS program. In 2015, she graduated from SFU with a major in English literature and minor in philosophy, precisely five years after her first cancer diagnosis. Shenul is a B.C. Cancer Foundation supporter of ongoing cancer research and programs.

Colleen Doty does some of her best writing while turning compost and watching her chickens. With an MA in Canadian history, she is a writer and professional researcher living on Galiano Island. Her novel manuscript, "All About Isaac," spans thirty years and explores themes of mental illness, addiction, class, and colonialism, and is set in an intimate world of one family and their years-long battle to truly understand each other. Also a writer of short stories and poems, Colleen's most recent story, "What the Sea Eats," appears in the anthology *Rising Tides: Reflections for Climate Changing Times*.

Diane Dubas is a writer based in Ontario, Canada. She has a number of short stories published or forthcoming with *AEscifi, Inaccurate Realities, Saturday Night Reader*, and the following anthologies: *Wings of Renewal, Don't Open Till Doomsday*, and *Circuits and Slippers*. She is a graduate of numerous writing programs, including the Writer's Studio at SFU and the Humber School for Writers. In her spare time Diane likes to daydream about dragons and space, and more importantly, dragons in space.

Michael Edwards is a poet, writer, and busy dad living in Vancouver, B.C. on traditional unceded Musqueam and Coast Salish territories. His work has been published in various online journals, including *Cypress Poetry Journal, Cabinet of Heed*, and *Headline Poetry*. Michael also edits *Red Alder Review*, an online publication focused on building connections between writers and the wider community.

DK Eve returned to her hometown in 1992 after living in Victoria, Regina, Ottawa, and Montreal. Her mother said she had come back to the Sooke River to spawn. She's been a journalist, public servant, hockey mom, and failed politician. She draws on Vancouver Island's characters and settings in poetry and short prose, published in six anthologies for the Sooke Writers' Collective and *Art & Word* (Sooke Arts Council, 2018). She's an active volunteer on the Federation of B.C. Writers board. Her home in Sooke is a haven for hummingbirds, deer, other critters, and a couple of humans.

Katherine Fawcett is a Squamish-based writer, teacher, musician, and mountain enthusiast. She has published two short story collections: *The Swan Suit* (Douglas & McIntyre, 2020) and *The Little Washer of Sorrows* (Thistledown Press, 2015). She has also written a book about living in bear territory: *A Whistler Bear Story* (Get Bear Smart, 2010). Her writing has been featured in *Geist*, *Event*, *subTerrain*, and *Grain* magazines, and in numerous anthologies. She prefers blueberry but will eat rhubarb pie in a pinch.

A native of New Westminster, **Deborah Folka** has been writing stories since she taught herself to read at the age of three. After earning communications and journalism degrees at the University of Washington and the University of Arizona, she worked in communications for a variety of public, private, and not-for-profit organizations in both Canada and the United States. For over twenty years she has been an independent consultant with expertise in crisis communications and issues management. She currently edits *No Good Deed*, an ethics column for the Canadian Public Relations Society, as well as numerous other client publications.

Maryanna Gabriel is an artist, writer, and forest dweller on Salt Spring Island, B.C. Formerly a web designer, she is studying for her MFA in creative non-fiction at King's College, Dalhousie University. Her interests include gardening, cooking with style, and bandying with the voices in her head. She is the author of *Memento: A Coastal Recipe Treasure*, *Owen's Grandmother and the Little Black Box*, and *The Book of Days*. She is a graduate of Emily Carr University with a certificate in art and design and has studied creative writing at the University of Toronto.

Elliott Gish wants to make you sleep with the lights on. A writer and librarian from Halifax, Nova Scotia, she holds a master's degree in library and information studies from Dalhousie University. Her work has been published in *Psychopomp Magazine*, *Understorey Magazine*, *Vastarien*, the *Dalhousie Review*, and others. Her novel manuscript, "Grey Dog," follows a turn-of-the-century schoolteacher whose post in a small town puts her in the grasp of an ancient and malevolent power.

Lori Greenfield is a retired RN with a strong interest in, and passion for, women's issues, specifically the right to choice. She returned from Calgary to Vancouver in 2012 to begin her next phase of life as a writer. Her writing has been published in the collection of stories, *One Kind Word: Women Share Their Abortion Stories* (Three O'Clock Press, 2014) and on her blog. She strives daily to live an honest and authentic life. She is forever grateful for the friendship and support of the TWS non-fiction group and her mentor JJ Lee.

Hugh Griffith is a biologist, science writer, and natural sciences educator with a fondness for storytelling. His fiction often features wildlife and wilderness. His novel manuscript, "The Snake Club," is a fast-paced, suspenseful story of a family beset by an unknown stalker, set in the contrasting worlds of a luxurious cruise ship and the rugged desert of Baja California. Hugh is a recent graduate of the SFU Writer's Studio and lives in Richmond, B.C., where there are very few venomous snakes.

Brandon Houston is a health care worker, emerging writer, and labour activist. He writes poetry and short stories, focusing on narratives of working-class people, which reflects his upbringing and political values.

Nancy Jin emigrated to Vancouver in 2008. She obtained a master's degree in TEFL at the University of Salford in Britain. She has taught English writing at university level as well as in language training centres. She got SFU's creative writing certificate in 2020. She is now working on her first novel, a work that reflects the motif of women who were held back from self-awareness and self-actualization through the exploration of the life of her grandmother, a 94-year-old woman with bound feet, as well as the lives of other women in her family.

Prachi Kamble is a Canadian writer and journalist of Indian descent currently based in Vancouver, B.C., unceded land of the Squamish, Tsleil-Waututh, and Musqueam Nations. Prachi holds degrees in English literature from UBC and electrical engineering from the University of Calgary, and has lived in India, Italy, Malaysia, and the UAE. Prachi is the founder and editor of *The Vancouver Arts Review*, an online magazine that promotes the excellence of local female, BIPOC, and LGBTQ+ artists. She lives by the beach with her partner and their many houseplants, and loves to eat tacos.

Uttara Krishnadas does her best writing under the pressure of a deadline. Much to the chagrin of her mother, she has been making up stories since she was four years old. But, she has trouble putting them down on paper. The Writer's Studio has helped her take herself seriously as a fiction writer. A resident of Mumbai, India, she has an MA in film from Kingston University, London. Uttara recently made her directorial debut with a short film earlier this year.

Justyna Krol was born in Lublin, Poland, and currently lives and works on the traditional territories of the Squamish, Musqueam, and Tsleil-Waututh First Nations. She is a communications coordinator, graphic designer, poet, and writer. Her non-fiction has appeared in *Hayo Magazine* and she has performed her poetry at *SAD Mag*'s Sad Cosmos reading series. She writes a lot about her family, as they continue to be interesting. Like most Geminis, she prefers to have the last word.

Angela Kruger is a writer, scholar, and activist. Her work has been published in community and academic publications, including *Nikkei Images*, *Nikkei Voice*, *The Bulletin/Geppo*, *The Volcano*, and *Canadian Literature*. Growing up as a mixed Japanese Canadian settler in and around Vancouver, B.C., Angela's creative writing developed alongside her political activism. Involved in the Japanese Canadian and Downtown Eastside communities, her writing is an expression of her commitment to their fight for justice. Angela now lives with her partner in Kingston, Ontario. She's working on her next book, a collection of short stories—in between movies and bags of chips.

Christina Kruger-Woodrow is a fiction writer who lives with her partner in North Vancouver. Prior to TWS, she studied at SFU and graduated with a BA in philosophy. When she's not working, she lives a fast-paced and exciting life of gentle walks, bike rides on the Seymour Demonstration Forest Road, and looking up more pictures of cats on Instagram than is strictly decent.

Dora Larson is a graduate of the Jiménez-Porter Writers' House at the University of Maryland. She won second prize for prose at the University of Maryland's Litfest, and her writing has been published in *Stylus: A Journal of Literature and Art*. In addition to writing fiction, Dora is a practising lawyer. She lives in Los Angeles with her husband, son, and two cats.

Anna Lee-Popham is a white settler writer and editor. She will begin an MFA in creative writing at the University of Guelph in 2020 and is a recent graduate of Simon Fraser University's Writer's Studio Online program and the University of Toronto's Certificate in Creative Writing. Anna facilitates community writing workshops with the Toronto Writers Collective and lives with her partner and child in Toronto on the traditional territories of the Huron-Wendat Nation, Mississaugas of the New Credit First Nation, Mississaugas of Scugog Island First Nation, the Haudenosaunee, and the Métis Nation of Ontario, home to many diverse Indigenous peoples.

Katie Lewis is a Vancouver-based journalist. Her work has appeared in publications such as the *Ottawa Citizen,* the *National Post,* the *Globe and Mail,* the *Toronto Star, Al Jazeera,* NPR, and CBC. She has reported from countries around the globe—including Uganda, South Sudan, DRC, Somalia, Colombia, and China. Previously, she worked in a senior communications role with Canada's largest investment bank. Katie holds both a BA and MA in journalism from Carleton University in Ottawa, Canada. Outside of work, she volunteers with VOKRA, is VP of the Strathcona Residents Association, and is raising five-year-old twins.

Pinki Li is an artist/facilitator living and learning on the unceded ancestral lands of the Musqueum, Squamish, and Tsleil-Waututh First Nations. At the age of five, she picked up the English language and a pen with a vengeance. Her writing has filled more than 25 journals and nine years' worth of online blog entries, which she now reads aloud professionally. Pinki writes for and about contemporary performance—contemplating its relations to food, race, and the anti-colonial body. She is a late sleeper, a late riser, a late bloomer, a latecomer, and a late-night snacker.

Danica Longair will look after you, if you consent. Her current care-receivers include her young son, middle-aged husband, and two old cats. She also tends to the extensive collections of tea she drinks daily, plants she sometimes waters, and books she'll hopefully read. She is revising a novel manuscript titled "Hope Is a Necessary Delusion," a mental health dystopia, while living in somewhat dystopian times. Her work appears in *Prairie Fire* and the anthologies *Sustenance* and *The Walls Between Us.* In addition to fiction, she writes creative nonfiction and attempts poetry. Join her on her journey at danicalongair.com.

Magnus Lu was born in Vancouver and is a graduate of the Writer's Studio in the fiction cohort. She has a background in computer science and East Asian studies and works as a freelance project manager. Magnus lives in downtown Vancouver with her husband and their bullheaded Boston terrier, Huey.

Laura McGavin is a writer and editor who lives in Ottawa. Her poems appear in the *Literary Review of Canada, Room, cv2, The Maynard, Riddle Fence*, and elsewhere. Before TWS Online, Laura completed degrees in English at the University of Victoria and Queen's University. She is working on a manuscript of poetry about new motherhood.

As a youth services librarian, **Libby McKeever** is passionate about youth literature, both writing for and reading to kids and teens. Her book- and writing-club kids have been her beta readers and always keep her on task. As well as reviewing children's books for the Canadian Review of Materials, McKeever belongs to the Vicious Circle writing group. Her short story "Sand in My Oranges" was published in *Pique Newsmagazine* and her creative non-fiction piece, *Travels and Trails: The Story of the Burrard-Lillooet Cattle Trail*, was performed at the 2010 Olympics. Her current YA project is "Out of the Wreckage."

Clare McNamee-Annett is a writer in Surrey, B.C. If she found a matter-hole, she would pop her head inside, just to take a look.

Calvin McShane is a fisherman and writer living in Michigan's Upper Peninsula. He holds a BA in philosophy and after his day job spends his time fishing, gardening, practicing Soto Zen, and hanging out with his two dogs and partner, Miranda. Calvin hopes his writing is thought-provoking and entertaining. He is currently working on a collection of short stories that he hopes will offer him more time to fish.

Jenn Marx was born and raised in urban Ontario but answered a call to adventure in 2003, when she moved to remote northern B.C. for work as a registered nurse. When she's not writing, you'll find her exploring the wilderness right outside her back door with her husband, two children, and a dog who's convinced he's human. Her short stories have been placed on a few long lists, not enough short lists, and garnered a second-place win for "Wood Anemone," published online by *Northword Magazine* in December 2018.

Raised in a small town near Milan, **Francesca Mauri** has since lived in eight countries, from Macedonia to Australia. She has been daydreaming and solving riddles since childhood, as stray cats and weird smells always popped up in her garden. Now she creates her own dark mysteries on the page. She is currently working on her first novel, "Adriana," a psychological thriller set in the UK. Francesca has published articles about travel on *Futura—Corriere della Sera* and *Natural Born Vagabond*, and written short stories for children for K-5 Learning. English is her second language.

Marco Melfi is an Edmonton poet originally from Hamilton. He has had poems published in *The Prairie Journal, FreeFall, Funicular Magazine, 40 Below: Alberta's Winter Anthology,* the *Stroll of Poets Anthology,* and as part of the Edmonton Poetry Festival's Poetry Route. His chapbook, *In between trains,* was published in 2014 and received the Sharon Drummond Chapbook award.

Višnja Milidragović is a wanderer at heart, even when her body is in stillness. Born in Sarajevo, in the former Yugoslavia (current-day Bosnia), she's currently settled in Vancouver, where she works as a content strategist and editor. She is currently working on her first memoir, as well as other creative musings on themes of belonging, connection, and relationships. She has a BA in English literature from UBC and a master's in publishing from SFU and has only published things on the internet, mostly under the moniker @vishmili or with a corporate byline.

Margaret Miller has worked for environmental organizations in Vancouver, Toronto, Whitehorse, and New Delhi, and studied ecological theology at Vancouver School of Theology. Travelling the globe has been a passion, but for the past few years Margaret has enjoyed becoming more familiar with, and writing about, her Vancouver hometown. When she isn't riding around the city on her bicycle, taking in her surroundings, she writes personal essays, often about the environment.

Jack Murphy emigrated from Ireland to Canada in 2015, after receiving a degree in fine art. Most of his time is spent reading sci-fi and fantasy or tending to his two cat overlords. He is currently working on a fantasy novel with all the Dickensian murder mystery and gunpowder plots he can fit into it.

eve nixen's (Nicole Ebert) writing is visceral, expressive, and provocative. She is interested in experimenting with language and teases the boundaries of traditional storytelling. eve is a McGill graduate and professional non-profit fundraiser working in the arts. She won her first poetry contest when she was fifteen. For two years she was the director of operations of the Speakeasy Project, an online creative workshop space. She self-published a collection of poetry in 2019, *In Pursuit of Gravity*, and a chapbook of short stories in 2016, "Day Dreams of a Dull Girl."

Tim J. O'Connor shelved all his creative pursuits in the 1980s to "get a real job" in business. He started taking writing seriously in his fifties, when he was admitted to the Writer's Studio. It was there he began to listen to the muses and started penning his novel, "The Book of Watchers." Tim lives with his wife, Karen, who still puts up with him after thirty years. When he's not writing, he's playing hockey, on his bike, or poorly strumming a few chords on the guitar. All three of his children have pursued careers in the arts; he never told them to "get a real job."

Elizabeth Page is a graduate of the Writer's Studio at SFU. She was the 2018 second-prize recipient of the Northwestern Ontario Writers Workshop's Bill MacDonald Prize for Prose and was long listed for the CBC Poetry Prize in 2019. Elizabeth has written several articles for online parenting publications and has been an active member of the *Medium* writing community, where she has a portfolio of diverse styles and genres of self-published stories and poems.

Stephanie Peters is a fiction writer from British Columbia. She grew up in the suburbs on a hobby farm with peacocks and guinea fowl, and now resides in East Van. Her writing tends to revolve around family dynamics and women behaving badly.

Erin Pettit has had a strange, non-linear career that has involved grooming dogs and diving in sewers. While battling her own demons of procrastination and imposter syndrome, she prefers to write about fighting actual demons, monsters, and dragons. When not writing, Erin enjoys growing and preserving vegetables, baking bread, and riding her bike. She is happiest with a warm cup of something and an imaginary world to escape to.

Sofia Pezentte enjoys daydreaming, doodling, and yoga. When not writing speculative and historical fiction, she can be found eating vegan chicken strips and talking to her cat. She also works at a library. Her favourite sections in the Dewy decimal system are 292 (Greek and Roman Mythology), 398.2 (Folk and Fairy Tales), and 410 (Linguistics).

Sarah Phillips-Thin has a BA in English literature from UBC and completed two years at the Hagley Writers' Institute in New Zealand, where she wrote her first novel manuscript, "Manuka Hill." She's a fourth-generation Vancouverite but has lived in different places, most recently India with her husband and son for a few years, which inspired the novel she is currently working on at TWS. "Some Parts" is about a guy with a money problem who works as a driver for a foreign family in Bangalore.

Christine Pilgrim reached three score years and ten a while back. Now it's time to lay aside a comic acting career that began in London, England, in theatre, TV, and film, and ended in B.C. touring the one-woman history-based shows she authored and performed. Between gigs, Christine wrote for magazines and newspapers. Since moving to Vancouver, she reviews plays and concerts for vancouverpresents.com and contributes to the Roedde House Museum. Now she's applying her pen to her own past, before it's too late. Her website is christinepilgrim.com.

Dora Joella Prieto is a Mexican Canadian writer, who was born in Nova Scotia and grew up moving between her families in central México and the West Coast. She works in communications and development in the arts sector in Vancouver and has published freelance journalism in a variety of publications, including the *Georgia Straight*, *Adbusters Magazine*, and *BeatRoute Magazine*. She has been writing fiction and poetry for a few years and is working on upcoming submissions.

Ela Przybyło is an assistant professor in English and women's and gender studies at Illinois State University. She is the author of *Asexual Erotics: Intimate Readings of Compulsory Sexuality* (Ohio State University Press, 2019) and editor of *On the Politics of Ugliness* (Palgrave, 2018), as well as many other peer-reviewed publications, including in such journals as *Feminist Formations,* GLQ, and *Radical Teacher.* Her creative writing has been published in *Entropy* as part of the Name Tags series, in *Canadian Woman Studies,* and is forthcoming with *Borderlands: Texas Poetry Review.* Ela is a founding and managing editor of the peer-reviewed, open-access journal *Feral Feminisms.*

B. B. Randhawa was raised across two continents. Born in India, B. B. spent her formative years in B.C., Canada, and lived in Ireland for five years. Her fiction and poetry has been published in *Auroras & Blossoms Poetry Journal, Synergy: Psychiatric Writing Worth Reading,* PARO, and *From the Pier and Beyond.* She is a graduate of Simon Fraser University's creative writing program, the Writer's Studio. A psychiatrist in her other life, B. B. loves to hear and tell stories. She is based in Vancouver.

Sky Regina is a curious, ceaselessly wandering suitcase of nostalgia from Toronto. In more direct terms, she's a nosy teenager in an adult woman's body, which is why she decided to fulfill a perennial pipedream: to become an author of YA fiction (and perhaps a fly-by-night poet when she's feeling pensive). A recent graduate of SFU's TWS Online program, Sky is currently working on her debut novel, "We Are Apricots." When Sky needs a break from writing, she enjoys singing and dancing, cooking without recipes, and taking off to explore any unknown locale, always with a book nearby.

Anne (Louise) Rosenberg, named after her great-grannie Annie and great-grandpa Louis, is the middle of seven siblings and mother of one wonderful daughter. Anne has worked as a social worker, owned an art gallery, founded a global shoe company, and currently teaches guided autobiography, to name a few of her adventures. She's been in a lifelong love affair with beauty, finding it in nature, art, architecture, and people—beauty as not only aesthetic loveliness but a deep resonance that's a homecoming. Anne lives on the magnificent west coast of Canada. She shares her home with two male Scotties. One is a dog.

Daniel Ortiz Rubio was fashioned and molded in Venezuela, nutty notions and convictions included. He left his country of origin following puberty and his travels have taken him to the U.S. and, as of late, Canada. Originally a combination between financial advisor and leisurely musician, Daniel thought the best use of the complementary layers of paranoia that come with entertaining thoughts of solipsistic whimsy was not personal consumption but writing. Occurrences and spurs have arranged themselves to convince him that sitting alone in a room, assigning meaning to the inherently meaningless, is what he wishes to do with his time.

Frederic Sahyouni is a writer and head copywriter of a digital music marketing agency. Having backpacked to nearly two dozen countries across the world, he's written extensively of his travels and lives part time as a digital nomad. When he's not on the road photographing moments, he enjoys yoga, spirituality, and Beat poetry.

Amrit Kaur Sanghera is an Indo-Canadian writer and artist. She strives to paint the collective fantastical images floating around in her brain to paper, and hopes a story will bloom through as she jots it all down. She hopes to intertwine the warmth of the world with dark realities in order to capture parts of the human experience.

Kuldeep Singh lives and works as a mechanical engineer in India. He is currently enrolled in SFU's Writer's Studio program. His mentor, Kayla Czaga, and eight classmates discuss the writing world every Tuesday.

Libby Soper spent her early years in Iowa but lived in various regions of the United States and Canada, as well as France and the former Soviet Union, before making Vancouver her home. Her motley employment history includes but is not limited to tree planting, bread baking, translating, administering government-funded programs, and lecturing at universities. An avowed word nerd, she has been a teacher of Russian and French for over twenty years. Libby began writing when her youngest child was a baby, scribbling poems on scraps of paper between bouts of breastfeeding. Happily, she now can write at her desk.

Kim Spencer is a storyteller, emerging writer, and graduate of the SFU Writer's Studio program. She is working on a collection of narrative non-fiction stories and personal essays, with a particular focus on YA. The stories are from an Indigenous person's perspective of life growing up in the Northwest Coast. Her writing takes a close look at the significance traditional foods played in that upbringing, mixed with complicated family relationships and how interwoven the two are. Kim is from the Tsimshian Nation in Northern B.C. and currently resides in Vancouver.

Sandra Sugimoto is an emerging writer of Japanese Canadian heritage, born and raised on unceded Coast Salish lands. She is fascinated by the seemingly simple yet complex stories that arise out of everyday life. With a background in fine arts, and as an art teacher, she enjoys combining visual art with the written word.

Ola Szczecinska was born in Warsaw, grew up in Toronto, and lives in Vancouver. She studied history for many years at the University of Toronto, then spent a few years travelling and writing and teaching English overseas. She writes short stories and poetry, and has had some work appear in print and online. She cooks in bush camps in the warmer months and writes in the colder ones, usually in Vancouver but sometimes in Whitehorse, or northern Ontario, or places like that.

Susan Taite has BS and MS degrees in geoscience from the University of British Columbia. She has taught historical geology, physical geography, and structural geology at Kwantlen College and UBC. Susan also worked as an exploration geoscientist in Mexico and Canada, and believes that a properly created map can be an entirely narrative experience. She is presently a student at SFU's the Writer's Studio, where she is exploring near-future speculative fiction.

Léa Taranto is a biracial dreamer with spunk who has hard-won apocalypse survival skills. She is a member of SFU's the Writer's Studio and an MFA student at UBC. Her work has been published in *The Wayne Literary Review, Untethered Magazine, Transitions Magazine*, and is forthcoming in *Room* magazine. She and her fiancé Shaun live on traditionally unceded Musqueam land in British Columbia.

Sarah Jessie Tucker is a poet, writer, grant writer, and recent graduate of the Writer's Studio at SFU. Sarah grew up in Scarborough, Ontario, where she earned a law clerk diploma at Centennial College. She has worked with senior lawyers across the country and now resides in rural Alberta, where she is working on her first poetry collection.

Born and raised in Winnipeg, **Robert Weber** left home to go to school in Ottawa. After graduating from Carleton's journalism program, he began his career by producing documentary segments for CBC and TVOntario. He then went on to write for Prime Minister Jean Chretien, before running away to join the film industry. Since then, he has been writing spec screenplays while etching out a living as an assistant director. He currently lives in New Westminster with his infinitely more successful wife and their two much better-looking children, diligently working on literary and graphic novels.

Jess Wesley writes young adult novels and fairy tale-inspired short stories. Her writing is influenced by a family tradition of telling captivating tales at kitchen parties. Her short stories and novels have been featured on the social writing app Wattpad, where she is also a Wattpad Star. She lives in Smithers, B.C.

Anya Wyers was born and raised in Prince George, B.C. Following high school graduation, Anya moved to the lower mainland of B.C., where she still lives with her husband, their two sons Archer and Maverick, and their family dog, Eddie. She attended the paralegal program at Capilano College and worked as a paralegal for eleven years. Anya now writes full time. Anya's writing experience includes her self-published memoir, *Letters to the Mountain* (2019), a biweekly blog, and the Writer's Studio at SFU. Her other loves include crafting, wine, reading, and being outdoors.

F. J. Erica Yang is a writer, translator, and actor. Born in Taiwan, she moved to Vancouver in the late '90s as an international student in hope to start a remarkable new life for her and her parents. After her mother's passing in 2001, life led her on a different and unexpected path. This new journey pulls on her heart and soul to explore art, which she could not possibly imagine when she first moved to Canada. Her writing reflects on what we all have in common—unspoken words, unfelt feelings, and unexamined memories—what makes us all human.

Production Credits

Publisher
Laura Farina

Managing Editor
Emily E. A. Stringer

EDITORIAL TEAM
Section Editors
Emma Cleary — Fiction
Rebecca A. Coates — Speculative
   and Young Adult Fiction
Raoul Fernandes — Poetry and
   Lyric Prose
Christina Myers — Non-fiction

Copy Editors
Stephanie Charette
Danica Longair
Stephanie Peters
Erin Pettit
Amrit Kaur Sanghera
F. J. Erica Yang

PRODUCTION TEAM
Reese Kim Carrozzini —
   Production Editor

Acknowledgments

The students of the Writer's Studio would like to thank their mentors for the guidance and insight they have provided. We would also like to extend special thanks to the mentor apprentices for their support throughout the year.

We extend our gratitude to Hood 29 (4770 Main Street) for graciously hosting our monthly reading series.

We would all like to thank Vancouver's local independent bookstores for selling *emerge*. We urge our readers to support the booksellers that support local writers.

Elzevir A*a* Q*q* R*r*

The interior of *emerge* is set in DTL Elzevir. Originally created in the 1660s, Elzevir is a baroque typeface, cut by Christoffel van Dijck in Amsterdam. As noted in Robert Bringhurst's *The Elements of Typographic Style*, baroque typography thrived in the seventeenth century and is known for its axis variations from one letter to the next. During this time, typographers started mixing roman and *italic on the same line*. The Dutch Type Library created a digital version in 1993 called DTL Elzevir. It retains some of the weight that Monotype Van Dijck, an earlier digital version, possessed in metal but had lost in its digital translation.

This book is printed on FSC®-certified paper, containing post-consumer fibre and other controlled sources. The paper is manufactured in Canada, using renewable energy, and processed without the use of chlorine.

emerge

AVAILABLE AS AN EBOOK

Since 2011, *emerge* has been available
in print and ebook editions.

Visit
amazon.com
and
kobobooks.com